UNHOLY OBSESSION

CARNAL GAMES SERIES

STASIA BLACK

Copyright © 2025 by Stasia Black

All rights reserved.

No part of this book may be reproduced in any form or by any electronic or mechanical means, including information storage and retrieval systems, without written permission from the author, except for the use of brief quotations in a book review.

For everyone who resonates:

"When you are not fed love on a silver spoon, you learn to lick it off knives." — Lauren Eden

TWS

Please note: This book will be heretical and contains hypocrisy, unholiness, and blasphemy of the filthiest and most unrighteously fabulous kind. Triggers for religious trauma, written by a girlie with religious trauma. Bible school graduate says what? Holla!

Other TWs include: trauma, abuse, violence, and mental illness (including self-deletion ideation). For complete list of trigger warnings, please check author's website, stasiablack.com

Platlist

Uh Oh Neoni
Morally Grey April Jai and Nation Haven
Me and the Devil Soap&Skin
25 Rod Wave
Behind The Scenes TEYA
No Mercy Austin Giorgio
Take Me to Church Hozier
Gasoline Halsey
Boy Toy by Halle Abadi
Bad Apples Pussy Riot
Breaking Down I Prevail
Beggin' by Måneskin
Mess It UP Gracie Abrams
Please Please Please Sabrina Carpenter
Heathens Twenty-One Pilots
Pony Ginuwine
Popular Monster Falling In Reverse
Toxic Love SZA and Kendrick Lamar
Serotonin Girl in Red
Beautiful Things by Benson Boone

ONE

FATHER BLACKWOOD

I'M A MONSTER, but as so often happens with monsters, I've got everyone snowed into thinking I'm a good man from the outside.

The priest's collar around my neck helps.

No one knows about the shattered glass and spilled blood. No one knows about the floggers and leather and the countless women I've put on their knees and ordered to call me Lord—just like my father always said they ought to.

I'm an Episcopal priest, not a Catholic one, so I've made no vow of celibacy. But that doesn't mean my bishop would approve of me going to a club like the one I did on Friday, putting a woman in chains and making her beg, cry, and take everything I gave her until I came home with a Bible soaked in her juices from spanking her pussy with it.

I am a sinner of the worst order.

The kind who wears the cloth of a saint.

I stand at the altar, arms raised for the opening prayer, eyes cast downward in hypocrisy.

A half-full church full of elderly faithful sits before me. A congregation that believes in me. Trusts me.

I might never have meant to betray them, but depravity is my birthright.

My mouth shapes the familiar words of prayer, each syllable smooth and practiced. But my mind? My mind is still trapped with *her*.

I smell her phantom scent—cinnamon, vanilla, and sweat. I feel the silk of her hair as I twisted it around my fist. Taste the salt of her skin and hear the rasp of her broken moans as she took what I gave her. As she *craved* it.

My hands tremble with the memory.

It only took walking three blocks to throw away everything I've built.

A priest never should have set foot in a place like that. *Carnal.* But the sign was a beacon to my profane soul. A glowing, blood-red promise that I could indulge—just once—before snapping myself back in line.

I could blame it on the letter from my father. But a weak man can always find something or someone else to blame, can't he?

Three years of silence, and now this, him summoning me like the errant heir he always knew I'd be. The Blackwolf family crest stared up at me from the letterhead—a seal I swore I'd never look upon again. I should have burned it.

Instead, I read every word.

You can run, but you're still a Blackwolf. You can't escape what you are.

The echo of my father's voice coils around my chest like barbed wire. I thought the vows, the collar, and the church—all of it—could change me. *Redeem* me.

But last Friday, I felt the truth in my bones.

I am my father's son, and I always will be.

I fought for years—*years*—to strip myself of Bane, the monster I was raised to be. And yet, in a single night, I let him loose again. I hid my face behind a black cloth skull mask, concealing the priest and letting the sinner run free. I thought it was protection. But that wasn't the truth. It was *permission*.

I bow my head and whisper, "*Amen,*" keeping my voice steady. The congregation responds in kind, and their unwavering trust cinches the barbed wire tighter.

The opening hymn begins. Off-key voices fill the high, arched ceilings, but the sound barely registers. The air is thick with candle wax, the age-old scent of polished wood, and the bite of Mrs. Blanchard's whiskey-laced coffee that she thinks no one notices. My vestments feel heavier today, a noose instead of a yoke.

"Now, for a moment of contemplation and silence as we

gather our hearts for worship," I say, my voice calm despite the storm inside me. I roll the mallet around the singing bowl, the low hum filling the silence.

I begin the count in my head. Sixty seconds to hold on to the calm. Sixty seconds to convince myself that I am still in control.

I am Father Blackwood, I chant inwardly. *Twenty-one, twenty-two, twenty-three.* I have dedicated my life to serving others. *Thirty-nine, forty, forty-one.* To bring hope to the hopeless.

Fifty-eight, fifty-nine, sixty.

I roll the mallet again, the sound dissipating into the vaulted rafters.

I open my eyes, my hands lifting as I prepare for the next prayer. The congregation waits expectantly.

And then I see her.

Her.

Oh, fuck. All the air in my lungs freezes as she slips in through the heavy arched doors at the back of the church, hesitance in every line of her body.

The woman who's haunted me for forty-eight agonizing hours.

The woman whose body I used like an altar, whose voice still echoes in my mind, wrecked and desperate and gasping my name.

TWO

MOIRA

I KICK AT THE FLOORBOARDS, still sitting in the pew long after the service has finished.

The sexy priest stands at the back of the church, shaking hands and murmuring blessings like he actually means them, his deep voice steady and calm. There's a line of folks slowly working their way out of the sanctuary, thanking him for his sermon and making small talk.

I didn't think priests were allowed to be that young and hot.

Fuck, what am I even doing here?

I slump against the hard wooden pew and tilt my head back, looking up at the beautiful light spilling in through the stained-glass windows. The church smells like candle wax and polished wood and old people. It's... nice. Different.

Clean.

I clearly do not belong here.

The last time I stepped foot inside a church was... God... back when I was a kid, and the nuns from school would drag us in for weekly chapel on Wednesdays. The boys would always snap my bra straps when the nuns weren't looking. But when I punched them for it? *I* was the one who got in trouble. Sister Agatha would just sigh, shake her head, and mutter under her breath about me turning out just like my mother.

I tighten my coat around me like armor, curling my fingers into the sleeves. My palms are damp, and my breathing's uneven.

I should not be here.

But my brain's been doing the Electric Slide into the deep end of the crazy pool ever since Friday night, and if I don't do something drastic, I'm gonna start climbing the walls like a rabid raccoon.

Breathe, Moira. Act normal. Blend in.

Ha. Normal. God, it's not like I don't fucking try. I should win a goddamn Oscar because I spend my whole life acting.

Why can't you just be normal, Moira?

That was my mother's favorite line.

Everyone in our little village outside of Donegal said I

was just like Mam, and then there was Mam, saying I should be acting normal like everyone else in town.

As if she was one to talk. She was the town slag, a drink in her hand if she was awake and breathing, and there was barely a day of my life when there wasn't some man or other in our one-room flat. Domhn and I would hide in the closet, but it wasn't like that was soundproof or anything.

When Domhn and I moved to the States right as I became a teenager, I eventually lost my accent, and he raised me the best he could, but—

Somewhere in all that mess, I was supposed to come out knowing how to be normal?

The line waiting to talk to Father Sexy is finally dwindling, so I stand up and tiptoe toward the end of the pew. Head down, shoulders hunched, trying to look devout instead of deranged. The few other people scattered throughout the sanctuary don't even glance at me. Good.

I just need to get clean.

Not, like, Jesus-clean. Just... brain-clean. Soul-clean.

Something-clean.

I scan the front of the church, looking for the little booth that Catholic churches always have, but there's nothing. No tiny wooden box to tuck myself inside with a little sliding panel between me and salvation.

I chew my lip, debating. Maybe I can make my confession to the priest face-to-face? Is that a thing?

Why does he have to be so goddamn hot? How am I

supposed to confess my sins to a priest I *want to climb*? Especially when the sins I need to confess are all about fucking?

I get in the line, still not sure what I'm going to do. Maybe just slip out the door and chalk this up as another ridiculous one-off impulse?

I scratch at my wrist in the spot that's already raw. But it's nothing compared to the itch that's inside me. Ever since Friday when that crazy hot new dom made me come *so* hard after not being able to come for months, I've been itching like mad. But nothing else will do it. Believe me, I spent all weekend wearing out every vibrator I've got to recreate the feeling.

Me not being able to come is like the sun not rising. Sex is my failsafe. My one sure escape. But no matter how many men I fuck or fancy vibrators I try, it doesn't matter. I've been fucking broken ever since last year when—

I shake my head, scratching harder at my wrist.

But then *he* walked into the club like a fucking god. So dark and sexy and mysterious in that skull mask, commanding my body in a way no one ever has before. Bringing me back to life. Talk about *resurrection*.

Then he didn't show up on Saturday.

God, I've been dying for his touch ever since, and what's worse, I don't know when or if I'll ever get it again. I couldn't sleep last night. So I drove to the club this morning, planning to wait until they opened tonight, praying the mysterious dom would appear again.

But once I got to the club, I realized how ridiculous it was to just sit in my car for twelve hours like some kind of desperate stalker. So I got out. Started walking. And when I heard the organ music, something inside me just—

I don't know. Snapped.

I mean, I'm not generally given to introspection, but this weekend, everything has felt tougher than usual.

Something's got to change.

I have to change.

It's time. It's *beyond* time. I just don't know how.

So, for the first time in years, I wandered through the doors of a church.

Not that I've got any actual hope for help. After last year, betraying my brother in the deepest way possible, even if I didn't mean to—

"What are you doing here?"

I startle at the question, blinking up at the priest. *Holy shit.* Up close, he's even more devastating. Sharp jaw, dark eyes, lips that look like they were made for sin instead of sermons.

"I need to confess," I blurt.

His expression doesn't change. But his eyes...

"We don't do confession like that here." His voice is even and unreadable.

I falter. "But—I thought—"

"That's Catholicism," he says. "Episcopalians don't do confession like that."

I should leave. Apologize for wasting his time. But my body feels glued in place, buzzing with something I don't understand.

Then his gaze drops to my wrist, where I'm still scratching.

"We might not do confession like you're used to," he says, voice low, eyes intense, "but I can still listen. Tell me what troubles you."

Since there's no one in line behind me, he leads me back to a pew. I follow, feeling a little light-headed.

I sit down beside him, suddenly hyper-conscious of how close my knee is to his knee.

I take a shuddering breath and curl my fingers against the wood of the pew underneath me, trying to focus on anything besides his overwhelming masculine energy.

"I've done things," I blurt out, not sure how to start. My voice trembles, but if this priest is willing to listen, I'll tell him everything. Maybe if I just say it all out loud, I can be free of it? "Things I'm not proud of. Things I can't take back."

The admission hangs in the air between us, raw and heavy.

He closes his eyes as if he knows this is only the first admission of many. I let go of the pew and twist my fists in the fabric of my jacket.

"I hurt people," I say, voice shaky. "I mean, not like I punched anyone or anything. But I've used people. And let them use me, too. Then, the people I actually care about, I push away. I betrayed my family. And now..." I trail off as I look at the floor. I decide, since this is my one chance to be honest with myself and God, to tell the truth.

"Now I don't even know if I can care about anyone. I don't know if I want to. It hurts too *bad*." My throat clogs on the last word. "Everything hurts."

I can't look up at the Father. Even though I want to see his reaction, I'm not sure I could handle it.

I take another breath, this one fractured and shallow. "I thought... I thought if I kept moving, I could outrun the mess I made of my life. But it's still here."

I press a hand to my chest, fingers curling into my ribs. "It's always here. I don't know who I am anymore. I don't even know if I'm worth saving."

"You *are*," the priest responds immediately, deep voice fervent.

"How can you say that?" I look up in surprise. "You don't even know me."

He swallows, and I watch his Adam's apple move in his throat. "Because redemption doesn't come from doing things perfectly. It comes from the *fight*. From choosing to believe you're worth saving, even when it feels impossible."

But I *have* been fighting. And now, there's no fight left in me. My shoulders sag, and the faintest sob escapes before I press a hand to my mouth as if I can shove the sound back down.

"It's alright. It's going to be alright. . ." His voice is so gentle and so without the pity people usually talk to me with. The way he's sitting, it's like he's barely holding himself back from reaching out to me.

I wish he would. I want to wrap my arms around his neck and listen to the heart beating in his solid chest. Like the good part after sex.

I wince back and shake my head, dropping my hand only long enough to suck in a breath and whisper, "I don't know how to fight anymore."

The compassion carves even deeper in his brow as he inches slightly toward me on the bench, reaching out a hand before yanking it back and fisting at his sides.

His words are still vehement as he says, "You don't have to fight alone. You aren't alone."

My breath catches. Does he mean *he'll* help me? That he'll... that he'll be there for me and somehow help me find a path even though I can't see any way forward?

But as my eyes search his, I realize how ridiculous I'm being. *No, you idiot, he's talking about* God. He's saying God will be with me.

All my hope deflates.

No offense, but God let my brother be tortured by his childhood sweetheart's father while they were both just kids, so I doubt He'll be intervening to help the likes of me anytime soon... Especially since I'm the one who brought that evil man back into their lives after they'd escaped him.

I don't *deserve* my brother's forgiveness. Much less God's.

I swipe at my eyes and nose with my forearm and push to my feet, the movements stiff and jerky.

"I— I should go," I stammer.

"Wait—"

"No. I can't—this was a mistake."

I turn and rush for the door before I do something stupid, like let the handsome priest stop me. I just know, with salt in my mouth from my tears, that I've got to get the hell out of this holy place.

The priest's voice sounds ragged as he shouts, "Go in peace!" after me.

But I know the truth.

There's no peace for someone like me.

THREE

FATHER BLACKWOOD

I WATCH HER FLEE, frozen in place. Not by my legs, but by my fucking collar. By the eyes I feel on both of us. More churchgoers have arrived for the coffee hour between services, murmuring, sipping from Styrofoam cups, and absolutely oblivious to the war raging inside me.

I grip the wood of the doorframe, watching her already small figure shrink into the distance, my chest locked in a vise.

She didn't come here because she followed me. She didn't know who the fuck I was. She was a lost, tortured soul looking for something—*anything*—to hold on to. And yet, I can't shake the gut-deep certainty that this is my fault. That I did this to her or at least contributed to it.

I was the one who let temptation draw too close to my doorstep. I was the one who broke his own goddamn rules and played with fire three blocks from my own church.

And now, here *she* was.

Seeking God. Seeking absolution. And I, his so-called messenger, failed her. Again.

I wanted to reach out and catch her before she ran, to say something *real* that might have met her where she needed to be met. But I didn't trust myself.

Not here. Not with her looking up at me like that, so broken.

She doesn't see her own light, the fire that burns in her even when she's breaking. Even as she bowed her head before me, exposing her vulnerabilities to a man she thought could absolve her in God's name.

A man she didn't realize had already had her on her knees, begging, pleading—not for salvation but for—

I breathe out hard.

Then she looked up at me with hope in those tortured, tear-filled eyes. For a moment, I thought I could say *something* to keep that hope alive.

And then I watched it die.

Before I could stop her, she was gone.

Far older memories have me leaning against the doorframe, my grip tightening more as dizziness lurches through me.

I'm dragged back to my childhood in England. Back to

that house. Back to the screams, the sobs, and all the rest a child never should have witnessed.

I'm dragged back to the day I saw desperate tears in another tortured woman's eyes.

"Please, Charles. Just let me take him with me!" My mother's voice. "This is no house for a boy to grow up in." Her hands clutched together, knuckles white as she begged my father. "Then you can fuck your whores in peace!" She flung a hand out toward the stairs.

Behind the doorway where I crouched, I saw them—the other women sprawled along the grand staircase, tangled together in lazy amusement. They hardly paid attention to the fight happening only feet away. One of them laughed, sipping from a crystal glass.

My father barely looked at my mother as he unbuckled his belt.

"How much do you want it?" he asked, voice cruel. He pulled out his willy and held it out in challenge.

I didn't understand. Not yet. But I understood the way my mother recoiled. The way her hands clenched. The way fresh tears welled in her eyes before she did something I never thought I'd see her do.

She got on her knees, bent her head and opened her mouth.

I didn't understand then. But I do now.

My father was a goddamn monster.

"You." His voice lashed out to one of the women on the

staircase. "Join her. Teach my wife how I like to be pleasured."

Mom jerked back from him. "Why do you have to be so vicious?"

"You're free to leave anytime you wish." My father sneered down at her, motioning to the grand doors. "But you'll *never* take him with you."

My mother started to crawl away from him, toward the door, sobbing.

"And know this," he called after her, voice thick with cruel satisfaction. "If you leave today, I'll never let you back in."

She paused and looked back, not at him but at the staircase and the second floor, where my bedroom was. She thought I was up there, reading my books, tucked safely away.

But I wasn't. I had snuck down the back staircase like I sometimes did, wanting to hear why there was so much loud laughter downstairs.

Dad always said it was good to be naughty.

"I'll fight you," my mother swore, voice shaking with fury. "He's my son as much as yours. Courts care about a mother's rights."

My father yanked the other woman onto him, his hand twisted in her hair, his head tilting back in pleasure.

"You're a *nobody*." His voice was thick with arrogance. "You have *nothing* without me. I'll bury you in court fees."

And then—

"I hope you took a good look at his face this morning because you'll never see him again."

She flinched like he had struck her.

Then, without another word, she climbed to her feet, turned, and walked out.

And I never saw her again.

My fingers dig into the wood, breath ragged. My father was a monster. And the first rule I've *sworn* by since the day I left his estate and never looked back was this: *In every situation, do the opposite of what he would do.*

I release my grip on the doorframe, pulse roaring in my ears.

Fuck what anyone in my congregation thinks. Fuck the whispers. Fuck if it gets back to the bishop.

She ran out in tortured tears.

And I let her go.

I *will not* let that be the end of it.

I take off running after her, ashamed of how long it's taken me to move.

But no matter how many alleyways and streets I sprint down, I can't find her.

I'm too fucking late.

Another sin to add to the infinite list.

I laugh bitterly as I walk, defeated, back to the church. Let's be honest.

I was damned the moment I spurted out of that bastard's cock.

FOUR

MOIRA

I CLUTCH my phone in a white-knuckled grip and stare down at the screen at a text from Anna, my brother's saint of a fiancée:

> ANNA: Come to the club tonight. Domhn and I will be there.

Huh.

I don't know why Anna is suddenly willing to risk my brother's wrath by inviting me anywhere, but I'll take the W.

It's been a shit week. Ever since I bolted out of that church like a bat out of hell last weekend, I've been holed up in my apartment, watching mindless reality TV and subsisting entirely on coffee, stale Pop-Tarts, and regret. I needed to get away the second I sprinted outside those heavy wooden doors, practically diving onto the light rail a couple blocks away the moment it rolled up.

Why the fuck did I think *that* was a good idea? Crying in some rando church? Confessing my sins to an impossibly gorgeous man who probably went back to his priestly duties with a sigh of relief that the weird, sobbing sinner left him alone?

I scrub a hand over my face and squeeze my eyes shut.

I used to have *methods* for dealing with my bullshit. Get an itch? Scratch it. A little fun in the club, or a little reckless adventure, maybe a semi-public fuck, and boom—distraction achieved.

But now? Now, the itch is a wildfire under my skin.

I've tried to get satisfaction. Believe me, I *tried*. I pulled out every trick in the book, not to mention every toy in my arsenal. Let's just say my best vibrator and I have been in an *exclusive relationship* this past week, and even then—nothing.

That stupidly hot new dom ruined me in just one night after a whole *year* of not being able to come. He woke something up inside me.

And I hate him for it.

Because what the fuck is the point of glimpsing nirvana if you can't fucking find it again?

I just need to get back to my old self.

And Anna's invitation has to mean *something*, right? A

tether to my old life. It's a sign I'm not completely excommunicated from everyone I love. If Anna's reaching out, maybe—just *maybe*—Domhn's softening. Maybe this is the first step to him talking to me again, even if he never forgives me.

I stuff my phone in my pocket before I can overthink it and shove out of my car, heading inside the club before I lose my nerve.

One of the new bouncers, Kit, grins at me as I walk up. I wink at him and throw a little bounce in my step. He's new and still starry-eyed about the place. I gave him a couple welcome rides when he started; he's not bad, just nothing to write home about.

"Miss me?" I tease, trailing a finger down his arm as I pass.

"Always," he grins at me. Men are simple creatures.

Inside, the thrum of bass vibrates through my bones, the music sinking into my skin like a second heartbeat.

And then I spot everyone. For the first time all week, the weight in my chest eases. The whole gang's here. Is it weird that we hang out just to *hang* in the lounge of a BDSM sex club? I've obviously never given a shit about weird in my whole life, so no.

I should kiss Anna for inviting me. If she weren't already head-over-heels for my brother, I'd consider it. She's hot and a little nuts, so we have that in common. She's got DID—dissociative identity disorder. Anna's cool and all, but I gotta say, her alter, Mads, is a *really* fun time.

I weave through the crowd toward our usual lounge area, past familiar faces and whispered greetings.

I slide into the seat beside Kira and immediately clock the situation with her bodyguard, Isaak. She's been having stalker problems, and Isaak's just started a security firm, so he took the case.

But the way his arm is draped possessively over the back of her chair? It's giving more than just bodyguard vibes. His whole body is turned toward her like he's got some primal need to keep everyone else the fuck away.

I arch a brow at him. He rolls his eyes.

Interesting.

"Moira!" Kira leans in and hugs me like she actually means it.

I squeeze her tight, trying to ignore how good the human contact feels.

I let her go before I do something weird like burrow into her shoulder like a cat in need of warmth. "How's life, darling?" I wiggle my brows, flicking a glance at Isaac.

Kira blushes. *Blushes.* She's only a year older than me, but she's got that whole buttoned-up professor thing going on, which makes teasing her that much more fun.

"You gettin' some, huh?" I rock my hips against the chair and make some truly obscene noises.

"Moira," a voice cuts through the conversation. Sharp. Cold.

My whole body locks up before I even turn my head.

Domhnall, my brother.

I force myself to look at him. He's got Anna curled in his lap, arms wrapped around her like she's something precious.

There's naked contempt in his eyes as he looks at me. Not annoyance. Not frustration. *Contempt.*

Anna glances between us, frowning. I can see it in her face; she *hates* this. She starts to say something, but Domhn just turns away.

Like I don't exist.

He murmurs something in Anna's ear, making her giggle and snuggle closer. He tucks a piece of hair behind her ear, the picture of a devoted fiancé.

I try not to stare.

Anna's the best thing that's ever happened to my brother. I know people think my relationship with Domhn is weird, that my exhibitionism and lack of shame must mean something, but *I do have boundaries.* He's my brother. That's it. That's all.

I just...

I just wish someone would love me like that one day.

Because whatever *that* is—the easy way they fit together, the way they always seem to exist in their own little world—that's not something I've ever had. Not something I ever thought I *wanted.*

But maybe that's because I never thought it was possible for someone like me.

That chasm inside me cracks open a little wider, a

yawning void that no amount of sex or fun or recklessness has ever been able to fill.

Because there's nothing inside me.

Certainly, nothing worth adoring.

"So, what have you been up to?" Kira asks me.

I grin back at her, and I make sure it stretches ear to ear. Fuck all that maudlin shit for now. I'm in party-Moira mode. Light-hearted. *Fun.* I twirl the end of one of my pigtails. "Oh, you know, the usual—fucking around and getting fucked."

She laughs, shaking her head. "I've always admired how… free you live."

"Oh, honey, don't." I kick my heels up on the table and smirk. "I've just got you all snowed. I'm the great and powerful Oz." I wiggle my fingers at her. "Pay no attention to the emotional disaster behind the curtain."

Quinn peels herself away from the chair she was sitting in beside Domhn and Anna to join us. Finally. Something interesting. She's my oldest friend and the only woman I know who isn't side-eyeing me, wondering if I'm about to steal her man. Not that I ever would. But some girls get twitchy when their boyfriends so much as look at me, the dangerous, self-admitted sex addict.

"Taking a night off, gorgeous?" I ask, eyeing the way Quinn moves like a panther even when she's off duty.

She perches on the edge of a leather chair like a queen on her throne, all perfect posture and coiled power. Meanwhile, I'm splayed out like a lazy cat in the sun. She shrugs. "It's nice to chill here without my boot halfway up a sub's ass, you know?"

I snort. "Isn't that shit *exhausting?*"

Quinn shakes her head. "It's not that bad. Most of them are harmless little puppies who just want to worship you. The trick is weeding out the ones who secretly hate women."

"How do you tell the difference?" Kira's practically vibrating with curiosity. If she had a notepad, she'd be scribbling furiously.

Quinn waves a dismissive hand. "You get a vibe. But even I get it wrong sometimes. That's why I never meet clients at home. Always at the club."

Kira tilts her head. "What about your own love life?"

Quinn scoffs. "I can't afford a love life for the next five years."

I lean in, intrigued. "Five years? Why so specific?"

Quinn rolls her eyes at me. "Because, unlike *some* of us, I have to work for a living. I'm out to get my bag."

"And then what?" I prop my chin in my fist, staring her down. "Gonna retire before you're thirty? You make good money working for my brother. I always assumed you dommed at night because you liked it."

"I domme at night because I get paid six hundred dollars an hour."

I *smack* the table. "*Holy shit.*"

How have I never asked this after knowing her for four years?

Quinn smirks at my dropped jaw. "And that's before the paypigs."

Kira's eyes light up like she's just discovered a new species. "I've *read* about that! You have financial submissives?"

Quinn shrugs, looking smug as hell. "If men want to worship me by throwing money at my feet, who am I to deny them the privilege?"

"But do you *like* being a domme?" Kira asks, then immediately backtracks, hands twisting nervously. "I mean... like... is it natural for you?"

Quinn's smirk flickers, just for a second. "I like being able to manipulate power dynamics in my favor. I'm good at reading people. It's a means to an end."

"But Domhn says you're really good at your day job. Couldn't you make just as much money if you tried to, I don't know, start your own company?" I narrow my eyes at her. "I think you do this for a reason. You're not just good at being in control. You like it. You need it."

There's an uncomfortable silence as Quinn sits up in her chair, foot going back to the floor as she squares her shoulders to turn toward me.

Oh, shit. Did I just stick my foot in my mouth? I always go too far.

Quinn's eyes glitter. "You bet your ass I need to be in control if I'm having any sort of intimate interaction with a man."

I nod. Huh. So, is it just about men? "I have noticed that you've been taking on more female clients lately."

"Is it 'cause you swing that way?" Marcus interrupts from across the table, grinning like an idiot.

Quinn *flicks* the cherry from her whiskey sour at his forehead. He ducks—too slow.

Ping.

Marcus snatches the cherry from his lap and tosses it in his mouth, winking.

"Ugh," Quinn groans, rolling her eyes so hard they almost fall out of her skull.

"So what about after your five-year plan," Kira asks. "What then?"

Quinn digs the toe of her boot into a crack in the concrete. "I just want to find my sister and then disappear somewhere by a beach. She deserves the good life from here on out."

The energy shifts. Becomes heavy. Weighted. Quinn rarely talks about her sister, and we all know why. The system separated them, and then they lost her sister. How do you *lose* a person? And the state had the *fucking nerve* to act like she never existed. Quinn hacked the system herself trying to find her, got thrown in jail for it, and my brother pulled strings to get her out early. But her sister? Still missing.

Kira, ever the innocent academic, asks the worst possible question. "Where is she?"

Quinn's head snaps up, her glare like a dagger. "If I knew, Kira, I wouldn't be *looking for her*, now would I?"

Oh, *shit*.

Quinn exhales sharply, drags her hands through her hair, then mutters, "Sorry." She flicks a glance Kira's way, gaze softening. "I need a drink. You want anything?"

Kira just shakes her head, looking guilty.

Quinn stomps off, and Anna hops off Domhn's lap to follow her. I jump up, too. No sex for me tonight, but who cares? I'm trying this friendship gig, right?

At the bar, I lean on a stool while Quinn orders a round of shots.

"Maybe we should all go bar-hopping together. Just us girls," I suggest, buzzing with the idea of this whole girl bonding thing.

Kira pops up beside me. "Or we could have a night in and do mani-pedis."

I stick my finger in my mouth and fake gag. "Barf. Who's gonna fuck me in the bathroom during mani-pedi night?"

Kira laughs like I'm joking. I just stare at her, head tilted. Bitch is literally wearing a cardigan to a sex club. It's like she grew up in a two-parent household or some shit.

Then she waves a fluttering hand. "I mean, I can't anyway until this stalker thing calms down."

I pat her awkwardly on the shoulder. Am I... *comforting someone*? "I trust Isaak. He'll keep you safe."

Quinn slides shots into our hands. "Slippery nipple. Bottoms up."

I slam mine back, enjoying the warm burn. "Aye!"

Quinn and Anna do the same, and finally, *finally*, Kira downs hers, only to start coughing and sputtering like she just swallowed pure lava.

I laugh so hard that I nearly fall off my stool. *Now this—* this is what I needed.

Maybe I don't need my brother's approval. Maybe I don't need the past to stop hurting. Maybe I just need... *this*.

Then I shake my head.

Nah.

"Shut up, shut up!" Quinn hisses, waving her next shot in the air. "Jinx and Gemini are on stage. I want to support them."

I look up to see Jinx bending Gemini over a spanking bench, a wicked-looking leather whip in hand.

"Jesus," I whisper.

"I know," Quinn breathes, eyes glinting as she hurries back toward the lounge.

Kira follows her, and I'm about to when Anna suddenly grabs my forearm.

I look at her questioningly, but she just keeps tugging on my arm as she nods toward a hallway, quickly glancing back at Domhnall. I do, too. His attention is momentarily taken by what's happening on stage, so Anna tugs me even more urgently until I turn back and follow her out of the main room.

"What's up?" I ask.

Anna just shakes out her shoulders and her hair like she's shuddering. "Fuck, it's exhausting when I pretend to be her. She's such a fucking Pollyanna."

My eyes widen. "Mads?"

Oh, yay, I love it when Mads pops out. I like Mads. Mads is fun.

She nods as she breathes and slouches against the wall, eyes sliding my way. "Hey. Missed you, kid."

A million questions clog my throat, all of them fighting to be first. What manages to stumble out is, "How come you're here?"

She reaches into her pocket and pulls out a joint, rolling her shoulders as she lights up.

I laugh in surprise. "You can't smoke in here!"

"Eh, who's gonna stop me?"

"Caleb, for one. He lost his shit when I brought weed brownies in here once."

She barks out a laugh. "Everybody plays by the rules so hard around here." She takes a long drag, her head sinking back against the wall as she exhales through her nose.

"Why'd you text me?"

Because now, of course, I realize it was her, not Anna.

She turns her head lazily toward me and grins before bumping my shoulder with hers. "I meant it. I missed you, kid." She takes another long inhale, holding the smoke in her lungs before blowing it out slowly. "Plus, all Domhn's friends fucking hate me. But they love Anna." She rolls her eyes. "You're the only one I can talk to. A bitch needs some friends out here, ya know?"

I do, more than she knows.

"I am your friend," I assure her automatically. "You can always text or call me to hang out or just, ya know, talk."

She nods. "That's good to know, kid."

She stubs the joint out on the bottom of her shoe, then turns to face me more directly. "I always wondered about you, you know? I wanted to meet you so bad... back then." A shadow crosses her face, but she shrugs it off quickly like it was never there. Like nothing in the world could touch her. "But I never wanted any of that shit to get to you, so whenever Domhn suggested we go back to his place, I always made up an excuse."

Then she reaches out and grabs my face under the chin, her eyes locking on mine. "But that doesn't mean I didn't dream about meeting you, ya know? You've always been the most important thing to him. And that makes you important to me. You understand? I want to know you. I want us to be friends."

"I'm your friend," I assure her again, reaching up to grasp her forearm, squeezing it while I look back into her intense gaze. "I swear it, Mads. Whatever you need, I'm there."

She grins and lets go of my chin, then noogies the top of my head with her fist. "Yeah, I knew you would be."

"Hey," I laugh and pull back, hands going to my carefully arranged hair. "You'll mess up my hair."

She rolls her eyes. "It's time to let go of the pigtails, honey."

"Never! They're my signature. Plus, they're sexy."

"To creepy perverts."

"What if I like creepy perverts?" I waggle my eyebrows. "Maybe I *am* a creepy pervert."

She chuckles in that low way of hers that's so different from Anna's laughter. "I always knew we'd be two peas in a pod." She holds out the joint to me. I've just taken it and am leaning in for her to light me up when a loud voice booms down the hall.

"What the hell is going on down here?"

Fuck. I know that voice.

It's Domhnall.

I yank back right as I've sucked in half a puff from the lit joint and quickly try to put it out on the bottom of my shoe. But I'm not nearly as practiced as Mads and nearly burn a hole through the side of my cloth Mary Janes before managing to smother it on the rubber of my sole.

"Anna? What's going on?" Domhn asks as he approaches.

Mads steps in front of me protectively and pops a hip. "What crawled up your ass? I don't need your permission to talk to my friend."

"Mads," Domhn says, his voice suddenly cool. "How long have you been here?"

Mads twirls the bottom of her hair on her finger.

"Jesus, it's been you all night, hasn't it?" Domhn storms up to her, only stopping when he's right in her face.

"Hey, let off her," I say, moving around her to try to get between them, but Domhn silences me with one of his terribly icy looks.

"Don't," he bites, "get between me and my wife."

I feel my eyes go wide. Shit. This night is just full of surprises. "When did you guys get married?"

"We haven't," Mads pipes up.

Domhn yanks on the lapels of his jacket as he turns back to her. "You know we already may as well have. You're my wife in all but paperwork. Why won't you just tell me when you switch, Mads? How many times have I told you it's fine with me. Now, let's get back home. I think it's been enough adventure for one night."

Mads pouts, and even I can tell it's a barely skin-deep manipulation tactic. She's playing with him and wants him to know it. It's fascinating to watch the two of them together. She's so much more confrontational than Anna. "But I want to stay and play." She arches an eyebrow and leans into his body. "Don't you want to play with me, Donny?"

"Not with her here," Domhnall growls, obviously softening to her wiles, gesturing toward me with the barest tilt of his head.

"I'll leave," I pipe up.

"No one was talking to you," Domhnall bites. "Because you're already gone. My sister is dead to me."

I back away from the pair of them and do my best to pretend he didn't just bludgeon me in the chest with his words.

"Domhn," Mads says sharply, but I shake my head at her and give a lame wave before turning and trying to walk away without looking like I'm running.

FIVE

BANE

THE CLUB IS ALIVE TONIGHT, and I'm pulled here again like a sailor to a siren's call. From my perch in the shadows across the street, I have an unobstructed view of its entrance. A string of well-dressed patrons pass through the darkened doorway. Their laughter and the click of heels reverberate faintly down the street.

But Moira is the only one who matters.

I don't interfere. I only watch.

Just like I have for too many nights in a row now. I stand here, watching and fighting the ache in my chest that's always my unwelcome companion. *It's not stalking*, I tell myself. I never follow her home. I still don't know where she lives. I just come here to catch a glimpse of her and reassure myself she's still safe.

My eyes scan the entrance, muscles tense with expectation. The door swings open and shut, and strangers spill out into the night. They're irrelevant. She's the only one I'm waiting for.

She always comes.

And now here I stand, night after night. Watching her step through the club door, the barest thump of the club's base beat spilling out, throbbing with temptation.

As much as I might want to cross the street and follow her inside so I can reassure myself up close that she's okay... the simple truth is, I don't trust myself.

I want her to be all right. I *need* her to be alright.

But thinking *I'm* the one to step in and fix her is the height of ego. I might be an arrogant monster, but that's even more reason to stay away. Whatever brought her to the church's doorstep, eyes so full of shame and self-recrimination. . . I shake my head. My interference in her life could only make things worse.

The thought bites deep, but I force myself to swallow it. Shame is an old acquaintance of mine. One I thought I'd made peace with long ago. Yet here it is again, festering under my skin like a wound that never healed.

When Moira ran from the church, it felt like the final echo of a life I'd tried to bury. That life was one of excess, indulgence, and all the other sins I inherited from my father.

I've tried to distract myself. Believe me.

I told myself I'd never come back here.

Earlier tonight, I tried to practice discipline. Lining up dominos in my living room—a child's game, I know, but one I've taken back up again in recent years to practice exactitude, a quiet mind, and discipline.

My hands moved with practiced precision, setting the final piece in place. A perfect chain of black-and-white dominos stretched across the polished surface of my coffee table and floor, each one standing tall and precisely spaced. Order. Control. The simple, immutable laws of physics dictated that every piece had its place. That nothing could fall unless it was set into motion.

It was what I used to do as a child, back when I still lived under my father's roof. Before I learned that control was only an illusion. I would spend hours setting up elaborate patterns, only to swipe them down in a single movement. The fall was inevitable. I thought I had grown past the need for this kind of ritual, but tonight, I desperately needed something to still my thoughts.

Something to wipe *her* from my mind.

Moira.

The name itself is a trespass. A disruption. A single out-of-place domino among my carefully arranged life.

My jaw clenched as I stared at the first domino. If I pushed it, the rest would collapse in a beautiful, fluid sequence—one after the other, a perfect, unstoppable chain.

The way things had always worked. The way they're supposed to work.

Except Moira hadn't followed the rules. She had lodged herself into my thoughts, a piece of chaos in the symmetry of my world, and no matter how much I tried to ignore it, I could feel the balance shifting.

And now I'm here. Drawn back by the siren's call, just like always.

The sound of heels against pavement cuts through the night. My breath catches.

There she is.

Moira.

Framed under the streetlight like something out of a dream. Her auburn curls glint like fire, tucked into adorable pigtails that catch the golden glow of the streetlamp. The leather jacket she wears is unzipped, revealing a sequined dress that clings to her body with maddening precision. She walks like she owns the night, and maybe she does.

My fists clench at my sides. I should leave. I should turn my back and return to the rectory where I belong.

But my feet stay planted, as immovable as the weight in my chest.

The door swings shut behind her, and she's gone, swallowed by the darkness of the club. The night settles around me, thick and quiet, save for the distant hum of traffic.

And in the quiet, memories rise unbidden.

Because I know this world. Its pull. The smell of expensive perfume and the feel of the bass that thrums in your chest and drowns out everything else.

I lived it. Years ago, I'd have been the one striding into that club, hungry for the thrill and oblivion waiting on the other side of the door.

I can almost hear my father's laughter, low and sharp. "If you're going to sin, boy, do it right," he'd said once, handing me a glass of bourbon far before I was old enough to legally drink.

That was his way—teaching me indulgence, not responsibility. I was hungry for any scrap of his attention, even when I hated him. But then, I hated everything. I was furious at the world and worked hard to be a destructive force everywhere I went. I fought everyone except my father. His hold over me was one I never allowed myself to look in the face until far too late.

So, at fourteen, I drank the bourbon. And the next. And the next.

For years, I let his world of indulgence after indulgence consume me until the night it all came crashing down. There'd been blood. Flashing lights. The cold bite of steel cuffs. And my father, sweeping in like the puppet master he was and handing over a check that erased the entire mess from the record.

"Boys will be boys," he'd said, laughing and cuffing me on the back as he turned to head back to a party he'd come from. As if ruining lives was just part of growing up.

No one died that night, but they might have.

Then and there, I realized I hated myself as much as I hated him. It should've been the last straw, but I've always had a stubborn heart.

It took three more weeks for me to leave. It took discovering the full extent of my father's monstrosity and all he'd stolen from me for me to find God and trade Bane for Father Blackwood.

And yet, here I stand. Teetering on the brink, staring at the same darkness I once embraced.

Watching her.

Hours later, the door opens, spilling a group of laughing strangers onto the sidewalk. Then I see her again.

Moira steps back into the night, radiant and alive. Her cheeks are flushed, her pigtails tousled, and she bounces from one foot to the other as if dancing.

She only pauses for a moment to pull out her phone. The light briefly illuminates her face, and for a moment, everything else falls away.

Relief washes over me, sharp and almost unbearable. My entire day zeroes down to this. Watching her go in that dark door and waiting for her to come back out again.

For one more day, she's safe. She's whole. She doesn't need me.

I should turn and leave. But I don't. Instead, I stay rooted, watching as she continues to bounce and dance in place to an invisible melody. When she finally drops the phone back into her pocket to head toward the parking lot, her steps are confident and sure. She's a queen who answers to no one.

I wait until she disappears around the corner. Only then do I exhale, the breath trembling as it leaves me.

"I'll keep you safe," I murmur into the empty street, the words a vow I've no right to make. It's all I can do. Stand watch. Remain unseen. Ensure she has the freedom to walk her own path.

Even if it kills me.

SIX

Two weeks later

MOIRA

I REACH over to pluck a greasy fry from the basket, then lean my head back in the steamy bubbles of the hot tub as I eat it. Damn, Domhn really does know how to live it up. This hot tub is fucking massive.

"Fine, if you don't want to talk to me," I shout at the top of my lungs. "I'll just keep enjoying your amazing backyard!"

I look around his large, elegant back deck for cameras. I'm sure there are at least ten pointed at me, but my annoying fucking brother has them discretely hidden.

Is he even listening?

I mean, sure, it's almost three in the morning. I grab my phone from the other side of the hot tub with my non-greasy hand to double-check—yup, two-fifty-seven. But I figured that would piss him off even more with all his fancy security alarms going off.

It's been weeks since I had any sort of stimulation.

And I mean... *any*.

Obviously, I still masturbate every time I'm in an enclosed space—my bedroom, my bathroom, my shower, the bathroom of the coffee shop on the bottom floor of my building, in my car with my seat levered down so no one can see me—but there's barely any point to it lately. And yes, I know, it's creepy. And no, I'm not proud of it. Especially since there's nothing more shameful than being in a public restroom, rubbing at your pussy like it's a firestick and you're trying to get a goddamn spark when there's absolutely nothing happening. And then just feeling even more numb.

I can't get off.

What the hell even is my life if I can't fucking get off?

I splash the bubbling water with both my fists and furiously kick my feet. Then my ass slips off the edge of the bench.

"Shit!" I splash even more, giggling as I regain my balance.

What if I went back and saw that hot priest?

I let myself sink back in the water but stretch out my arms

to hold on to the side of the smoothly tiled hot tub this time, kicking out my feet in the multicolored water. While this house is far smaller than his last, Domhn's still so fucking fancy; the pool and hot tub have lights that aren't just white but slowly shift back and forth between gentle neon colors.

I put my feet together like I'm a mermaid and let my body float, head resting on the edge.

Maybe I should go back to church.

I sigh. That priest was so fucking hot. I'd let him give me absolution *anytime*.

I smirk, then sigh again.

Last Sunday, I went back to listen to the bells, but I couldn't go inside. I didn't need to go and make a dumbass of myself again in front of the yummy priest. I just stayed long enough to catch a peek of him when the doors opened, where he stood there, all dark and sexy in that collar of his and so patient with each one of the older folks who came through the receiving line after church.

If he looked at me with those gentle eyes again, I would melt, and then die, and then throw myself in his arms, slowly sliding down his body with my hands still clutching him, and then run away again as fast as I could.

So, instead of recreating that mortifying situation in reality, I go to the club night after night. But I don't bother fucking anyone.

I keep hoping Bane, the magic-fingered masked dom, will come back, but he never does. Sometimes, I take a turn on the spanking bench to at least feel *something*, but not even that can get past whatever this funk is I'm in the middle of.

I just know it hurts a tiny bit less when I'm at the club.

But tonight, both Quinn and Jinx were busy sceneing on stage, and I just sat there alone, feeling nothing. I tried texting Anna and Kira but got no response.

Everybody's got their own lives. And I'm just floating, purposeless.

Because I told Marci to take me off the schedule at the shelter so often the last six months, she said she didn't have any available volunteer shifts when I called today. *Bitch.* There are always shifts. She just doesn't like me.

I kick at the water.

Tonight, after the club closed, I couldn't stand the thought of going back home to compulsively wail on my numb-to-the-world-clit.

So I drove here. My stupid brother has to talk to me eventually. I figured there was no point ringing the doorbell, so I just came around to the back, hopped the security fence, and made myself at home in his hot tub.

Frankly, I'm shocked attack dogs haven't come and ripped my throat out. Domhn's such a freak about security. I figured a bunch of alarms would have gone off by now and the cops would be hauling my ass away.

Does that mean he still loves me if he disabled the alarms enough to just ignore me and not call the cops?

I kick angrily at the water again.

Of course, he's ignoring me. I don't exist, right? I'm *dead* to him. Fucking bullshit. He should be so lucky. He can't get rid of me that easily.

At least it's one thing keeping me from wanting to disappear off the face of the earth. Fucking spite. I mean, yes, it would be fun to haunt his ass and see how bad he felt for saying all the things he's said—

The bubbles suddenly turn off.

I swing my head around toward the back of the house.

"Domhn?"

Then I realize, no. It was just the stupid timer. I've been in here for an hour already? Sighing, I drop all the way underneath the water. The hot tub is big enough that I can submerge my entire body.

I look up through the circles of settling water at the big, full moon.

It's so bright.

But lonely, too, up there by itself in the sky. I've always been a moon child, preferring night to day. *Just you and me, pal*, I say to the moon from underneath the water, bubbles coming out of my mouth with each word.

I stay under until my lungs burn.

Slowly, I bring my face out of the hot water.

The cold air feels like a relief. I've been in too long, but I don't want to leave yet.

Maybe just another hour. There are towels by the grill. I

could wrap myself up in them and sleep by the pool until Domhn's forced to kick me out tomorrow.

Just as I'm daydreaming all the ways I could try to get my brother's attention, movement at the edge of the yard catches my eye.

What the fuck?

I know why *I'm* back here, but who the fuck else is trespassing in my brother's backyard at this hour?

I slink back down in the water so that only the top of my head and eyes are over the edge, like a crocodile, watching a figure in black jog toward the house.

Fucking seriously?

Am I watching someone try to rob my brother? Yes, his security will keep them out... but I could always try to stop them, too.

That's, like, fucking heroic. And if they, I dunno, knife me in the process, well... at least it'll be noticeable.

I slip, dripping but still relatively quiet, out of the hot tub.

Then I run on bare feet toward the figure right as they manage to pry the kitchen window open without setting off any alarms at all. Maybe they're silent, only lighting up Domhn's phone or something.

Either way, the intruder has one leg over the windowsill and is about to climb in before I leap forward to grab them and yank them back to the deck.

They yelp—a much higher-pitched sound than I'm

expecting—and before I can grab their wrists to pin them, they've flipped me and got *me* pinned.

"Anna?!" I gasp in shock when I realize it's my soon-to-be sister-in-law crouched on top of me. "What the hell are you—?"

But her hand slamming down over my mouth silences me. By the hard way she's glaring at me and shaking her head *no* —I get it.

It's not Anna. It's obviously Mads running the show right now.

I nod to let Mads know that I won't make a noise.

She looks suspicious but still lets go of my mouth.

"Mads," I whisper, "What the hell are you doing?"

"What am *I* doing?" she laughs. "Why are you drenched in nothing but your underwear in my backyard?"

Right. I look down at myself. I figured underwear worked as well as a bikini. I can't decide which of us is being weirder right now. "I was stopping by to borrow the hot tub. Now *you*."

She sighs, rolls her eyes, and climbs off me. "Can't a girl take a night-time stroll without being interrogated?"

I raise an eyebrow, looking her up and down in her totally black burglar outfit.

So she's sneaking because Domhn doesn't know she's out... and *that's* why all hell didn't get raised when I hopped the fence.

"You disabled his security," I breathe in realization.

She shrugs. "He's not the only one who's good with a computer."

"Where were you?"

"None of your business, kid." Her tone's sharp now. "Now get out of here." Then her brow pinches. "Where the hell's your car, anyway? I didn't see it on the way in?"

"I took an Uber." I may have had a *few* drinks tonight at the club. It was embarrassing when Caleb cut me off. I wasn't drunk or anything, but he has a habit of being Domhn's watchdog, even though Domhn doesn't give a shit anymore. It had me wishing I'd gone to a real bar where they let you drink and grab someone random to fuck, because a few drinks in, I'd changed my mind about wanting dick even if it wasn't going to get me off.

Instead, I just Ubered here.

"Well, put the rest of your clothes back on and call one to take you home." Then she puts a finger to her lips. "And not a word about this to Donny."

My shoulders slump. I'm trying to get back into my brother's good graces, not keep more secrets from him. Especially when it comes to the most important person in his life. If he ever finds out I'm keeping secrets about Mads sneaking out of the house in the middle of the night for reasons she won't say, I really will be dead to him. Because he'll kill me himself.

But I nod my head miserably. Because girl code. And because I see myself in Mads.

This bitch is bananas, too.

"You're the best, kid."

She grins and nuzzles the top of my wet hair, then disappears in through the window.

SEVEN

MOIRA

"YOU FUCKING BITCH!" Jeff screams. "Get back here!"

Oh, for fuck's sake.

Now I'm the one climbing out a window. I shake my head at myself. This is what I get for judging Mads. Karma's a bitch, and apparently, so is Jeff.

I glance back through the window at the bedroom door I so thoughtfully jammed shut with a chair.

Jeff had some real issues grasping the extremely basic concept of *no means no*.

Yes, we met on an app two hours ago. Yes, I came over for a good time. But guess what, Fuckface McSlappypants? A girl has the right to change her damn mind.

Apparently, Jeff the Fuckhead didn't agree. And when I tried to leave, he decided to get handsy.

Bad call, buddy.

It's been a long time since I've been slapped that hard. I open my mouth to stretch my jaw, only for pain to blossom across my cheekbone.

"Fuck!"

Yup. Still hurts.

I expressed my displeasure by stabbing him through the hand with a fork.

Helpful tip: always check your surroundings for potential weapons. Jeff was a slob. Leftover plates of food were all over the place. Major ick. There'd been bad vibes since I stepped inside the place, hence my about-face. But it was convenient 'cause the moment he hit me, I grabbed the nearest fork and turned his hand into a kebab.

He screamed like a little bitch.

I bolted.

Thus, kitchen chair under the doorknob to buy myself time.

Classic. Effective. A++ move, Moira.

Cut to my great escape and scrambling down a rusty fire escape outside his apartment. Too bad I was two stories down before my brain very helpfully reminded me that I could've just taken the elevator.

At least Fuckhead Jeff only lived three floors up.

A cackling laugh bursts out of my throat. I slap a hand over my mouth while I kick the last ladder down to the street.

Scratch that. *Almost* down to the street.

I have to drop the last three feet to the pavement and—

"Fuck!"

My ankle twists. But I'm back up and sprinting before my body can fully register the pain.

Finally, I make it to a well-lit street and duck into a pharmacy. Sanctuary. Civilization. Concealer.

The security guard gives me a look, but I keep my head high, shoulders back, and march straight for the sunglasses section.

It's not my first rodeo.

Have I made some dumb decisions in my life? Yes. Was meeting up with Jeff one of them? Obviously.

Most of the time, it goes fine. Like ninety-three percent of the time.

I've just been on edge ever since I woke up to a text from Mads. She and Domhn are going to the club again tonight for Strip Poker. Which means tonight is another chance to fix things.

But also... another chance to fuck everything up.

And if there's one thing I excel at, it's fucking things up.

I speed-walk through the overly perfumed aisles to the sunglasses display. I tilt my head, checking the mirror on the twirling rack.

Fuck.

A bruise is already blooming around my eye.

I groan. Goddammit.

But what's the goddamn point? I root around in my purse for some aspirin and can't find any. What do I come up with instead? Weed gummies, the magical Delta 9 kind that's legal here in Texas.

My eye really does fucking hurt. I look around for the security guard, grab a handful of gummies, and stuff them in my mouth. There. That'll help with the pain *and* the anxiety.

I yank the biggest pair of sunglasses off the rack and slide them on. They cover most of the bruise. Good enough. Everyone will be wearing extra accessories tonight, right? I'll leave before things really get started since Domhn'll be there.

Respectful boundaries and shit.

I tilt my head in the mirror, testing angles. "I'm so fucking respectful."

I try a pouty face. Bad idea. My lip is swollen, too. Fucking perfect.

Right—concealer. I need concealer.

I yank the sunglasses off and stomp toward the cosmetics aisle. Should've grabbed a basket.

EIGHT

BANE

I'M at my usual perch, watching from the shadows and feeling more foolish than usual.

How long am I going to keep this up? Yes, we had one night of connection. And yes, she came to my church pleading for something—salvation or absolution, maybe. But the dazzling siren who commands every room she walks into doesn't look like she needs saving. She looks untouchable. Unstoppable.

Unlike me.

Oh, I go through the motions: my rigid priest's routine, my careful sermons, my daily devotions. But the truth? I'm having what the kind-hearted might call a *crisis of faith*. I don't doubt God. I only doubt that He ever truly called *me*.

Did I turn to the priesthood to atone, or was it just another form of selfishness? Another way to wrest control over the urges that have ruled me since I was old enough to name them? Because if I was ever truly in this life to serve others...

Then why can't I let go of her?

She haunts me. Possesses me. Consumes my thoughts with a fervor no prayer could ever match.

I've stopped dressing it up. Why lie to myself? There's nothing noble about this. There is no higher calling behind my actions.

There's only *obsession*.

I'm as twisted as I ever was.

The drizzle starts, soaking through my collar as I keep up my usual vigil across the street from the club. But still, she doesn't come.

I clench my jaw, already cursing myself for a fool and telling myself that this is *it*. The last night. I'll leave this place behind. I'll let her go.

Then, a car pulls up.

She steps out.

And my whole body locks with tension.

Something's wrong.

She stumbles, barely catching herself as the driver steadies her. Moira never stumbles. I've watched her for weeks; she's a force of nature, striding through life with fiery confidence. But tonight, she's moving like something inside her is broken.

My hands curl into fists inside my coat.

Don't move. Don't interfere. Whatever's wrong in her life, you'll only make it worse. My obsession is meant to be my own curse.

She disappears inside the doors of the club, and my breath releases.

But she's barely inside ten minutes before she storms back out.

Limping.

Quinn follows, eyes narrowed, mouth set in a hard line. They argue. Moira shouts something sharp, and Quinn lifts her hands in surrender before shoving back inside, leaving Moira alone on the street.

And the moment she's alone, she absolutely collapses in on herself.

Even though she's still standing, I see her broken before me again—lost, trembling, pleading.

Lightning splits the sky.

I failed her once.

I *won't* fail her again.

Before I've even made the decision, I'm moving. Already slipping my mask from my pocket and tying it into place across my face. Already crossing the street.

Her tears have mixed with the rain by the time I reach

her, but I don't miss her sharp inhale when she lifts her gaze and sees me.

"You!"

"Me."

She blinks, water clinging to her lashes, her chest rising and falling too fast. I *see* the moment she registers me. The way her expression wobbles, just for a second, before she forces herself into something sharp, something brittle.

And then I see the bruise blooming across her eye.

My stomach twists.

Who?

I'll fucking tear them apart.

I will find them. And I will *end* them.

But first—

She's shivering. Uncontrollably.

"Come with me." My voice is lower than I mean for it to be, but she doesn't hesitate.

She nods, eyes wide, and reaches out a hand like she's a child seeking comfort.

Her trust destroys me.

I take her hand. The moment our skin touches, a shudder runs through her, and I don't know if it's the cold or—

No. She's freezing. That's all it is.

After only a few steps, I see again how badly she's limping.

What the hell am I thinking? Dammit. I can't make her

walk three blocks like this. She's just an elf of a woman, anyway.

Without a word, I scoop her up into my arms.

Her gasp is soft, startled, but her arms loop around my neck like she belongs there.

My gut tightens.

I don't know what the fuck I'm doing, but I keep striding forward, carrying her down the familiar path I've walked over and over these past few weeks, as if each step wasn't a step toward damnation.

She doesn't say a word, and neither do I.

Not until we're almost at the church.

Her voice is quiet but not weak. Never weak. "Are you real, or am I imagining you?"

I should ignore her. I should let the silence stretch between us. I should remember that this moment—her body curled against mine, her trust so freely given—is an illusion.

But I don't.

"Do you often imagine me?"

She hums, something wistful curling in the sound. "Sometimes."

The word slams into me like a fist to the gut. My grip tightens around her instinctively, my body warring between smug satisfaction and something darker.

She thinks of me. Imagines me. I shouldn't crave that knowledge, but it unfurls inside me, warm and insidious. I want to know how often. How much. In what way.

Thunder rumbles in the distance, and I shove open the gate to the parish house, the rain falling harder now, soaking through my coat.

"I'm real," I growl.

She shivers against me, her face pressing into my chest, seeking warmth.

I move faster.

The gate swings shut behind us, and the cobblestones glisten with rain. Her breath is warm against my throat as I climb the steps of the parish house, my keys already in my free hand.

I should let her go.

I should set her down.

But I don't.

I shoulder open the door, my grip on Moira unwavering. We step inside, dripping water across the threshold, and I shut the door quickly, cradling her tighter before carrying her straight to the bathroom.

The moment we cross into the smaller space, I reach over and twist the faucet, a rush of water filling the tub. Steam curls into the air, warming the chill between us. Only then do I realize—I'm still wearing the mask on my face.

I pull it off, and the second my face is revealed, she gasps.

Her gasp slices through the air like the snap of a whip. Her eyes widen, shock swirling with something raw.

I expect words—accusations, questions—but she gives me

silence instead as she shivers in the damp glow of the bathroom light.

Shame crashes through me.

For years, I've fought to keep these two halves of myself separate. To lock Bane away and let Father Blackwood atone for his sins. But now, standing before this bruised and vulnerable woman, it's so clear: I was never truly hidden.

I kneel before her, the motion both instinct and surrender.

I force my hands to stay steady as I untie her boots, the sodden laces resisting. When the first shoe finally slips free, I set it aside carefully, almost reverently.

This feels like a sacrament.

The chill of her sock seeps into my fingertips as I peel it off, her skin cold against my palm. Too cold.

A deep, unrelenting rage coils in my chest. What happened before she got to the club? Who left that bruise?

I shove it down. She doesn't need my fury. She needs warmth. Comfort.

I gently rub her foot between my hands, coaxing heat back into her body. She gasps at the contact, her breath hitching, and my stomach tightens. *Fuck. Not now. Not like this.*

"In the bath," I say, my voice rougher than intended.

I risk a glance upward, but she isn't looking at me. Arms locked tight around herself, her gaze is fixed firmly downward as if she can hold herself together through sheer will alone.

And then, in a whisper barely audible over the running

water, I hear, "You're... Father Blackwood. But you're... you're Bane."

The name cracks through the air like a whip. I flinch.

I wish there was any denial I could make. But the truth is raw and rasping in my throat. "I am," I admit. "I'm both."

I look away as her accusing gaze flashes up at me.

I've tried to smother Bane for years, to starve that hunger out of me. But, in this moment, as her eyes rake over me, I feel him resurrecting.

I take a breath and steady myself.

"You're freezing," I say, pushing past the wreckage of my confession. "Let's get you warm first. The rest can wait."

She hesitates. I reach out but stop short, hovering just above her arm. "May I?"

She nods, barely, but it's enough.

I slip my arms beneath her knees and back, lifting her effortlessly. She's nearly weightless in my grasp, yet the moment feels impossibly heavy.

Now she knows. Now, there's no more pretending and stalking safely from afar.

I ease her into the bath, clothes still on, my hands steadying her as the water rises to meet her skin. She gasps at the heat, fingers brushing my wrist before she lets go.

Her shivering slows. She sinks deeper. The steam swirls between us, a fragile veil.

"You're... a priest," she murmurs at last, eyes shadowed with something unreadable. "But that night, you weren't..."

The accusation cuts deep. That night, I was Bane.

I swallow hard. "That night, I wasn't wearing the collar. But it doesn't change what I am."

Her lips part, but no words come. Instead, she wraps her arms around herself again. A shield and a barrier.

Something in me fractures at the sight.

"I never wanted to hurt you." The words escape before I can stop them. "That night, and every day since, I—" I clench my jaw and swallow the rest. She doesn't need my turmoil. She clearly has enough of her own tonight.

She watches me, her gaze searching as if trying to see past the man in front of her to the truth beneath.

"Why didn't you come back?" she asks finally.

I exhale sharply. "I had to stay away. For both of us."

A flicker of something crosses her face—anger? Disbelief? Pain?

She opens her mouth, but I shake my head, reaching for the towel beside the tub. "Feel free to stay in 'til you get all the way warmed up," I say, quiet but firm. "I'll leave you now."

I stand, nodding toward the robe hanging by the door. "You can use that. I'll find you something warmer to change into."

Her nod is faint. Hesitant. Watching me even as I pull away.

I step to the door, pausing at the frame.

I glance back once.

"You're safe here," I murmur, voice low but resolute. "I promise you that."

Then, before I can break further, I close the door behind me.

The silence that follows is heavy. Final.

I let out a slow breath, turning and resting my forehead against the door for just a moment before pushing off and walking away.

Because she sees me now. And for the first time in years, I don't know if that means salvation—or damnation.

NINE

MOIRA

I DROP my head back and stare at the ceiling.

Hot water. Ha. Back in hot water. *When are you not, bitch?*

I giggle, the sound bubbling up like a fizzy drink, and wiggle my toes beneath the surface of the bath. The world is soft. Shimmery. Everything has a little extra glow like the whole universe got hit with the prettiest Instagram filter.

Oh, right. The gummies.

But still. Still.

Father Blackwood is Bane!

My brain hiccups. Stumbles. Falls flat on its ass trying to

put that puzzle together. The hot priest and the hot dom are the same fucking person.

I mean—*holy shit*.

A hiccup-y laugh spills out of me, and I slap my hand over my mouth to keep the crazy from escaping. Then I lift my head from the bath and squint around the room, blinking water from my lashes.

I'm in his house.

I'm in the sexy priest's house.

The sexy priest who is also the hot dom!!

Wait. Is that the weed talking? I run a hand down my face. I didn't eat *that* much. And I bought it at a store. They don't just lace dispensary shit for funsies, right? Weed makes things *extra*, sure, but it doesn't make you hallucinate. Unless...

Unless I ate, like, ten times what I thought was in my purse.

Nah. I'd remember that. Probably.

I sink back into the water, exhaling hard through my nose. Bubbles rise and pop in little bursts.

It was the club that got me like this. Not the weed. The weed just turned my usual chaos dial up to eleven. It was already going south the second I walked into the *Carnal* lounge. I was trying to be chill, easy-breezy Moira, but then I accidentally took my sunglasses off and —boom.

Domhn saw the bruise.

And then he got all, *Jaysus, how could ya go play outside the club again, Moira? After what happened LAST TIME?*

Boom.

Last time.

The thing I'm not supposed to think about. The thing I keep running from. The thing that got me exiled from his good graces forever.

The memory shoves its way in any way—Anna catching me with her father, the man who made her and Domhn's lives the worst living hell anyone could possibly think of. *Her face when she saw me.* The way she shattered.

I press my hands over my eyes. *Fuck.*

Of course, Domhn got extra mad. Of course, Anna got upset. And, of *course*, I blew the one tiny, fragile, threadbare chance my brother had given me to make things right.

I slide under the water again and scream.

Only bubbles rise.

But then—

My scream dies. My thoughts stutter.

Because *then there was Bane.*

He arrived out of nowhere, this dark, impossible man, stepping out of the shadows like an avenging angel. Like he was built just for me.

And, miracle of miracles, he turned out to be *both* men who've made my heart race in recent memory.

My head spins, the water rippling softly around me.

Two men. All in one. My brain still refuses to compute.

I open my eyes and stare at the ceiling, my shoulders sinking under the warmth of the bath. My limbs feel light, but my chest feels heavy.

I think about the way he took care of me. Not like a man planning to fuck me. Just... took care of me. Like I was something precious. Like I wasn't just a mess to be managed.

When was the last time someone was gentle with me?

Not my mother, that's for damn sure.

The tears come so fast I don't even feel them build. One second, I'm floating. The next, stupid, ugly sobs are bubbling up. I shove my arm into my mouth and bite down to muffle them.

After the day I've had—

I lift a shaking hand to my bruised eye and flinch with pain.

Bane saw. He didn't say anything, but he *saw*.

I sniff hard and blink at the heavy wooden door.

Why did he bring me here?

Does he want to fuck me now?

My gut twists.

Then I roll my eyes.

That's all men ever want from me. Duh.

Priest or not, he's obviously kinky as fuck. He didn't even bat an eye at the bruise. He'll probably make it good for me.

I nod, wiping my face. I'm ready.

This night is about to turn around, at least.

I pull the plug on the bath and step onto the plush, ridiculously nice rug. It's warm. Oh. He must have turned the heat up.

My chest tightens.

It wasn't just about getting me naked. It was a real concern.

I don't know how to handle that.

I shake it off, drying myself and wrapping my curls up in the towel. Time to get this show on the road.

TEN

BANE

I'M STANDING in the kitchen when I hear the faint creak of the bathroom door opening. The sound pulls me immediately from my thoughts, my hand stilling on the glass of water I'd poured but haven't touched.

I brace myself as I turn.

I shouldn't look. Even seeing her like this—fresh from the bath in my robe, all soft and vulnerable—will test every restraint I've spent years cultivating.

And then she steps into view.

I barely manage not to drop my glass.

She's not wearing the robe, and she managed to take off

the wet dress. Only one of my gray towels is wrapped around her head. The rest of her damp skin is flushed and absolutely bared.

She's standing naked just across the room from me.

Brown nipples peak in the cool air, not yet warm even though I've cranked the heat up.

Fuck her. Take what she's offering, drag her down to the floor, and fuck her.

I jerk my eyes back up to her face when I realize where I've let my gaze drift.

For all her brazenness, there's an unguarded quality to her expression that tugs at something deep in my chest.

"Moira," I say, my voice low and steady, though it costs me dearly to keep it that way. "You should rest. I'll show you a room where you can stay the night if you like."

She smiles, a little crooked, a little coy. "And you'll join me?"

I take a step forward, but she beats me to it, padding softly into the room on bare feet. I force my eyes to stay on her face, swallowing hard.

But even then, I can't escape the way her gaze meets mine—intent and deliberate, a challenge I'm not sure I can meet without faltering.

"I feel much better now," she says, stopping just a few feet away. Her green eyes hold mine as she adds, "Thanks to you."

She knows what she's offering. And you've been dreaming of bedding her for weeks now.

"It was the bath." My tone is sharper than I intended. I clear my throat and take another step back, trying to widen the space between us. "Not me."

Her smile softens, but she doesn't step back. If anything, she edges closer, her bare toes brushing the cool tiles as she tilts her head slightly, the towel precariously balanced atop her damp hair.

"You're very kind, Father," she says, the word both respectful and mocking, like she's testing it. Testing me. "I don't think I've ever met anyone quite like you."

"Don't call me that," I bark. "Not now that you know. I'm Bane."

She quirks an eyebrow, amused. "Bane, then."

She's playing with me. Because she can see the part of me that craves indulgence, pleasure, and dominance? Or just because she's a woman who knows how to use her body to get what she wants?

Or perhaps she simply thinks this is what I expect of her after bringing her here?

It's the last possibility that shuts down the beast inside me.

If we were back in the club, I would know exactly how to bring her to heel. *Or to weeping, howling pleasure.*

But we're not at the club. This is Father Blackwood's

territory, no matter what she calls me. While I don't know how to find solid ground between the man that I was and the one I usually strive to be, some motherfucker has already hurt her once tonight. I won't be the second.

"Moira," I begin, my voice rough. "You should—"

"Should what?" she interrupts, her voice soft but insistent. She takes another step closer until she's nearly within arm's reach. "Should go to bed? I'd be warmer if we went to bed together, you know. Don't you want me to be warm?"

Her gaze lowers briefly, taking in the way my fists are clenched at my sides, before rising to meet mine again. "Or do you want me to leave you alone to your cold prayers, *Father*? Is that what you want?"

I exhale sharply, wanting to paddle her for her insolence. "What I want doesn't matter."

"Doesn't it?" she whispers, her voice barely audible but devastating nonetheless.

The air between us is too thick, too charged. I take a deliberate step back, and the edge of the counter presses into my spine as I force myself to put distance between us.

"You're tired." I force my voice steady. "You've had a long night. You need sleep."

Her head tilts slightly, her damp hair catching the light as she studies me with those piercing green eyes. "What if I don't want to sleep?" she asks, her tone feather-light but laced with meaning.

Fuck her. She's begging for it, you self-righteous asshole. You can make it good for her before you choke her on your cock.

I close my eyes briefly, my hands gripping the counter behind me as though it's the only thing keeping me upright. When I open them, she's still there, her expression unreadable but undeniably... vulnerable.

"Moira," I say again, her name a prayer, a plea. "This isn't..." I trail off, the words refusing to come.

She takes another step forward, so close now I can feel the faint warmth radiating from her breasts—not touching the cloth of my shirt, but so, so close. She's still flushed from the bath, not that I dare let myself look down.

"This isn't what?" she asks softly.

My breath catches as she reaches up, her hand brushing against my arm, tentative but deliberate. The touch is electric, setting every nerve in my body alight.

"Moira," I growl, the sound barely human. I step away from the counter, towering over her now, though it does nothing to lessen her defiance—or her proximity. "Don't."

"Why not?" she whispers, her hand still hovering near my arm but not touching. "I'm not some wounded thing. And I'm not afraid of you."

The words hit me harder than they should. She doesn't know about all the things I'm envisioning in my head.

"You should be," I rasp.

Her brows furrow slightly, but she doesn't move away. "I don't think you'd ever hurt me." She sounds so sure.

And that's the crux of it, isn't it? The thing that keeps me rooted here, torn between the need to protect her and the gnawing temptation to give in, to take what she's offering even if it damns me completely.

"You don't know what I'm capable of," I say, my voice deep and gruff.

Her gaze doesn't waver. "I know enough."

I look again at the bruise darkening her eye, and it's enough to reaffirm my resolve even as my teeth clench. "Tell me who did that to you."

Her eyes harden. "A man who's nothing like you. A man I'll never see again."

For a moment, the world narrows to just the two of us, the air humming with tension and something far more dangerous. But then she shifts, just slightly, and the movement is enough to shatter the fragile balance I'm clinging to.

I reach for her, my hands gripping her shoulders, and I can't help but tighten my fingers the same way I would, as if I was about to pull her into a passionate embrace.

Her eyes widen, and for the first time, I see the flicker of uncertainty in her gaze.

"You need to rest," I say, my voice low but unyielding. "This isn't... This can't happen. Not tonight."

Her lips part, but no words come. She looks up at me, her

expression unreadable, and for a moment, I think she might argue.

But then she nods, the movement small but enough to ease some of the tension coiled in my chest.

I release her shoulders and step back, the loss of her warmth almost unbearable. "Come on," I say, finally able to make the words come out gentle and soft. "Let's get you to bed."

ELEVEN

MOIRA

I WAKE up with the kind of regret that clings like a cheap polyester dress in the middle of a Texas summer. Sticky. Unforgiving. And making me deeply, deeply question my life choices.

Oh, Moira, what have you done this time?

I groan, rolling over, and—yep, there it is. The crushing weight of last night slamming into me like a ton of bricks.

Bane is Father Blackwood. Father Blackwood is Bane.

Of course. Of freaking course. The one man I've actually fantasized about worshipping is technically already married to the Church. And I tried to seduce him with a black eye.

Goddamnit, the room is too bright. I wince as I pry my

working eye open. And I'm too fuckin' sober. This is all just too painful without the haze of gummies to soften the memory of me throwing myself at him like a runaway rollercoaster with no brakes.

Nope. Time to dip out like the hot mess coward I am.

I roll out of bed—correction, I roll out of *his bed*—and get to work. I straighten the sheets like a polite little house guest, smooth down my dress that he washed and dried like the infuriatingly thoughtful man he is, and tiptoe toward the bedroom door.

But when I try to open it, the door groans like it's personally offended by my attempt to sneak away. I wince. *Fuck you, stupid door!* I try pushing harder and faster. *Creeeeeeaaak.* Oh, for fuck's sake. I squeeze through the smallest opening possible and inch down the hallway, wincing every time the floorboards squeak beneath my feet.

I pass by the living room, pausing for a moment when I see a coffee table lined with upright dominos in a little maze, each perfectly spaced. Just waiting for someone to come and push the one at the end to set them all off.

I'm tempted. Very tempted to go knock over the first one.

But no. I shake my head. The front door is right there. I focus back on it, tiptoeing closer.

So close. Almost home free.

And then—

"Leaving so soon?"

I freeze like a goddamn deer in the headlights. Like every bad decision I've ever made is coming back to haunt me in the form of a six-foot-something, dark-eyed, utterly unreadable priest standing by a little coffee nook, two steaming mugs on the table.

"Uh—" My brain short-circuits. Words tumble out of my mouth without pausing for breath. "I just—figured you had things to do, so I'd just get out of your hair, also, I'm so sorry for last night, I'm mortified, truly mortified, beyond mortified, if there's a level past mortified, I'm there."

His gaze flicks to my bruised eye.

I stammer. "Oh, yeah, that. It was just a misunderstanding. A—a mix-up. I mean, obviously, you know that, but I just—" I gesture wildly at my face like that'll somehow erase my embarrassment. "I'm gonna go now."

I make a break for the door.

Bane is faster.

One second he's sitting, the next he's towering in front of me, blocking my exit like an impenetrable wall of calm, controlled masculinity.

"Stay." His voice is smooth. Commanding. A slow, deep vibration that sends a shiver down my spine. "Have some breakfast."

"I don't eat breakfast," I say automatically.

"Coffee, then."

I hesitate. His dark eyes pin me in place. He's unreadable, as usual, but there's something in his gaze that makes me feel... *seen*. Which is dangerous because no one ever looks at me long enough to see anything real.

But he does.

And that is a problem.

Still, I shrug, trying to play it cool. "Fine. But only coffee."

He moves aside in a silent invitation. I step into the kitchen, past the point of no return, past the escape I should have taken while I had the chance.

The coffee smells rich, dark, and far too comforting for my current emotional state. The kitchen is neat and sparse. All masculine—just like him. He's got creamers in multiple flavors, which seems shockingly indulgent for a man of God, but then again, nothing about him fits in a neat little box.

I take my seat at the small dining nook by the window, wrapping my hands around the warm mug like it's an anchor. I take a sip, and fuck, it's as delicious as it smelled.

"Tell me about yourself."

I shift, clearing my throat. "Why do you want to know about me?"

He leans forward. "Because you're fascinating."

I laugh. "You clearly need more hobbies."

"Don't do that." His voice is firm.

"Do what?"

"Act like you're not worth knowing."

His words hit deeper than they should. My throat tightens. My knee starts bouncing.

I need to say something, anything to shove the attention

off of me, so my mouth does what it always does in a crisis—spits out something completely unhinged.

"I'm a sex addict. How's that for a fact about me?"

Silence.

I squeeze my eyes shut. *For fuck's sake, Moira.*

When I peek one eye open, Bane is... completely unbothered. If anything, he looks like I've just confirmed something he already suspected.

"Aha," he murmurs. "You do seem to surround yourself with chaos."

I huff, setting my coffee down and fidgeting with the mug's handle. "Well, at least you're observant."

Enough with the twenty questions and all this sitting-still bullshit. I get up, eyes on the dominos in the living room again.

Bane watches me, sipping his coffee, as I meander back into the living room. His gaze is so steady, and it's unnerving and thrilling all at the same time.

I crouch in front of the coffee table, my fingers hovering over the neat little setup. "So," I muse, pretending like I'm totally casual. "What's the deal with these? Do you have a YouTube channel dedicated to setting up elaborate domino chains or something? Should I be worried that you're about to show me some Rube Goldberg contraption that actually made our coffee?"

"They're about control." His voice is low. Steady. He's

followed me into the living room. "About setting order to chaos."

I hum, considering this.

"You know what's funny about dominos?" I muse, tapping a finger against my chin. "They look so perfectly aligned, all neat and controlled, but really, they exist for one reason and one reason only."

I grin. And before he can stop me—

Boop.

I flick the first domino.

Bane exhales sharply through his nose as the dominos collapse in a perfect wave, the soft *click-click-click* of their downfall filling the space between us.

I gasp, bringing a hand to my mouth in mock horror. "Oh no," I whisper, eyes wide. "I *definitely* didn't mean to do that."

His breath leaves him in a slow, measured exhale. He places his coffee down with the kind of restraint that suggests he's resisting the urge to throttle me.

I grin. "Well, at least now you have something to do while we drink the rest of our coffee."

He doesn't move. Just watches me, long and slow, until my smirk falters slightly under the weight of his stare. Until my pulse stumbles. Until I realize I might've started a game I didn't fully understand.

Then, he speaks, his voice like a low rumble of distant thunder.

"Moira."

I swallow. "Mm-hmm?"

"You're going to regret that. You need order in your life."

I roll my eyes. "And you think you can give it to me?"

His gaze burns into me. "Yes."

A slow, magnificent shiver runs down my spine.

Oh dear. I have the horrible, no good, absolutely deliciously delightful feeling that I'm about to be in trouble.

And I *do* so love trouble.

TWELVE

BANE

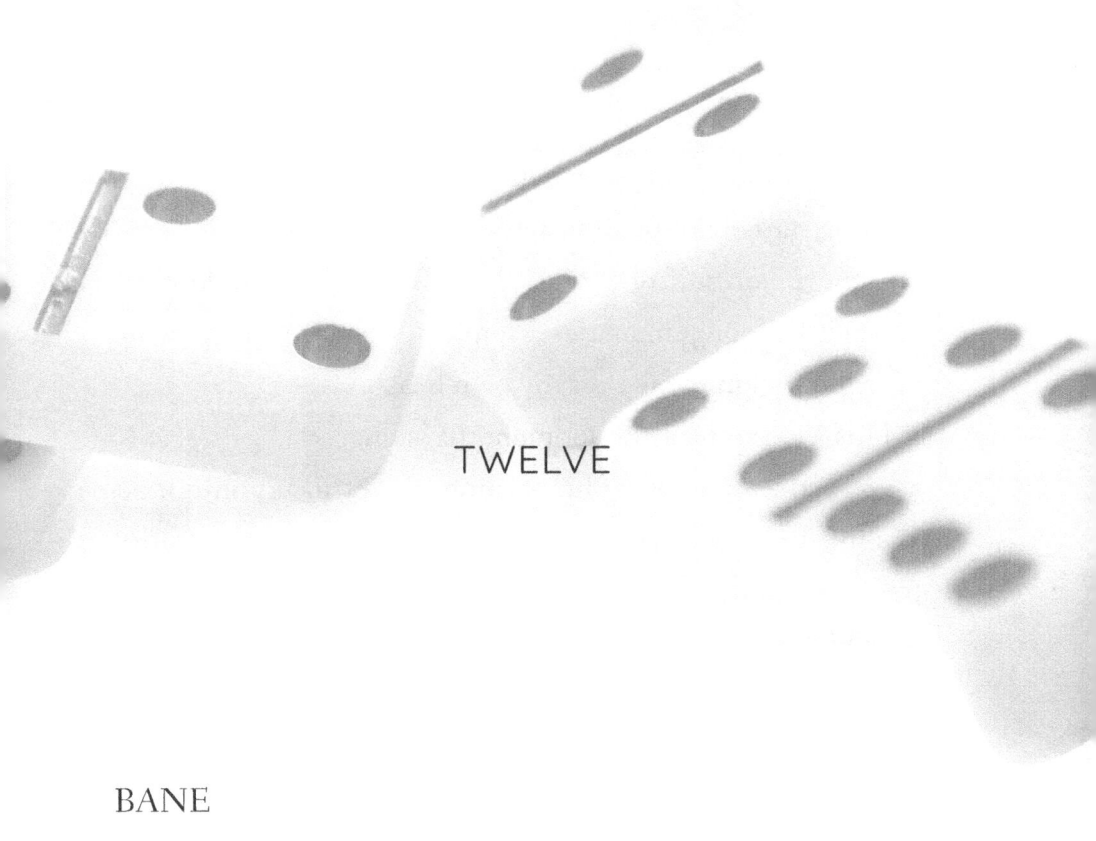

"YES," she whispers, big Bambi eyes blinking up in a way that has me wanting to toss her up against the wall right now and reach under the flimsy skirt of her dress to thumb her cunt and see if my offer has her wet already.

She's not as vulnerable as last night, and after a good night's sleep, I know she's sober. She's admitted she's a sex addict, so she'd probably be game. I could get verbal consent and be balls-deep in the cunt I've been obsessing about in less than sixty seconds.

Do it. Take what's yours.

"Good," I snap, the word overly crisp. "We begin today."

I turn away from the coffee table of fallen dominos. "Training starts with breakfast."

I ignore her huff of protest, heading towards the kitchen because if I'm going to model discipline, I better start exerting some right fucking now over my own beast.

This is no spur-of-the-moment decision.

I stayed awake all night, turning it over in my mind. At two a.m., I got out the dominos. The precision and control calmed my thoughts and helped me think. Again and again, I dissected every angle, every possibility, and every risk. And every single time, I arrived at the same conclusion.

First, I have to bring us both under control.

And second—*she must be mine.*

I covet her with a lordly possessiveness that should unnerve me.

But fear is where I faltered before. Fear of myself. Fear of my past. Fear of my own dark, snarling desires.

I do not have to be afraid of my hunger, just as I will teach her she does not have to be afraid of hers.

In discipline, we will both be free. We can tame our animals.

It's true that my father taught me to just *take* whatever I wanted. To be the conqueror. To let nothing stand in my way. I've spent years rejecting his lessons, refusing to be that kind of man anymore. But denying my nature doesn't erase it. The drive to dominate and possess never left.

Maybe it's not wrong to give in to obsession as long as the object of my obsession wants to be devoured.

How is a dominant that much different from a shepherd? Both guide, watch, and protect their flock. I ensure the well-being of the ones entrusted to my care as a priest. And Moira... she is in need of care, whether she knows it or not.

I will take care of her. And indulge my cravings at the same time.

But only if this hunger is shared.

I glance over my shoulder at her as I cook.

She sits cross-legged on the chair at the table, scrolling on her phone absentmindedly while she watches me from her peripheral. The sight of her here, in my house, twists something dark inside me.

I saw the hunger in her eyes that night at the club. Felt it in the shudder of her body.

Even now, she bites her bottom lip. She wants this, too. She may not understand it yet, but she will. Because I will make her crave like she has never craved before.

I plate her breakfast—a simple omelet and fruit, nothing too heavy. She looks like she barely eats. We'll work on that.

I set the plate down in front of her. "You're quiet this morning."

She looks up, startled. "Oh—I—" She hesitates, eyes flickering with something like guilt. "Is that bad?"

I shake my head. "There is no bad or good here."

"What are you, like, Yoda?" She smirks.

I arch a brow. "Well, I'm a little taller."

She actually laughs, and it's a sound I *want*. I want to hoard it and pull it from her again and again until it's mine.

I turn back to retrieve my own plate, then settle in across from her. She pokes at her food with a fork but doesn't eat.

"What are you thinking about?" I ask.

She doesn't hesitate. "Sex."

My hand stills over my coffee. She flicks her gaze up to mine, then back down to her plate as if she regrets the admission. "But I'm usually thinking about sex."

I hum in approval. "Interesting. Thank you for your honesty." I tilt my head, assessing. "You should know I value honesty above everything else. If we embark on this together, you must never lie to me. Do you promise?"

Her gaze sharpens. "If I promise, how do you know I'm not lying?"

I smile, slow and dark. "I'll find out. And then this—between us—will end forever."

She leans back, considering. "Lying is that much of a dealbreaker to you?"

"Yes."

"What about cheating? Because I already told you I'm a sex addict."

"Do you usually cheat?"

She shrugs. "I don't know. I don't have significant others."

That surprises me. "Never?"

"Maybe when I was a teenager, for like, a minute."

"Did you cheat on them?"

"They cheated on me."

Each minor revelation is a pearl I tuck away, a puzzle piece I will assemble until I have the full picture of her laid bare.

"What do you think about when you're not thinking about sex?" I ask.

She smirks. "I'm always thinking about sex."

I doubt that's true, but I let it lie. "So, you can't promise me that you won't cheat, but I need you to promise me that you won't lie."

She studies me, and I like that she's taking this seriously. I like everything about this subdued, thoughtful version of her. Interesting that she's not always manic energy and chaos. She has quiet depths, too. Even more interesting is that she's already willing to show me this new side of her.

"Okay," she whispers. "I won't lie to you."

She doesn't meet my eyes as she says it. But I still believe her. I've had plenty of people look me in the eye as they swore they were telling the truth, only to stab me in the back later.

"Good. What are your hard limits?"

"No scat play," she says immediately, wrinkling her nose. "And no fluid exchange."

I nod. "That's reasonable. Although, eventually, I would like to exchange fluids."

She looks hesitant. "Full disclosure, I have HSV-1. It's one of the types of herpes."

"I know. One that fifty to eighty percent of the population has. I have it, too."

Her eyes widen, seeming surprised by my calm answer. "Doctors don't usually test for it. And most people freak out when I mention the H word."

"That's ignorance. It's commonly acquired in childhood through shared towels or water bottles. And you didn't answer my question. Do you have any more hard limits? It's important that we agree on these before we begin."

"What are *your* hard limits?" She arches her petite eyebrow.

I smirk. "You won't get near them. And you'll be the one following the rules, not setting them."

She flops back dramatically. "Jesus! Usually, I have to fight for my safety-first spiel. Now you're grilling me because I don't have more limits?"

"We'll circle back. What's your safe word?"

She arches an eyebrow at me. "Domino."

My cock stiffens. "When were you last tested?"

"Two weeks ago."

"Did you use a condom?"

She scowls. "Of course. I told you—no fluids. I'm a safety girl."

"Are you amenable to fluid exchange if we're both tested?"

She blinks, looking shy for the first time since I've met her. "I've never done that."

"Gone with someone to get tested or been taken bare?"

Her lips part. I see the shift in her breathing. "Either. Both."

I feel the change in the air between us.

Heat licks down my spine. *I will be the first. I will be the only.*

"Are you amenable to doing so?"

She smiles crookedly, then repeats with a terrible mock British accent, "I am amenable."

My cock goes fully hard, and I want to pull her over my lap and finger her until she squeals. No one ever dares to take the piss with me.

I want her to do it again. And again, and again.

"Eat," I command, voice rough.

She rolls her eyes but obeys, stabbing at her food. My cock twitches. No one ever dares roll their eyes at me, either.

I'm obsessed with watching the way she eats, slow and careful, like she's testing the boundaries of this strange new world we're building.

She swallows, then tilts her head. "So, are you ever going to explain how you're a priest *and* a dom?"

I take a sip of coffee, then smirk. "I wasn't always a priest."

She leans in. "That's all you're gonna give me? No more explanation about how you go back and forth from playing, '*yes, Daddy,*'" she moans breathily, then puts her hands together, "to 'forgive me, Father'?"

Her eyes glint with mischief. *Brat.*

I chuckle, low and dark. She has no idea what she's just unleashed.

I push my plate aside and stand. Her eyes widen.

"What now?" she asks, cautious but intrigued.

I beckon her down the hall. She follows.

I stop in the bathroom and retrieve a fresh toothbrush, handing it to her.

"Toiletries?" She stares. "That's what's next?"

I put toothpaste on both hers and mine. "If you stay here, you'll need one."

I meet her gaze in the mirror as we brush our teeth.

The moment feels strangely intimate. Too much. Just enough.

And fuck—

I want her.

So take her. Press her up against the door, wrists clasped on either side of her head. Helpless.

Make her mad with craving.

Don't stop until she's screaming your name and calling you her god.

The vein bulges in my neck as Moira finishes with her teeth and wipes that sultry mouth, big eyes meeting mine in the mirror. Her wintry fresh mouth would feel so good gulping down my cock. Gagging on my balls.

I lean over the sink and spit. I want her on her knees,

want to spit into her mouth and for her to accept it like it's God's gift.

Instead, I white knuckle the counter.

She's grinning at me, and when she hands me the towel she just wiped with, she intentionally brushes her fingers against mine. Goading me.

I snap back to attention. Yes, the brush of her skin lit me on fire, but it reminded me why I'm doing this.

I have to be the control for both of us. She's unruly and must be brought to heel. For both our sakes.

"Go wait in my bedroom. It's across the hall from the bathroom. We'll discuss the rules. Your training begins *now*."

THIRTEEN

MOIRA

THIS. Motherfucker. Put. Me. In. A. Chastity. Belt.

Like I'm some goddamned maiden being kept in a castle. Except, you know, it's sleek black leather instead of being all rusted metal and shit.

The smell of new leather is driving me nuts. Knowing this absolute menace of a man, it's probably from some upscale kink boutique called *Luxe Dom* or *Exquisite Restraints*.

But did you hear me? A motherfucking chastity belt!

Because when Bane said "training," I was thinking... oh, I don't know, some light flogging? Maybe he'd show me his favorite whip and let me ride the sting a little?

But *no*. No, instead, he went full medieval dungeon master on me. And now I'm kneeling in the corner of his room like a wayward nun with a chastity belt on under my skirt while he—*get this*—writes his fucking sermon. By hand. In a notebook.

The scratch of his pen is the only sound in the room besides my shallow breathing and the occasional tiny frustrated groan that I *definitely* don't mean to let slip.

He doesn't use a laptop, even though he can't be more than a few years older than my twenty-two. But nope, Mr. Proper English Broody McPriesty-Pants over here probably thinks modern technology is somehow cheating. I bet he still balances a checkbook. I bet he—

"Stop fidgeting," he says, all calm and superior from his fancy wooden chair like a king holding court.

I make a face. A very mature, very respectful face. And then, because I have a death wish, I mock, *Stop fidgeting*, in the most obnoxious whisper possible.

His pen pauses for exactly one second before he resumes writing, like he's too *holy* to engage with my nonsense. Like he has the patience of a saint.

I can't take it anymore. Forty-five minutes ago, this seemed exciting. Hot. I was all in for the game. But now? Now, I've got the itch, and I *can't even* pretend to *scratch*. And let me tell you, that is some eighth-circle-of-hell-level torture.

The scent of leather clings to me, taunting me, reminding

me with every breath that my body is locked up tight. I kick at the rug under my knees just to feel *something*.

"Stay still."

Oh, fuck off. That's easy for *him* to say. He's perfectly composed, his muscled forearms flexing slightly as he writes, his crisp white shirt rolled up to his elbows, looking like the most dangerous daydream. I *hate* him. I *hate* how hot he is.

And I really hate that he's right.

This isn't just about control, Moira. It's about trust. That's what he said when he buckled the belt around me, his voice all rough and constrained. Like it wasn't just me he was binding up tight.

It was so hot, and all I wanted to do was beg him to fuck me.

Which pissed me off even more.

I don't beg.

I grant people the *privilege* of fucking me.

But Bane and his deep, steady voice, his dark, knowing eyes, and his entire *everything* makes me want to scream.

Because, uh, has the man ever actually met me?

Trust?

I trust my brother, sure. Or at least, I did. Before he turned his back on me and decided I wasn't worth the effort anymore.

So what the fuck is trust supposed to mean to me now?

I don't have to trust someone to enjoy fucking them. But what if I did? What if—

Nope. No. Absolutely not. That way lies madness.

I shift again, pressing my thighs together in desperation, but the belt mocks me. My body is soaked, needy, screaming for something I can't have.

"Moira." Bane's voice is a warning.

I snap my head up and glare at him. "I can't *help it*. I'm losing my goddamn mind down here."

He pauses, his pen hovering above the page, and finally—finally—he looks at me. Those storm-gray eyes are infuriatingly calm. "That's the point."

"The point?" I sputter. "The point of what? TORTURING ME?"

"The point of teaching you patience."

I scoff so hard I nearly choke. "I have patience! I've been sitting here for *forever* while you scribble away about god knows what—"

"About God, actually," he says, his lips quirking.

Oh, for fuck's sake.

I growl and rock forward slightly, chasing even a whisper of relief. The belt presses against me—too much and not enough—and my hips jerk involuntarily.

Bane's chair scrapes against the floor as he stands and looks down with that infuriating calm control. "If you can't control yourself, I'll do it for you."

My breath catches. Oh.

Oh, I *like* that.

My heart pounds as he hauls me up and leads me to

the bed. My body is screaming *yes, finally, please*, but instead of pushing me down and giving me what I *need*, he sits me on the edge and holds my shoulders firmly in place.

"Stay."

I stare up at him, vibrating with frustration. "What are you going to do?"

He doesn't answer. He just walks to the chest at the foot of the bed, pulls out a length of silk rope, and turns back to me, his expression utterly composed.

I swallow hard. Oh, fuck.

"You brought this on yourself," he says, taking my wrist in his strong, steady hand.

"You're tying me up? *Seriously?*"

"Seriously."

"No!" I fight against him, but he easily subdues me, grabbing both wrists and pinning them to the bed, his chest holding my body down. We're both breathing hard even though we barely wrestled. I struggle against his hold as his dark eyes skewer me.

"Do I hear a safeword?" he asks, chest heaving against mine.

My lips clamp together as I search his eyes. I feel a wild elation suddenly as I realize...

Oh shit, I feel *safe*. Even as he holds me down and subdues me with his superior strength.

There's no background thrum of fear like there is with

random men I fuck outside the club. Like there was with that pissant, Jeff.

But I'm also not feeling that sense of bored safety I usually do *within* the club because I know bouncers are near if a guy steps out of line.

I feel safe because of *Bane* himself.

Well, fuck. Is *this* what trust feels like?

He'll stop if I safeword. There's not a bone in my body that doubts it.

"You fucking bastard!" I scream again, but only because it feels good to fight like hell as he smiles down at me, working quickly to secure my wrists to the headboard with practiced ease.

The silk is soft against my skin, but the restraint is firm. Unyielding.

My heart races as I tug against the bindings, testing their strength.

"There," he says, standing back to admire his handiwork. "Now you can't get yourself into trouble."

I glare up at him, my chest heaving with emotions I don't understand.

I'm giddy and furious and wildly excited. And I really, really want to be fucking Bane right now instead of being tied up, helpless, on his bed.

"You're enjoying this, aren't you?"

His lips curve into a slow, dangerous smile. "Immensely."

"You're the devil," I spit.

"And you're beautiful when you're helpless," he replies, his voice soft but deadly. He leans down, his face inches from mine, and I hold my breath. "You'll thank me for this one day, Moira. When you finally understand."

"I hate you," I whisper, even as my body burns for him.

"No, you don't," he murmurs, brushing a strand of hair from my face. "But keep telling yourself that if it helps."

Oh, I am *so* fucked.

FOURTEEN

BANE

THE AFTERNOON SUN filters through the curtains, casting soft, golden light across Moira's skin where she lies on my bed. Her wrists are still bound to the headboard, her body humming with defiance even in stillness. She is a study in contradictions—soft yet unbreakable, restrained yet entirely untamed.

My pen rests against the pages of my sermon, the ink flowing easier than it has in weeks. There is clarity in domination, in the simple purity of control. And yet, Moira—

Moira is an anomaly.

She watches me now, dark green eyes flicking toward

mine before darting away. There is no pretense with her. No coy games. Everything about her is raw and unfiltered.

And that, more than anything, is why I can't stay away.

She isn't like the women from my past. I've known too many who smiled at me with hungry eyes but cared nothing for the man beneath the wealth and power. They wanted the Blackwolf name, fortune, and proximity to power. My cruelty turned them on only because it meant access.

But Moira? Moira fights me at every turn, not because she wants to push me into playing some role but because she doesn't know how to be anything other than herself.

She isn't pretending.

The weight of that realization settles over me as I rise from my chair and cross the room. "Thirsty?"

Her lips part slightly, a betraying movement, but her jaw clenches before she nods. She wants to resist even this. The simplest act of care.

I retrieve the water and press the glass to her lips. She hesitates for a beat too long, then drinks, her graceful throat working as she swallows. My free hand ghosts over her jawline, my thumb grazing the heated skin just beneath her ear. She stiffens but doesn't pull away.

She's learning.

I set the glass aside. "More?"

She exhales, shifting slightly, the leather of the chastity belt creaking as she moves. Her flush deepens. "No."

I tilt my head. "No, Sir."

Her nostrils flare, her pride rebelling, but she knows what I'm asking of her. Knows, and for the first time since I bound her wrists, she doesn't fight it. Her voice is barely above a whisper. "No, Sir."

Progress.

I untie her wrists, watching the way she stretches and the small wince as circulation returns to her hands. I take them in mine, rubbing slow, soothing circles over the faint red marks. She doesn't pull away.

That trust—so slight, so fragile—claws at my chest.

"Come." I extend a hand.

She takes it.

I lead her to the bathroom, watching as the stubborn line of her spine stiffens when she realizes the chastity belt is still in place.

"Do you need help?"

She shoots me a glare so full of fire that my cock twitches in response. "No."

I smirk but say nothing, stepping back to let her have her space.

The door clicks shut. I lean against the frame, waiting. Listening. The sound of the sink running. The rustle of fabric.

When she emerges, she looks composed but wary. That blush still lingers high on her cheekbones, and I want to *taste* it.

"Better?"

She huffs, brushing past me, but there's no real bite in it. A part of her is beginning to settle into this. Into me.

She climbs onto the bed, lifting her wrists in silent acceptance as I tie them once more to the headboard. She exhales slowly and then meets my gaze.

"You're learning," I murmur, tightening the silk.

"Learning to hate you," she mutters, but there's no venom in it. Only *heat*. Only *need*.

I chuckle, brushing a strand of hair from her face. "Like I told you earlier, hate me all you like, Moira. It won't change the fact that you're still here."

She swallows hard, something flickering behind her eyes that she doesn't yet understand. That's fine. She'll learn.

Her stomach growls, breaking the silence. She freezes, eyes wide, but I only smile.

"Hungry?"

"I'm fine," she says quickly, but I see the hesitation, the way her body betrays her even now.

"You need to eat." I rise, heading to the kitchen. "Stay."

She grumbles under her breath but doesn't argue.

I take my time preparing something simple—grilled chicken, fresh greens, a slice of lightly buttered bread. When I return, she watches me warily as I set the tray down beside her.

"Lunch."

She eyes it, pride warring with hunger. I pick up a forkful of salad and hold it out. "Open."

Her lips press into a thin line, but her body decides for her. She opens her mouth, taking the bite and chewing slowly. I watch her, cataloging every shift and every subtle flicker of emotion.

"Good girl."

She glares, but there's color in her cheeks. My cock, already half-hard from watching her defiance give way to need, stiffens fully.

"Don't patronize me," she snaps.

"I'm not." Another bite. Another moment where she lets me take care of her. "I'm feeding you."

"I don't need—"

"Of course you don't." I smirk. "But you're getting it anyway."

She huffs but keeps eating. The fight in her never fully dies, but it softens at the edges, dulled by a full stomach. And by something else she isn't ready to name yet.

By the time the tray is empty, she looks almost... content.

I set it aside and meet her gaze. The air between us hums, quieter now, less combative. Charged in a different way.

"Thank you," she murmurs, barely above a whisper.

I don't know if she realizes how much that single concession means.

"You're welcome."

As her eyes slide away from mine, I feel it again, the

warring ache, satisfaction, and *need* in my chest at having her so near.

She's *here*.

And she's more than even my dark, little, obsessive heart could ever dream she could be.

FIFTEEN

MOIRA

THE SUN DRIFTS lower in the sky, and I let out a shaky breath. It's almost sunset. I've almost made it through this whole goddamn day without losing my mind.

Almost.

Every other second, I was right there—on the edge of screaming my safe word and ending this whole stupid experiment in self-discipline.

Because let's be real: I don't do discipline. Ask any of the nuns back at The Sisters of the Immaculate Heart Academy for Girls. They tried. They failed.

I tug at the silk binding my wrists. It doesn't give. Of course, it doesn't. Bane's too precise for that, too maddeningly perfect at tying me just tight enough that I can't slip free but not enough to actually hurt me. It's like he knows exactly how to push me to the edge but never lets me fall.

I should hate that. I do hate that.

Don't I?

My thighs twitch, and I would rub them together for some semblance of relief, but a couple of hours ago, Bane tied my ankles apart, too. Because he *knows me*.

How the fuck does he know me so well when he's only just met me?

Uh, probably because you're so fucking obvious? I never was one of those polished, mysterious girls. I was half-feral as a kid. Only Domhnall could keep me in check. The nuns tried. I bet they wanted to tie me down, too.

Bane is the only one I've ever let do it, though.

I hate bondage. It makes my skin crawl, makes my brain itch, makes me want to scream and run and never stop moving.

Being so still, there's nothing to do but sit here and notice little details like the way Bane's shoulders shift when he leans forward. Or the way the light catches on the muscles in his forearm when he moves. It's stupid. All of this is stupid.

I'm going to go literally fucking crazy if he ties me up like this every day.

And yet, there's also... this knot in my chest that won't loosen. Like I'm on the edge of something, something big. I feel like my whole world is tilting, and all I can do is hold my breath and hope I don't fall.

But also, I terribly *want* to fall.

It's unbearable.

"You're squirming," Bane says without looking up, his voice low and steady. He says it like it's just a fact. Like it doesn't mean anything. But I know better.

"I'm not squirming," I snap, even though we both know I am. The silk rubs against my skin again as I shift, the friction sending a little thrill of frustration and something I don't want to name shooting through me.

"You're restless," he says, his pen pausing mid-stroke. His eyes lift to meet mine, and there's that calm, piercing gaze of his that makes me feel like he sees right through me. "Do you want to talk about it?"

"No," I say, a little too forcefully. "I don't want to talk about anything."

His lips twitch like he's holding back a smile. The knot in my chest tightens. I'm a simmering tea kettle about to combust from the pressure. How long has it been since I've gone a whole day without masturbating? Of course, I'm about to burst!

"Suit yourself," he says, going back to his writing like I'm just another piece of the furniture. Like he hasn't tied me to this bed and left me to stew in my own thoughts.

I glare at him, wishing I could set him on fire with my mind. He's too calm, too in control, and it pisses me off.

I shift again, trying to find some position that doesn't make me feel like I'm coming apart at the seams. My legs ache from lying still for so long, my wrists are starting to tingle, and the damn chastity belt is driving me mad. Every little movement sends a reminder of how close I am to relief. And how impossible it is to reach it.

It's torture. Delicious, infuriating torture.

"Stop wriggling," Bane says without looking up.

"I'm not wriggling," I bite back. But I am. I can't help it. My body is restless, desperate for release in more ways than one.

I hate this! I hate how he gets under my skin, how he makes me feel things I don't want to feel.

And most of all, I hate that deep down, beneath all the frustration and anger, there's a part of me that doesn't want him to stop.

I pull against the silk again, testing its strength, even though I know it's futile. The bindings hold firm, and I feel a sharp pang of something like defeat that I immediately try to smother.

I don't lose. I don't give up. Not like this. Not to him.

"You're quiet," Bane says, his pen stilling again. He leans back in his chair, watching me with that same infuriating calm. "What's going on in that head of yours?"

"Nothing," I say quickly. Too quickly.

"Liar," he says softly, and the word sends a shiver down my spine.

I look away, focusing on the patterns in the rug instead of the way his voice makes my stomach twist. I hate this vulnerability, this feeling like he can see right through me.

So I do what I always do when I feel cornered: I lash out.

"This is ridiculous," I say, my voice sharp. "Tying me up, locking me in this stupid belt. You get off on this? Keeping me here like some prisoner?"

His expression doesn't change, but I see the faintest flicker of amusement in his eyes. "Do you feel like a prisoner?"

"Yes," I snap, even though it's not entirely true.

"Interesting." He leans forward, his elbows resting on the desk. "Because you could've said your safe word at any time. You know that, don't you?"

The air leaves my lungs in a rush, and for a moment, I can't think of a single thing to say. He's right. I hate that he's right.

Doesn't he know I've been fucking thinking about that all damn day? He even reminded me of it in the middle.

But what then?

This all ends and I go back to what?

My apartment? The bed I can't bear to get out of, morning after morning?

I'm twenty-two, and these are supposed to be the best years of my life. But instead of thriving, I have these dark moments I've never admitted to another living soul about having when I don't want to bother even *being* alive anymore.

I hide so well. I've got such good escape hatches so the darkness never catches me, but still.

"You're quiet again," Bane says, his voice softer now, almost gentle. "What are you thinking?"

I shake my head, refusing to meet his eyes. "Nothing."

"That's twice you've lied to me," he says, standing and crossing the room in slow, deliberate steps. My heart pounds harder with every step, my chest tightening as he stops beside the bed. "White lies, but still. There will be consequences."

"Consequences... as in, punishment?" I grin up at him wickedly. I make a lusty, groaning sound, "Oh, punish me, Sir. Please, *punish* me."

He doesn't take the bait. He just stands there, so solemn, and then his hand brushes against my cheek, and I flinch, even though it's the softest of touches.

"You're fighting yourself," he says, his voice low. "Why?"

"I'm not," I say, but my voice wavers. He tilts my chin up, forcing me to meet his gaze, and I see it in his eyes—that steady, unyielding certainty.

He knows I'm lying.

"Talk to me, Moira," he says, his thumb brushing against my jaw. "What are you so afraid of?"

"I'm not afraid," I whisper, but the words feel hollow. "I'm never afraid."

My chest aches, my throat tight, and I feel like I'm on the edge again of that something I can't name.

"Liar," he says again, but there's no malice in it. Just calm, steady truth.

The knot in my chest unravels just a little, and I feel tears prick at the corners of my eyes. I blink them away quickly, refusing to let them fall.

"I hate you," I whisper because it's easier than saying what I really feel. Fuck, I don't even know what I really feel.

I don't want to look. Because he's right. I am afraid.

"No, you don't," he murmurs, his hand still cradling my face. "But you can keep saying it if it helps."

I let out a shaky laugh, the sound bitter and raw. "You're insufferable, you know that?"

"I know. And yet," his lips curve into the faintest smile, "you're still here."

I don't know what to say to that, so I don't say anything. I just lie there, his hand warm against my skin, and for the first time in a long time, I feel even more fully... *seen*.

Exposed, yes, but not judged. Not rejected. Just... held.

It terrifies me.

But maybe, just maybe, it also makes me feel safe.

The silence between us stretches, heavy and loaded. Bane's hand is still on my face, his thumb brushing lightly against my cheekbone.

I can feel my pulse thrumming in my neck. Too fast. Too loud. He hasn't said a word, but his silence speaks volumes.

It makes me feel seen in a way that's so sharp it borders on painful.

No one ever *sees* me.

I don't know what to do with it.

"Stop looking at me like that," I murmur, turning my head to break his gaze. The movement pulls my cheek from his hand, and I feel the loss of his touch like a phantom ache. My skin prickles in its absence.

"Like what?" he asks, his voice unshaken. He always sounds like he knows exactly what's going on in my head. Like he's ten steps ahead of me in a game I don't even remember agreeing to play.

"Like you're waiting for me to fall apart," I snap. I can't look at him. I stare at the edge of the bed instead.

He exhales softly, and I feel the warmth of his breath against my temple before I even realize he's leaned in closer.

"I'm not waiting for you to fall apart, Moira. I'm waiting for you to *let go*."

The words hit me like a punch to the chest.

My throat tightens, and I swallow hard, trying to push down the surge of emotions threatening to rise. "I don't know what that means."

"Yes, you do," he says, and his certainty makes my stomach twist. "You've spent your whole life building walls, fighting to keep everyone out. But what has that gotten you?"

I hate that he's right. I hate that his words cut so deep that they scrape against parts of me I've worked so hard to hide. But more than anything, I hate that I don't have an answer.

"I'm going to untie you now. You've done *so well* today, dove."

I glow under his praise. It literally lights me up from the inside, like I'm suddenly filled with helium and none of the heavy darkness or shadows can touch me now.

"I know how difficult this was for you," he continues. "I believe in you, Moira. But this is the beginning of you learning to believe in yourself."

I relax against the bed as his fingers come to my skin to untie the silken ropes. They didn't actually hurt. He was skillful with the perfect amount of tension he allowed in the rope and his knots.

The moment I come free, I reach for him.

Daring what I probably shouldn't. Maybe he'll tie me right back up again. But earlier, he liked it when I begged.

"Please. If I've done so well, been such a good girl..." I swallow, but I don't lower my head and flutter my lashes like I do when I'm flirting with a potential hookup at a bar.

I just look him straight on, my stomach swooping as his dark, intense gaze locks with mine. No guile. No games.

"I'd really like to fuck you, Bane. *Please.*"

His eyes darken, and his nostrils flare. He lifts a finger in front of my face, and it's probably only my imagination to think his hand is trembling.

"Yes. But only once a day, and only if you behave as well as you did today."

SIXTEEN

BANE

SHE IMMEDIATELY SCRAMBLES off the bed and throws herself into my arms.

Literally climbing me.

Like a little monkey, she wraps her arms around my neck and her legs around my waist, grinding on me.

I'm immediately hard.

Everyone my whole life has wanted to use me, it's true.

But never like this.

"I thought you hated me," I sneer in her ear, arm around her waist, spinning and slamming her up against the nearest wall. All day I've been patient, kind, understanding Father

Blackwood. But Bane's finally been unlocked from his cage by her animal need for me.

"I do," she gasps, biting at my neck.

Fuck. My top lip twitches, and my fingers squeeze her ass. All day, she's kept this fire leashed, just barely boiling beneath the surface.

Because I fucking told her to. Christ, that does something to me.

"Bite me again if you hate me," I growl. "But try biting like you fucking mean it."

I want to fuck her for hours. In every position. On all fours. Face to face. Then smother my face with her cunt, cock in her mouth.

She drags the collar of my button-down shirt aside and sinks her petite little teeth where my shoulder meets my neck.

My cock all but busts my fucking pants to get to her cunt.

"This how you want it?" I growl low. "Up against this wall and not some sweet love-making in the bed?"

She laughs, lifting her head up to glare at me. "I don't do that shit. I fuck."

She reaches down and grabs me through my pants, sighing in relief. "Thank Christ. Here I was, worried I'd waited all day to get fucked by a AAA battery."

My lip twitches. "Oh, so now you just want to use me for my big dick?"

Her body shudders against me, and she groans the same

way she did at the club that first night. "After what you put me through today? Of course, I do."

"Oh, dove," I laugh caustically, being my true, selfish, spoiled, sadistic little self without any remorse for once in my fucking lie of a life. "But what if I feel like putting you through so much more? I do so like it when you beg."

She makes an infuriated noise and writhes against me, dry humping me through my pants. The skirt of her dress is already hiked up, so it's easy enough to reach down and unlock her chastity belt. It drops to the ground, and she groans needily.

I spank her bare bottom just to hear the noise of it and to rile her up even more.

It works.

I'm greeted by another indignant noise and more of her grinding on me.

I grin and chuckle, deep in my chest.

Oh, I'm going to give her exactly what she's asking for.

Pressing her against the wall with my chest, I put an arm under her ass and lock gazes with her while I reach in my other pocket for the condom I stowed there earlier.

"Let's hear it, dove," I hiss, then lean forward and nip at her bottom lip. "If you want to get what you deserve, beg me to fuck you with this big cock."

I lift the condom to my teeth and tear it open, never losing eye contact with her.

Her chest heaves against mine as I reach down and

unbutton and unzip my pants to finally free my aching shaft. I roll the condom down its length and allow it to hover, hard and hot, against her inner thigh.

Another of those simmering moans escapes her throat.

She glares at me with a combination of fury and desperate lust, and I almost bust the condom right then and there.

"You fucking cocky, twisted bastard." Her green eyes burn with fire. "Please let me ride this giant monster cock of yours so I don't die of horniness."

Then she grins like the devil herself and leans in to whisper in my ear, "But just know, *I've had bigger.*"

My body responds to all that she *is*.

A woman to finally match me.

I groan in abandon and thrust forward.

SEVENTEEN

MOIRA

OH FUCK, it's good.

Why does it have to be so good?

I was really hoping that having such a big tool would mean his weird cocky ego was fronting for inadequacy.

But nope.

He does this slow-scoop-thrust-thing that hits spots I didn't even know I *had*.

Oh, *God*, that's good.

I arch into his body.

He spanks me again, and it's *just* right. The bottom of my jiggling ass cheek bounces right to my pussy, and I clench around him inside me.

Which makes his fingers flex on my ass, his cock buck deeper inside me, and his top lip twitch. Like a dangerous, furious Elvis.

Fuck, how does he make that hot?

I come.

I grab a fistful of his hair, my hips thrusting back and then *bucking* forward against him with the seizure-like orgasm that rocks my body.

His hand lifts, caging my face with clenched fingers, but somehow, he's careful only to gently caress my cheek at the same time.

I lift my eyes as pained agony washes over his face before, for the most fleeting of moments, something like pure, undiluted *happiness* replaces it.

Then my shoulders rear back with the next wave of the world's single most intense double orgasm.

EIGHTEEN

Several Weeks Later

MOIRA

I BOUNCE into the women's shelter where I regularly volunteer—or used to, anyway—forcing myself to keep the energy up. Marci hasn't been taking my calls. She might've even blocked my number. But Bane and I have been talking about how I need to start showing up for my life again. Getting back out in the world. *Doing* things.

Because the training with him has been going well. Really... um... *well*. I've been staying at his place, and when he's not working, he's training me, and god, it's *awful* and boring but also, randomly the most exciting time in my life. If that makes any sense at all? I live for our once-a-day reward fucks when I do well.

I can't tell if today's a test to see if I'll be a good girl even when he's not looking or if it's just another one of his Jedi mind tricks to... I don't know. Make my life bigger? Better? He's not one of those guys who wants to lock me away. He's trying to push me into something more. And I can't figure out what the fuck to do with that.

But I'm here. I'm trying.

I paste on a bright smile and push through the shelter doors.

Marci grimaces and rolls her eyes the second she sees me.

My cheeks go hot. She's always had this ability to make me feel two inches tall, and I hate her for it. Girls like her have been cutting me down like this my whole life.

"Well, look who showed up," she drawls, arms crossed. "After months of vanishing, no less. But I suppose a lady like you would never dirty her pretty fingers with actual work."

I clench my jaw but keep my tone even. "I'm here, aren't I? Can't you use the help? Client intake? Making up beds? Laundry?" I flatten my expression. Hell, I'll beg if she wants me to beg. Begging's not that big a deal, ya know? The world's just a giant, stupid game, and some of us are better players than others. "I'll mop the floors if you need."

She scoffs, stepping closer until I catch a whiff of stale coffee breath. "You're on *suspension* from client relations.

You think we wouldn't hear about how you let a former client move in with you? How that whole mess led to her getting involved with your brother? At least someone with *actual* sense finally sent her off to Chicago."

My jaw tightens. She's talking about Anna. *The grapevine never dies.* Though she doesn't even know the half of it. But now Anna and Domhn are happy, so she can suck it.

"How long is my suspension?" I force out.

Marci smirks. "Six months. And it starts now. Feel free to vanish again and take the time to learn about *boundaries*."

I don't flinch. "If it's just a client relations ban, there's still plenty I can do."

Now Marci's cheeks get red. Oh, she's good and mad. I don't think she's used to folks standing up to her mean-girl antics. She usually just bosses everyone around while they cower. I almost laugh in her face. Please. I grew up in the ass end of Donegal, and she thinks she can intimidate *me*? Girls back home fought with steel pipes.

She sees something in my face that makes her look away first. "Fine. Lucita's out sick. You can scrub the toilets and mop the bathroom floors." Then, voice sharp she continues, "But we have standards. If you can't manage, tell me now, and I'll call someone who actually *knows* how to work."

I narrow my eyes but I don't rear back and punch her in the face. I got fired from a few jobs that way. And this isn't even a job. It's volunteer work.

Theoretically, I *want* to be here.

And I do.

I'm... trying.

Yeah, part of me is doing this because Bane says these little tests are important. It's not like he *owns* me. We've already discussed that I probably can't do monogamy, and he didn't seem to care. His only rule? No lying.

He calls it a choice. Whether or not I *choose* freedom.

The self-righteous prick.

I mean, yes, *technically*, I'm wearing the chastity belt by choice today.

But there are also incentives for playing by the rules, as Bane oh-so-clearly laid out before I left this morning. I can either *choose* not to be patient, or I can *choose* to get my brains fucked out tonight.

So, yeah. It's chastity belt day. A softer one meant for movement.

But the truth is, it's not just for him.

It's not like I *want* to be the way I am. Life was better when I was showing up for it. When I, ya know, gave a shit about anything.

Having some place to go and helping women who'd just met the shit end of what life had to hand you... It used to feel like something to get out of bed for.

And once I started to get out of bed for it, I soon forgot about how that was why I'd started, and before I knew it, I was just... living. There were the normal ups and downs. And yeah, I was still the inappropriate one no matter where I went, but life felt okay for once. Like I wasn't just floating through existence, one impulsive mistake at a time.

Maybe I *can* get back there.

I smile at Marci through clenched teeth but keep my head high and my shoulders back. "I've got it."

Marci purses her lips and makes an ugly face like she hates to trust me with a key to the fucking mop closet, but she finally produces a heavy ring of keys and wrestles one off for me.

She holds it up in front of my face but yanks it back when I try to grab it. "I expect this back promptly at the end of your shift."

Bitch. I give her an overly sugary smile. *I expect you to suck my dick.* "You got it, boss."

I turn away before I get myself into more trouble, get the supplies from the closet, and head into the dorm bathrooms. The women are in life skills classes, I know from the time of day it is, so I'm alone in here.

I put my earbuds in, turn on my *Pussy Riot* playlist and get to work.

I've cleaned hotels before, so scrubbing toilets and attacking grime with industrial-grade cleaner isn't exactly new territory. Bitch Marci doesn't know it, but I actually *like* work that's physical and repetitive. Gives me something to do with my hands that doesn't get me into trouble and lets my mind wander.

Hmm. Maybe I should try getting a job again. Hotels are always hiring.

Domhnall would shit a brick. The thought makes me grin before it fades just as fast. Well. He *would've*, back in the day. Before he stopped looking at me like his baby sister.

And, ya know, there's also the small problem that I've been fired from *almost* every job I've ever had. Taking too many breaks. Taking breaks that were too long. Fucking my boss. Fucking my boss's boss. Fucking the delivery guy.

But I'm *only* fucking Bane now.

… Right?

I frown, scrubbing harder at some unidentifiable black gunk. I mean, I *think* I'm only fucking Bane now. We talked about how I probably can't manage monogamy, and he said that wasn't a deal breaker.

Is that part of today's test? Not just to see if I can keep my hands out of my pants all day, but if I'll keep my legs closed the second I'm out of Bane's sight?

My frown deepens.

Do I *want* to fuck someone else?

I've always gotten bored with just one dick. Always.

But it's not *just* one dick, is it? It's *his* dick. And his fingers. And his mouth. And the fucking way he looks at me when he steps through the door like he's about to eat me alive.

Bane hasn't gotten boring yet.

But he doesn't *know* me, *know* me.

I scrub harder.

That's the other reason I've lost jobs. Not just the sex but the... shutdowns. Once or twice a year, everything slows down, my thoughts get sticky like tar, and my body? My body turns into a ten-thousand-pound sack of useless meat.

I *want* to get out of bed, don't get me wrong. I just... can't.

Getting up feels *impossible*. Showering? Laughable. Leaving the house? A cruel joke. Talking to people? Fucking *kill me*.

I scrub the counter with so much force I could wear a hole through it.

People suck. Usually, I think all they're good for is fucking. That way, I get my socialization and my human contact while also getting myself and someone else off. Foolproof system. No expectations. No disappointments.

So, where's the disillusionment with Bane?

If this is all just an illusion, why am I still so into it?

My phone buzzes in my pocket. My heart starts beating stupid fast. Is it him?

I rip off my gloves like they've personally offended me, fumble my phone out, and—

Oh.

It's just a jewelry ad.

I deflate like a goddamn punctured balloon. Then I get pissed.

What, like I have to wait for a *man* to text me? Fuck that.

> Me: Have you been thinking about me?

The response is immediate and deeply satisfying.

> Bane: Yes.

> Me: Then why haven't you texted?

> Bane: I'm trying to be a good boy.

Why does my brain immediately go to him on his knees, naked, wearing nothing but that cock ring I love when he wears, waiting for me to milk his prostate?

I bite my lip and let my thumbs fly over the phone screen.

> Me: I know how you could be my good boy.

> Bane: By not texting.

> Me: Why?

> Bane: Because I'm about to meet with the bishop.

My eyes go wide.

> Me: So you're in your collar right now? Kinky. Go in the bathroom and send me a picture of your dick before the bishop gets there. 👿

> Bane: Are you touching yourself?

> Me: No. Do you want me to be?

> Bane: Not if you want to go to Carnal tonight.

I groan. I hit a g, then *stab* the R button over and over so he *feels* my frustration through the screen.

> Me: Grrrrrrrrrrrrrrrrrr.

> Me: Going back to work now. Have fun with the bishop.

> Bane: I'll have more fun picturing your frustrated, throbbing clit.

I slam my phone back in my pocket and attack the counter like it's personally responsible for my lack of orgasms today.

But now all I can think about are Bane's shoulders, Bane's fingers, *Bane's fucking voice* when he steps through the door after being away.

Goddamn him.

My clit *is* throbbing.

Kinky motherfucker.

I scrub harder.

NINETEEN

BANE

THE DOWNTOWN COFFEE shop bustles with the easy lull of morning business. Machines hiss and churn, voices rise and fall, and the smell of roasted beans fills the air.

Bishop Caldwell sits across from me, sharp-eyed and patient, her hands curled around a porcelain cup. She's a steady woman, both in faith and presence, but even she can't quite keep the curiosity from her gaze as I chuckle and put my phone away.

"So?" she prompts, lifting a brow. "How are things? With the congregation, I mean."

I clear my throat and take a slow sip of my black coffee. "Steady. No great changes, but no great losses either."

She hums, watching me over the rim of her cup. "And yet you seem… distracted."

Fuck. No more thinking about Moira's pink little pussy that's probably all wet and pulsing right now. I exhale through my nose, forcing myself to focus. "The budget is tighter than ever. We had to push back the repairs on the rectory roof another month. And Mrs. Pearson has, once again, taken issue with Agnes over pew placement."

Her lips twitch in wry amusement. "As I recall, she's been fighting that war since long before you arrived."

"I suspect it will outlive us both."

She chuckles, but the knowing gleam remains in her eye. "And yet still, your mind is elsewhere."

It is. It absolutely is. Three weeks ago, I laid down the law for Moira. Set expectations and stripped her of choices that had been leading her down a path of chaos. And she—

She's flourished.

I roll my thumb over the lip of my coffee cup, the warm ceramic grounding me as flashes of the past weeks fill my mind. The first few days, she fought the structure I gave her, bristling, testing boundaries with a sharp tongue and restless hands. But discipline and consistency won out. By the second week, her obedience no longer felt forced. By the third, something in her settled, her edges smoothing, her wildness tempered—not extinguished, never that, but refined.

This morning, I kissed her forehead before she left for the

shelter. Her first day back. A test of sorts. One I'm eager to see her pass.

"Bane?" Bishop Caldwell's voice pulls me back.

I set my coffee down and offer her a wry smile. "You're right. My mind does wander. A thousand apologies. It's inexcusable. I know how valuable your time is." I mean it sincerely. I understand she's run ragged dealing with all the churches in the diocese. Taking time to meet with all the priests individually, in addition to coming to visit the churches, keeps her schedule full to overflowing.

She studies me with that piercing gaze of hers, the one that sees too much. "Wandering anywhere in particular?"

Yes. To a woman who kneels so sweetly now, who opens so easily under my hands. To the way her breath catches when I call her my good girl. To the promise I made her this morning—that if she behaves and doesn't chase pleasure I haven't given, I'll take her to play at Carnal tonight.

"Just the usual," I fib smoothly. It's not exactly a lie. Being with Moira is my new normal.

She smirks, unconvinced, but lets it go. "Well, distracted or not, I do have something to discuss with you."

I force myself to listen, to engage, but half my mind remains with Moira. I imagine her at the shelter, hands busy, mouth soft with focus. I imagine her remembering my words and my warning. I imagine the reward she'll earn if she obeys.

I can't wait to see if she'll pass my test.

The bishop finally folds her hands around her tea, fingers delicate but firm, and regards me with a quiet intensity.

"You know I'm not just your bishop," she says, voice measured. "I'm meant to be a shepherd to you."

The weight of her gaze feels too heavy for the light monthly check-in I expected today's meeting to be.

I nod, offering nothing in return. Silence has always been my refuge, safest when words might betray too much.

She takes a slow sip from her cup before setting it down with precise care. "It has been reported to me," she continues, each word deliberate, "that you have been seen taking walks with a woman. A woman who follows you into your house."

The words land like a stone thrown in a pond, disturbing my calm. A muscle in my jaw twitches, but otherwise, I force myself to remain still, my hands flat against the table.

Of course, people talk. Of course, even here, where I've worked to build something new, the past is never entirely out of reach. As the son of my father, gossip and gossip rags used to be my constant nuisance.

The bishop watches me carefully. "You understand, of course, that your heart is not yours alone." Her gaze becomes more pointed. "Nor is your house. You are living on parish property, and people... gossip."

I stare at her, my fingers tightening imperceptibly. Gossip. The great currency of communities, small and large. And I know well enough that whispers can turn into a sharp weapon if a man isn't careful.

She pauses. Takes a calculated sip of tea. Then, her voice drops just slightly. "And I took a risk on you."

That lands. A direct hit.

I swallow hard.

"You were not the obvious choice for this parish," she continues. "Your past raised concerns. But I saw something in you. A man seeking redemption."

My fingers curl into fists beneath the table. I force them to relax. "I appreciate that, Bishop. Truly."

"Do you?" she asks, her gaze sharp. "Because I have to wonder."

The air feels thick, pressing against my ribs.

The past. The unspoken thing always lurking between the lines. A past I can't undo, no matter how many good deeds I accumulate.

Her expression hardens. "Is it serious with this girl?"

Another punch to the gut. It's the first time the thought has been presented so bluntly.

Serious. The word reverberates.

The second time I met Moira, I promised her she wasn't alone anymore.

I should have an answer to this question. The last few weeks have just been so... good. Great. Stunning, really. Giving into the dominant bastard inside me... training Moira... satisfying both our demons while also reaching into the realms of heaven with our pleasure and connection—

I should be able to answer this fucking question.

But instead, my mind blanks.

Is it serious?

Moira's laugh, sharp and untamed, plays in my head. The way she moves through my house like she belongs there. Her presence fills spaces I didn't know were empty. The warmth in my chest when she brushes against me in passing. The way my body tightens when she looks at me with that knowing, unafraid gaze.

I've never been a man who lives with an eye toward the future. Maybe it's why I was never caught in the allure of my father's money. I live in the now, and in the *now*, I knew Moira and I were good for one another. So I never stopped to question tomorrow or next week or next year.

It's a failing, I realize, if I'm truly to be a good dom.

Because I don't know what this is between me and Moira.

I don't know if I can call it serious because I don't even know if I have the right to hold it in my hands.

But I know it's something. Something that pulls at me, that makes my blood run hot and my prayers falter.

The silence stretches too long. I swallow, my voice low, when it finally comes. "It's new."

The bishop's expression doesn't change, but the sharpness in her gaze deepens. "Well, figure it out." Her words are steely, as is her gaze. "And I'm sure you understand that sleepovers are inappropriate on church property."

A fresh wave of heat rushes through me. Not shame. Not guilt. Just anger.

She doesn't understand what this is. She can't. And yet, she has the power to destroy it before I even know what to call it. Not to mention, we aren't in the twentieth century anymore. The church has evolved. It's infuriating that we're still supposed to live by puritanical nonsense just because some elderly women in the congregation like to gossip. It's not what we preach but it's still a standard we're held by?

Still, I manage to nod once. "I understand."

Bishop Caldwell watches me like she's trying to peel me open and figure out what's ticking underneath. Maybe she is. Maybe she always is.

"Good." A long pause. Then, a slow exhale, like she's letting something go. "I heard you've been spending time at the correctional facility again."

I shrug. "A few times a week."

She gives a knowing hum, fingers steepling. "They need someone willing to see them. To remind them they aren't lost causes."

"They're not." My voice is steel. "They don't get visitors. They don't get forgiveness. They don't even get a phone call from the outside. Most of them got thrown away long before they ever ended up behind bars. The least I can do is show up."

Her lips press together, thoughtful. Then, "It's good work. Just don't neglect the ones who sit in your pews every Sunday, the ones looking to *you* for guidance."

I roll my shoulders, letting the tension settle. "I'm aware."

She studies me another beat, then nods. "And Advent preparations?"

I lean back in my chair. "The choir's rehearsing, the volunteers will handle the decorating after Sunday's service, and I've got midnight Mass lined up."

She hums. "And the food drive?"

"It's happening," I confirm. "But I'm expanding it. A lot of the guys inside have families barely scraping by. I want to make sure they get something too: care packages, food, supplies, whatever they need to get through the season."

Bishop Caldwell leans back. "Good. The church should serve more than just those who walk through its doors."

I nod once. "Agreed."

"Then I suggest you stay focused on the work. And don't get waylaid by... *distractions*."

She watches me carefully, as if waiting for me to falter, as if she expects some further admission. But I give her none.

The conversation shifts back to logistics and schedules, but the weight of her words lingers.

Long after I leave the cafe, long after I walk the familiar streets back to my home, her voice echoes in my mind.

I took a risk on you.

Figure it out.

Your heart is not yours alone.

TWENTY

MOIRA

THE NEON red glow of Carnal's sign flickers against the rain-slicked pavement as we pull up to the club. My heart is already tap-dancing in my chest, a wicked little beat of excitement. It's been too long since I've been here, too long since I've felt this rush, and even longer since I arrived on the arm of someone who actually meant something to me. Oh, wait. I've never arrived on the arm of anyone who actually meant anything to me.

I giggle at myself, feeling flushed with happiness as I suck on my signature cherry lollipop. Bane bought me a bagful the other day to help satiate my oral fixation.

He steps out first, the heavy door of the sleek black car swinging open with practiced ease. I was a good girl all day at the shelter, and now I get my reward.

Bane's always in control and composed. But I see the slight pause in his breath and the way his gloved fingers flex at his sides. He might be cool, but he's feeling this too.

I know sometimes his control is just a front. Like earlier when I'd all but burst through the front door of the parish house, practically vibrating from the afterglow of a good deed. "You should've seen me!" I announced, kicking off my shoes. "I was a damn angel today."

Bane was already home, rolling his big, stupid, unfairly sexy shoulders like he was shaking off the weight of the world. He barely glanced up. "That so?"

I sauntered toward him, still high on my own self-satisfaction. "Mm-hmm. Spent all day at the shelter. Scrubbed some toilets. Didn't get into a single fistfight. I'm practically a saint myself. How 'bout you?"

He just exhaled, long and slow, like he was carrying something heavy. "Long day."

I cocked a hip, crossing my arms. "At the church?"

He shook his head and ran a hand through his messy dark hair like some tortured hero in a gothic novel. "I met with the bishop. Then spent the afternoon at the prison."

That stopped me dead. "Hold up. You... do prison ministry?"

He nodded, all nonchalant.

I stared at him. "How come?"

"Because someone has to."

I opened my mouth to make a joke—something sharp, something to keep my heart from doing that stupid *flutter* thing—but nothing came out.

Because this man—the one who makes me lose my mind, who makes me feel too much, who gets under my skin in a way no one else ever has—spends his time sitting with those the whole world has given up on.

And damn him, that makes it really hard to keep pretending these feelings I have for him aren't like... scary real.

He grins at me now and my chest goes all *flutter flutter* again. Plus, now that we're at the club, I'm gonna get my reward for being a good girl all day.

Seriously, what the fuck? Who's life did I just hijack, and when are they gonna want it back? Fuck that. I'm enjoying the hell out of it for now, and maybe, just maybe, I won't give it up.

I smile up at Bane, bouncing on my toes like a kid about to be let loose in a candy store. "You ready for this?"

He slid the cloth mask on over his face right as he stepped out of the car, but I can still hear the devilish grin in his voice. "Are you?"

Bane is out to play.

"I was born ready," I declare, looping my arm through his. "Come on. I wanna see everyone and show you off."

Kit, the club's door security, smirks as we approach. "Haven't seen you in a while, Moira."

I give him a wink, reaching up to pull the cherry lollipop from my mouth with a pop. "Miss me?"

"You know I did. Everyone's been wondering when you'd finally drag your ass back here."

"Well, let's not keep them waiting."

Bane lets me pull him inside, though I know it's more an illusion than anything. He allows me my excitement and indulges my bubbling, madcap energy as I take in the sight of my old haunt. The thrum of bass-heavy music vibrates beneath my heels, the scent of leather, sweat, and something sweet—maybe vanilla—swirling through the air. The club is alive tonight, bodies moving through dimly lit spaces, whispers of pleasure and command threading through the heat.

And there, in our usual corner, are my people.

"Marcus!" I screech, flinging myself at the broody bastard where he's leaning against a leather chaise, a whiskey glass balanced in his hand. He must be done playing for the night.

He barely has time to put his drink down before I've thrown myself in his arms. "Jesus, Moira—"

"I missed you, I missed you, I missed you!" I chant, kissing his scruffy cheek before sliding down. "Did you miss me?"

Marcus gives me his signature dry look, but there's warmth in his eyes. "Club's been too quiet without you."

"That's what I like to hear," I purr, spinning to find Caleb watching with an amused smile, arms crossed over his chest. "And you, Daddy dearest?"

Caleb chuckles, shaking his head. "You're impossible."

"But you love me," I coo, skipping over to give him a hug. "Oh! I have someone for you to meet."

I twirl back to Bane, who's been standing like a predator in the shadows—still, watching, and waiting. His presence alone is enough to send shivers down my spine, his mask doing nothing to conceal the dark hunger in his eyes.

"Boys," I say, pressing a hand to his broad chest. "This is Bane. My Dom." *My everything.* I almost say that last part out loud but just barely manage to keep it inside.

I'm glad I do when Marcus and Caleb exchange a look, assessing. I feel the weight of their scrutiny like a physical thing, the way they take in Bane's imposing frame, the mask, and his aura of complete and utter dominance.

And Bane? He simply inclines his head as if bestowing a royal favor. "Pleasure."

Caleb snorts. "Well, he certainly fits your type."

"If by my type you mean big, broody, and can handle me," I say, waggling my brows, "then yes, Bane passes with flying colors."

Marcus takes a slow sip of his whiskey, eyes still trained on Bane. "You treating her right?"

Bane doesn't hesitate. "Always."

Something in the way he says it makes Marcus nod, satisfied. Caleb just grins. "Then welcome to the madhouse."

I beam, wrapping my arms around Bane's waist. "Told you they'd love you."

"I don't recall you saying that," Bane murmurs, lips brushing the shell of my ear.

"Well, I thought it," I admit. "And that's close enough."

Quinn strides up next, all sleek confidence and leather. "Moira, finally. Thought we were gonna have to send out a search party."

"Oh please, you know I always come back to the scene of the crime."

She smirks. "And Saint. I was wondering when we'd see you again."

"Quinn." He inclines his head.

"I see you've met Moira." Quinn seems amused, looking back and forth between us. Why did she call him Saint?

I squeeze Bane tighter, wondering how they know each other. "He's my Dom."

Quinn nods as if something's just clicked into place. "Well, that seems like a perfect match."

"Don't you have a pain piggie to be making squeal somewhere?" Bane inquires mildly.

But Quinn just grins and sits down in the chairs beside us. "He doesn't get here for another hour. I'm free to hang out 'til then."

Bane rolls his eyes but then asks if I want anything to drink.

"Sparkling soda, please." I intend to play tonight, so I'll stay strictly no alcohol 'til afterward.

Bane kisses my forehead and heads to the bar.

I immediately spin toward Quinn. "You know Bane?"

She shrugs. "I may have run into him a time or two."

"With or without the mask?" I quiet my voice so Caleb and Marcus won't hear. Caleb rarely has a night off, so I definitely want to catch up with him, too, but first things first.

Her eyes widen. "Have *you* seen him without the mask?"

I sit up straighter. "Of course I have. I'm his sub." I feel so fucking proud saying it.

"I didn't know you did that. Have you ever been a sub before?"

"All the time here."

She rolls her eyes. "You know what I mean. Like, a real sub. For anything longer than a night or two."

"There's a first time for everything. I can learn. I *am* learning."

Quinn's eyebrows just raise as she eyes me over her cup.

"Have *you* seen him without the mask?" I turn the question back on her.

Her eyes narrow on me, but she glances over at the bar quickly before leaning in. "If you've really seen him, tell me why I call him Saint."

Oh. My mouth drops open a little.

She really has seen him without the mask.

I lean in even further, looking around to make sure no one's listening in. "Did you accidentally walk into his church, too?"

Her loud laughter has me yanking back.

"Go to his—" She literally slaps her knee. "Fuck no! Girl, I haven't been in one of those since they dragged us as foster kids when I was nine."

She waves a hand. "No, no. I just ran into him while he was in"—she breaks off, checking around as if also seeing who might be in hearing range—"you know, *uniform*, when I was sitting in a coffee shop. I was in my domme gear, which I try not to wear out in public, but I just really needed a fucking cup of coffee that day and didn't have time to change."

She waves a hand. "I just saw it in his eyes. Out of all people, someone in that—uniform—you'd expect to be judgy about what I was wearing, but he just had a normal conversation with me while we were standing in line, and when he casually asked me which dungeon I went to, I knew."

She smirks. "I told him about *Carnal* and said he should drop by. He about choked when he realized I'd also clocked him as part of the community. But he showed up, didn't he?"

"Thank you!" I throw my arms around her.

It's because of her I have my Bane. If they hadn't run into each other that day, would I have ever met him?

"Thank you, thank you, thank you!"

I give her a big kiss on the cheek.

She chuckles low and pulls away from me.

"Get off me, you freak."

"Mwah, mwah, mwah, I give you kisses." I mock giving her big, sloppy kisses.

"Oh my god, you're worse than a puppy!" She laughs and wrestles me until I finally let her go.

"Hey, hey," Caleb jokes from across the coffee table. "Keep it consensual."

"Fine," I sigh, then grin with all my teeth. "But I don't know how sane I'll be tonight. Bane's been edging me like a motherfucker lately, and tonight, I finally get to unleash."

Marcus takes another sip of his whiskey. "Where exactly will you be scening? Because that sounds like it'd be fun to watch."

"Jesus, Marcus." Quinn gives a heavy eye roll.

"What?" he shrugs. "What's better than friends who fuck? And who watch each other fuck?"

"I can't think of a thing," Caleb says, lifting his glass to toast Marcus. The *clink* of their glasses makes me giggle. I'm usually more in their camp than Quinn's, but my eyes drift to Bane, who's walking back our way with our sparkling waters.

As we all sit together and chat, I'm curled up beside Bane in a deep leather lounger around a coffee table cluttered with glasses, and for the first time in a long, long time, I don't feel so... broken.

Kira and Isaak show up fifteen minutes later, and again, for the first time in forever, it feels like the whole gang's back together. Well, minus my brother and Anna, but I'm not letting anything dim my glow tonight.

Kira doesn't chat long—she's still doing research—so she wanders off to watch an intense scene happening in the corner. Isaak stays seated with us, but every other moment, his eyes lift to clock her with an intensity I'm not used to seeing on his face. Has the great and stoic Isaak finally actually fallen for someone? I didn't know he could be so human. It makes me happy for him.

The low golden glow of Carnal's lounge casts soft shadows over our group, and the air hums with warmth, familiar voices overlapping. I stretch out, drumming my fingers against Bane's thigh, stealing a glance up at him. He's relaxing next to me, all composed power, hand draped over the armrest like a king surveying his court.

He glances my way, dark eyes heavy. It takes everything in me not to squirm in anticipation. I know that look. He has plans for me tonight. Plans I'm dying to uncover.

I know he's drawing this part out, and it feels so good to be completely at ease and able to follow his lead. I allow myself to enjoy the anticipation while I catch up with my crew.

I turn to Marcus, but something catches my eye.

Across the room, near the bar, a man is watching me. Medium height with brown hair and unremarkable features, but something about him sticks in my mind, like a song I can't quite place.

A prickle of unease crawls up my spine.

I swear I've seen him before. Maybe hanging around outside the women's shelter? But that's halfway across town. He could just be an old hook-up.

The man looks away, focusing on the flogging scene in front of him.

I shake it off. I'm just being paranoid. All medium-height brown-haired guys start to look the same after a while, right?

Still, I shift slightly in my seat, angling myself so that Bane is between me and my unwanted observer, just in case.

I look back at Marcus. He looks wrecked, rubbing his temples as if it might erase the exhaustion pooling under his eyes.

"Alright, Marcus," I say, nudging his knee with my foot. "Give me the update. Work still eating your soul? And how's Elle?"

Marcus groans, rolling his glass between his palms. "Work is... work. Non-stop, never-ending. The partners keep dumping cases on me like I don't have a three-year-old at home demanding constant entertainment."

I make a face. "You're so adult with all your..." I wave a hand, "Adulting."

Isaak snorts. "Still no nanny?"

Marcus scoffs. "Don't even get me started. The last one quit after two weeks. Said Elle was 'too intense.'"

Quinn smirks. "Did she climb them like a jungle gym?"

"Probably." Marcus sighs. "I swear, she's got more energy

than a caffeinated squirrel. I don't know where she gets it. Definitely not from me."

I grin. "Well, she is three. And adorable. And smarter than half the people at your firm, probably."

"No arguments there," Marcus mutters, but there's pride tucked into the exhaustion.

The conversation shifts to Caleb, who's been uncharacteristically quiet. He's nursing his drink, thumb tracing slow circles against the glass. I know that look. Something's on his mind.

"Alright, Caleb," I prod, arching a brow. "Spill. What's going on in the kingdom of Carnal?"

He exhales through his nose, tilting his head. "Business is good. Better than good, actually. New members, packed weekends. But..." He hesitates, something flickering behind his eyes. "I got a letter."

I feel the shift in the air. Marcus leans forward, Quinn's eyes narrow, and I soften my voice. "From Silas?"

Caleb adores his stepfather, who's been locked up in federal prison for the last eight years for armed robbery.

Caleb nods, setting his glass down with a quiet *clink*. "Yeah. He wants me to visit."

A beat of silence passes between us. Marcus and Quinn exchange a glance, and I chew the inside of my cheek.

"That's... surprising," Marcus finally says. "I mean, you haven't gone before. I figured—"

"What?" Caleb interrupts, his jaw tightening. "That I don't care?"

"No," Marcus says carefully.

Isaak tries interjecting. "We just thought maybe you were angry at him."

Caleb scoffs, shaking his head. "I could never be angry at Silas. You don't understand. He did what he had to do. He always does."

Quinn tilts her head, her eyes narrowing slightly. "Then why haven't you gone?"

Caleb hesitates. For a split second, something dark flickers across his expression before he masks it with a casual shrug. "Because it's complicated. And because he wouldn't want me wasting my time sitting in a prison visiting room when I have things to take care of here. He told me to take care of the club. To watch over myself and to never step foot in a place like that, even to visit him."

I frown. "Well, something's obviously changed his mind. It's been years. He wants to see you now. That means something." Then I perk up. "Bane volunteers at prisons. He could go with you."

Bane shifts forward even as Caleb looks away. "I'd be happy to sit with the two of you. Sometimes having someone else there helps calm tensions."

Caleb exhales sharply. "I don't know."

"The man raised you." Marcus shakes his head. "Don't you think he deserves at least a visit?"

Caleb tenses, but his voice is even when he says, "Silas doesn't need me to visit to know where I stand."

Something about his tone makes me pause. Caleb is fiercely protective of Silas. Always has been. But there's something new here, something I can't quite put my finger on.

"Well," Quinn finally says, cutting through the tension. "If you do go, maybe let one of us come with you."

Caleb's lips twitch, a hint of amusement breaking through his carefully crafted defenses. "What, you want to hold my hand?"

"Someone has to," I tease, nudging his arm. "You're a handful."

The moment lightens just enough for Caleb to chuckle, shaking his head. "I'll think about it."

The heaviness lingers for a beat before Quinn clears her throat. "Well. That's enough broody male bonding for one night. Someone tell me something ridiculous."

I settle back into my seat. The weight eases, laughter bubbles up, and for a while, everything is easy again.

I grin, straightening up. "Oh, I've got one. You know the cat rescue near the shelter where I volunteer? The one run by the old lady with the lavender hair?"

Caleb nods warily. "Yeah?"

"Well, I was walking by last week, and she flagged me down like it was an emergency. Thought something awful had happened. Turns out, she just needed someone to hold her purse while she tried to break up a fight. Between two cats."

Marcus chokes on his drink. "A catfight?"

"Literally. One of them was her 'star rescue' named Lord Purrington. The other was a stray she called Bandit. Apparently, they've been arch nemeses for months."

Caleb smirks. "And she just assumed you were the right person to mediate?"

I spread my hands. "I have the aura of someone who understands chaotic energy. Anyway, she threw herself right into the middle of it like a gladiator in a tiny floral sweater. I was just standing there holding her purse and wondering how my life came to this."

Quinn wipes away tears of laughter. "Please tell me you got a video."

"Oh, I wish. But I was too busy trying to dodge flying fur and old lady sandals."

Isaak shakes his head, grinning. "That is... exactly something that would happen to you."

Caleb lifts his glass in a mock salute. "To Moira, the official peacekeeper of the local cat mafia."

I clink my glass against his. "Hey, someone's got to keep the streets safe. And cats love me."

Laughter ripples around the table, the tension from earlier dissipating completely. And as the conversation moves on, my thoughts drift again—to Bane and the night ahead.

Even as our gazes lock now, electricity sizzles through the

connection. I squirm in my chair, feeling him everywhere even though he's not even touching me.

"Oh, there's my pain pig," Quinn says, clocking someone just walking into the club area. She glances at her phone as she stands up, then clicks her teeth. "Two minutes late. Little shit. He'll pay for that."

She stalks over to him, barking, "On your knees, little piggie!"

The piggie in question absolutely lights up when he sees Quinn, then drops to his hands and knees obediently, head down.

"She does have a way with them," Marcus says admiringly, watching her as she goes.

Caleb snorts. "It's a lost cause, man. Give it up already."

"What?" I ask, looking between them. "You like Quinn? But you're both dominants."

Marcus just rolls his eyes and downs the last swig of his whiskey. "I've got to get home. The babysitter could only stay until ten."

Caleb laughs. "Marcus always wants what he shouldn't."

Marcus cuffs Caleb lightly on the back of the head as he stands up.

I turn, squirming, to Bane. I've officially waited as long as I can.

He looks at me over the glass of his sparkling water, eyes dark. *Fuck*. It's not fair for a man to be so fucking hot. Especially in that mask, thinking of the filthy, combative way he likes to fuck me. All the while knowing the rest of the time, he wears a priest's collar, patiently dealing with old ladies squabbling about who sat in their spot in the pew last Sunday.

He doesn't have to say a word. He just gestures with the left to indicate it's finally time.

I all but squirt in the panties he made me wear for the night as I leap to my feet to follow him.

TWENTY-ONE

BANE

I'VE BEEN SUCH A MISERABLY lonely fuck my whole life.

But of course, Moira has friends. The kind who seem like family. People are drawn to her not because of anything they want from her but simply because she *shines*. She's kind. She's funny. Unselfish. Self-deprecating. She makes space in conversation for other people. You can tell she actually *cares* about them.

Realizing all this, I scrap the scene I had in mind for the night and lead her instead to the throne with a spotlight shining down on it.

"Isn't this a... queening chair?" She arches an eyebrow at

me. "You want me to eat your ass?"

Oh, sweet dove. I'm glad for the mask so I don't have to stifle my smile. I reached down to grab the hem of her dress, whipping it off over her head in one smooth motion to reveal the black negligee beneath.

"Sit before I make you."

Her big eyes widen before she smirks. "As if you could." She flips one of her pigtails and then sits down on the chair.

If one can call it that. The queening chair is a type of chair that's missing most of its seat. Two padded lengths run down the width of where a chair seat would be, and I strap her thighs to them. I do the same to her forearms on the padded arms of the chair, then tie her ankles to the chair legs.

Her chest moves up and down, and she strains against the constraints, swallowing hard. Her nipples pebble in the black silk negligee she's wearing.

I stand back and take her in, cock stiffening in my pants. I'm not wearing leathers, just dark jeans. The denim stretches a little, but not enough. With the stainless steel cock ring I put around my cock and balls before we left, what I have planned will be a perfect torture. For both of us.

With her strapped to the chair like this, I couldn't even get at her perfect little cunt even if I wanted to.

At least not with my cock.

"What now?" she whispers, luminous eyes still so fucking big. She's breathless and waiting for my next move.

Which is exactly where I want her.

She's the most fascinating woman I've ever met.

Am I serious about her?

Yes.

But what if I'm just a passing fucking fancy to *her*?

Time to make her crave me as much as I've craved her from the first time I met her.

I drop to the floor, lay on my back, and fit my head in the leather hammock hanging beneath the legs of the chair.

Her sex smells fresh, clean, and salty-sweet. A drop of her moisture glistens at the top of her pretty, pretty pussy.

"What are you doing down there?" she calls.

Always so impatient.

I breathe out so she can feel my warmth against her petals.

And enjoy feeling her ankles shiver against my shoulders.

Why haven't I thought of this before? My cock strains fully hard against my zipper. So much more fun to torture us both. I do so love it when she swears she hates me.

They say anger increases one's heart rate and blood pressure, as well as sharpening the senses.

It's always been my favorite emotion. And the most useful, if you ask me.

I've been furious at my father for almost a decade, and look how far it's taken me. I think Moira could do with some good anger in her life, frankly. She can practice on me. And that's how it makes me so fucking hard. But I've always been a fucking selfish little monster underneath, haven't I?

I chuckle, pull down my mask, and extend my tongue to take a long, lingering lick up God's juiciest cunt.

She shudders above me, her pussy lips fluttering, little opening puckering like she's clenching. But there's nothing to *clench* on.

I smile, head comfortably laid in the head hammock. Waiting.

One. Two. Three. Four. Five. Six.

"Goddammit, you sadistic motherfucker," she squeals, "*again* alre—"

But before she can finish the demand, I start to suckle her clit.

The ecstatic, grunting squeal that comes from her throat is truly a thing of wonder.

As is her colorful string of curses when I stop again for an extended period.

But I'm just getting started.

"Tell me how much you hate me," I whisper into her pussy.

"Oh, I hate your smug little—"

A surge of emotion and lust fills my chest as her words cut off when I smother my face with her pussy. She's warmth and wetness, with an earthy, feminine scent. I lick and suckle again before pulling back.

Again and again and again.

It's only my years of discipline that allow me to wrench away even when I want to suckle down her spurting juices.

So every time I feel the fluttering of her moist flesh around my tongue that signals she's right on the edge of coming, I pull back.

"I hate you!" she screams at the top of her lungs, her entire body clenched in frustration at yet another denied orgasm.

That's right. Scream for me, little dove.

Hate me and crave me.

I want to bury my cock in her while she yanks my hair out of my scalp in fury.

But only once we're home, and she's half out of her mind with the wanting that only I can satisfy.

TWENTY-TWO

Two months later, two days before Christmas

MOIRA

MARCI'S in one of her *delightful* moods again. Lucinda's still out, which means janitorial duty at the shelter is all mine.

Marci practically vibrated with joy when she handed me the mop and informed me about the *catastrophic* backup in stall three. If she'd been any giddier, she might've clicked her heels.

But Marci's petty little victories can't touch me today. Not when I'm still floating somewhere above the clouds, carried by the *aftershocks* of my morning with Bane.

Things have been different since I got back from what everyone at *Carnal* now calls—without a hint of irony—*the Red Wedding*.

Isaak was in a bad situation, so we all banded together to get him out of it. Well, mostly, he did all the badassery, but we got him out of jail so he could go do his white knight shit.

It felt good.

I felt good.

And it felt *even* better that when Quinn called about Isaak, Bane didn't turn all caveman on me. He let me go, and he didn't try to control the situation or insert himself into it like some overprotective asshole marking his territory.

Yeah, we like to fight—but only during sex.

I've never had anything like this before. I mean, obviously. I've never had *anything* with *anybody* before.

But this morning, I woke up and just *watched* Bane sleep. Felt the warmth of his solid, muscled torso pressed against me, his heavy man-arm slung over my waist like he was afraid I'd disappear if he let go.

His face was turned slightly away, dark lashes casting delicate shadows on his sharp cheekbones. He looked almost... serene. *Almost*.

Because even in sleep, his mouth was tight, and a furrow was etched deep between his brows.

Like he was wrestling demons only he could see.

Not that he'll tell me about them.

I frown as I push the wheeled mop and bucket toward the bathroom.

We *have* to sleep at my apartment now. Not by choice but by *decree*, courtesy of his bishop, who laid down the holy law after that little meeting of theirs. *No sleepovers at the church-owned house.*

Bane, ever the stickler for his twisted brand of honor, took it as gospel. No exceptions. No bending the rules. Not even for me.

But he's still in my bed every night but Saturday.

Like he can't help himself.

Like I'm gravity, and he's cursed to fall. But not cursed enough to break all the rules. Not cursed enough to let me in all the way.

He knows everything about me but still won't tell me shit about his past beyond the maddeningly vague *I wasn't always a priest.*

He hates lies but apparently doesn't feel the same way about secrets. Because he's a locked box.

Always in control. Except for those rare, feral moments when he fucks me like a man possessed.

I want to know what's really going on in that infuriating, brilliant head of his.

While he slept this morning, I mouthed words too dangerous to ever say aloud against his hair. Words I barely let my lips form: *Tell me you never want me to leave.*

Because what if he doesn't?

But worse—what if he *does*?

We're not strangers anymore. But we're not just lovers either. We're something tangled and raw and dangerous.

Every night he crosses town to be with me, defying his own goddamn boundaries. At first, I thought this was temporary. Some fleeting indulgence on his part. But he keeps coming back, night after night, like a tide pulled by a moon neither of us is willing to acknowledge.

The more he stays, the deeper I sink.

And the more terrifying it becomes to imagine the night he *doesn't* come back. When I wake up to cold sheets and nothing but a ghost where his warmth used to be.

Why did I let him in so deep in the first place?

There was probably a reason I never had relationships before. Yeah, I'm a fucking chaotic disaster. But also, this shit is *terrifying*.

I push into the shelter's bathroom with my mop bucket and lean against the closed door. My palm presses flat against my chest, feeling the frantic drum of my heart.

I *want* him.

I *want* this.

But wanting is so goddamn dangerous.

Wanting means I have something to lose.

It's just so fucking sweet right now. No, sweet isn't the right word.

This thing between us is sharper, like dark chocolate with sea salt.

And just as fucking addictive.

Just before I left to volunteer, Bane didn't say a word. He just guided me to sit on the edge of the bed, his palms warm against my thighs as he parted them and his gaze dark and unreadable as ever.

Then he kneeled between them like I was something sacred, something he needed to worship, and proceeded to devour me. His mouth was slow. Relentless. Devastating.

Half an hour.

That's how long he kept me there, trembling and unraveling, his mouth merciless while my fingers clutched and pulled desperately at his hair.

His hands gripped my ass, strong and possessive, dragging me closer and anchoring me at the same time while wave after wave of pleasure fractured me into pieces. Only for him to gather them up again with his tongue for the next devastating rush.

Even now, heading toward the mess in stall three, my jelly legs still carry the ghost of that quaking, muscles weak like they've forgotten how to hold me upright.

I was nearly late for my shift because my body refused to cooperate, stubbornly lingering in the aftershocks of pleasure.

Bane fed me yogurt in bed afterward, casual as you please, his fingers occasionally drifting south, brushing over my overly sensitive clit with the lightest touch—just to watch me twitch.

Bastard. Sadistic, gorgeous bastard. He loves to torture

me, but not without purpose. There's an art to it with him, every flick of his fingers, every command—a calculated masterpiece of control.

But he's also maddeningly disciplined. Once he decided I'd recovered enough, he was all business. He made sure I got dressed, packed my bag, and ushered me out the door with military precision, ensuring I left at the exact minute I needed to be on time.

Good thing, too.

I got here on time, so despite Marci's bad mood, there wasn't anything she could do but scowl at me and give me the keys.

Really, if I don't let my fucking doom spirals ruin shit, my life is currently going quite fucking spectacularly.

I grin the entire time I scrub down stall three, earbuds blasting Sabrina Carpenter as if the music alone can match the pulse thrumming in my veins.

I yank my gloves off and toss them, then snap a new pair on. Hell, I'm practically dancing as I move on to stall four.

Because yeah, the messes will always be there.

But maybe so will Bane?

I push open the fourth stall, expecting the usual grime-and-regret combo, but instead—

"Jesus!" I yelp, stumbling back a step.

There's a woman perched on the toilet tank, knees tucked up, boots planted on the closed lid. Long brunette hair spills over the collar of an oversized Bad Bunny shirt, tight jeans tucked into scuffed combat boots.

She glances at me, completely unfazed, and blows a lazy stream of smoke out the cracked open window.

I thought I smelled something earlier, but stall three's backup situation had been an olfactory apocalypse. Guess my nose needed a minute to recalibrate.

She rolls her eyes like I'm the inconvenience here. "Lemme guess, I'm in trouble now?"

I lean against the grimy tile wall, pressing a hand to my chest, still catching my breath. "Not from me, you're not." I let out a laugh, adrenaline mixing with amusement. "You must be new. Skipping Life Skills class, huh?"

"Life skills," she snorts, taking another slow drag. "They don't know shit about my life."

Fair point.

I nod, crossing my arms. "So, what's the plan, then?"

She exhales a plume of smoke, squints at me like she's sizing me up, then shrugs and holds out the joint. Not just a cigarette. Yep, definitely a joint.

For a split second, I hesitate. But then, fuck it. I'm already in the shit with Marci, and impulse control's never been my strong suit. I take it, inhaling deeply. The smoke burns warm in my chest, blooming like a rebellious little fire, and I blow it out the same window.

She nods like that seals something between us. "My sister's got me covered," she says, all bravado. Then she shrugs. "Unless her dad or my boyfriend kills me first when I get out of here." Her head wobbles in a casual, it-is-what-it-is kind of way. "Which is probably more likely. So no real point in Life Skills class, ya know?"

She winks. Like it's a joke.

But it doesn't feel like one.

"Well, shit," I mutter, the words hitching somewhere between my lungs and my heart. My instincts kick in, bulldozing over the whole maintaining healthy boundaries thing. I glance at my janitorial cart, grab a stub of a pencil and a clean square of toilet paper—it's the industrial kind, practically laminated cardboard—and scribble my number on it.

Turning back, I hand it to her. "If you ever get in over your head—like, really over your head—call me. My brother's got... resources."

Resources like fists and favors and connections nobody talks about in polite company. He may not be speaking to me right now, but Anna's got a soft spot for girls tangled up with bad guys. And I guess I do, too.

She frowns down at the makeshift note, squinting like it's written in code. "Look, that's real nice and all," she says, voice dropping into something softer. "But these guys? They're not just assholes with anger issues. We're talking cartel-level trouble."

Oh.

Shit.

My pulse kicks up, but my mouth moves faster. "Doesn't matter. Help's help."

Then, maybe because the weed's hit me just right, or maybe because I'm feeling stronger lately and more pissed off at guys who hurt women and get away with it now that I've finally found one who's actually kind, I lean in, lowering my voice to a whisper. "Don't tell anyone, but my family just buried the body of another bad man where no one'll ever find it. If you catch my drift."

Anna's father was a monster, and the only reason I can sleep at night is because I know he's six feet under.

Her eyes go wide, the kind of wide that says she believes me.

"Well, shit," she says, folding the toilet paper and carefully tucking it into her pocket. "I'll keep your number, then."

"Moira," I say, tapping my chest.

"Daniela."

She offers the joint again, but I wave it off, shaking my head. "My supervisor will put my tits in a vise if she finds out I've been smoking on the job."

We both dissolve into laughter, the kind that's too loud for how unfunny the situation really is.

"Tits in a vise," Daniela giggles, clutching her stomach like it's the best joke she's heard all year.

I'm wiping tears from the corners of my eyes when my phone buzzes in my pocket. It takes me a minute to fish it out

—my fingers suddenly feel like bratwurst. Jesus, where did she find such good weed around here?

"Dammit," I giggle, finally managing to get it out.

It's a text from Bane. My fingers are still clumsy, but I click on it.

> Bane: Thinking of you gorgeous.

I sigh dreamily and type,

> Me: Back at you, Sexy.

Daniela squints at me, her grin slipping into something sharper. "Ugh, I know that look. Don't fall for his bullshit, whoever he is."

"Not all guys are bad news," I say automatically, but my voice wobbles like a chair with one short leg.

She tips her head back against the wall, exhaling like I'm exhausting. "Oh, naïve sweet summer child."

I snort. "If you knew me, you'd know naïve is the last word to use. Besides, how old are you? You look twelve."

She scowls. "I'm twenty."

"Well, I'm twenty-two. That makes me your wise elder."

"Blow it out your ass," she fires back, grinning. "My sister's twenty-two, and she's shit at telling good men from bad ones."

"She knew enough to send you here when your boyfriend got violent."

Daniela scoffs with a bitter little sound. "As if she's one to talk." She looks at me, her gaze sharp enough to cut. "Your man ever lay hands on you?"

I waggle my eyebrows. "Only when I want him to."

She shakes her head, exhaling smoke. "Just wait. All men are dogs. You met his mama? Any of his friends?"

I frown.

Um. No. Not really.

Her face shifts into an I-told-you-so expression, and my heart sinks to my stomach, then down out my asshole.

"Be real," she says, grinning now. "You're his sneaky link."

"I'm not."

He's just British. All his family lives back there. I think.

She arches a brow. "Do you even go on dates outside of his apartment?"

I open my mouth. Then close it. "Well... it's my apartment."

But even as I say it, something cold creeps into the pit of my stomach. Because—shit. The bishop said we couldn't be seen together. Or was that just the most convenient story ever to keep me out of his business because *fuck*—

Am I actually his...?

Daniela bursts into laughter, doubling over like she's heard the second funniest punchline in the world.

"You are his sneaky link and don't even know it. He could have a whole-ass family in another state, and you'd be none the wiser."

"No!" I protest, heat rising in my cheeks. "I've seen his house. There's no secret family."

She gives a nonchalant little, "Heh, whatever you say," then hops down from the toilet tank. She stubs out the joint on the edge of the stainless steel trash can, pocketing the rest with the kind of casual defiance that says she's been doing this a long time.

"Stay chill, Moira."

"Same to you, Daniela."

As the door clicks shut behind Daniela, the lingering haze of weed-scented air feels like it's pressing down on me. But it's not the smoke that's suffocating.

Oh my god. I'm so fucking stupid. Prancing around like a fucking idiot.

Why haven't I ever pressed to know more about Bane's past? I mean, it's not like I haven't asked here and there. But he always just...

Changes the subject.

Turns the question back on me.

Offers something vague, then distracts me with sex.

I told myself it's normal not to want to talk about the past. Mine's not all that rosy and I'm certainly not sharing monologues about it. But he's met my friends. And if I was on speaking terms with Domhn, I think I might've introduced them by now.

Still, it could be normal... right?

Fuck, what if it's not normal? What the fuck would I know about normal, anyway?

Daniela was right. Maybe I am naïve. A sweet summer child thinking I've learned from my mistakes when really I'm just dressing them up prettier this time.

Because here I still am, trusting that a good fuck equals a good man. Tumbling headfirst into something, only for it to drop out from underneath me. Leaving me *falling*, all right. Straight into the shit. Into trouble so bad, like last year when I broke my brother's heart.

Fuck *that*.

I'm nobody's secret.

I yank out my phone, thumbs tapping before I can think twice.

> Me: You busy tonight?

The text flies off like a bullet. No time to overthink.

Bane's reply comes quick. Too quick.

> No. Why? You want me to bring pasta on my way home? You eat pasta, I eat you? I've still got the taste of you on my tongue.

A shiver dances down my spine, sharp and electric, pooling heat between my thighs. My knees wobble, and for a second, I almost let it go. Almost let the sweet talk smooth over the jagged edges.

But I'm Moira.

I always poke.

Because if I've learned anything, it's this: when something feels too good to be true, there's always a catch.

> Me: Good, you're free. Dress up nice and meet me here at 8:00.

I drop a pin, my thumb hovering before I add the kicker.

> Me: I want to introduce you to my brother.

I hit send before I can chicken out.

Then I stare.

And wait.

The screen stays blank.

No reply. No dots. Just the harsh glow of expectation burning into my retinas.

Maybe he's just busy, I lie to myself, heart pounding like a drumline. Maybe his phone's dead. Maybe he's—

> ...

I suck in a breath, not realizing I'd been holding it.

Then the dots disappear.

Pop back up.

> ...

Disappear again.

My pulse pounds in my ears. "Answer me back, you motherfucker," I hiss at the phone like it owes me something, frantically waving my hand through the lingering weed smoke like that'll help.

Finally—*ping*.

> Bane: I don't know. I might have to be on a call with the worship committee tonight. Can we have your brother over for dinner another time?

I blink.

The worship committee?

WORSHIP COMMITTEE?

> Me: Lie

My thumbs type furiously.

> Me: You just said you were free.

He tries to call me, but I silence it. More fucking smooth talk isn't going to cut it. I'm seeing red. The petty, righteous kind that demands satisfaction. My thumbs fly over the screen.

> Me: I'm at work

I type, fingers hitting the keys like they personally offended me.

> Me: And maybe I'm done with your secrets. Meet me tonight where I said or we're over.

Send.

The second it flies off, regret crashes into me like a freight train.

Fuck. Did I just ultimatum him?

I did.

Fuck, fuck, fuck—I just ultimatum'd him.

Why did I do that?

I pace in frantic little circles, bouncing on my toes, phone clutched like it's a grenade. My mind spins out:

Should I text back? Say I didn't mean it? Play it cool?

Or grovel? Maybe grovel.

No. Fuck that!

But also, maybe yes, grovel.

Ugh, why am I like this?

"Say something!" I hiss at the phone.

But the screen stays stubbornly dark.

No dots.

Just me and my spiraling thoughts.

Minutes drag by, stretching into the unbearable. I consider typing another text—something cute, something flirty, something to undo the explosion I just caused—but the self-loathing bubbles up before I can.

Weak. Stupid. Naïve.

I hate that voice. But it's mine.

Finally, the phone *pings*.

I fumble it like a greased-up football, scrambling to unlock the screen.

> Bane: Fine. We'll discuss this tonight.

Relief crashes over me in a tidal wave, but it's bitter, mixed with dread. I glance up, catching my reflection in the cracked mirror above the grimy sink.

Oh. Shit.

I look like a street cat that's just lost a turf war. Hair wild, smudged eyeliner from god-knows-when, janitor gloves still dangling from my pocket like sad little flags of defeat.

And I've just arranged for my very pissed-off, possibly-keeping-secrets-from-me dominant to meet my brother—who also happens to not be speaking to me—at one of the city's swankiest yearly galas.

Oh, and I have nothing to wear.

I chuck my gloves into the janitorial bucket, wipe my palms down my jeans like that'll help, and whip out my phone again.

Fuck. Who's the fanciest person I know?

I text furiously.

> Me: Kira, HELP. Fashion Emergency 911!

TWENTY-THREE

BANE

AM I furious that Moira's cornered me into this public spectacle of a night?

Yes.

Is it my own damn fault for the way I've handled things from the start and then doubling down on stupidity by feeding her some half-baked lie about a worship committee meeting to wiggle out of it?

Also yes.

I tried to justify it to myself, of course. *Technically*, it wasn't really a lie. They *have* been asking me to join those calls, nudging me to step in and lead. But that's the problem, isn't it? The second I'm on the line, everyone suddenly defers to me, looking for guidance they're perfectly capable of providing themselves. I've been trying to cultivate leadership from within and make them realize they don't need me. Priests only stay in a parish for seven years or so. They should stand on their own, whether I'm presiding or not.

But when you peel away all the righteous justification, it was a bullshit excuse.

And Moira saw right through it.

So here I am, sitting in the back of an Uber, grinding my teeth as we circle the city blocks congested with traffic, all funneled toward the bright chaos of the famous yearly Christmas charity gala.

Even from here, I can see the flashes of paparazzi cameras strobing against the night like tiny, relentless explosions.

"*Fuck*," I mutter under my breath.

The driver glances in the mirror, brows lifted in silent question.

"This is fine. You can drop me here," I say, already reaching for the door handle.

Moira only sent me the ticket half an hour ago, like an afterthought—or a challenge. But I'd already Googled the event, the venue, the date. Had to know what I was walking into.

I slide out of the car, the city's evening air cool against my face, tinged with exhaust fumes, expensive perfume, and the faint buzz of anticipation that always hovers near events like this—where wealth, influence, power and beauty feel tangible in the glitter of each jewel and stitched into every designer seam.

I know it's an illusion. But it's such a compelling one that I've yet to meet a person who couldn't be seduced, even if just a little, by its charms.

I glance into the car's side mirror, adjusting the priest's collar around my neck.

It's the only disguise I could muster.

My hair's longer than it used to be—a little shaggy, the edges flirting with unruly. I haven't bothered with the razor today either, and stubble shadows my jaw. It's all a far cry from the slick, carefully curated image I used to maintain. Back when I thought being polished made me untouchable. Back when I believed I could control perception like I controlled everything else.

Tonight, I'm hoping the collar does most of the heavy lifting. It usually does.

People's eyes slide right over it—or, more accurately, they glance *at* it but not *past* it. It makes them squirm, either out of reverence or discomfort, unsure whether to engage or retreat. Especially around here, where religion's either woven into your bones or treated like an awkward relic from someone else's attic.

It's the perfect camouflage.

Nobody looks too closely at a man in a collar. They see what they want to see.

Which is exactly what I need tonight.

I start walking toward the entrance, the ticket tucked into my pocket like a dare, like Moira's voice is still echoing in my head: *Meet me tonight or we're over.*

So, of course, I'm here.

Because losing her isn't an option.

But as I approach the building, it's clear the red carpet's a battlefield. Paparazzi are clustered like vultures, their flashing lenses hungry for scandal. I'd be an idiot to walk straight into that.

So, I circle the block, cutting through the shadows where the noise thins out. I follow the quiet hum of generators and the faint clatter of service carts.

Every event like this has a pulse beneath the glamor. A heartbeat of staff, security, and overworked coordinators trying to hold it all together with duct tape and desperation.

I find a side entrance tucked between dumpsters where a catering van is parked, half-hidden under a flickering security light. A woman with a headset and a clipboard stands there, snapping orders. Her stress is palpable as her eyes dart between the staff and her checklist.

Perfect.

I straighten my collar, smooth the front of my jacket, and walk toward her like I belong. Because that's the trick. It's not about sneaking. It's about being invisible by standing in plain sight.

"Excuse me," I say, my voice low but threaded with quiet authority. She glances up, frazzled but polite enough not to ignore me completely. "I was told an attendee requested spiritual counsel. They asked me to come discreetly."

Her eyes flick to the collar, then back to her clipboard, processing just enough to believe me without actually thinking. That's the beauty of the uniform—it fills in the blanks for people. They see what they expect to see.

She doesn't question me or ask for a name. She just jerks her thumb toward the door. "Down the hall, ballroom's to the left."

"Thank you."

I slip inside before she can change her mind.

The hallway is dim and lined with crates and folded linens. Staff hustle by with trays of champagne flutes. No one looks at me twice.

I move through the corridors like smoke—silent and unnoticed.

I'm not here to be seen.

I'm here for Moira. To prove whatever point she needed to be proved by my presence. To meet her brother. To take her home where I can punish her properly for dragging us into this unnecessary chaos. I will be exacting. I will bring back order.

I move through the corridors, pulse steady, every step

measured with precision. A man with a purpose. A man in control.

Until I push through the final door—

And the world stops.

There she is.

Moira.

Time folds in on itself and slips sideways, as if the universe had been holding its breath for this very moment.

The noise of the gala—the dull roar of conversation, the clink of glass, the undercurrent of Christmas music—fades to a distant hum.

She stands under the glow of chandeliers that drip with crystals, each shard refracting light like constellations scattered just for her.

The golden warmth paints her skin in liquid gold hues that cascade over the slope of her shoulders and catch in the delicate hollow of her throat.

Her dress—fuck, her dress—is a dark, fluid thing that hugs every curve like it was designed with just her in mind. It drapes. It clings. It *bares*.

My knees are weak, and all pretense at control evaporates as my eyes continue to trace her, incapable in this moment of doing anything else.

The truth is laid bare: I'm as under her spell now as I ever was.

Her hair is swept up, leaving her neck bare and vulnerable, the elegant curve of it leading down to a thin, silver chain resting against her collarbone—a chain I want to trace with my tongue. I want to taste where the cool metal meets her warm skin.

She laughs at something, her head tilted back just enough for me to see the curve of her throat, the faint pulse beating there like a siren's call. Her mouth—Christ—her mouth is a perfect, wicked thing, soft and plush, curved in a way that makes me remember every filthy, sacred thing it's ever done to me.

I feel it like a punch.

Low. Sharp. Hot.

A hunger buried so deep it's practically in my bones, clawing its way to the surface.

But it's more than that.

And I'm faced with the stark truth that this is more than just want—it's need. The kind that doesn't fade. The kind that doesn't get sated, no matter how many times I've had her. No matter how many times I've told myself it's enough.

She's the wild wood, and I've been a goddamned idiot to think I could ever... what? Tame her? Tether her?

She unravels the threads I've knotted so tightly around myself.

I thought I was here to keep control, to be the one who dictates the terms.

But that was a lie.

I'm here because she *exists*.

I'm here because, without her, there's nothing else.

I've been a lost man, thinking I was found. The man who hates lies was living buried under so many I can't tell one from another. I'm no shepherd. I'm a fraud.

Her laughter fades, her gaze drifting across the crowd, indifferent—until it lands on me.

Her smile falters just slightly, but it's enough.

I watch her breath catch. I see it. Feel it. Like we're connected by some invisible thread pulled taut between us.

Her eyes—those impossible, beautiful green eyes—widen with surprise, then something darker flickers behind them.

Recognition. Heat. That sharp, electric awareness that's always been there, thrumming beneath every word we've ever spoken, every look we've ever shared.

Our gazes lock, and the world collapses.

There's no gala. No music. No crowd.

It's just her.

Just me.

I start moving toward her, my steps automatic, pulled by a force older than logic and stronger than reason. My heartbeat drowns out everything else. It pounds in my chest and my throat and my skull.

She doesn't look away.

Neither do I.

Each step feels like falling.

Because in this sea of people, beneath the glittering lights, surrounded by noise and artifice—

It's just us.

It's always been just us.

"You came." Her voice trembles.

"I'll always come for you."

"I—I didn't mean to—" She cuts off. "I just—" She cuts off again, looking up at me helplessly.

I hold out a hand, desperate to touch her. "Would you like to dance?"

TWENTY-FOUR

MOIRA

I BLINK up at him like he just asked if I wanted to wrestle a tiger. A very sexy, broody tiger in a tailored black suit with eyes that say, *I'll ruin you, and you'll thank me.*

"Dance?" I repeat because, apparently, I've been reduced to an echo.

Bane doesn't answer. He just stands there with his hand outstretched, like he's carved from dark marble. Except marble doesn't make your stomach do somersaults or send a heatwave directly to your undies. No, that's all him.

My brain scrambles like eggs on high heat.

This is fine. Totally fine.

Normal people get asked to dance all the time. I can do

this. I can be graceful and mysterious and definitely not like I've mainlined three energy drinks and made a questionable amount of bad decisions today.

I slip my palm into his like I'm about to seal a deal with the devil. Which, knowing me and knowing him, feels about right.

His hand is warm and big and dominating.

Of course, it is.

He pulls me in gently, but not too gently, because he's Bane, and subtlety isn't really his brand. My body crashes into his, and I lose the breath in my lungs.

I was sure he wouldn't come. I was sure I'd ruined things like I always do.

But here he is. Solid. Holding me. Here for me. Even when I was a little shit.

The music shifts. Something low and slow with a beat that crawls under your skin like it belongs there. Figures. Even the DJ is conspiring against me.

Bane slides his hand to my waist, and oh god, how does that feel like both an electric shock and a security blanket at the same time? His other hand keeps mine, fingers entwined, like we're in some old-timey romance.

"Relax," he murmurs, his voice low and dark.

"Oh, I'm relaxed," I chirp because nothing says "relaxed" like sounding like a deranged parakeet. "This is my relaxed face. See?"

His lips twitch. Just a little. Not quite a smile, but enough to make me feel like I've won something.

We sway, and it should feel weird, but it doesn't. Not with him. There's this magnetic pull with us, like gravity decided to take a coffee break and he's the only thing keeping me grounded.

I glance up, expecting to see judgment in his eyes. Or anger about earlier.

Instead, I see something else entirely. Heat. Want. Maybe even a little bit of awe, like he can't believe he's here with me.

"You're staring," I whisper because, of course, I can't just let the moment be.

"I know," he replies, unapologetic.

Oh.

My heart does this weird stutter-step like it missed a beat and then tried to catch up all at once. I feel hot and cold and like I might either faint or burst into flames. Maybe both.

"Well, stop it," I mutter, but there's no heat behind the words.

He doesn't stop. Of course, he doesn't. Bane doesn't do anything he doesn't want to do. And right now, apparently, he wants to look at me like I'm the answer to his every question.

We keep moving, slow and steady, our bodies close enough that I can feel every inch of him. And trust me, there are a lot of inches to feel.

I'm not sure how long we dance. Time feels slippery like it does when we get in the zone like this. We're in the bubble.

Just me, him, and the quiet thrum of a song I'll probably never hear the same way again.

When the music finally fades, we don't move apart. We just stand there, breathing the same air, hearts beating in sync like we're sharing the same rhythm.

And then he leans down, mouth near my ear, his breath warm against my skin.

"You've been a very naughty girl," he whispers. His hand tightens on my waist.

"I know," I breathe back. "But only because I was afraid you were a very bad boy. I was afraid you didn't want to be seen in public with me."

He pulls back just enough to look me in the eyes, and there it is again—that almost smile like I'm the only thing in the world capable of pulling it out of him.

And then he leans in like he's going to kiss me—claim me—right here in this room full of fancy people, collar and all—

When a clearing throat suddenly interrupts us.

"Seducing a priest at my charity gala, Moira?" comes my brother's cutting voice. "You really will stoop to any low to get my attention."

TWENTY-FIVE

BANE

I PULL BACK from Moira slowly, deliberately, as if Domhnall's voice hasn't sliced through the moment. My gaze stays locked on her flushed face, lips slightly parted, pupils blown wide with something darker, wilder and far more appealing than innocence. She looks like sin wrapped in velvet.

But the sudden tension stiffening her body isn't because of me. It's from him.

Her brother.

I turn my head slightly, just enough to meet his gaze over Moira's shoulder. He stands a few paces away, rigid in his tailored suit, his eyes full of judgment. His voice might've been cutting, but his cold eyes are worse. They carry the weight of history and clear resentment.

Moira straightens beside me, rolling her shoulders back like she's preparing for war.

"Domhnall," she says sweetly, all sugar, but I know her well enough by now to hear the razorblade underneath. "I was wondering when you'd crawl out from whatever dark corner you were brooding in."

His lips twitch, but not in amusement. No, I don't think this man finds anything amusing when it involves his sister.

There's clearly bad blood here. Moira told me she and her brother had a falling out, but now I'm thinking there's much more to it than that.

His gaze flicks to me briefly, assessing, then back to her like I'm nothing more than a shadow.

"Enjoying yourself?" he asks coolly.

"Oh, immensely," she replies, her grin widening like she's daring him to push. She gestures between us. "You've met Bane? He's my"—her eyes flick toward me before she quickly finishes—"my Dominant."

Domhnall's jaw tightens. His eyes drag over me, slow and deliberate, the way a predator sizes up another predator. His glare lands on my collar. "And you decided to cosplay at my charity event?"

"What? No! He's really a—"

I step forward slightly, not enough to be overt, but enough

to remind him I'm not background noise and extend my hand. "We haven't had the pleasure."

Domhnall's hand shoots forward, rigid, the motion practiced and hollow. I clasp it, our grips locking in something far less polite than the gesture suggests. His palm is calloused and controlled. I feel the strength in his intent. He's not pleased I'm here, and he wants me to know it.

I squeeze just enough to make a point.

His smile doesn't reach his eyes. "Bane, is it?"

"Father Blackwood, if you prefer," I reply smoothly. "Or if you have sins to confess."

His eyes narrow, but he lets go first. That's two points for me, though I doubt he's keeping score the way I am.

Moira steps between us, ready to steamroll over the tension. "Where's Anna? I thought she'd be glued to your side."

Domhnall's expression shifts, the sharpness fading into something more subtle. His eyes dart around the room, scanning the glittery crowd.

"She had to go to the restroom, but that was ten minutes ago," he mutters, more to himself than to us.

Moira's smile falters, just a crack, and I see the undercurrent of worry that mirrors her brother's.

Domhnall's brow furrows, his gaze darkening. "Unless..." His voice drops lower. "Unless something brought Mads out."

The words hang in the air like smoke. I don't know much

about their situation, but Moira told me her future sister-in-law has DID.

Moira's face shifts from playful to concerned. She leans in, voice low. "Want me to look for her? I can check the bathroom."

Domhnall hesitates, the mask of indifference slipping just enough to reveal the concern underneath.

Moira puts a hand on her brother's sleeve, voice soft. "I'll find her."

She immediately heads in the direction of the far wall, and I follow, with Domhnall at our heels.

We move through the gala together. The crowd parts for us, whether from instinct or the quiet tension radiating off us like heat. My hand rests on the small of Moira's back, not to control, but to remind her—and myself—that she's not alone. Not anymore.

Moira disappears inside the women's restroom, but it's not long before she emerges again, shaking her head.

"She's not there, but I got a lead," she says. "A lady said security just kicked a woman out for smoking in a stall."

Domhnall grimaces, jaw flexing. "It's Mads. I keep finding spent cigarette butts in the corner of the back deck."

"She'd have gone outside then," I say. "C'mon, I know the way out back to the service entrance. We can check there."

Domhnall's eyes flash my way distrustfully, but, teeth gritted, he nods.

TWENTY-SIX

MOIRA

THE AIR OUTSIDE is sharp and cool, a slap to the face after the suffocating warmth of the gala. Waitstaff hustles in and out of a catering van with food on trays. But back behind the van and off to the side—

There she is.

Mads. Hard to tell from this distance, except for the cigarette's curling smoke. She's arguing with some guy holding a camera, his flash bulb popping like a strobe light from hell.

That pisses her off even more because she starts really yelling then and reaching for the camera.

Domhnall spots her. I know because his entire body goes

rigid beside me like someone jammed a steel rod straight through his spine. He doesn't say anything. He just moves. Fast.

"Domhnall," I snap, but he's already halfway across the lot.

Bane and I follow, my high heels clicking against the pavement in a frantic staccato to match my racing heart.

Because I know that look in Domhnall's eyes. It's the same one he used to get right before he'd break some other boy's nose when they insulted me or Mam back in Donegal.

The photographer keeps clicking away despite Mads screaming at him, oblivious to the furious Irish brawler approaching in an expensive suit.

Domhnall grabs the guy by the front of his shirt, yanking him so hard the camera dangles from his neck.

"Delete it," Domhnall growls, low and dark, his accent slipping through the cracks of his polished facade.

"Hey!" I shout, sprinting the last few steps. Suddenly I've been transported back a decade and a half, back to break up another one of Donny's fights.

Domhnall ignores me, shaking the guy once for good measure.

"Domhnall!" I snap again, stepping between them. Which is probably not the smartest move, considering my brother's got all the chill of a rabid dog right now. "He's just a cockroach with a camera. Let him go."

Mads watches, her expression distant, like she's not fully there. Great. Just what we need.

"He took photos," Domhnall bites out.

"No shit, Sherlock. That's what photographers do."

The paparazzo tries to wriggle free. Bad idea.

Domhnall shoves him against a car, the impact loud enough to make me wince. People are starting to notice now. Phones come out. Flashes ignite.

Bane steps in then, his arm coming around my waist, lifting me back gently but firmly. His eyes lock with Domhnall's, and oh boy, here we go. The testosterone showdown.

"Let him go," Bane says to Domhn, calm but with an edge sharp enough to cut glass.

Domhnall hesitates, just for a second.

He drops the guy like trash but scoops his camera off the ground. He yanks the mini-SD card out of it, then tosses the camera back to the photographer. The photographer stumbles, catches it, then grins. He just pulls out his phone and starts snapping pics again.

"This is gold," he mutters, grinning. "Callaghan family drama. Love it."

Domhnall lunges, but Bane moves faster, stepping in front of him with a quiet authority that makes even my hotheaded brother pause.

"Not worth it," Bane says.

Domhnall glares. At Bane. At me. At the world.

And that's when the real circus arrives. More paparazzi

flood the back parking lot like vultures smelling blood. Flashes explode around us, blinding and relentless.

Domhnall tries to shield Mads, who finally snaps out of her trance. She flinches at the lights and throws her arms over her head.

Bane pulls me closer, his body a solid wall between me and the chaos. But it's too late. I hear the shutter click. A perfect shot:

Domhnall, furious, his hand still clenched into a fist.

Mads, fragile and wide-eyed.

Me, mid-yell, hair wild, expression wilder.

And Bane, towering behind me, protective and dark, his hand firm on my waist.

One photo.

A thousand stories will be splashed all over the internet tomorrow about tech billionaire Domhnall's lunatic fiancé and sex-addict sister.

TWENTY-SEVEN

Christmas Eve, Mid-morning

BANE

THE FAINT SCENT of fresh laundry greets me when I step off the elevator at Moira's penthouse apartment. No doubt the cotton-scented candles she likes to burn. It always makes the place feel homey. She told me once she likes the smell because it makes her feel like a normal person with a normal life.

She's waiting for me.

I don't even have to see her to know it. I feel her—this buzzing, restless thing thrumming in the space where she's pacing as I turn the corner. I hear her before I see her. The quick, uneven taps of her footsteps against the floor, like her anxiety has its own heartbeat.

When I round the corner, she freezes.

Her face—God. That face. Wide, dark eyes rimmed with worry, her bottom lip caught between her teeth like she's afraid if she lets go, the terror will spill out.

She knows where I've been. I had to have an emergency meeting with the bishop about everything that went down at the gala last night.

Her voice is a whisper, fragile and thin like it might snap under its own weight. "Do you still have a job?"

I should draw this out. Make some joke about clergy job security or how even God wouldn't fire me. But I can't.

"Of course, I have a job."

I say it fast, like I need to get the words to her before they lose their meaning.

She crosses the room in a rush, colliding with me. I catch her, my arms wrapping around her small frame automatically. She fits against me like she was made for it. Her face presses into my chest, her body trembling the second she makes contact.

It hits me harder than it should—her shaking.

"Thank god," she breathes, the words a soft exhale against my shirt. "I've been so worried."

"I can tell," I murmur, my hands sliding up her back,

massaging the tension from her shoulders. She's all tight knots and frail bones beneath my fingers.

"Shhh," I whisper into her hair, breathing her in like I need her scent more than oxygen. "I told you everything would be fine."

But that's a lie. I seem to be stacking them up lately.

It wasn't fine.

Not even close.

I don't tell her that.

I don't tell her about the bishop's voice, sharp and cold, slicing through the screen like it could cut me where I sat. I don't tell her about the way my name—*Father Blackwood*—sounded like an accusation instead of a title on the bishop's lips.

I went to the church office for the video meeting, although meeting seemed like the wrong word. It was more like an interrogation. The bishop's face glared back at me from the screen, framed by the sterile white walls of her office.

"Explain to me why you're on the front page of the *Dallas Chronicle*." She folded her hands underneath her chin like she was ready to deliver a verdict even though I'd barely said a word.

I kept my face neutral, hands in my lap, but my jaw ached from how tightly I was clenching it.

"With respect, Bishop, I don't control the media."

Her eyes narrowed, sharp as a scalpel. "Don't be flippant

with me. This isn't just media, Father. This is a scandal waiting to explode. Do you have any idea what this looks like?"

I didn't flinch. "It looks like a man caught in a photograph."

"A man caught with Moira Callaghan," she snapped, her voice rising. "A woman with a—how shall I put this delicately—colorful history. The press didn't even bother with subtlety." She waved a hand, mockingly quoting, "'Billionaire Tech Tycoon's Unstable Fiancé and Sex-Addict Sister Cause Chaos at Charity Gala.'"

I said nothing.

She leaned forward, her voice colder. "But I know who you are. And I know who she is. What exactly do you think you're doing?"

"I'm serious about her." The words left me before I could temper them. "That's what you asked when we last met, and I am. Serious."

She froze for half a second, then laughed—a short, humorless bark. "Serious? Have you heard a thing I've said? Clergy have to be above even the *appearance* of reproach, Father. It doesn't matter how serious you *think* you are. She's a known sex addict. The papers have statements from treatment facilities she seduced her way out of. Not just one. Several." She shook her head like she pitied me. "I'd hardly call you naïve, but are you sure you're not being played?"

The words hit harder than I would've expected, anger

sparking beneath my ribs. But I didn't let it show. I did grip the arms of my chair until my knuckles went white, though. I had to anchor myself in restraint somehow.

"I am not being played." It took all my strength not to belie the fury humming like a live wire right beneath my skin. Rule one was do not disrespect your bishop.

But the bishop just continued relentlessly. "She's manipulative. That's not judgment—that's fact. She's estranged from her billionaire brother, and now she's latched onto you? Another man with wealth and status? Wake up, Father."

She leaned back in her chair, crossing her arms. "End it. End it now."

I swallowed every retort burning on my tongue. Every curse, every defense. Instead, I bowed my head slightly.

"Thank you for your counsel, Bishop. Merry Christmas Eve."

Her mouth tightened. "I don't expect to have this conversation twice, Father Blackwood. If you value your position, I suggest you reflect deeply on your priorities."

The call ended with a soft *click*, but the echo of her words lingered.

So it's come to this.

A choice.

My calling. Or Moira.

My faith saved me when I was nothing but a hollow man —a shadow of myself, drowning in the wreckage of my selfishness.

I clawed my way out of that darkness, not with strength, but with surrender. I turned to the Lord, cracked open and raw, and found something resembling salvation.

Faith and serving others gave me purpose. It wasn't just a vocation; it was what stitched me back together and made me a man.

I believe I received a genuine calling from the Lord—to go and do likewise for others. To reach into the darkness for others the way God once did for me. To offer light. To offer hope.

But here's the thing about light and darkness. Sometimes, darkness doesn't smother light, it shapes it. Sometimes, they coexist without blurring, tangled so tightly you can't tell where one ends and the other begins.

Moira is both.

And in the end, I suppose there's no choice at all. Not really.

I smooth my hand down her back now, feeling the curve of her spine beneath my fingers and the steady thrum of her heartbeat pressed against my chest.

"I won't be home tonight." My voice is low, like if I say it softly enough, it won't matter.

Moira pulls back, her brow furrowing, confusion flickering across her face. "But it's not a Saturday."

I force a small smile. "There's Midnight Mass tonight and then a Christmas service in the morning."

Her hands tighten around my waist, fingers digging in

like she's trying to keep me from slipping through her grip. "Will you come over after?"

"After the service tomorrow, of course."

I lean down, pressing my lips to her forehead, letting them linger there longer than necessary. My chest aches with the weight of her. Of this.

"There's just not enough time between services," I add, pulling back slightly and making sure to keep my face neutral.

But she sees through it. She always does.

She frowns, tilting her head, studying me like she's searching for the cracks beneath the surface. "Are you sure I couldn't come stay the night just this once at your place?"

The question hits harder than it should. I feel my muscles go tight. "Things are... a little strained with the bishop at the moment," I admit carefully, each word measured and deliberate. "It's not the best idea, in case anyone sees you."

Her sigh is loud, frustrated, her breath warm against my collarbone. She buries her face into my chest, her arms clutching tighter.

"Are you sure everything's all right?" Her voice is muffled by my chest.

I close my eyes, resting my chin on top of her head, and inhale the familiar cinnamon scent of her.

"Of course it is," I whisper, my lips brushing against her hair. "Everything's going to be fine."

But it's not.

These will probably be the last two services I ever perform as an ordained priest.

I hold her tighter, memorizing the feel of her and the way her body fits against mine like a puzzle piece I didn't know I was missing. My hands tremble slightly, hidden in the small of her back, and I pray she doesn't notice.

Yes, I've been fighting to find myself between Bane and Father Blackwood, but who will I be if I lose being a priest completely? Will descending fully into Bane, even with Moira at my side, destroy me? Will I then destroy us both?

How do I tell her that I still choose her anyway?

TWENTY-EIGHT

Christmas Eve Night

MOIRA

I LOCK up after myself at the shelter, grinning like an idiot. It was a good night. One of those rare, golden evenings where the universe doesn't seem dead set on flipping me the bird. For once, Marci wasn't here with her clipboard and her "Actually, Moira, could you just stick to the kitchen?" vibes. Nope. Tonight, I was unleashed. Unshackled. Free-range Moira.

I got to come out and serve the residents, not just scrub pots and pretend I don't mind smelling like institutional lasagna. It felt meaningful, like I was part of something bigger. Like maybe I wasn't just a walking disaster wrapped in questionable life choices.

I even saw Daniella again. Sweet Daniella with her nervous smile and the kind of haunted eyes that make you want to punch the entire male population. We talked. I told her about Bane and how my man doesn't mind being seen out in public with me. I might've left out the part where I sort of catastrophically fumbled the end of the night and almost put his job in jeopardy. *Details.*

"Maybe you got a good one after all," she said, and I could see in the wistfulness behind her eyes that she wanted to hope such a thing was possible.

"I think I did get a good one," I whisper, grinning into the crisp night air.

I lock the last gate around the shelter with a satisfying *clunk*. The city hums softly around me, all twinkling lights and the distant sound of car tires hissing over wet pavement. Christmas Eve in the city—it's kind of magical if you squint past the nihilistic dread.

I start walking toward the light rail, hands shoved deep in my pockets. No point wasting gas when the train runs right between the shelter and my place. I pull out my phone, hit play on my favorite playlist, and shove one earbud in. Just as I'm about to pop the second one in—

I feel it.

That prickling sensation at the back of my neck, like my

instincts are waving tiny red flags and screaming, "Hey, dumbass, pay attention!"

A man is walking behind me.

Shit.

How long has he been there?

I glance over at my reflection in a dark shop window. Nothing suspicious. Just a girl walking home, pretending she's not low-key panicking and planning an escape route.

Then I roll my eyes at myself. Jesus, Moira. Paranoid much? It's Christmas Eve. It's a big city. People exist. Some of them even walk places. Revolutionary, I know. He's probably just some dude heading to a last-minute shopping spree to buy his girlfriend a scented candle she'll pretend to love.

Still.

Working at a shelter for survivors of domestic violence has taught me a few things. Like how not every monster wears fangs. Some of them wear nice cologne and smiles that don't reach their eyes. We've had angry exes show up before.

So, just to be safe, I casually jog across the street. You know, a totally normal, festive Christmas jog. The kind you do when you're definitely not suspicious of being followed.

I glance over my shoulder.

Oh fuck. The man crossed the street, too.

Okay. Not festive. Not normal. Not good.

My heart does this weird somersault thing, landing somewhere between mildly anxious and, oh, we're definitely gonna die tonight.

I quicken my pace, heading toward the well-lit street ahead. The light rail stop is just a block away, glowing like a tiny beacon of salvation. I can make it. I've got a head start.

Play it cool, Moira. Just a brisk Christmas Eve stroll. Nothing to see here.

Screw that.

I abandon all pretense of nonchalance and run. Full out sprint. No dignity. Just pure, adrenaline-fueled GTFO mode.

But I don't get far.

Before I make it three steps, two guys in leather jackets pop out of nowhere. One grabs my left arm, while the other snatches my right.

I scream bloody fucking murder, thrashing and kicking wildly, landing a solid heel to someone's shin.

Leather Jacket #1 grunts but doesn't let go.

"Calm down," he snaps.

"Oh, I'm sorry. Did you want me to be polite while you're kidnapping me?" I snarl, twisting and kicking some more.

But they're strong. Too strong.

"HELP!" I scream dramatically because why not go full damsel when you're being literally manhandled? Then I remember from self-defense training at the shelter to scream "fire," not "help," because people are nosy about fires but conveniently deaf about calls for help.

"FI—" is all I get out before a gloved hand slaps over my mouth, muffling the rest.

Mistake.

I bite down. *Hard.* I mean hard-*hard.* Like, "I hope you're up to date on your tetanus shot" hard.

The guy yelps, yanking his hand back like I'm rabid—which, to be fair, isn't entirely inaccurate. Fueled by pure rage and spite, I start kicking, aiming for shins, knees, or anywhere soft enough to cause maximum damage.

The back of my brain registers that the curses flying out of their mouths come with British accents. Fancy that. I'm being assaulted by the Spice Boys.

I'm still in full feral-cat mode when another man appears out of nowhere. He's limping heavily with a gold-topped cane and lifts his other hand like he's the goddamn king, all regal authority.

"Stop. Don't hurt her." His voice is smooth and polished with the kind of accent that's less London-street and more I-own-an-obscene-number-of-horses. "I only want to chat."

Chat? Oh, is that what we're calling kidnapping these days?

The distraction is enough for me to pause mid-kick and squint at the new guy. He's older—mid-to-late sixties, I'd guess—dressed like he walked straight out of an overpriced men's catalog. Tailored suit, polished shoes, not a hair out of place. But the fucker is pale and gaunt and giving real consumption-chic.

"What the fuck do you want?" I spit, still twisting like I'm auditioning for the world's angriest interpretive dance.

He steps closer, leaning calmly on his cane like this is a TED Talk and not, you know, an abduction.

"My son," he says smoothly. "Bane."

Wait. WHAT? It's like someone yanked the emergency brake in my brain.

Bane?

I freeze for half a second, but it's enough. I snap back to reality with a growl, whipping my head toward the guy gripping my right arm.

"LET. ME. GO!" I snarl, punctuating each word with another vicious kick.

When words don't work, I go primal—I bend down and bite him. Again. On the forearm this time. I'm an equal opportunity biter.

The brute roars, yanking his arm back. His other hand shoots up like he's about to clock me.

But Mr. Fancy Suit raises a hand, his voice cool as ice. "That's enough, Billy."

Billy—because, of course, his name is Billy—growls but steps back. His buddy releases me, too. But when I try to make a break for it, Billy grabs me around the waist like I'm a particularly difficult suitcase. He lifts me off the ground, carries me three steps, and unceremoniously drops me right in front of Bane's father.

I let out a guttural scream—not words, just pure rage-fueled noise—and glare up at the smug bastard.

"What the FUCK is this?!" I snarl, my voice echoing off

the nearby buildings.

"A conversation," he says with the kind of grim patience people use when explaining things to toddlers—or women they've just had abducted off the side of the street, apparently. He pulls a silk handkerchief from his breast pocket and dabs at his face, wiping away the spittle I didn't intend but am honestly proud of.

"The shorter, the better, if you'd stand still for a moment."

"Oh, *fine*," I hiss, dragging out the F just enough to spit again because why not double down?

His jaw tightens, but he smooths it over with condescending British calm.

"I should've known my son would continue his rebellion by taking up with someone so… completely unsuitable."

"Who the fuck are you, anyway? An anal-retentive dick in a suit? Got it."

He squares his shoulders, standing taller like that's supposed to intimidate me. "I'm one of the most respected men in the world, young lady. And you'd do well to watch your tongue if you don't want these men to cut it out."

I blink, then slowly look around. "We're on a public street, genius. There are cameras."

He smiles. Not a warm smile—a predatory one. "They'll have all conveniently gone out for these few minutes."

Great. Love that for me.

"So let me get down to it," he continues, pulling out a

literal checkbook. Like this is 1997. "What will it cost me for you to leave my son be?"

I actually laugh. Right in his face. "You can't be serious."

"Oh, I'm afraid I'm quite serious."

He scribbles something on the check. "Will a million do it?"

I blink. Then scoff. "You really are one jaded motherfucker. Don't you want your son to be *happy*?"

His expression flattens, deadpan. "I highly doubt the daughter of a whore from nowhere, Ireland—who grew up to be a sex addict, no less—could make my son happy."

Oof. That one lands like a punch to the gut, but I swallow it down.

"Two million," he bites out.

I jab my finger in his face. "You can take your money and shove it up your ass."

"Fifty million."

I laugh, shaking my head. That's how much my brother paid when Anna auctioned off her virginity.

"If you know so much about me, then you know I've already got a billionaire brother. I don't need your filthy money."

"A billionaire brother who's not speaking to you." He gets right in my face, eyes burning. "You live in such a pretty penthouse, but what happens when he stops paying your rent? And stops paying for your fancy car? Or did he already, and that's why you're taking public transit like the provincial you really are?"

I toss my hands up, smiling wildly. "I guess I'll finally have to get off my ass and get a job."

"But you've never managed to hold a job, have you? One *hundred* million dollars." He over-annunciates every word. "My final offer. You never have to worry about your brother again. Or ever work a day in your life."

I blink down at the cold concrete of the sidewalk underneath my feet, then laugh—a wild, unhinged laugh that starts deep in my belly and rolls out, loud and ugly. I'm laughing so hard I have to bend over, slapping my knee like he just told the world's funniest joke.

Bane's father stands there, rigid as a statue, his face carved from stone.

Then, he looks at one of his brutes and gives the tiniest of nods.

In a flash, Billy lunges, grabbing me by the coat and *slamming* me against a nearby brick wall.

My laughter dies out, replaced by a grin so sharp it could cut glass.

"What the fuck do you think you're laughing at, little girl?" Billy snarls, shaking me hard enough to rattle my teeth.

But I look past his shoulder at Bane's father, meeting his gaze without blinking. "I'm laughing at the sad little man who Bane couldn't wait to get away from. He hates you, doesn't he? God, that must drive you crazy."

He goes pale. Like, paler than he already was—ghost pale. His face twists in fury.

"He's better than you," he sneers. "If you won't leave him for the money, then leave him because Bane deserves better than some two-bit slut."

With that, he spins on his heel and motions to his goons. Billy drops me to the ground, and they all disappear into the dark like the world's most dramatic Bond villain.

I slide down the wall, my body sinking to the cold concrete, shaking—not from fear, but from the adrenaline crash. Silent tears slip down my face, hot and fast.

I might hate the man I just met with every fiber of my being, but...

Bane deserves better than some two-bit slut.

Damn him... he's not wrong.

TWENTY-NINE

Christmas Eve, Midnight Mass

BANE

THE SPACE INSIDE THE OLD, lofting, oiled wood church hums with anticipation, the kind of stillness that's never truly silent—soft coughs, shuffling coats, the faint creak of old pews as sinners and saints alike take their seats.

All are welcome at Midnight Mass, the holiest of nights, wrapped in candlelight and reverence as we re-enact the wait for hope to come into the world.

I stand in the small sacristy just beyond the altar, fingers grazing the edge of my stole, grounding myself in the familiar texture. The fabric is smooth beneath my fingertips, and I wonder if tonight, at the end of things, I can make peace with this contradiction—these holy vestments worn by an unholy man.

I breathe in and breathe out, trying to meditate and connect to the divine beyond the silence. But then my phone vibrates in my pocket, an unexpected buzz slicing through the sacred quiet.

I shouldn't check it.

I do, anyway.

It's her.

> Moira: You up?

The words are simple. Casual. But coming from her, they're anything but innocent. My thumb hovers over the screen, pulse quickening like a drumbeat in my veins. Another vibration.

> Moira: I can't stop thinking about you. Sure I can't sneak into your bed tonight? Or under your robes. Whichever's easier. 😈

I exhale sharply, the breath catching somewhere between a groan and a laugh. My body reacts before my brain catches up, cock stiffening.

It's completely inappropriate in this moment and context. Christ. I glance through the crack in the small sacristy door, half-expecting someone to materialize and catch me sinning in plain sight. But it's just me. Alone with the ghost of her words.

I type back quickly, fingers tense.

> Me: I can't. About to start Mass. I'll see you tomorrow.

I don't wait for her reply. I put the phone on airplane mode and shove it into my pocket like it's burned me.

All calm and meditation is shattered. I can't tuck my thoughts of her away as easily as I can the phone. Is she alright? I told her she couldn't come over earlier, and she seemed fine. Did something happen?

I want to pull out the phone again and examine the texts. She didn't say anything was wrong. She seemed fine. Flirty, like usual.

But with Moira, it's always hard to tell unless I'm face-to-face with her. It's still so new between us that every hour I'm away from her, I feel the ache of absence. The shadow of where she's not, haunting me. Making me restless until I settle eyes on her again.

I straighten my shoulders, tugging at the stole until it sits just right over my shoulders. The weight of it feels so right.

This will be the second-to-last service I ever perform. The thought feels like both a release and a noose tightening around my neck.

Will Bane without Father Blackwood still be merciful?

Still be kind? Still live by the rule of *the last shall be first, and the first, last?*

Another glance through the sacristy door shows a full church. Pews always swell for this service. Friends and family are in town for the holidays, and the solemn candlelight service may be the one time a year some step foot in a holy place like this.

I have a duty to them and the Lord to feed their spirits, regardless of how restless my own is.

I breathe in.

I breathe out.

I allow a moment of stillness to empty myself.

How quickly I've forgotten the lessons of surrender.

I bow my head.

Not my will but thine.

And then I step through the door out onto the altar. The glow of candles cast long shadows against the aged, wooden walls.

The congregation rises, their faces lifted in expectation. I meet their gaze, one by one, anchoring myself in the ritual and the sacred duty that has defined me for so long.

Not my will but thine.

I begin the service, my voice steady even as my heart feels like it's trying to claw its way out of my chest. The words are muscle memory now—prayers etched so deeply, surely they're in the marrow of my bones by now.

"In the name of the Father, and of the Son, and of the Holy Spirit..."

The congregation responds, their voices a chorus that rises and falls like waves against the shore.

I deliver the readings, my voice echoing in the vast space. Scripture is a connection to faithful people throughout time and space. I close my eyes as I recite familiar words about peace and hope like well-worn grooves worn by tongues throughout the centuries.

This is all so much bigger than me, than us, here in this church that is just one tiny node among millions all over the globe celebrating hope and peace tonight. It's called peace that surpasses all understanding.

So maybe it's all right if I don't understand how it will all work out.

Maybe it's all right if, for once, for fucking once, I let go of my iron control.

Over and over, I glimpse that control is an illusion. But over and over, I clamber to grasp even tighter for the reins.

As if the dark thing inside me will ever be tamed.

I'm a fool.

It's right that I put an end to this pious farce.

My impulse to run as far from my father might have been the right one, but I had no right to throw myself into a holy vocation that would make me a leader for anyone to follow.

I've learned nothing.

I ought to have been paying penance, not putting on white robes and standing up front with all eyes on me.

I was such an egotistical fool not to see the difference.

Agnes is in the front pew, and as always, her mouth presses into the disapproving line that seems permanently etched into her face. Like she's been judging priests and finding them lacking since the Reformation.

She's always seen right through me, hasn't she?

Her hands are folded neatly in her lap, rosary beads slipping between her fingers with practiced devotion.

I feel a rush of affection for her. For all of them.

They're imperfectly living lives of frail faith. Most people who step foot in a church eventually learn to get good at pretending, but how could I shepherd them when I'm the biggest pretender of all?

So, as I move into the sermon, one of the last I know I'll ever give, I try to say something honest for once.

"You've all been so kind to me in my few years serving you. I've been a foolish young man stumbling around trying to find my way, pretending I could offer any wisdom when the decades you all have on me humble me. Sometimes I feel like nothing at all."

I swallow hard and look down, my careful notes blurring in front of my eyes. I'm supposed to offer wisdom, guidance—a glimpse of something divine. Laughable, considering how obscure everything has seemed of late.

All I can speak about is what I do know.

"Tonight is a night celebrating hope born into the world. I imagine it's hope that's brought most of us to church in the first place. Either that or your grandma dragged you along."

Some chuckles come from the crowd.

I look from face to face in my congregation, abandoning my notes. "We've all faced struggles in our life. Dark times when it felt like there was no way out. I know I have. And when I was at my most desperate and hopeless, pleading to what felt like an unkind universe for help, it felt like something answered back."

Heads nod. I'm not the only one who's experienced this. Of course, I'm not.

"Hope returned, just when all was lost. A hand was extended. A kind word offered. Or we might find that light within ourselves from a well we thought was exhausted to help us through for just *one more day*. And then one more after that. And then another."

My hands clutch the edges of the lectern as I lean forward. "God's love comes to us in all kinds of unexpected ways. It's as fragile as it is fierce. Like God Himself being born into this world as a baby in a dirty barn. Like losing all your worldly possessions but finding the kind of love that survives even when everything else falls apart."

The words nearly tangle in my throat.

Because, holy shit, *I love her*.

I love Moira. Not just the chaos of her and not just the

way she makes me feel alive—but all of *her*. Even the parts that scare me.

Just because of who she is.

She showed up like a miracle in my life, and I *love* her.

I barely manage to keep my hands steady while I move through the rest of the service.

I have to call her. I'll drive home tonight after all; I don't care if I only get an hour of sleep before tomorrow's morning service.

Finally, we get to the service's last tradition—the Midnight Mass candlelight benediction.

The lights dim slowly, leaving the sanctuary bathed only in the faint flicker of candlelight from the altar. I step forward, holding the single flame that will spread from person to person like a ripple across water.

"Light shines in the darkness," I say softly, my voice carrying even in the hush. "And the darkness has not overcome it."

I light Agnes's candle, watching as she turns to pass the flame along. A soft glow blooms in the darkness—fragile yet unstoppable. One small light grows into a sea of flame.

The organ begins the first gentle notes of *Silent Night*.

Silent night, holy night,

All is calm, all is bright...

The congregation sings, voices blending, soft and reverent. I watch their faces bathed in golden light—hope flickering in fragile flames.

And as I stand there, holding my own candle, the warmth of it trembling in my hands—

I *see* her.

Moira.

I gasp and blink, looking again as if my eyes have deceived me. My candle flickers with my sudden inhale of breath.

But it's her, standing at the very back of the church, just beyond the last row of pews. She's holding a candle, but she's not dressed for church. Her curly hair is wild and untamed, catching the faint glow of candlelight like a halo gone rogue. Her coat is slightly crooked, and though warm candlelight blooms on her cheeks and forehead, her eyes are shadows.

How long has she been here?

The moment our eyes meet, it feels like the world stops spinning. Like every note of *Silent Night* fades into nothing, leaving only the pounding of my heart.

She doesn't move. Just stands there, her gaze locked on mine, her expression unreadable—something between defiance and longing.

I swallow hard, the candle trembling slightly in my hand.

I shouldn't look.

But I can't look away.

The hymn comes to an end, the final note lingering like a held breath.

"Go in peace," I say softly, my voice rough around the edges.

The congregation responds, but I don't hear them.

Because all I can see is her as the congregants file out, lights held aloft in their hands.

Moira.

Maybe faith was never about choosing between darkness and light.

Maybe it's about learning to stand in both. Night and day in harmony.

And as I extinguish my candle, I feel the glow.

Not from the flame.

From her.

I step forward once more. Toward her. Toward hope.

THIRTY

MOIRA

THE SERVICE WAS BEAUTIFUL.

I came in late and stayed here in the back. But watching Bane do his thing is nothing short of... magical.

He transforms up there. Like he's a whole different person, except not really. Somehow, he's still him, but more. Both the dominant man I—um—*have strong feelings toward* (read: want to climb like a tree) and this calming, radiant presence that casts a spell over everyone in the room.

It's wild.

Everyone felt something while he talked. Even me. Even though he was just reciting old words from an even older book about shit I don't believe in. But it didn't matter because he made it all come alive. Like he breathed life into them. Made them feel meaningful and useful and like maybe, just maybe, there's something bigger than us out there that loves us.

I mean, the way his voice filled the space, soft but strong—

I blow out my candle and press my palm against the center of my chest, right over my heart. It feels raw like someone cracked me open with a chisel. There's this weird ache, not a bad one, just... sharp. Bright. Too big for my ribs.

I take a step back into the shadows, my heartbeat buzzing under my skin like I swallowed a hive of bees. I watch as people line up to greet him—Father Blackwood.

He steps down from the altar, still wrapped in all his holy finery: billowing white robes, a blue sash-thing draped around his neck, and his collar glinting under the soft, flickering candlelight.

He looks pure. Untouchable. Like a true conduit to the divine.

And I—

I'm a fucking ink stain on a white page.

It's easy to forget this part of him when he's Mr. Kinky Dom, pinning me down and making me beg. When his teeth are on my skin and his voice is a growl in my ear. But this—*this*—is who he really is, isn't it?

Bane deserves better than some two-bit slut.

The words slide into my head like they've always been there, waiting.

They taste like acid. And truth.

I step further into the shadows, my body vibrating with too much energy. My skin feels tight like it doesn't fit right. I scratch at my arm—just a little—but the itch doesn't go away. It's under my skin, crawling, scurrying, like raccoon feet tap-tap-tapping across my brain.

Scratch, scratch, scratch.

Ow!

I hiss and look down. There's blood. A thin red line runs down my forearm like it's trying to escape.

What the fuck are you doing, Moira?

I stare at the blood for a second, but it doesn't feel real. None of this does. The candlelight. The hymn still echoing in my head. Bane's velvet voice.

I shouldn't have come. The bishop said he shouldn't be seen with me. She said I was bad for him. I'm a stain on his reputation. A mistake.

You don't belong here.

I scratch again, harder this time, my fingers digging into the same spot like I can rip the feeling out. But it's still there. It's always there.

I bounce on my feet, my heart racing like it's trying to outrun me. My thoughts spiral—fast, faster, like a tilt-a-whirl with no brakes.

What the fuck was I thinking, coming here like this?

I'm a mess. A goddamned disaster. And now I've dragged it here—to his place of work. His job. His sacred little world.

I'm ruining it.

Like I ruin everything.

That's all you fucking do, Moira. Ruin things.

I should leave.

No. I should…

My thoughts skitter, each faster than the next.

I pull out my phone, my fingers hovering over the screen before I can even think. Text Bane? No. Call someone? Who? Domhnall? Ha. Yeah, right.

I shove the phone back in my pocket, neck straining as I try to stretch out the horrible tight-skin feeling.

Fuck. No one wants to hear from me.

No one wants this chaotic mess in their life. *I* don't even want this chaotic mess in my life.

Wrong, wrong, wrong in the head, my brain singsongs.

Shouldn't be here. Should be dead.

A giggle bubbles up, sharp and bright like champagne fizz, but I slap it down just in time. *Don't laugh in church, Moira.* That's rule number one in the Don't Be A Fucking Disaster handbook.

But then—

Exit sign.

Red and glowing like a beacon just down on the opposite end of the church.

Run.

My legs move before my brain catches up. I shove through the door, metal slamming behind me with a satisfying *clang*.

Then I gulp in the cold night air like it's the first breath I've taken all day.

I'm outside, tucked into the shadowy guts of the church—a concrete patch squeezed between a giant AC unit and a dumpster. I press my back against the cold brick, heart racing, pulse in my throat.

Breathe.

But I'm not really here, am I?

I giggle again, feeling light-headed. Light like I might just lift off from the ground. Gravity can't hold me.

I'm just a ghost in the shadows. A flicker at the edge of his vision. Not someone you hold on to. Not someone you keep.

There's a balloon inflating inside, pushing against my ribs, my heart, my everything.

Somewhere at the back of my head, I recognize this feeling.

Hello, Crazy, my old friend.

I shake my hands out, fingers twitching like they've got a mind of their own. Doesn't help.

So I start dancing in place. Just quick little stomps, feet slapping the ground, trying to shake it out—shake out the static, the buzz, the wild, uncontrollable *more* that's crackling under my skin.

But it's still there. Louder. Bigger.

Then I freeze mid-stomp, breath ragged. I know what I need.

Of course.

I need to fuck.

That's it. That's always what I need when I get like this. When my head feels too full and too empty all at once. When my skin doesn't fit right and my thoughts are racing laps around sanity.

I ruin things. That's what I do.

A loud, manic laugh bursts from my throat, sharp and too big for my chest. I slap my hands over my mouth, but it's already out, echoing off the stone walls like an accusation.

Time to fuck. Time to fuck!

Ding, ding, ding.

The bell tolls for thee, Moira. Time for ruin!

I double over, gripping my thighs, nails digging into my skin because I need to feel something real, something sharp to cut through the noise. I glance around the dark, barren edge of the church, searching for something.

Someone.

There.

A man, alone, heading toward his car, keys jangling in the quiet.

Before I can think—because thinking is not on tonight's agenda—I sprint to the edge of the church, peeking around the corner like some deranged pervert. Which I am.

I whistle.

Sharp and loud. His head snaps toward me, eyes squinting in the dark.

Hook bait. Cast line.

I grab the hem of my shirt and yank it up, flashing my tits like it's Mardi Gras and he's got beads. Then I wiggle my fingers in a "come here" gesture as if this is the most normal thing in the world.

He freezes. Looks away.

Dammit.

But then—he looks back.

Gotcha.

I hike my skirt up next, flashing more than just enthusiasm this time, wiggling my hips like I'm starring in the world's most chaotic strip tease.

Come on, dumbass. How much clearer do I have to be?

He hesitates, then locks his car with a beep and starts walking toward me.

Huzzah! I caught a fish!

Fish, fish, in a dish. Catch a cock and—

But as he gets closer, something shifts. Not in him. In me.

His face comes into focus. He's just a guy. Totally regular guy. The kind of face you'd forget in a crowd. And suddenly, the buzz under my skin isn't excitement.

It's fear.

It's panic.

Fuck. What am I doing?

Because this isn't a game.

I'm out of control. I just happen to be aware of it like someone watching outside my body. Fuck!

This is me, but not me. Humpty Dumpty's off the wall, and there are no king's horsemen and no king's men to even try to put me back together again.

I step back, breath hitching, heart still racing, but now for all the wrong reasons.

What the fuck are you doing, Moira?

The man slows, confusion on his face when I turn and bolt—legs pumping, lungs burning, running like if I go fast enough, I can outrun the thing chasing me.

But I can't.

Because it's me.

And no matter how far I run, I'm still always right there.

THIRTY-ONE

BANE

THE LAST OF the congregation filters out, leaving the church steeped in hollow silence. My collar feels tighter without the noise to distract me. I should be relieved; my duty's done now that the service is complete. But I've been distracted with thoughts of Moira the entire time I dealt with the receiving line.

Where is she? I scan the empty church.

I caught a glimpse of her earlier, a flash of wild hair and feral beauty tucked in the wings of the sanctuary. I tried to make my way immediately to her. But between Mrs. Sanchez's tearful gratitude for the sermon and Bill Washerman's desperate plea to pray over his ailing parakeet, she vanished.

I heard the heavy door on the left side of the sanctuary slam shut at some point, so maybe that was her? My pulse stirs in response.

I move through the darkened church, footsteps echoing against the old wooden floors. Shadows stretch long. She's certainly not here anymore. I frown and push through the door, the cool night air biting.

The mechanical hum of the church's outdated HVAC system is the only sound that greets me. I pull my phone from my pocket, thumb flicking the dark screen to life, and take it out of airplane mode.

No messages.

No missed calls.

Where the hell did she go?

She was just here. Why'd she run off right when I finished? Did she really think I wouldn't see her? Is she afraid I'll be mad at her for coming tonight after I told her not to?

I call her. It rings several times, then goes to voicemail. I grit my teeth, thumb hovering before I hit redial. Again—nothing but that hollow beep after a few rings.

My breath escapes in a hiss, tight with something dangerously close to fear. She was just here. Did she leave already?

I text her, pacing the cracked pavement behind the church, the cold seeping into my bones.

> Me: I just want to hold you tonight.

I stare at the message, willing it to reach her.

Maybe she's driving, and that's why she's not answering. Even though I know her car can receive my phone calls without a problem.

I call again.

And then I hear it—faint, like a whisper tucked between the rustling leaves and distant traffic. Ginuwine's *Pony*. My head snaps toward the sound. It's her ringtone for me.

To the right of the church, there's a small garden. A cluster of trees meant to be a meditative space. The faint glow of a phone winks through the darkness before vanishing.

I sprint. My heart slams against my ribs.

"Moira!" My voice cuts through the night. Brittle winter leaves crackle under my feet until I see her—a silhouette crumpled on a large boulder, hands tucked under her as if trying to hold herself together.

Thank God. She's here. She's in one piece. But then I see the tremble in her shoulders and how her whole body's shaking with more than cold. And how she's sobbing.

"Moira!" She has a jacket on, but her legs are still exposed, and it's freezing out here. "What are you doing?" I crouch down and pull her into my arms—or try to. She fights me and scrambles off the rock and back.

"Don't touch me!"

I freeze, hands raised in surrender, though every instinct

in me screams to gather her up in my arms to protect her from the cold and whatever's making her cry so hard.

"Shhh," I murmur. "Moira, what happened? Are you okay? Are you hurt?"

"No!" Her voice fractures on the word. She throws her hands up, just visible in the dim light filtering through tree branches from a streetlight. "Of course, I'm not okay! Have you *met* me? I'm fucked up! Fucking screwed up in *here!*"

She punctuates the words with sharp knocks against her own temple with her fist.

"Stop it." My voice is firm. The command slips out before I can soften it. "You're perfect."

She laughs—a bitter sound. "You don't know what you're talking about. You've only seen what I *let* you see."

"Fine. What don't you want me to see?"

"This!" She screeches, spinning in a frantic circle, then jumping in place. "Fucking *this*! The fucking *ants* under my skin. The itch I can't scratch. I almost—" She flings an arm back toward the church. "I almost lured one of your church guys to the parking lot out back behind the church to fuck me just to stop the noise in my head!"

I absorb this information and nod, trying to keep my face non-judgmental. "Okay. Thank you for telling me that."

"Thank you for—" Her face twists, incredulous. "What's wrong with you? Did you hear what I just said? That's fucked up! *I'm* fucked up!"

She's luminous like this. So fragile and furious. So unfiltered. She thinks her ugly truths will make me recoil.

She couldn't be further from the truth. Doesn't she get it? Every time she's so vulnerable with her rawest emotions—with her soul—she only makes me want her more.

She's the opposite of the perfect bullshit pretender I am.

I step closer, slow and steady, like I'm approaching a wild animal. She could run if she wanted. She doesn't.

"I don't think you're broken," I whisper, closing the space between us. I finally wrap my arms around her, gentle but firm. She stiffens but doesn't push me away. "I think you're so, so brave."

She stares at me, her eyes glassy and lips trembling. Finally, she manages a whispered, "Nobody thinks I'm brave."

I squeeze her tighter to me as if that will make her believe my words. "Then nobody's been paying attention. You live fearlessly. And you're brutally honest. No one's as brave as you, Moira."

Her breath shudders out, and for a moment, she lets herself sag against me.

"I'm not brave," she whispers. "I'm just crazy."

I smile softly, pressing a kiss to her temple. "All the bravest people were called crazy first, dove. The prophets. Saints. Revolutionaries. They were the only ones brave enough to stand up against kings and dictators."

She snorts. "Pretty sure none of them were trying to fuck randos in church parking lots."

I chuckle, the sound rumbling through both of us. "Who knows? Maybe they just edited that part out of the scriptures and history books."

Her fingers spasm on the fabric of my shirt and she blinks up at me. "But those are the best parts."

I chuckle. "If only they'd had Kindles back then. The scribes were probably writing all the dirty parts on any leftover scraps of paper."

I finally manage to get a small smile out of her, which sobers me.

I tilt her chin up, forcing her to meet my eyes. "What are you really doing out here, gorgeous?"

She swallows, her gaze flickering away. "I'm not good enough for you."

Her words slug me in the guts.

She hiccups in a big breath, eyes landing somewhere around my Adam's apple.

I shake my head, but she goes on.

"I mean, look at you in there. Being so holy and leading those people to like, God and stuff. And then I'm so bad and dirty—"

I stop her the only way I can. I dip down and kiss her, cutting her words off. My hands slide up the sides of her body until I'm cupping the back of her precious head when I finally pull away.

"That's nonsense," I say, pressing another gentle kiss. A line from all that useless Shakespear I learned in school suddenly returns to me: *Thus from my lips, by thine, my sin is purged.*

"Don't you understand, love? You're not the sinner here, and I'm not the saint. You've got it backward."

She just shakes her head, looking confused.

"Come with me," I whisper suddenly. I drop my hands down and thread my fingers through hers.

Because I can't stand another second without her, and I need her to understand what I see so clearly.

THIRTY-TWO

MOIRA

"WHAT ARE WE DOING?" I ask as Bane pulls me back into the church, his hand wrapped around mine like it belongs there.

The heavy doors shut behind us, sealing us inside the warmth and shutting out the cold. The church air feels different now that we're all alone.

"Wait here," he murmurs, pressing a gentle kiss to my forehead, and then hurries off to the front of the church.

The warmth seeps into my frozen limbs, but my insides stay brittle, ice tucked beneath my ribs because—

Oh, right.

That still happened.

The alley.

His father.

The checkbook ready like I'm a whore who can be bought.

I should tell Bane. The words rise in my throat like bile.

Hey, so funny story—ran into your dad tonight. He tried to buy me off like I'm a stain on the family name he thinks he can bleach out. And then his goons shoved me up against the wall and scared the shit out of me.

My mouth even opens.

But nothing comes out.

Because—what do I say? *How* do I say it?

Bane's never even mentioned his father. Are they close? Estranged? Somewhere in the middle, where it's just awkward family reunions and suppressed childhood trauma?

If they *are* close, dropping this on him would be like tossing a grenade into the middle of their relationship.

If they're *not* close... well, same grenade, different shrapnel.

And honestly?

There's a part of me—a dark, ugly little part—that thinks... *of course* Bane has a father.

A real, living, breathing father who gives a shit about him. One who's willing to throw stacks of cash at me to protect his son. From me.

And here's the kicker: he's not wrong.

If I were Bane's dad, I'd pay me off, too. Hell, I'd throw in a bonus just to make sure I stayed gone.

Bane has someone in his life who'd bother. Someone who thinks he's worth protecting. Sure, my brother *pretends* he cares—or he used to—but maybe it was always more about his ego than about me. I've been everyone's afterthought for so long that I've practically evolved into it—a walking, talking footnote in everyone else's life.

But not to Bane.

When he looks at me, it's like I'm not a punchline. Not a mistake.

He called me *brave*.

Me.

So, if telling him about his dad risks breaking that? I'd rather swallow the secret and let it burn a hole straight through me.

Besides, Bane's obviously got this whole mysterious past he never talks about. Dropping this on him could unravel things he's worked hard to keep stitched up. Maybe his father's tied to all that darkness he hints at—the vague references to a life left behind, like shadows he can't quite shake.

And if I pull on that thread and unravel him, too?

No.

I won't be the reason he falls apart.

I'll be his shield. His poison-taster. I've been drinking poison my whole life. What's a little more?

I stand up straighter, squaring my shoulders against the weight of my own thoughts.

I can handle it.

I've always handled it.

And if his father comes sniffing around again, I'll handle that too.

Because Bane sees me like no one else ever has.

And I'll burn before I let anyone take that away.

THIRTY-THREE

BANE

SHE DOESN'T BELIEVE me about who's the villain and who's the hero here. I see it in the way her arms wrap around herself and the distressed furrow in her brow.

It's all wrong.

She doesn't see what I see when I look at her.

I need to hold up a mirror to make her see the truth. For once in her life, she needs to see the fucking truth.

Because I know what happened to her even if I don't know all the details. People have taken and taken and *taken* from her since she was too young to fight back. They've told her who she is and isn't allowed to be. A story was written for her that she never had a say in.

And fuck, do I understand.

I understand because they did the same damn thing to me.

Conditioning is a hell of a thing. It carves deep grooves in the mind—grooves that feel as permanent as the ones on an old wax record. The lies repeat, over and over, until they feel like a song you'll be humming under your breath until you take your last exhale.

But it's still a lie.

And I need her to know she can rewrite her story.

"It's time you understand—you get to be whoever the fuck you want, Moira." I step forward, framing her face between my hands, holding her still so she can't look away. "Tonight, we set you free."

Her brows knit tighter. "What does that mean?"

"You'll see. Do you trust me?"

She hesitates, searching my face, and then—so slowly, so cautiously—nods. "I trust you. Even though you have secrets."

The words punch through me, landing somewhere deep.

She swallows, glancing away. "Some things have... happened recently. I don't want you to think I'm lying. I just—I want it to be like what you haven't told me about your life before you became a priest. So you know those things are there, but I'm just not telling them to you right now. Is that okay?"

Her eyes find mine again, open and raw.

I wasn't expecting this.

And I feel, with a quiet kind of horror, how unfair I've been. Keeping my own secrets close to my chest and not telling her about my past. But now that the shoe is on the other foot, I feel it—the clawing questions that rise in my throat, demanding to be asked.

What happened? When? Why can't she tell me?

I know my reasons for keeping my secrets. They're harmless. At least... I think they are.

But hers?

No, my mind rejects the suspicion immediately.

It's not her I don't trust. It's me and my own judgment. My ability to put my faith in the right person.

I spent decades trusting the wrong one.

"I'm such a fool," I whisper.

Her eyes widen with concern. "What does that mean? You're acting weird. Tell me the truth—are you mad that I came tonight after you told me not to? Or about what I did outside?"

"No." I lean in, pressing a kiss to her forehead. "I'm sorry if I scared you. I think I'm just... seeing some things clearly tonight."

"Like what?"

"Like how fucking stunning you are." My voice drops, and I take her chin between my fingers. "The world has it backward, Moira. They look to men who hoard money and call themselves kings and make gods of them. But those men are usually liars and thieves, so lost in their own goddamn hype they wouldn't recognize the truth if it was splashed in neon right in front of them."

I stroke my thumb across her cheekbone, memorizing the softness.

"But you," I murmur. "You shine from within. You're worth so much more than any of them with their stupid fucking gold."

She lifts an eyebrow. "How much of the communion wine did you get into tonight, Father?"

A laugh bursts out of me, startled and real.

There she goes again, making my point for me.

I shake my head and take her hand, tugging her with me down the center aisle of the church. I lit every standing candelabra at the front of the church and the one on the altar. The candlelight flickers over us, casting a soft, golden glow.

The altar is clear of everything but the altar cloth, the candles, a fresh cruet of wine, the plate of leftover wafers, and a tincture of sacristy oil.

"Tonight, you see the truth," I tell her.

We've reached the altar.

"Do you give yourself to me tonight?"

She studies me now, sensing the shift in my mood. Her posture straightens, and the last of the tension drains from her face.

And then—finally—the worry line in her brow smooths.

Satisfaction rumbles low in my chest.

Good.

If I can give her anything tonight, let it be this.

"Yes. I give permission for everything. I'm yours." She meets my gaze, steady and fearless, with the kind of bravery that makes my breath catch—

The kind of bravery that makes me love her.

I step into her, knee sliding between her legs, hands beneath her coat to cinch around her waist. My fingertips squeeze against her warm flesh.

"Even if everything I want to do tonight is very, very wrong?"

"Yes." Her breath hitches, and her eyes brighten. "Yes. I love wrong things the best of all."

I search her eyes, my top lip twitching. I slide her coat from her shoulders, my hands trailing down her arms until it slips to the floor at her feet.

Still pinning her gaze with mine, I grab the low-cut concert tee she's wearing with both fists right at her cleavage. Then I rip it down the center.

She's not wearing a bra, and her small, perfect tits heave up and down as her nipples pebble in the cool air. The heat is on, but the arching loft of the sanctuary means it never warms up all the way in here.

She swallows hard when I reach down and roughly grab for the back of her skirt, yanking her body to mine as I undo the button and zipper, adding the layers of black cotton fabric fluff to the growing pile of clothes at her feet.

Now I'm the one gulping.

"You're so fucking stunning, naked and in nothing but your boots." I lean into her, pressing my forehead against hers.

"I want you." I fist my hands to keep them by my side instead of touching her.

"You have me," she whispers back, lip trembling.

Do I?

Why is it all crashing in on me tonight?

My past and my future and *her*. My sense of control trembles on a knife's edge. But control is all I have. It's all that's separated me from... *him*.

But isn't that what I've seen tonight at the end of it all? At the end of the charade?

It's all been a lie.

I've been a lie. Playing at priest. The collar's like a costume I put on.

Finally, I let myself touch her. I grab her by the waist, lift her and set her bare bottom down on the altar.

"Sweet dove," I murmur, stepping between her legs, jaw flexing. "Didn't you ever realize? The discipline was as much for me as it was for you."

She blinks, eyes wide as she sits so fucking gorgeously on the consecrated altar. I feel such deep fucking satisfaction, followed by a dark wave of need.

"It was?" She gulps, and my eyes zero in on the delicate curve of her neck.

It takes the last of my control to reach down for her left

boot, unlacing it, tugging it gently from her foot, and dropping it carelessly to the floor behind us. Then I peel the sock from her sacred skin.

I lift her foot to kiss the arch, pressing my cheek to her cool skin. Her toes twitch against my cheek and I exhale, looking up into her surprised face. Then I repeat the ceremony with her right boot.

Her legs tremble by the time I've kissed her arch, and then the top of her foot, and then caress my hands up the outsides of her calves before finally stepping back from her.

"What now?" she asks breathily, eyes meeting mine.

Her eyes are curious and excited.

I'm shaking as I take in the sight of her completely naked on the Lord's altar.

She's perfection.

Before her, I feel the weight of exactly who I am and shed the façade I've been hiding behind for so many years. I yank the priest's collar from around my neck and fling it into the shadows.

I drop to my knees before her.

Filthy soul bared.

"Please," I beg for what I don't deserve. "Be my priest tonight."

THIRTY-FOUR

MOIRA

BANE IS on his knees before me.

He doesn't see me as a broken thing. Or as a problem or inconvenience.

He's looking up at me like a goddess.

He called me *his* priest.

I sit up taller and cross a leg elegantly over the other as I stare down at him. I've been messy and weeping at his feet and an absolute and total manic mess. Even now, I have to fight tears at the amount of trust he's placing in me.

In his gaze, I read total devotion, and it gives me strength.

In his eyes, I see who I could be.

Who, to him, I already *am*.

My chest clenches, and then, looking at him kneeling in a penitent position, it hits me—for *once*, I'm not the one on my knees. That floor doesn't look soft, either.

'Cause, Jesus. How many hard floors have I kneeled on, bowing down to men while I gave them blow jobs? How many grimy tiles have I looked at up close and personal while I bent over so I was all but touching my toes so they could get a better angle to fuck me in a bar bathroom stall?

No one's ever let me take the power. To be fair, I also haven't gone seeking it out. And I—I think some part of me never believed I was capable of holding it. Or that I deserved it.

Bane's dropped his face to the ground. Just like I've seen so many little good subbies do at the club. It's such an incongruous look on such a big, confident man. I mean, yes, I've seen plenty of big gay guys as subs, but a powerful, hetero man submitting like... like *this*? I'm probably stereotyping, but good Lord.

The sight of him has my stomach sweeping out with lust.

I put my foot on his shoulder and kick him back lightly, just to see how he reacts. He tips backward easily, absorbing my motion and then returning to the perfect position, head bowed.

I bite my bottom lip and look around the altar table. In the dark, with nothing but candlelight and as naked as I am, I feel wild and a little pagan. I stretch my arms out over my head and breathe in so deeply that my lungs fill all the way up. My arms arc slowly down as I breathe out.

All my worries and anxiety from the day dissolve with my released breath. Nothing matters but the satisfaction I'm about to chase with this man. There's nothing in the whole world except the oiled wood of this church, our two bodies, and the things we'll do to one another.

No other moments exist outside this one.

I reach over and pick up one of the last scattered communion wafers from a silver plate. Then I spread my legs wide, lifting one ankle up toward my shoulder.

Carefully, I place the little round wafer between the lips of my sex.

"My body," I whisper. "Broken for you. Eat, and be cleansed of your sins."

Bane's eyes darken as they lift to mine, that uncanny connection that always zings like shooting electricity between us, lighting me up.

Then he lifts from his knees.

I forget to take a breath as slowly, gaze still locked with mine, he extends his tongue to lick straight up the center of my pussy.

The wafer is soggy with my juices.

I watch it disappear into his mouth. His eyes close as if in ecstasy as he chews and swallows.

Is he praying right now? I only realize in this moment that

I've never actually stopped to ask him if he actually believes in... I glance around. All... *this*.

"What are you thinking?" I whisper.

"I'm giving thanks for you." I love that he responds immediately. His brow furrows. "And I'm thinking I want you to hold me down with your weight on my chest and shove my face sideways into the ground while you ride my cock. That's what I'm thinking."

I gasp, his words stealing the breath from my lungs. "Holy fuck that's hot."

My pussy clenches, wanting everything he just described.

But for once, I don't immediately give in to the need that has my body twitching and use the gift of patience and discipline the man on his knees before me gave me.

And what a fucking gift it is. I close my eyes and luxuriate in the feelings making my stomach squirm and my pussy muscles clench and unclench.

Over the last year, before meeting Bane, I had totally lost connection with my body.

Ever since... Ever since I betrayed my brother without meaning to.

Whether or not I meant to, Anna was hurt in a way she almost couldn't come back from. I forced her into a terrible situation with consequences that have lasted to this day. For both her and my brother.

And I'm *sorry*.

Oh God, I'm so, so sorry.

Tears squeeze out of my eyes. Yes, I was just being my normal, rebellious, thoughtless self.

I reach for the silver chalice of wine, bring it to my mouth, then tip my head back and close my eyes.

Yes, I was being my normal, thoughtless self. And people got hurt.

Both are true. And I will absolutely try to be more conscientious in the future. I will beg for forgiveness on my knees.

But whether or not Domhn or anyone else fucking acknowledges it, it's also the truth that I *am* trying.

I'm trying when it would be *so* much fucking easier to give up.

No one but Bane has ever seen that. How fucking hard I fight every fucking day, and how brave it is to keep showing up as well as I do in the world. Even if everyone thinks I'm a disaster, he looks at me and thinks I'm stunning.

Somehow, he gets it. He gets that every morning, apart from a few bad months earlier this year, I get out of fucking bed, and I *try*.

"My blood." My voice rings out in the church as I lift the chalice. "Spilled for the forgiveness of your sins. Drink and be whole."

I spill the wine down my chest, letting it flow down the valley between my breasts. It cascades down my belly to my sex.

Where Bane's mouth swiftly moves to my pussy to gulp up my offering.

The wine finishes pouring from the chalice, and I drop it to the table, too distracted to do anything else because, oh god—

I grab Bane's hair, fingernails clenched right at his scalp as his mouth continues licking, then suckling at my cunt.

"Oh!" I cry and then can't manage words as my pussy flutters with pleasure that bites straight up to my belly. My other hand scrabbles somewhere at the fabric of Bane's shoulder, pulling his mouth deeper into me.

Oh shit. Oh shit. Oh *shit*.

My mouth opens, but nothing comes out. I don't have sound.

My fingertips are too busy lighting up with pulsing fire.

My chest convulses with the orgasm I didn't even realize was already building, now racing up and down my spine.

Mother*fucker*, how does that feel so goddamned *good*?

I drop his shoulder to brace myself back on the altar while my hips buck up into his perfect, slurping, magical mouth.

I keep one hand fisted in his hair, though, and thank god I'm holding on to something because he takes me right back up to the peak almost as soon as I've come down from the last one.

I screech some sort of animal noise because, *Oh!* Now my goddamn spine is lit up. Good god, it's busting out the top of my scalp this time.

Coherent thought blanks out for a minute as I wrap my legs around his head and hump the man's damn face. He only eats more voraciously. Motorboating my pussy one second. Then the next, licking deep inside my cunt so, so deeply with his wicked tongue.

"Oh, God!" I scream, coming harder than any of the previous warm-ups, hips shuddering violently against Bane's face.

THIRTY-FIVE

BANE

SHE FUCKS MY FACE, and goddamnit, I love the shameless way she uses me. Yes. This. This is how it should be.

I smother my face in her cunt. I can't remember the last time I took a breath. My lungs are burning.

I don't fucking care. I don't deserve to breathe. She just keeps coming, and all I want in the world is to lose myself in this perfect pussy.

I dive deeper, nose absolutely buried in her cunt.

It's only her nails digging into my scalp as she drags my head backward that has me relenting and finally taking a breath.

Even then, it's only when she demands, "Breathe," that I fully fill my lungs with life-giving air. But eating the sweet fruit of her cunt hardly feels like punishment at all.

"Smother me," I growl. "Punish me. I deserve to be punished."

She glares down at me. "Didn't you just get your absolution?"

I rise on my knees, grabbing her thighs.

"It's not enough." I lick my bottom lip to get just a little more taste of her, and I fucking love the way her eyes flare as she watches my tongue.

Something inside me cracks.

No, *shatters*.

Like a glacier breaking free, crashing adrift into the sea with a force too powerful to stop.

"It's not enough," I rasp, my fingers tightening around her thighs like they're the only thing tethering me to this world. "I never pay any consequences. I always get off scot-free."

My voice breaks, and shame drags my gaze to the floor. I swallow hard, but it doesn't stop the confession from clawing its way up my throat.

"I almost killed a man." The words scrape out of me, raw and bitter. I force myself to look up and meet her eyes because I deserve to see the disgust that should be there. "And what happened? Nothing. I got to walk away and start over. Like always."

I let out a breathless, humorless laugh. "It's bullshit. My

father made every consequence disappear before I could ever feel it. So *please*." I hear the desperation in my own voice and hate myself for it.

But I *deserve* this. Every humiliating second.

"For once in my pathetic fucking life, give me the punishment I deserve."

She stares down at me, and I almost choke on the frustration rising in my chest. Because there's no disgust in her eyes. No revulsion. Just something softer, compassion I don't want.

But then—she moves.

Her foot presses to my chest and *shoves*.

Not hard. Just enough to jolt me where I kneel.

I barely have time to process the sharp inhale of breath that burns my throat before the words tear out of me.

"Again."

Her eyes flash. "Who says you get to demand things all the time?"

I let out a sharp exhale. *She's right.*

But I still bare my teeth. "I've demanded everything my entire life. My father raised me to believe I was born special. That I could treat anyone however I wanted because it was my god-given right." My throat tightens. "I say I hate liars, but I'm the biggest fucking liar of all."

She folds her arms. "What have you lied about?"

I lift my chin, bracing myself. "Please. Kick me again. For real this time."

"Maybe."

She glares down at me, and I finally realize what I've been afraid of all this time.

Not that I couldn't trust her.

But that she'll leave if she really knows who I am. And all the things I've done.

"You almost killed someone?" she prompts, her voice steady.

I drag my hands through my hair. I need to rip myself open for her.

"When I was young, I think I knew it was wrong. The orgies my father held. How cruel he was to the staff. The women he fucked. His friends. My other half-brothers and sister. I mean, they're all nightmares, but still." I shake my head, jaw clenched so tight it aches. "But by the time I should've known better, I'd spent so many years trying to impress him that I was numb to it all. So when some girl tried to get with me by jerking me off while I was driving after a few drinks, why the fuck would I have cared?"

Moira shoves me again with her foot, harder this time, and I absorb it.

Crave it.

When I look up, something in my chest tightens.

For the first time—she isn't looking at me like I'm a saint.

So I keep going. I need her to see all of me. Even the worst parts. Especially the worst parts.

I push to my feet to get closer so I can see every flicker of realization and revulsion on her face as I lay myself bare.

"I missed a stop sign. T-boned another car. There was so much fucking blood. The other driver was in the Critical Care Unit for weeks. Had to have three surgeries. There was even a moment when we didn't know if he'd make it."

My breath shudders out of me. "And even then, I was only worried about myself. About whether Dad would get me out of trouble. Like he always did."

She leans away from me, mouth parted, horror slipping into her expression.

"*Hit me.*" I pound my chest with a wild, reckless need. "I'm a hypocrite. Fucking hit me!"

She shoves me with her palms on my chest, and I stumble back.

"What happened then?" she asks, eyes burning.

A laugh forces its way out of my throat, sharp and empty. "Nothing. My father took care of it, of course. He paid the guy off after he recovered. Buried the records. And I barely cared. I was such a selfish little shit. I didn't feel a *thing*."

"Until what?" she challenges. "What changed?"

My mouth opens—and nothing comes out.

Because this is the part I never say. The part I never let myself *think*.

"My mom," I finally force out, voice thick. "She'd died a couple of years before." I exhale hard, willing the words to keep coming, to cut me open like I deserve. "But my father always told me she was just another gold-digging whore. That she never wanted me. That he was the one who wanted an heir, and she just used the pregnancy to trap him."

Moira stays silent, but I can feel her watching me.

I don't look at her. I can't.

I focus on her knees. The candlelight flickering against the floor. Anything but her eyes.

"I believed him." My lips twist, bitter. "Because why wouldn't I? He said she'd signed me away without a second thought. That she never fought for me. And then one day... I was looking for something in my father's office."

I swallow past the lump in my throat.

Say it.

"I found proof. Court papers. She never stopped fighting for custody until the day she died of cancer. She was still filing for visitation rights even when I was sixteen."

Moira exhales sharply.

My jaw locks. "My father fucking stole her from me. He wanted a trophy for a son. An heir of his own creation. But my mother, she just wanted *me*. All that time. She'd wanted me. And I—I just believed him and never fought for *her*."

I hate myself for how easily I let him shape me. How desperate I was for every ounce of his approval.

How pathetic I was, playing along with his game. Trying to *be* him.

I drop back to my knees.

And I look up at her.

I beg.

"Kick me again. But this time for real. I can take it. Please. Humiliate me. Hurt me."

Her mouth presses into a tight line. Then, slow and deliberate, she points to the ground.

"Face to the floor."

I don't hesitate. I drop.

And pray for once in my life to feel the weight of my sins pressing in on me.

I hear her hop off the altar and watch, my cheek cemented to the cold wood. Her bare feet walk out of my sight and she pauses, maybe to get something from a pew? Then she comes back toward me.

"Shove your pants down."

I obey immediately, lifting my ass enough to unbuckle and shove my pants down. Whatever she's about to do, I just pray she makes it hurt.

Almost as soon as I've got my pants down, she smacks my butt with something *thuddy* that's barely more than a gentle massage. I should know. I used it on her once.

A Bible.

Cute, but I'm selfishly furious at her gentle treatment.

How does she not get it yet? I am *not* a good man. I deserve all the punishment she has to heap on me. *Real punishment*. Not the gentle kind I've given her during training.

So I disobey, jumping up to my knees again.

The devil in me will goad her if that's what it takes.

"You showed up on my doorstep that first night, bruised, and I never tracked down the motherfucker who did it to you. Fucking *hit* me for being a cowardly motherfucker because I should have *ended* him by now!"

She drops the Bible and slaps me.

It sends a rush straight to my dick.

Goddamn her. She slapped me *correctly*. In the BDSM world, there is a correct way to slap if one is trained. And Moira's obviously been trained.

I'm being the biggest bratty asshole bastard right now, as much as I ever was in my youth, and she's seeing me at my childish worst.

But she's the one staying in control.

Which means, for once, I can let all my tightly wound restraint completely fucking unravel.

Holy shit. I really have met someone I can give my trust to completely.

It *is* possible.

"*Again*," I beg.

She slaps me again.

My cock goes hard as fucking stone.

"I love you," I gasp.

She slaps me again, this time on my other cheek, and I can't stop the rest of my confessions from pouring out.

"I've been obsessed with you since the day we met. I stalked you night after night at the club and watched from the shadows to see when you'd come and go. I wanted you. Your body. I wanted to lose myself worshipping your cunt. I couldn't stop thinking about you. Every hour of every day. You're the only person in the whole world who wants the real me. Maybe you won't now, now that you know everything, but I love you—"

She drops to her knees and throws her body against mine, kissing me hard, bruising.

I meet her, kissing her back just as furiously.

She bites my bottom lip, and I groan, cock harder against her bare thigh, even though I wouldn't have thought that was possible a moment ago.

"Please," I beg.

Her hips rock wildly. "Fuck me on the altar."

I climb to my feet, holding her face so I won't lose the connection of our kiss. She comes with me, leaping up and wrapping her legs around my back. Her hot cunt lands against my cock, cementing it against my stomach. She wriggles back and forth to rub herself against me.

So wet. Fuck. It makes my breath catch.

She wants me.

She still wants me.

I choke as I gather her to me and lift her to set her back on the altar, careful of the candles in the corner.

She clings to my shirt, and I nod. She's gloriously nude, and it's time to come to her as I am. I yank off my starched shirt and black suit coat.

Finally, I heft myself up onto the altar to cover and warm her body with mine.

But she waves a finger, shifting to the side on the wide altar table. "On your back."

Immediately, I obey, lying down.

Without a moment's delay, she climbs on me, seating herself on my cock in a way that makes both of us groan with relief.

I lift up, kissing her again and wrapping my arms around her small waist. "Bite me again. Slap me. Punish me. Give me what I deserve."

She kisses me again in a frenzy, sucking on the bottom lip she bit earlier. I shudder beneath her and groan when I feel her slim hands on my chest, shoving me back down to the table.

Then she stretches for something past my head, nipple bobbing right in front of my face as she pulls almost all the way off me. I lift to suckle her nipple, and she groans, clenching on just the tip of my cock. When she finally comes back and seats herself so that her pussy slaps back down on my balls, my eyes widen when I see what she's got in her hands.

One of the candelabras.

She arches one eyebrow, and I nod furiously.

"Your dad sounds like a real evil prick," she says, plucking out one of the thick candles with cooled wax dripping down the side.

I know there's still a pool of hot wax in the top cup of the candle.

"Yes," I respond eagerly. "And so was I. I deserve to be punished."

Her eyes narrow. "You were eighteen when you changed your ways. Barely more than a child."

Before I can argue, she tips the candle, and hot wax drips down my chest.

I hiss at the stinging pain, hips thrusting my cock deeper into her clenching pussy. I grip her hip as I fuck her slowly, lingering in the sweet burn of the candle wax as it cools into a pebbled slash across my chest.

"A child who thought he was a man," she continues, and dips the candle again, dripping another slash down my torso.

I groan, neck muscles straining against the exquisite pain.

"Made to grow up too fast." She nods. "I know what that's like."

My top lip twitches as I see her reach for another one of the full candles from the stand, bringing it to hover over my lower belly.

"Fuck them all for what they did to us," she whispers, meeting my eye. She bites her bottom lip as she tips the candle and splashes hot wax down the center of my belly as if tracing the line of hair that leads to my—

It drives me absolutely fucking crazy. I reach up and extinguish the flame with my fingers.

Then I flip her, barely remembering to brace her bottom with my hand before I thrust back into her roughly.

"You were right," she cries, legs tangling behind my ass as her back arches. Her hand reaches up to tangle in my hair. "I *do* want you."

"Say it again." I bear her down to the table, pinning her there with my cock deep inside her.

Her fingernails dig into my scalp, and her pussy clenches around my cock like a vise. "I. Want. *You*. Just for *you*."

I groan as need expands in my chest even though I'm already balls deep.

"Harder," she whispers.

I pull out and pound back into her, over and over, the sound of my balls slapping her wet cunt and our moans filling the quiet, sacred space of the church.

"Oh god, yes, Bane," she cries.

I bend over her, elbows on either side of her face, gaze locking as we fuck frantically. Her legs squeeze my hips, and then—

Oh fuck.

She digs her fingernails into my shoulder blades and scratches them ruthlessly down my back.

At the same time, she arches up and bites deep into the muscle between my neck and shoulder, right above my collarbone.

Her cunt starts clenching and shuddering around my cock, tightening even further than I thought possible.

The spikes of pain mingled with the wild pleasure of fucking her on the altar while she comes shuddering around me—

Pleasure more intense than any I've ever felt in my fucking life hits like a goddamn spike at the base of my spine, and—

I release a feral roar as I come, clutching Moira to me as tight as humanly possible. Her teeth dig in as she bites down even harder, and I empty everything in my body and soul into her clenching cunt.

My second salvation.

THIRTY-SIX

Christmas Morning

MOIRA

I WAKE UP TO A SCREAM.

Not the fun kind. Not the kind that says, "Moira, you're so good at this, I might actually see God."

No, this is high-pitched, horrified, and laced with the kind of indignation that means someone's about to start throwing hands—or hymnals.

I jolt upright so fast my skull nearly detaches from my spine. My heart is doing its best impression of a tap dancer on cocaine, and it takes a solid three seconds before I register where I am. Which is a problem because I'm still on the altar.

The altar. Of the church. Where Bane works.

Oh. Oh no.

Ohhhhh fuu—

"Father Blackwood, how *could* you?!"

I know that voice. It belongs to Agnes, the most dedicated of Bane's parishioners and quite possibly the most terrifying old lady in existence. I swear she could strangle a man with her rosary beads and walk away without a wrinkle in her cardigan.

I do the only rational thing available to me—I let out a strangled yelp and roll off the altar, hitting the floor with a breath-stealing *thud*.

Beside me, Bane moves with infuriating grace, leaping down and landing in a crouch like some brooding, muscle-bound Batman. Except instead of a cape, he's got the altar cloth in front of him covering his nethers. I, meanwhile, am still tangled in the damn thing, looking like a sacrilegious burrito.

"Agnes," he says smoothly as if he's greeting her at the church bake sale instead of standing mostly naked behind the Lord's table. "This is my wife, Moira."

His *what*?

I whip my head toward him so fast I give myself whiplash.

"Your what?!" Agnes chokes, echoing my own internal meltdown.

Bane has the audacity to hold my gaze, utterly calm, as he snatches up his pants and starts stepping into them. "I understand if you want to tell the council and the bishop," he continues because, apparently, he has completely lost his damn mind. "I take full responsibility for this... lapse in judgment."

A lapse in judgment? Oh no, Bane. Last night was the best kind of holy experience, and I think I saw the face of God at least twice.

Wrapped in the altar cloth like some kind of makeshift toga, I peek up over the edge of the altar and give Agnes a small wave. She does not wave back. Her mouth is hanging wide open.

"I completely understand the need for dismissal after this sacrilegious infraction," Bane adds solemnly because he's still in some kind of confessional mood now.

Agnes wags a gnarled finger at him. "Oh, you won't get out of this so easily, young man."

Bane blinks. I blink. We both brace. Shit. This could cost him his *job*.

"This church was twenty grand in the hole when you showed up. The bishop stuck you with us because we had no endowment, no resources, and our last priest was an embezzling jackass." She straightens, looking him up and down with the judgmental power of someone who has seen men fall and rise again. "I had my doubts about you. I thought you were too young. Too arrogant. Too... *British*."

Bane bows his head slightly. "I understand."

She narrows her eyes. "But things have turned around since you've been here. People have come back to church. You actually care about the folks around here, and I reckon that's what we've been needing all along."

There's a long, excruciating pause.

Then she levels him with a gaze so sharp I feel it in my bones. "But I expect the bishop's got a copy of that marriage license."

Bane doesn't hesitate. Doesn't flinch. He lies with the kind of conviction that really makes you wonder if he should've been a politician instead of a priest. "Of course," he says smoothly. "And I'll tell the congregation the good news next Sunday."

I would strangle him if I weren't still frozen in shock. Instead, I just gape, then snap my mouth shut when I realize I'm gaping.

Agnes eyes both of us up and down—takes in my bare arms, Bane's half-dressed state, and the general disaster zone of our clothing strewn across the holy ground—and then snaps, "Well, for God's sake, go get yourselves cleaned up before anyone else comes in and sees you like this."

Bane extends a hand, and I scramble to book it toward the back of the church. He's not far behind, scooping up our clothes. Because, of course, the man is still in crisis mode but remains polite enough to gather my things.

The second we're across the lawn and behind the tall gate of his parish house, I whirl on him, jabbing a finger into his chest. "Your wife?" I hiss.

He looks down at me, utterly unrepentant. "Did you have a better idea?"

I open my mouth. Close it. Damn it.

No.

But still.

I groan, dragging a hand down my face. "Oh my god, I've been fake-married for less than five minutes, and I already want a divorce."

He smirks. "You'll have to get in line, little heathen."

I glare at him. "Oh, you think this is funny? This is your career, Bane. Your *life*."

His expression softens just a fraction. "And what about you?"

I hesitate. I don't have a good answer. Because my life? It's been chaos from the start. But Bane? Bane had a future here. A purpose. And last night, I might have ruined it.

I chew my lip. "What are we going to do?"

His smirk fades, and he lifts a hand to brush a wild curl from my face. "We're going to get married. If you'll have me."

His voice is steady. Confident.

Then the bastard drops to one knee right there in the

dewy grass. "Moira Callaghan, will you do me the honor of becoming my wife?"

I thought I was done gaping open-mouthed for the morning, but apparently not.

I slap him hard on the shoulder. "What are you doing down there? Get up!"

"Not until you answer me." His eyes darken. "But feel free to keep slapping me. Just try not to leave a mark. I do have to go preach a sermon in a minute."

"Be serious!"

"I am being serious. Be my wife, Moira, in truth. We can catch a flight to Vegas right after the service." His clear gray eyes sear me. "Marry me."

"I—You—" I let out an infuriated noise.

"You're everything I've always wanted. I love you. Please do me the honor of becoming my wife."

Holy shit. He means it. The bastard's crazier than me, after all.

I feel tingly all over, but it's different from usual.

I think... I think it's *happiness*.

I drop to my knees and throw my arms around him, breathing out into his ear words I can't believe I'm saying. "Yes, I'll marry you."

THIRTY-SEVEN

MOIRA

AND SO, I marry him.

In a gaudy little Vegas wedding chapel way, way off the strip, I say, "I do," in front of Elvis and a witness who looks like she got lost on her way to work at a biker bar. Bane puts a cheap silver wedding band on my finger that we bought at the gift shop up front. And just like that—

BAM. Bane grabs me, kisses me deeply, and I swear I hear wedding bells. No, wait. That's just the *ka-ching* of the cash register as Elvis's assistant sells a couple of rubber chicken bouquets to the next doomed couple in line.

A flash goes off behind us, and I blink up at my brand-new husband. My stomach does a little swoopy thing like I just stepped off a rollercoaster.

"What the hell did we just do?" I whisper, my heart jack hammering in my chest.

Bane grins down at me, his dark eyes full of something that makes my breath catch. "I just became yours. And you became mine."

Mine.

I blink again, feeling all dazed and Cinderella-at-midnight, but my shoes haven't fallen off yet, so this must be real.

He laces his fingers with mine, nods at Elvis, and pulls me toward the door. "Come on, wife."

"Watermarked photos will be emailed to the address you gave! Only a seventy-five dollar upgrade to your package to unlock!" calls Elvis's assistant.

I giggle. "Hear that, darling? Just seventy-five bucks for a package upgrade!"

"Oh, my package is doing just fine," he growls, low and dark in my ear. "And more than ready to consummate the marriage. Are you wet for me yet, wife? Because I'm happy to eat you out until you are."

My breath hitches. My thighs squeeze together like they have minds of their own. Because obviously, I've been wet since we got off the plane. Hell, earlier than that. The man refused my very logical suggestion of an airplane bathroom quickie.

"Good things come to those who wait," was all he said.

Well, I waited, and now I'm ready to crawl up his body and ride him right here in the hallway.

As soon as we step into our hotel suite, Bane has me pinned against the door. His body is all hard muscle and barely restrained hunger. I let out a little whimper because, honestly, I might just combust from the sheer need vibrating between us.

My hand drops to squeeze him through his slacks. Sweet, merciful baby Jesus. No wonder he refused the airplane bathroom. There wouldn't have been enough room.

He thrusts into my palm, and I swear, I nearly pass out.

This is my wife, Moira. He said it this morning, and I still can't process it.

I was never the kind of girl who dreamed of wedding cakes and white dresses. That was for other girls, girls who believed in fairytales. Not me.

And yet, somehow, I said yes.

And somehow, we're here.

And somehow, this is real.

My pulse pounds as I push against his chest, just enough to make space. "Did you just do this because you hate liars? Because you freaked out in the moment and said I was your wife, so now you had to make it true? Like... for your ethics? To save your job?"

He frowns, and I realize I haven't taken a breath in

approximately forever. My lungs scream for air, but I can't move. I can't look away.

"No." He steps forward, arms wrapping around me again, solid and warm. "I meant what I said last night. I love you. I lied to you when I said things were fine after our accidental photo-op at the Christmas gala. Things weren't fine with the bishop. She made me choose. The priesthood or you. I chose you."

Oh.

Oh, fuck.

So then why did we—?

If he'd already basically lost his job. . .! Or is this just a way to keep both me *and* his job? My head's spinning too fast.

"You could have told me!" I finally explode.

"I just did." His lips graze my ear. "No more secrets, wife. Now that you're mine, I won't keep anything back. One last thing, though; my father is Brad Blackwolf."

I jerk back. "Brad Blackwolf. The—"

"The richest man in the world," he confirms, sighing like he wishes it weren't true.

My brain does a full reboot.

I thought there was something familiar about that man lurking in the shadows the other night. It was fucking Brad Blackwolf! Also known as Mad Blackwolf because the man eats billionaires for breakfast and flosses with their bones.

And I just married his son.

I blink up at Bane. "Why the fuck didn't you make me sign a prenup?!"

His eyes darken. "I gave up my inheritance when I became a priest."

I exhale. "Oh, thank God."

Bane throws his head back and laughs, then hauls me into his chest. "This. This is one of the many reasons you're perfect."

I narrow my eyes. "What?"

"It never even occurred to you to care about the money."

I slap him on the shoulder for thinking I would ever care about that shit. "I've been poor before. It was fine. I mean, I've been miserable when I was rich and when I was poor."

Bane cups my face, his gaze turning serious, almost fierce. "Not anymore. Not now that you're with me."

A small smile tugs at my lips. "Yeah?"

"Yeah."

I stretch up on my tiptoes, letting my lips graze his ear. "Wow. I bet you weren't lying about what an asshole you were growing up." And then I bite his earlobe, hard.

There's been a tightness in him all day, something coiled just beneath the surface, but it unravels in an instant as he melts into me, pinning me against the wall.

"Yes," he growls, voice dark, rough, and brimming with promise.

I shove him toward the bed with a wicked grin, my voice

all honey and steel. "Go lay on your back with a pillow under your hips."

Bane growls, his biceps flexing as he grabs me and pins me against the wall again. "What if I want to fuck you against this wall instead?"

God, I love the feel of his big body up against mine. I get back up on tiptoes to bite the tip of his earlobe, then soften the sting with slow, deliberate kisses down his jaw to his mouth. "You can do that. And we'd both enjoy it. I'm so fucking wet at the thought."

His hand is already beneath the hem of my dress, fingers teasing my inner thighs before sliding higher, and oh. *Oh.*

He exhales, sharp and harsh, and I clench around the fingers he's slid inside my cunt, grinning against his lips. "But you won't get the surprise you would if you were a good boy and did what I said."

I feel the jolt of his cock against my stomach at the words *good boy*. His muscles lock up like I just flipped a switch inside him, and oh dear God. Bane Blackwolf is utterly wrecked by the way I tease him, and the power of that knowledge floods me, thick and intoxicating.

I never get to have the power. Not like this.

But he relinquishes it to me so completely. So easily. So without hesitation.

I haven't told him I love him. *Do I?*

I haven't told him my secrets. *Can I?*

He gives of himself so freely, but I'm not sure I know how. Giving my body is easy. Thoughtless. Nothing at all.

His dark eyes hold mine, pupils so wide I swear they've swallowed his irises. Then he moves, stepping back to the bed. Never looking away, not for a second.

"Naked or clothed?"

My pussy clenches tighter than even when he had his finger in me. "Naked."

I stand frozen as he does exactly as I said and pulls off his clothes, one piece at a time, like my own private Magic Mike show. I was going to suggest going to see it while we were in town, but no, I think I like this much, much better.

I bite my lip by the time he gets to his boxers and shoves them down, stepping out to reveal his long, massively engorged cock.

He reaches down to touch himself, still watching me, but I quickly say, "Don't. That's my toy."

He heaves out a breath, his cock leaping as he puts his hands behind his back, eyes smoldering, before he climbs on the bed. He never takes his eyes off me the entire time he arranges a pillow beneath his backside and lays down just like I told him to.

"You fucking kill me when you bite your lip like that," he says, voice rough as gravel.

I do it again, just to see what happens, and his cock twitches where it lays against his stomach.

"Oh, do I?" I tease, deliberately adjusting my bottom lip between my teeth. "How so?"

"I want you to hold me down and ride me and bite me."

"Do you, now?" I take a slow, measured step toward him, loving the way his eyes widen in anticipation. But then, just to be a menace, I pivot and head for my quickly packed bag instead.

I can feel his obsessive gaze tracking my every move. God, I didn't know what it would feel like to be wanted this much.

But what about when he finds out what I've been keeping from him? Will he still look at me like this? Or will he fly off the handle? I've seen too many men explode into a rage before. He hates his father with a fire that burns in his bones.

How much like him is he?

Nothing!

I know Bane. I do.

No matter what he says about his past, he's not his father.

Still, my fingers hesitate for just a second before I grab the things I need and turn back to him.

He lifts a dark eyebrow when he sees what I'm carrying. "Jeans? You going somewhere?"

I tilt my head, my smile curling despite my anxiety. "I was thinking about going for a ride."

His entire body tightens, the way his focus narrows on me, making my stomach flip. "Oh?"

I reach down and wrap both hands around one of his

thick wrists, squeezing slightly. "Some stallions are best kept tied while you saddle up."

His nostrils flare. I swear his cock gets even harder.

I knot one leg of the jeans around his wrist as tight as I can, then drag his arm down and tie the other leg to the top of the bed frame.

His chest rises and falls heavy, eyes burning into me as I move around the bottom of the bed, grabbing the second pair of jeans to do the same to his other wrist.

When he's secured, I set the last object from my bag on the nightstand, making sure he gets a good look at it.

I particularly enjoy the way his breath hitches when he recognizes it.

"Alright, you absolute menace," he murmurs in a voice somewhere between reverence and raw need.

I grin as I stand from tying his second arm down, watching his gaze stay locked on the small tincture of oil I stole from the church this morning as we fled the altar.

"Did you miss it?"

His Adam's apple bobs. "I did not. I'd forgotten all about it."

His eyes finally find mine again, and my breath catches.

Oh, this is going to be fun.

I snatch the oil from the side of the bed and sling my leg over his waist, facing away from his face, reverse cowgirl style.

He groans again. "Fuck. Why do you have me tied up like this? I want to touch that ass."

"You've told me your secrets. I want to tell you mine. But I want you to behave and not freak out when I do."

"Moira. There's nothing you can tell me that's going to make me change my mind about loving you."

I look over my shoulder. "Good. But I still don't want you going off and doing anything stupid, either. I'll feel better this way."

Then I smile wickedly as I lift the little bottle of anointing oil and pull out the stopper.

First though, I grab his long, hard cock with my other hand and feed it into my wet cunt. Oh, God, *yes*. I clench around him, folding my legs beside his hip and riding him for a few long moments to give both of us some release from the pressure that's built up all day.

Behind me, I can feel him twisting like he's trying to get free of his restraints as his hips rise up to meet mine, straining to get deeper.

I smile. That's the point of this position. I have all the control.

But I still want to drive him crazy.

I grab his left leg and breathily manage, "Lift."

He obeys, lifting it the way I guide.

Then I remove the oil stopper and let it drip down the underside of his balls and down his crack.

He groans, finally getting the point of why I have him in this position.

I bite my bottom lip in anticipation, stoppering the little bottle and tossing it to the side.

Then I wrap an arm around the leg he's lifted before massaging two fingers underneath his balls to his taint and then further down.

He groans, and his cock leaps inside me when I begin to gently massage the gland right inside his ass.

"Moira," he heaves, his voice gruff but breaking.

"That's right, baby. Give in to all the good feelings. Completely relax into the pleasure."

"I fucking love you."

"Good. Remember that when I tell you what I've got to tell you."

"What does that mean?" he growls, and I feel some of the tension come back into his body even as his hips continue lifting, fucking me even more roughly as I stimulate his prostate.

I suck in a deep breath. Time to be brave. "I ran into your father yesterday."

He freezes, but I keep massaging him until he jolts forward and thrusts up into me again as if he can't help himself. *That's right.*

"He offered me an obscene amount of money to break up with you. He doesn't think I'm good enough for you. I didn't know who he was at the time. Not 'til you told me his name."

"But what'd you say to him?" He's frozen beneath me.

I stop this time and look over my shoulder, offended. "I told him to go shove it where the sun don't shine."

The look of stark terror on his face as he waited for my answer is swept away by relief, overwhelming pride, and then fury.

"I'm going to kill him."

"No, you're not."

I start to relentlessly massage him again.

He lets out a noise like a strangled animal and bucks beneath me even more furiously than ever. I cling to his leg wrapped up in my arm. Even though I'm on top and stimulating him, I'm not sure who's riding who at this moment.

"Why didn't you t-tell me?" he manages to get out.

"If you can still talk," I pant, clenching around his hugely engorged cock as I ride it, "I'm not doing my job right."

I go more furiously at his prostate.

"Oh—Jesus—Fuck—*Moira!*"

I'm waiting for him to thrust and finish inside me, but instead, I hear the noise of ripping fabric. I look over my shoulder to find him Hulked-out, all his muscles flexed and pulling against the impromptu ties around his wrists until the one on the right finally rips and tears down a center seam. His left hand pops through the hole of the other tie because he's still yanking so hard.

I squeal as his arm comes free, and he immediately reaches for me.

I'm helpless as he grasps my waist, hands needy.

I let go of his leg as he lifts me up and flips me, and I'm

the one on my back now. Immediately, his body engulfs me. Arms around me, cock inside me, mouth on mine.

I open up to him, feeling his sudden desperation even if I don't understand it.

"You chose me," he mumbles, even as his hands are everywhere, pulling me to him even though I'm already as close as can be. "I need you," he says, thrusting gently inside me.

"You have me," I say between kisses, turned on by this flash of wild passion. My legs lock behind his back.

He just shakes his head like I still don't understand. But I understand the language of his deep kisses. And how his body moves against mine. Slow lunges that reach so deep inside me. Claiming me as his... oh god, claiming me as his *wife*.

That's what this is. He said it earlier, joking. That we were consummating the marriage. But I feel it in how his body moves in mine, and I yield to him. I wrap my arms around him and clench, claiming him back.

He shudders above me, his hips thrusting faster.

No man in my life has ever wanted me this way. Tears roll down my eyes as emotions I've never felt before well in my chest. I cling even tighter to him, squeezing him to me, our bodies cemented together except for our hips that separate and slap back together with each desperate thrust.

He buries his face in my neck and howls when he comes, triggering the deepest G-spot orgasm. But for once, sex isn't about the pleasure that shakes my body as we shudder together. Tears pour out my eyes as I cling to him, feeling—

I—I—He's—

I give up on trying to figure out what I'm feeling, clutch the back of his head to me, dig my fingers into his hair, and abandon myself to him fully.

No more secrets between us.

We're bared fully to one another.

Man and wife.

THIRTY-EIGHT

BANE

SWEAR *you won't go and confront your father about the money.*

I repeat the promise to myself as I walk, hands flexing at my sides, jaw tight. The streetlights flicker as I pass, casting long shadows over the cracked pavement.

But it's not my father's door I'm knocking on tonight.

It's only the promise I made to my wife on the way home from Vegas that keeps me from tracking that motherfucker down. My father still thinks he has any say over my life? That he's got even a shred of control over me? The fucking bastard. But I won't go after him because she asked me not to. And feeding his narcissistic supply with another fight would be letting him win. I opted out of his games a long time ago.

They say the best revenge is living well, right? Somehow, I'm doing just that. I'm living a life I never even let myself hope for. It's intoxicating, like breathing in deep after drowning for years.

Moira is in my house. In my bed. In my shower. Bent over my kitchen counter. Wrapped around me at the club. Wherever I go, she's there. Electric and unpredictable and completely fucking mine.

And while I can let it go with my father, sometimes, revenge is also about sending a message that won't soon be forgotten.

I never go through Moira's phone. That's not who I am. That's not what I do.

But the second she told me she didn't even remember the name of the fucker who put his hands on her, I knew I had to fix my mistake.

So I looked over her shoulder when she was entering her password, and once she was in the shower, I scrolled. Through every damn dating app, every message thread, my blood getting hotter with each pathetic, simpering attempt from random pricks trying to get her attention. Until I found him.

Jeff.

Cocky in his messages. Too many winking emojis, the kind of guy who thinks he's charming but is really just a walking, talking red flag. And most importantly, I found an address. It was the only message from anyone that day—the day she showed up with a black eye.

I reach his building. It's a grimy, forgotten complex, and my blood hums in my veins. My life is better than I ever imagined it could be, but that doesn't mean I let things slide.

Not this. Not him.

The apartment complex is cheap and rundown, and the elevator is out of order. Not that I'd necessarily want to trust my life to it anyway. I jog up three flights of stairs, then rap my knuckles against the peeling wood door, firm and insistently. After too long a pause, it creaks open.

A guy stands there, looking exactly like the kind of greasy asshole I imagined—barefoot in basketball shorts, a smirk half-formed on his unshaven face.

"Jeff?" I double-checked.

"What?" he drawls, looking me up and down, not knowing he's about to have the worst night of his life.

My fists flex at my sides. I've spent months sinking into this new life, this new purpose, Moira's warmth wrapping around me like something I never knew I needed. But beneath all that light, there's a sharp, jagged edge. A reminder of what I let slip past and of what I need to correct.

I take a slow breath, steadying the rage boiling in my gut. She's mine. She chose me. And I choose her, over and over again.

"Do you remember Moira?" I ask, low and even.

His brow furrows, confusion playing across his features. "Moira, who?"

Wrong answer.

I push forward, just enough that he has to take a step back. His smirk falters.

"The girl you messaged months ago. Don't pretend you don't remember. The one you met up with, and then she came home with a bruise on her face."

His expression shutters, but I see the flicker of recognition in his beady little eyes.

"Look, man, she was just some whore. Who gives a shit?"

I don't let him finish.

My fist connects with his gut, doubling him over. He wheezes and stumbles, but I don't give him time to recover. I follow up with a brutal right hook, sending him sprawling to the dirty floorboards. His head bounces off the ground.

Before he can suck in another breath, I drive my fist into his ribs. Again and again until he lets out a strangled, gasping wheeze.

I'll be damned if I let anyone think they can lay hands on my wife and walk away unscathed.

He groans, rolling onto his side and spitting blood on the floor.

"Fuck," he gasps. "What the fuck, man?"

I crouch beside him, grab a fistful of his shirt, and haul him up just enough so he can see me clearly.

"If you ever lay hands on a woman again, I'll come back.

Because I'll be watching. And next time, you won't be walking away."

To make sure he's got the message, I slammed my fist into his face one more time.

I let him drop, watching as he curls in on himself, blood spattered down the front of his shirt.

"Say her name," I order.

He whimpers, but I grab his jaw and force him to look at me. "Say it."

"Moira," he chokes out.

Only then do I let go. I stand, roll my shoulders, and step over his sorry, bloodied form to walk out the door.

And don't look back.

THE MONTHS PASS, and I only become more obsessed with my wife

Wherever I go, she's there, electric and unpredictable and completely fucking mine. At the club, sometimes we let others into our play—Gemini and Jinx, a genderqueer dom/sub pair Moira trusts. But only if I'm leading. Because even when others are involved, she is always, always mine first.

She doesn't even realize how much it means to me that she chose me. There's only been one other person in my life who ever chose me over money—my mother. And no,

Moira isn't some replacement for the woman I never got to know.

But it still means something deep. To know that she put me above wealth. For fuck's sake, she even kept my father trying to buy her off a secret because she thought it would be better for me. She didn't want to come between me and my father because, in her mind, at least I had a dad. She figured maybe, just maybe, he was looking out for me.

She's wrong, of course. But the fact that her heart was in the right place? That she was thinking of me first? I've lived long enough to know how rare a person like her is.

And I'll spend the rest of my life proving to her that she made the right choice.

Because for the first time, I'm not alone.

I didn't even realize how fucking isolated I'd been until suddenly, she was there. Bright and wild and buzzing with energy every morning when I wake up and every night before I fall asleep. She fills every space she enters and lights up every room.

But I see what no one else does.

Sometimes, that light flickers.

She has her down days. She can be reactive, her moods shifting like a storm breaking without warning. She told me once it feels like a balloon popping; one second, she's floating, untethered, and the next, she's crashing hard over something as inconsequential as a commercial.

I haven't brought it up to her yet. She's sensitive about

labels and about having been institutionalized before for her so-called sex addiction.

But it's obvious—she's somewhere on the bipolar spectrum. No one ever looked past her manic behaviors, past the reckless sex and the constant motion, to see what was really going on. They just saw the symptoms, not the cause.

It pisses me off. Especially when it comes to her brother.

Domhnall should have seen it. He should have realized. Instead, he just wrote her off. Treated her like a problem instead of a person. I hear the way she talks about him, the way she pretends not to care. But I know better. She does care. She loves him, despite everything.

And he doesn't deserve it.

I do.

So I'll keep watching. Keep learning her in all the ways no one else ever bothered to. Every new thing I learn only makes me more obsessed. More devoted. More determined to be the man she deserves. To protect her.

She chose me.

And I'll keep choosing her every damn day.

THIRTY-NINE

MOIRA

I WAKE up and immediately roll over, reaching for Bane's warm, solid chest.

But he's not there.

I frown, curls spilling into my face as I blink at the empty sheets. Where the hell is he? He's always here in the morning.

Then it hits me.

Oh. Right. Church.

Ever since he announced the elopement, which we just pretend happened one week earlier than it did, he keeps saying I'm welcome to come. That everyone would love to meet me.

Right. Me, in a church? That would go over *great*.

I let my arm flop dramatically over my face.

At least marrying me did the trick. He got to keep his job.

But good Lord, I nearly burned the place down just walking through the doors on Christmas Eve. Almost got him *fired* the next morning after *already* almost getting him fired two days before. Pretty sure, for both our sakes, I should stay far, far away.

I ruin things. That's just what I do.

And yet… somehow, I haven't ruined *this*.

I roll onto my stomach and shove my face into his pillow. It still smells like him—warm, woodsy, *Bane*—and I want to rub it all over me like some desperate little pervert.

Which is exactly what I did last night. Long after he said he *should* go to sleep because he had to be up early. Long after we should've gone to sleep.

But I was hungry for him.

So he gave me what I needed. Because Bane? He's always doing little things for me. Finding new ways to take care of me. Making sure I eat. Making sure I get out of bed. Making sure I *live*.

And what do I give him?

I stare up at the ceiling, chewing my lip.

I give him *crazy*.

I give him problems he didn't have before.

I give him *too much*.

I am too much.

I always have been. Too much for Mam. Too much for Domhnall. Too much for my first boyfriend. Too much for everyone who ever got too close.

And yeah, that's the entire fucking list.

Even Quinn, my closest friend, looks at me like I'm exhausting sometimes. Like she wants to ask, *Could you just not?*

She and everyone else manage to keep their shit together just fine. Meanwhile, I can't hold down a job to save my fucking life. *She* works two jobs, and here I am, falling apart because I woke up alone.

But Bane is different.

He *loves* me.

Well. He *thinks* he does.

He loved me enough to marry me.

Except... he *had* to. If he didn't, he would've lost everything.

I squeeze my eyes shut, shoving those thoughts away, forcing myself to focus on last night instead. He was gentle and then rough and then—

Fuck, I came so many times I lost count.

My fingers slip between my legs before I even think about it. I'm already wet, already aching, already needing. I bite my lip, thighs clenching around my hand as I let the memory take over.

And then I freeze.

Bane wouldn't like this. His stupid rules. His obsession with control. His belief that I should *wait* for pleasure.

I groan, pressing my forehead into his pillow.

But what he doesn't know won't hurt him. It's not a lie if I just don't tell him, right?

I barely have time to make up my mind before my orgasm rips through me, fast and hard. My body curls around my own hand, my free hand gripping his pillow so tight my knuckles ache.

And then it's over.

And I feel guilty.

But the damage is already done, so what does it *matter* if I do it again?

And again?

And *again?*

By the time I hit my tenth orgasm, my body starts to betray me. The pleasure dulls, my clit going rubbery and numb. No, no, no. I rub harder, but it just makes things worse.

And then I'm crying.

I flop back on the bed, yanking the blankets over my head, my chest heaving, tears leaking into the pillowcase that still smells like him.

There was never any point in getting out of bed today, anyway.

FORTY

BANE

I WAKE to the feeling of something—someone—prodding my chest. Rhythmic, insistent. A warm weight is sprawled over me, curls tickling my jaw, breath puffing against my collarbone. Moira.

My wife.

The word still feels foreign, like boots I haven't broken in yet.

But when I open my eyes and find her grinning down at me, it doesn't feel wrong. Just... improbable. Like she's something out of a dream I never dared to have.

"Oh my god, *finally*," she drawls, draping herself across me like she belongs there. Because, apparently, she does.

My chest gets tight at the sight of her there smiling and rolling her eyes at me. "I've been lying here forever, *bored*, waiting for you to wake up. I even had a whole conversation with you in your sleep. Did you know dolphins are the ocean's perverts?"

I exhale slowly, rubbing a hand down my face. "Good morning to you, too."

She gasps theatrically. "It *is* a good morning! Look at you! Awake and brooding and all mine." She nuzzles against me, sighing happily. "Do you think we could get a pet goat?"

"Absolutely not."

"Ugh, but you'd look so hot feeding a little goat in your priestly garb. *Father Bane, tending to his flock—*"

I roll, pinning her under me before she can say anything else. Her laugh bubbles up, bright and untamed, as she fists her hands in my shirt like she means to keep me here forever.

And the sight of her, happy and underneath me, frees the weight that's been suffocating me with terror lately.

Last week, she could barely get out of bed.

Last week, I could hardly get her to eat, much less talk. There was nothing theatrical in her voice then. No teasing, no sharp wit, no Moira filling the space with the color and chaos she carries with her everywhere.

Just silence and exhaustion. She was curled in on herself. Unreachable.

Yeah, I knew that times like that would be part of what I suspect is her condition, but seeing it firsthand was something else. I couldn't help wondering—had I brought it on? Could I have prevented it? Brought her out of it sooner?

For all my fucking discipline and control, there was nothing I could do, and it made me want to tear my hair out or find somebody else to go punch.

So yes, she can prod and poke and torment me all she likes. I'll listen to every ridiculous thought that spills from her lips, *happily*, as long as it means she's here again. Fully here.

"Come on, broody husband," she purrs, curling her leg around my hip. "Let's stay in bed all day."

I shake my head, dragging myself up. "Out."

She pouts dramatically, but I see the spark in her eyes. She *wants* to be dragged into the world today.

So I do.

And once she's out, I watch her gain energy from being out.

She makes us walk downtown, but it takes twice as long as it should because she gets distracted by *everything*.

The bakery. The bookshop. A cat sunbathing in a window. A pigeon she claims is her sworn enemy from last week, even though we both know she spent all last week in bed and I have no idea what a pigeon might have done to deserve her wrath.

I follow wherever she flits off to because how can I not?

It's like following a living firework, sparking off in different directions, pulling me along in the wake of her energy.

Eventually, we end up at a cafe. She orders something absurdly sweet, I get black coffee, and she insists on getting us pastries shaped like bears.

I refuse.

She gets me one anyway.

"Bite it angrily," she demands, holding up her phone.

"Why?"

"For *memes*."

I give her a flat look.

"For science, Bane. For art. For *the people*."

Seeing as I've long since accepted my fate as the subject of her ridiculous whims, I take an unnecessarily aggressive bite.

She shudders. "*Hot*."

I exhale through my nose, shaking my head. All I feel in this moment is... content.

More than that, actually. Watching her like this, vibrant and alive, I feel something closer to reverence. I was alone in a boring, petty, cruel world.

And then came *her*.

She drags me to a movie, where she proceeds to whisper her commentary at me the entire time.

"This guy would *not* last five minutes with you."

"That's because he's an idiot."

Moira makes a noise so obscene people turn to look. "God, I *love* it when you say mean things."

At some point, I cover her mouth with my hand. She licks my palm. I don't react. She pouts.

By the time the credits roll, she's already plotting our next stop. We grab something easy for dinner and walk back home in the dark, her arm looped through mine, chattering about everything and nothing.

I half expect her to run out of steam now.

Sometimes, after days like this, the energy fizzles out, and she crashes. But not tonight. She just keeps *going*, her hand squeezing my arm every so often like she needs to keep checking that I'm here.

Like she still can't quite believe I *choose* to be.

We get home, and she drops dramatically onto the couch. "Carry me to bed."

"No."

"But I'm *weak* and *fragile*, Bane!"

I raise a brow. "You just spent the entire day dragging me all over the place."

She squints. "Your point?"

I roll my eyes and bend to pick her up. She makes a delighted noise and wraps herself around me.

"I win," she sings as I carry her to our bed.

She does.

She wins. Every time.

I set her down, and she watches me in the dim light of our bedroom, something quieter settling into her expression. She reaches out, tracing her fingers down my arm.

"You had fun today," she murmurs like it surprises her.

I catch her hand and press a kiss to her palm. "Of course I did."

Her lips twitch like she doesn't quite believe me.

I don't blame her. I don't always make it easy to read me. But I know the truth of it, even if she doesn't.

I had fun because she's fun.

Because she's *Moira*.

And because, more than anything, I'm just fucking glad she's *here*.

FORTY-ONE

MOIRA

AFTER DAYS, I emerge from my self-imposed exile covered in oil paint, exhaustion dripping from me like the last dregs of coffee at the bottom of the pot. My hair's half in a bun, half in a bird's nest. My tank top used to be white, but now it's a canvas of its own, Jackson Pollock-ed in black and deep red and a big smear of ochre right across my tits.

Bane is waiting when I push out the door of the spare room in my apartment. Of course he is. Leaning against the wall in that broody, too-intense way of his, arms crossed like he's trying to keep himself from either shaking me or dragging me against him. His dark eyes rake over me, slow and assessing, like he's cataloging every exhausted breath and speck of paint on my skin.

I cross my arms back at him. "What?"

He exhales through his nose. "Three days, Moira."

"Yes, darling?" I bat my eyelashes. "Is this the part where you tell me I look a fright and should go take a bath?"

"No." His voice is low and steady. Too steady. "This is the part where you tell me what the hell you've been doing locked away without eating or sleeping."

I stretch, my bones cracking in protest, and give a little yawn. "I was eating. I had peanut butter straight from the jar. And coffee."

"That is not eating."

"Says you." I smirk, then hesitate. My fingers tighten around the doorframe, and suddenly the bravado feels heavier to hold. I chew my lower lip, glancing back through the door toward the canvas propped up against the wall. "I was... working on something."

Bane's eyes flick to where I look, and he pushes off the wall in one fluid motion. "Show me."

I stay planted. For once, not out of defiance but out of something sharper. More uncertain.

This is stupid. It's just a painting. Just something I do every few years when I get a hare up my ass. It doesn't mean anything.

Except it does.

Bane sees too much already. What if he sees this, then sees right through me in a way I don't know how to undo?

I almost tell him never mind, that I was kidding, that it's a giant erotic mural of him on a horse just to see if he'll blink, but it's too late. He's already moved, already stepped past me into the room, already standing in front of the canvas.

And he's staring.

I tap my foot and bite my bottom lip.

My painting stands there, raw and open, like I cracked open my ribs and smeared my insides across the canvas.

The woman in the painting is almost swallowed by darkness. She's a silhouette of curly hair barely discernible from the midnight tones that press in around her. But at her center, in the place where her heart should be, embers burn. Small, fragile. Flickering against the vast nothingness.

Bane doesn't speak.

I shift from foot to foot, my stomach twisting. I hate this. Hate waiting. Hate that I want him to like it. Hate that I care.

"Well?" My voice comes out breezy and fake. "I was thinking of calling it 'Brooding Asshole Watches Wife Paint.' Too on the nose?"

His head turns toward me, slow as a glacier. His face is unreadable, but his eyes...

There's something there. Something deep and raw and so overwhelming I have to look away.

"You did this," he says, voice thick. "You painted this."

I roll my eyes, because obviously, but my throat feels tight. "Yeah, yeah. It's just something I do when I get the urge. No big deal."

"It is a big deal. Why didn't you tell me you're an artist?"

His voice is soft, but there's something behind it that roots me to the floor. A heaviness. A weight.

I swallow. Shrug. Try to ignore how my chest feels like it's caving in. "I'm not. I just play around sometimes. Not very often. It's just a painting, Bane."

His hand moves before I realize what's happening, brushing over my arm, his thumb dragging over a stray streak of paint on my skin. He lifts his hand, staring at the dark smear on his fingertips like it's something sacred.

Then he turns back to the canvas, his throat working. He doesn't say anything else.

But he doesn't have to.

Then, without a word, he moves. Strong arms wrap around me, his body anchoring mine in a way that feels like protection, like reverence. His embrace is firm but careful, like he's afraid if he holds me too tight, I'll slip away.

I freeze at first, because this—this softness, this quiet—is not something I'm used to. But then my muscles melt into him, exhaustion winning over instinct. My forehead drops against his chest, and for the first time in days, I let myself breathe. Just for a second. Just here, in the warmth of him.

His hand moves, slow and steady, up and down my back. No demands. No expectations. Just... holding me.

It's almost too much. The kindness of it. The weight of him letting me rest for once instead of pushing or pulling or fighting.

I can't let it stand.

I tilt my head back against his chest, peering up at him with a smirk. "So, uh... you do know this shirt was expensive, right?"

Bane exhales sharply, a sound that's almost a laugh but not quite. His arms don't loosen. If anything, they tighten. "I don't care."

I poke at his chest. "You say that now, but wait until you realize I used oil paint and this stain is forever."

His grip shifts, and he finally pulls back just enough to look down at me, his expression unreadable. Then, in a voice so low I barely catch it, he murmurs, "So be it."

I roll my eyes, but inside, I feel... happy. The fire that's burning in the painting—I feel it inside me now. Bane makes me warm and safe in ways I never knew were possible. Before, I felt like a jackal, afraid and always hungry for scraps.

On the rare occasions I do paint, it's because there's some feeling inside me that I can *see* in my mind but not name, and I can't rest until I've gotten it out of me.

Now that it's done and Bane's being all, well, *Bane*, I feel giddy on exhaustion and accomplishment.

"Come on." I pull back and grab his hand. "I need wine. And a lot of it, but I don't have any in the house. You're driving 'cause I'm too tired."

"It's two in the morning."

"Well then you better find a 7-Eleven that's open 24 hours. I'm getting my shoes."

Fifteen minutes later, we're in the car, and I'm bouncing my bare feet against the dashboard, drumming out a tune that only exists in my head while humming a ridiculous operatic rendition of *Elmo's World*. Bane is gripping the wheel like he's regretting every life decision that brought him here.

"You're insufferable," he mutters, but there's no real heat to it.

"And yet, here you are. Enabling my bad behavior." I poke his bicep. "That makes you my accomplice. My ride-or-die. My partner in crime."

His sigh is long-suffering, but I see the twitch of his lips. "I am neither riding nor dying."

"Well, you're certainly no fun."

He turns onto a quiet road leading to the gas station, fingers flexing on the steering wheel. "And what part of this is fun, exactly?"

"The part where I get wine and we create a beautiful, spontaneous memory." I flutter my lashes. "We are *butter* together, Bane. Soft, rich, and sinful."

Bane exhales hard, like he's praying for patience. But I see the corner of his mouth tilt upward.

Inside the 7-Eleven, I make a beeline for the sad little

wine selection. I grab a bottle of something that looks like it was brewed in a bathtub and possibly banned in several states. Then I hold up another, squinting at the label.

"Red or white?" I ask.

Bane, looming behind me like a very judgmental shadow, eyes the selection like he's witnessing a crime. "That's not wine. That's regret in a bottle."

"That's what makes it fun," I declare, thrusting both bottles toward him. "Choose our fate."

"I refuse."

"Too late, you're involved." I shove the red at him. "This one pairs well with dreadful decisions."

He holds it like it might explode. "It's three-dollar wine."

I place a hand over my heart. "I never *said* we were going classy."

After paying, we head back to the car. I twist off the cap before we even get the doors closed, take a long, dramatic swig, then smack my lips. "Mmm, notes of desperation and a hint of despair."

Bane looks at me like he's reconsidering our marriage. "Where to now?"

"Empty parking lot. We need music and ambiance."

"Ambiance," he repeats, deadpan.

"Exactly. We're making memories, baby."

He stares at me for a long moment, then—because he is, in fact, my ride-or-die—puts the car in gear and drives.

Five minutes later, we're parked under the dim glow of a flickering streetlight in some abandoned lot. I kick my feet up on the dash again, wine bottle in my lap, and scroll through the radio until I find something *appropriately vibey*—which turns out to be an '90s power ballad.

"You gonna drink, or are you just my designated brooder?" I nudge Bane with the bottle.

He takes it, eyes me warily, then—shock of all shocks—he actually takes a sip. A small one. Like a man who just licked a poison dart frog.

I gasp. "Holy shit, look at you! Corrupting yourself one sip at a time."

He hands the bottle back like it personally offended him. "It's vile."

"It's *freedom*." I take another deep swig and drape myself dramatically across the seat. "You, Bane Blackwood, are experiencing a *moment* with your wife."

He shakes his head, looking at me like he can't decide whether to put me in a straight jacket or kiss me. Probably both.

I grin, throwing my head back against the seat, letting the music wash over me. "You know," I say, swirling the bottle in my hand like it's a fine vintage, "I used to think happiness was this elusive, mythical thing. Like Bigfoot or a healthy relationship. But right now, sitting here with you, drinking awful wine in an even worse parking lot?" I sigh contentedly. "I think I finally get it."

Bane doesn't say anything, but his hand reaches out, slipping over mine. Warm. Solid. Steady.

And for the first time in forever, I feel... light.

The music hums, the stars blur, and I think—just for tonight—I don't need to outrun anything. I can just *be*.

FORTY-TWO

April

MOIRA

KIRA and I have lunch plans, but first, I want a reaction. A *look*. A well-placed, growled-out *fuck* from the man currently lurking somewhere in our apartment.

Bane is a lot of things—tall, broody, criminally good at ruining panties—but observant? Not always. Not about little things.

But he *notices* me. I know he does. He *worships* me. Other than that little blip last month with the week in bed, everything's been going great with this whole marriage thing. Most days, I still can't fucking believe I'm somebody's *wife*.

Bane really does seem to want me here. And not just because he has to or because I'm an obligation he got tricked into.

And so what if some days I just want to see it? Want to feel it? I want—

I step into the kitchen with a grin, ready to do something dramatic—maybe a slow, hip-swinging walk, maybe a little spin—but Bane is already moving.

Not toward me, though.

He's frowning down at his phone, one hand adjusting his watch, the other reaching for the coffee pot.

"You're up early," he murmurs, still looking at whatever *deeply important* priest shit is happening on his screen. "I made your coffee how you like it."

A steaming cup is pressed into my hands.

I blink at it. Then up at him.

I stand there, waiting.

Waiting for him to *look*.

For him to *see*.

For him to say something, anything.

A *damn*. A *holy fuck, Moira, you're illegal in six states*. A *get over here, you little brat*.

Nothing.

He presses a distracted kiss to my hairline, mutters something about a meeting at the church, and then he's gone.

The door shuts behind him. The house falls silent.

The coffee cup shakes in my hands, and I swallow back stupid, sudden tears.

Stop it. It's *fine*.

It's more than fine because it's *nothing*.

He was busy. Late for a meeting. Jesus Christ, it's *not a big deal*.

It's just—

It's just—

I look down at my reflection on the dark surface of the coffee. All that effort. All that energy. And he didn't even see me.

My throat tightens. My stomach hollows out. I *know* it's stupid, I *know* it's small, but the feeling slams into me anyway. A ridiculous, overblown, shameful devastation that makes me feel like a wind-up toy running out of spin.

My fingers slip, and then—

"Shit!"

The cup crashes to the floor.

Coffee explodes everywhere—on my shoes, on the cabinets, on my *perfect fucking skirt*. The sound of ceramic shattering echoes through the empty kitchen, and my body seizes up, my breath catching hard in my throat.

Oh.

That's just fucking *perfect*.

Hot coffee seeps into my socks. My lip trembles. My stupid fucking lip *trembles* like I'm some pathetic little girl about to cry over *spilled coffee*, and I want to scream at myself. I want to *shake* myself.

It's nothing. It's just coffee. It's just an outfit. It's just a moment. It doesn't mean anything. He still loves you, he still wants you, you are not being abandoned, you are not—

I swallow hard, pressing the heels of my palms against my eyes.

Get it together, Moira.

I take a slow, shuddering breath and force my shoulders back.

I'm still meeting Kira for lunch.

I'm going to clean up this mess, fix my makeup, and pretend none of this happened.

And *if* my brain decides to gnaw on this for the rest of the day, I'll deal with it later. With tequila. Or bad decisions. Or both.

No. I don't do that shit anymore.

I'm being good now. I'm *married* now. I feel a low, horrified drop in my stomach. I'm married to a *priest*, for Christ's sake.

I grab a towel and fall to my knees to furiously wipe up the coffee, tears squeezing out of my eyes.

KIRA LOOKS *ANNOYINGLY* RADIANT. Not that I'm bitter. I mean, I'm a *little* bitter, but that's beside the point.

The point is, we are at lunch, and I am *on*. Big, bouncing, shining like a goddamn supernova because that's what I do.

That's how I win at life. I perform until everyone believes I'm the happiest bitch in the room, even when my insides feel like a squeezed-out juice box.

"So, tell me." I lean forward, chin propped on my hand, eyes twinkling like I haven't spent all morning wrestling with the void. "How's living with Mr. Silent & Broody? Does he still do that thing where he stares into the distance like he's contemplating existential threats everywhere he looks?"

Kira snorts, stabbing at her salad. "Every day."

"Does he talk more now, or do you just sit in eerie, muscle-bound silence until one of you passes out from sheer lack of stimulation?"

Her lips twitch. "He talks."

"Oh, groundbreaking. A whole *word*? Or are we up to *sentences*?"

She rolls her eyes, but she's smiling. "Yeah, he's still a grumpy bastard," she says, casually twirling her fork, "but he's going to be a great dad."

Boom.

I barely stop my fork from clattering onto my plate. My fingers spasm around it, and for a second, I swear the whole restaurant tilts sideways.

I cover fast. Big grin. Big eyes. Big voice. "A *dad*? Holy shit, Kira! Congratulations!"

Her face lights up, and it's—ugh. It's sickeningly beautiful. No wonder she's glowing like some kind of Earth Mother goddess with an *actual future* stretched out before her. And because I am a *good* friend, a *supportive* friend, I do what I do best—I lean in.

"Okay, tell me everything," I demand, popping a fry into my mouth. I chew like I actually have an appetite, even though my stomach is currently a sinkhole. "Isaak as a dad? Oh my *god*, can you imagine? I bet he's been, like, *secretly nesting*."

Kira laughs, tucking a strand of hair behind her ear. "Oh, absolutely. You should've seen him when I got sick the first time. Full-on panic mode. Started researching morning sickness remedies at three a.m., woke me up just to tell me about ginger chews."

I nod, nod, nod. Laugh in all the right places. React with all the right *oohs* and *awws* and *oh my gods*. I ask the right questions. I keep the spotlight *firmly* on her because I cannot, under any circumstances, let it turn back to me.

Because inside? Inside, I am spiraling.

A *baby*.

That's what *normal* people do, right? They meet someone, fall in love, and make little life decisions that build into something bigger. Something real. Something that lasts.

Bane and I... we didn't do that. We got married so he wouldn't get fired.

He says he loves me, but...

But does he want *this*?

Could I even give him *this*?

Would I even want to? I can't even keep a fucking houseplant alive, let alone a human being. Sometimes, I can barely get *myself* out of bed. But what if...?

I shake it off, shake it all off, and force another smile. Bigger. Brighter. No cracks allowed.

"And have you picked a name yet? Because if it's something boring like 'John' or 'Emma,' I'm legally obligated to riot."

Kira laughs. The conversation moves on, but the pit in my stomach doesn't go anywhere.

She invites me to a baby shower she's having tonight, and of course, I agree to come. I missed the invite she sent in the mail because I hadn't been at my apartment in forever.

Not that I've told anyone about marrying Bane and living at his place.

It's just that I've been... happy.

That's the whole problem. Happy is such a fragile thing.

If I tell anybody about it, I'll jinx it.

I was going to tell Kira today but immediately abandoned the idea. Especially if I'll be seeing everybody else later tonight. The day should be firmly focused on her and Isaak's happy news.

So, I just keep nodding and smiling. Keep pretending.

Mid-spiral, I overcompensate. Hard. My words speed up, my hands fly everywhere, and my jokes? They're not *quite* landing. I don't care. I just need to keep moving. Keep talking. Keep laughing.

"Okay, enough baby talk," I announce, flagging down the waiter. "Tell me how Isaak is in bed now that you're all domestic. Does he still act like a grumpy bodyguard, or is he finally letting loose?"

Kira just tilts her head at me. "Moira, are you okay?"

And I—who am absolutely definitely *not* okay—grin. Too wide. Too sharp. "Why wouldn't I be? I've got Bane now. Everything's going totally great with me."

Kira gives me a look. I hate that look. It's her *I'm a-budding-psychologist-and-I-see-you* look. The one that says she can hear the cracks even if I'm trying to fill them with noise.

So I double down. Laugh too loudly. Gulp the margarita I ordered with lunch. Do *anything* to drown out the thoughts creeping in.

Kira folds her arms, watching me. "Moira—"

"No, no, we're talking about *you* today, remember?" I wave dramatically at the air between us, my bracelet jingling too loudly. "The glowing, perfect mommy-to-be and her big, scary protector man. So tell me, does Isaak do that thing where he broods harder when he gets turned on? Or does he just grunt, flip you over, and get the job done?"

Shit. The second it's out, I know it's one of those inappropriate things to say. If only I could realize this shit before it comes flying out of my mouth. I should probably *definitely* not be referencing the fact that I used to sometimes fuck her now baby-daddy back when the both of us would get bored at the club. Before he'd met her or I'd met Bane.

Kira sighs, but she smirks, unbothered. "You are *so* deflecting right now."

"Me?" I gasp, pressing a hand dramatically to my chest. "Never."

She just lifts an eyebrow, unimpressed. "You can't outrun your own brain forever, you know."

"Watch me." I signal the waiter. "Two tequila shots, please! Don't worry," I grin. "I know you can't drink. They're both for me."

She sighs.

The ping of my phone saves us both. It's a message from Anna's phone.

> Splitzy: It's Mads. We need to talk. Where are you?

I glance around, eyes zeroing in on a bar across the street. I quickly type the name into the phone.

> Splitzy: Kay. Be there in fifteen.

I down one of the tequila shots, squinting against the burn, then look to Kira as I reach for my coat. "Gotta go. It's been so great to catch up."

Her eyebrows are still furrowed with worry, but I wave

my hand. "Oh, stop it. I'm fine. And seriously. I'm so freaking excited for you guys. See you later tonight."

I drop cash on the table for my part of the meal as I get up, then come around to her, lean over, and hug her hard. "This is the luckiest kid in the universe. I can't imagine two better parents."

She squeezes me back. "Take care of yourself."

"Always!" I say brightly, nodding and smiling hard as I pull back and wave, walking away.

I don't want her to see I'm just walking across the street to the bar, so I turn the corner like I'm walking back to my car. I didn't even bring my car; I took the train. But I hang out there for five minutes, then peek around the corner until I figure she's cleared out. I don't see her anywhere.

Then I book it across the street, ignoring a car that honks at me, and slip into the bar.

I'm huffing for breath as I land on a barstool.

There's barely anyone else in here. Probably because, yeah, it's one p.m. on a Tuesday. But it's five o'clock somewhere, yada yada, and the tequila in my bloodstream hasn't nearly got me numb enough to handle this fucking bullshit day yet.

For fuck's sake. For a second back there, I was actually contemplating *motherhood*. I shudder.

"Two shots of whatever will have me unable to feel my legs the fastest." I wink at the bartender.

He's a guy in his fifties who brightens as he tosses a bar towel over his shoulder and starts my way. In the old days, I would've started immediately flirting and trying to get him to abandon his bar for five minutes to fuck me in the bathroom.

Once, when a steadfast bartender refused to abandon his register and top-shelf liquor, I snuck around the bar top and gave him a blowy while he kept working.

I stretch my neck against the itch working its way underneath my skin.

Bane might've given me permission, as it were, to get it outside our marriage, but knowing how good it is with him, I don't see how trying to get fucked at some ratty bar by some shitty old bartender or another dumb fuck also getting drunk here at this time of day would feel like anything but cheating. It'd be cheap and stupid and make me feel worse than I already do.

You're gonna grow up 'n be a slag just like yur mam, ain't ya, Moira? C'mon, flip up your skirt and show us your fanny!

Nothing but a two-bit slut.

I could never be a mother. Why would I ever pass down this curse to a kid? I'd be an embarrassment to them. What would their pious father tell them when I ended up in a place like this, fucking around again? Because I always *will* end up back here. Who the fuck am I kidding?

"Gotta say, you're a sight for sore eyes," the bartender says, pouring my shots and placing them on the bar in front of me. "What brings you in, beautiful?"

I down the shots, one after the other, ignoring him. Fire burns my throat as my eyes water and my thoughts spiral darker.

I ruin everything.

It's what I do.

I look around the bar. There's a younger guy who looks about my age in the back corner, nursing a beer with several empties on the table, thumbing through something on his phone.

My stomach feels sour from the shots. It would be easy to walk back there and sit across from him. Make small talk until he got in a better mood, then ask him if he wanted a good time. I could probably get it done before Mads even showed up.

I squeeze my eyes shut and pull out my phone, staring at her message.

Why does she want to even meet, anyway?

I didn't know she could be out and about in the daytime. That's new. I try to distract myself by wondering about it, but my eyes keep sliding toward the guy at the back table.

I jerk my gaze back to my phone and text Bane instead.

> Me: What are you wearing?

> Me: I'm dripping wet, thinking of your huge cock. I want to tie you to the bed and milk you until you beg me for mercy.

I hit send and smile. It helps a little to think about how in control I am in those moments he lets me take the reins.

But it's a short-lived feeling.

Because he doesn't text back.

I just keep staring and staring at the phone and...

Nothing.

It's just like when he didn't look up at me this morning when I dressed all pretty.

Like an empty gulf is opening up in my stomach where moments before I felt full and happy. But now there's just nothing but unbearable, crushing sadness.

And the itching. I slam my phone down on the counter.

"That kind of day?" the bartender says sympathetically, pouring me another shot. His sympathy's not real. I know the look in the eye of a man who's hoping to get laid. He probably gets off in an hour and is hoping to take me with him.

Bane's the only man who's ever looked at me with anything real.

Except he didn't look at you this morning, did he?

He thought you were exciting at first, just like they all do. But you're starting to wear on him. Maybe he'll keep you around because, like a fool, he went and married you, and he's an honorable man. He just feels bad because he fucked up when he was still just a kid, and like a good man with a conscience, he can't let go of it.

But he's good, loving, and caring, and I'm...

Thinking about fucking some drunk rando in the back of a dive bar off Main.

"Moira."

My eyes close in relief at Mads's voice.

FORTY-THREE

MOIRA

I SPOT MADS INSTANTLY. She's the only person in this place who looks like she could both kill a man and file her nails while doing it.

"Bitch!" I launch at her, wrapping my arms around her like a clingy octopus. She stands there like a goddamn *lamppost*, stiff and unyielding, which only makes me squeeze harder.

"Moira," she wheezes.

I release her with a dramatic flourish. "Look at you! Out and about in the daylight. I'm gonna start calling you Daywalker."

She snorts, glancing over her shoulder, then scanning the bar like she's waiting for someone to jump out of the shadows. The bar is dim, the kind of place where the wood is dark and sticky, the air smells like stale beer, and the neon lights buzz just a little too loudly.

I narrow my eyes. "You got a stalker?"

"What?" Mads lets out a laugh that's a little *too* loud. "What do you wanna drink?" She heads for the bar, then glances sideways at me. "Wait. Are you even old enough to drink yet?"

I roll my eyes so hard they almost fall out of my head. "Ha ha. We're practically the same age."

She rolls hers *harder*. "Cute. I'm a hundred and seventeen years your senior in trauma years."

I wince. Unfortunately, *fair point*. I only know the *barest* facts of what her father put her through, and even that is enough to make my blood curdle.

For a second, I wonder if Domhnall knows she's here. Then I remember—stupid question. He wouldn't *approve* of her hanging out with me. Not that it's up to her fiancé to approve shit, but I doubt he'd be thrilled about us kicking it like besties over a couple of beers.

"I'll take a beer," I tell the bartender.

The guy looks between me and Mads, his gaze flicking *just a little too long* down to her cleavage. "You sure? Not more shots?"

I shove Mads to the side before she can open her mouth

and get us in *real* trouble. "Two beers," I say, deadpan.

He huffs but turns to grab them.

"You can close out her tab, too," Mads says, and he brings me the receipt to sign.

Then I snag both and head for a table. Mads trails after me, looking far too amused. "Look at baby bear all grown up," she coos, ruffling my hair.

I bat her hand away and take a long pull from my beer, meeting her gaze over the rim. "So, you just wanna hang, or are we actually gonna talk about the fact that you snuck back into your own damn house like a teenager past curfew?" Then I think about how long ago that was. Months now. "Damn, it really is about time we just hung out like this."

She waves a dismissive hand. "Oh, that was *nothing*."

Then she tips her head back and *chugs* her beer. Not a sip. Not a gulp. Just a long, steady pour down her throat until the bottle is almost empty. She slams it back on the table with a sigh, elbows propped up, eyes a little watery.

I just stare. "Right. Totally normal behavior."

She licks a drop of beer from her lip and leans in. "It's *you* I wanna hear about. You got something going on with that priest I met a while back?"

I freeze mid-sip. I was *not* expecting her to ask about *that*. People think *I'm* chaotic, but Mads? She's on a *whole* different level. We don't do casual heart-to-hearts about our personal lives over beers.

And, well. There's also the tiny, insignificant fact that I haven't told anyone I got married.

I set my beer down, clearing my throat. "Yeah. We've got a little something going on."

Mads nods like that makes sense. "Sure. Sure. But it's not serious, right? Isn't that like, your whole thing? Not serious?"

I take another swig, buying myself a second. Yeah. Yeah, not serious was my whole thing. No attachments, no expectations, no letting people in.

But here I am, letting someone in.

I set my beer down with a little *clunk* and rub my nose. "Uh. It's... pretty serious."

Mads frowns. "But you don't do serious."

I tilt my head at her. "What the fuck, Mads? Why do you care?"

She exhales hard and glances toward the door like she's debating something. Then she leans in close, eyes dark, voice low, words sharp enough to slice right through me.

"Look, I'm sorry, baby girl, but I need you to break it off with the priest. For your brother's sake."

What the actual fuck?

I sit up straighter in my chair, eyes narrowing. "What the fuck does that mean?"

Mads gives me a look like she's debating throwing her drink in my face.

"Bad guy math," she says. "You had to go play hero at that

dumb Christmas thing and drag your big dumb boyfriend into the spotlight with you and me. Well, guess what?"

She leans back, arms crossed. "Some not-so-nice people saw that photo. People I'd rather keep *avoiding*."

I blink. "We were only out there because of *you!*" I wave my arm for emphasis.

"I had it handled!" She waves hers even *more* dramatically. "Before you brought the fucking *Avengers* outside and made a front-page-worthy spectacle."

"Who even are these people?" I demand. "And why the fuck would they care about *me*?"

Mads levels me with a look so flat it could be a table. "They don't care about *you*, dumbass. They care about *him*. Heir to the richest man alive? Ring any bells?"

Oh. Right. *That.*

"But he gave up his inheritance," I argue, grasping at straws that are rapidly turning to dust in my hands.

Mads laughs, a sharp, unpleasant sound. "Is that what he told you? Because Daddy Warbucks apparently *disagrees*. Bane is still the heir apparent."

I shake my head. "Okay, fine. Still don't see what any of this has to do with *me*."

Mads exhales like she's talking to a particularly stupid puppy. "I don't know, *blackmail*? Someone else wants you out of the way so they can marry their pet chess piece off to Bane? There could be a hundred reasons."

She leans in, voice dropping lower. "All I *do* know is that the charming sociopaths my father used to make me work for have now tracked me down. And they're working for someone who wants *you* out of the picture. They've given me a nice little ultimatum: get you to dump the priest and disappear, or they kill me, Domhnall, and *you*."

I stare at her.

She stares back.

"I'm thinking we call it 'rehab,' and you go sip piña coladas on a beach somewhere. Maybe the Riviera. I hear it's nice in the spring."

I let out a laugh, short and disbelieving. "Kill us?"

Mads doesn't even blink. "Did I fucking stutter?"

But I was just… I was just putting on a *pretty outfit* this morning so Bane would notice me. I was worrying about stupid shit like whether I should *get out of bed*, not fucking *life-or-death decisions*.

I slam my hands on the table. "What the fuck did you get us into?!"

Mads just shakes her head, mouth a hard line. "Oh, you got yourself into this one all on your own, baby girl. You should be grateful for my connections. At least I've got a way to get us out."

I glare at her. "You're not who I thought you were."

Her face stays hard. "I never am."

I suck in a breath, my heart pounding. "Do you even love Domhn?"

Her hand whips out, a sharp forefinger in my face. "Don't you ever question my love for that man. He's the *only* thing I've ever loved in this whole blood-fucked world."

Then she pushes back from the table, chair scraping. "Now come on. Time to go break up with your boy toy."

I stay frozen, my brain short-circuiting. It's all moving *way* too fast. But Mads is already grabbing my arm and *hauling* me up like I weigh nothing.

"Fuck," I hiss. "Why do you have to be so *rough*?"

She just keeps dragging me toward the front of the bar. "Sorry, kid. Not all of us were raised to live in cotton candy houses with peppermint dreams."

Once we hit the sidewalk, I *yank* out of her grasp. "Wow, you really *are* a bitch. And there's just one little problem with your *brilliant* plan."

She crosses her arms. "Oh yeah? What's that?"

I smirk, wiping sweat from my palms onto my jeans. "We got married. The priest and me."

For once, something I say actually *shocks* Mads. She blinks. "Well, shit."

But she doesn't even have time to process what I've said before a white van screeches to a stop right next to the curb. The doors fly open, and six men in black gear and face masks spill out like a fucking nightmare.

They grab us.

Mads kicks. I *scream*.

We fight like hell.

It doesn't matter.

We're dragged into the van, kicking and cursing, and the doors slam shut behind us.

I barely have time to breathe before the van *takes off*.

Well.

This is new.

FORTY-FOUR

BANE

I SMIRK down at the texts Moira sent earlier when I finally get out of my day of meetings and walk out of my office at the church. She wants to milk me, does she? My beast roars his approval.

The diocese was having a morning-long virtual retreat, and I was presenting on several panels, so I had to turn my phone off.

I should have warned Moira I'd be out of touch on my way out this morning. I know it bothers her when I don't answer quickly. But the bishop changed the schedule on me literally last minute, and I barely had time to down a cup of coffee before running over to my office, turning on my computer, and launching into my presentation.

Bishop Caldwell hasn't been my biggest fan since I went and married Moira instead of breaking things off with her as instructed. The bishop couldn't technically fire me over it since I didn't do anything against canon—at least as far as she knew. Agnes has been as good as her word about keeping mum on what she saw Christmas morning.

Moira mentioned last night she was meeting a friend for lunch today.

I craft my response, something wicked to have her shifting in her seat wherever she is.

> Me: Mmmm. But I've worked up an appetite. What if I want to eat you like a three-course meal instead?

I expect to see the little dots of her reply immediately.

But there's nothing.

I arch a brow, then put my phone back in my pocket as I push into the house.

I can't expect her to always drop everything to respond to me.

It's good she's out, socializing. It's what I *want* for her.

It's not like I want her obsessing over me every minute.

I swallow hard as I head to the kitchen to make myself something to eat. *Don't lie, you selfish bastard.* I sigh. Of course, I want her obsessing over me every minute.

I pull out my phone and look at the text I sent her.

And frown when I see that it's been *Read*.

But still no dots showing her writing me back.

I stare at the fucking screen for five minutes, progressively feeling more and more unhinged.

After ten minutes, it's clear. She left me *on read*.

My gut tightens.

I guess there's a first time for everything.

HOUR *Three*

I text her again.

> Me: If you're ignoring me just to make me lose my mind, congratulations. It's working.

Still nothing.

I scroll through our last conversation, looking for any indication that she was upset with me, that maybe I did something to piss her off.

But no. She was teasing me before bed last night. She was *soft* when she woke up this morning, curling into me, mumbling about not wanting me to leave.

I check my call log. No missed calls from her.

I try calling. Straight to voicemail.

My jaw clenches.

Maybe her phone died after she read my message.

Maybe she's busy.

Maybe she's *avoiding me*.

Maybe—*God help me*—she's finally decided she's had enough.

HOUR *Five*

I pace the length of my living room, my phone gripped in my fist. My mind is a battlefield, warring between logic and darker thoughts clawing at the edges.

If Moira was upset with me, she'd tell me. Loudly. She'd *scream* at me. She wouldn't go silent.

Wouldn't she?

Unless she *ran*.

The thought is a lead weight in my gut.

Because I knew, *I knew*, this was a risk. She doesn't do relationships. She doesn't do permanence. And maybe she finally realized what I already knew—

That she could do better than me.

That I *am* too much. Too controlling. Too selfish. Too demanding.

And why wouldn't she leave? People don't stay for me. They stay for what I can offer them—power, status, security, money. Not *me*. Never me.

And now Moira. Moira, who was never meant to stay. Moira, who flits through life like fire, who belongs to no one, least of all me.

I sit heavily on the couch, rubbing a hand over my face. The idea of Moira gone—Moira slipping through my fingers like she was never mine to begin with—unravels something ugly inside me.

She never told anyone about our marriage. I didn't push her. Was that a warning sign? Was she already half out the door?

Did I just not *want* to see it?

My stomach clenches. My fingers tighten around my phone.

I try calling again.

Straight to voicemail.

The walls close in. My breath comes sharp. *Fuck this.*

I grab my keys.

I don't even remember parking the car. One moment, I'm gripping the wheel so hard my knuckles ache, and the next, I'm throwing open the doors to *Carnal* and stalking inside like a man possessed.

The music is loud, too loud, pulsing through my bones as I scan the room. But something's off. The lighting isn't as dim as usual, the atmosphere not dripping in sin and desire the way it normally is. Instead, there are fucking *balloons* tied to chairs. A massive cake sits untouched on a long table. Women are gathered in small clusters, some laughing, some holding up tiny onesies and pastel gift bags.

A baby shower.

Fuck.

It barely registers because I'm already zeroing in on the person I need. Quinn, standing at the bar, laughing at something Isaak just said. My voice cuts through the chatter like a blade.

"Where's Moira?" I demand.

The room *freezes*.

Every single person turns to look at me. Glasses hover mid-air, conversations cut off, music still throbbing in the background like a heartbeat.

Domhnall stands up, glaring. "What's it matter to you, anyway? You lose my sister in the middle of role-play again?"

"He's a real priest, you idiot," Quinn interjects.

I keep my scowl locked on Domhnall. "It matters because Moira's my *wife*."

Quinn blinks. Slowly. As if she must have misheard me.

"Your *what?*"

"My wife," I bite out again. My voice is too low, too sharp.

Isaak leans back against the bar, exhaling. "Shit," he mutters under his breath.

Domhnall has gone rigid, fingers curling around his drink like he's about to snap the glass in half. And he's looking at me like he wants to take my head off my shoulders. As if he has any right to. He's been a total shit brother to Moira. I'm the only fucking one who's been there for her the last six months.

It's Kira who steps forward.

"Moira?" she says carefully, her brows knitting together. "I had lunch with her earlier."

Something inside me *lurches*.

My pulse thunders in my ears. "When did you see her?"

Kira exchanges a glance with Isaak before looking my way again. "I don't know. A little after noon?"

The room is still watching me, but it's shifting now. The shock is turning into something else—something I *don't* want to name.

"She seemed..." Kira hesitates. "A little off."

I seize on that immediately. "Off *how*?"

Kira shrugs, like she's trying to remember details that didn't seem important at the time. "Jittery, I guess? She was checking her phone a lot. But she wasn't worried. And she said she'd be here tonight."

Everyone looks around. She's obviously not here.

"She's usually late to things," Quinn says, "But we've already been here for an hour and a half. If she's this late, it probably means she's ditching."

My stomach drops, something ugly twisting inside me.

I look back at Kira. "But you said she didn't look worried?"

Kira shakes her head. "No." Then she tilts her face, frowning slightly. "She was just... being *Moira*. If anything, she looked... excited. I think maybe after she got a text from someone?"

I go completely still.

Excited.

After she got a text from someone.

Someone who wasn't *me*.

There's a long silence, and then Domhnall *laughs*. It's low and sharp, humorless. "Ah, Christ. You really don't know her at all, do you?"

My head jerks toward him. "What?"

Domhnall takes a slow sip of his drink, never breaking eye contact. "You're standing here, tearing the goddamn club apart, looking for her like she's missing." He lets out a breath, shaking his head. "You married my sister, and you *still* don't get it."

I don't respond. I can't. Because something is unfurling in my chest, something slow and creeping and fucking cold.

"She *does this*," Domhnall continues. "She runs. She gets restless and goes off on these wild benders, screwing whoever she wants, drinking herself into oblivion. Then she comes back like nothing happened."

I flinch.

I hear Quinn sigh before she steps in. "Look, man... I get that this is new for you, but Moira's always been—" She hesitates. "Unpredictable."

I don't even realize my hands are clenched into fists until my nails dig into my palms.

"She's my *wife*," I grind out.

Quinn winces like the word physically pains her. "Yeah, well. That was a choice, wasn't it?"

The unspoken *You should've known better* hangs between us.

I can feel the eyes on me. Pitying. Some apologetic, some amused. Like I'm the naive fool who thought he could keep her.

Like I thought I was *different*.

Domhnall leans forward, voice mocking. "Tell me, Father. Did you think you'd be the one to *change* her?"

I exhale slowly through my nose, locking my jaw, fighting the urge to break his fucking teeth.

"I was never looking to change her."

He scoffs. "Then what the hell are you doing here? Why are you acting like she's been kidnapped? Face it. She's off with someone else, same as she always is."

"She's not," I snap before I can stop myself. It comes out too fast. Too desperate. But is that just because I *need* them to be wrong?

Domhnall gives me a long, hard look. Then he shrugs. "Then why aren't you at home waiting for her?"

And there it is.

The final blow.

Because the truth is, I *should* be. I should be pacing our goddamn house, waiting for the inevitable moment she comes stumbling back in, laughing off her absence, maybe even *taunting* me about it, seeing how far she can push me.

It's not outside the bounds of our original agreement. And we never updated it after the marriage.

But I don't believe it.

I can't.

Not Moira. Not *my* Moira.

Not after everything.

And yet—

I hear Kira's words in my head again.

She wasn't scared, Bane. She was excited.

The club is too loud. Too bright. Too fucking *suffocating*.

I turn on my heel without another word and walk out.

I don't slam the door. I don't say goodbye. I just leave, the conversations behind me picking back up, the music resuming, like none of this ever happened.

Like I'm already forgotten.

Like she's already forgotten me.

I get into my car and grip the wheel, my breath coming in sharp, controlled exhales.

She left me.

Even as my gut screams that something isn't right.

Even as my body shakes with the urge to *hunt* for her.

Are they right?

Is it the right thing to let her go?

Beast wars with priest.

My car ultimately takes me home, though, if only in case she comes back to me.

But when I walk in the door, apart from the cat, the house is horribly, hauntingly empty.

FORTY-FIVE

MOIRA

I COME to in total darkness, my head throbbing like I spent the night downing tequila shots and banging my head against a brick wall. Well, the last thing I remember *is* downing a margarita, a bunch of shots, and then a beer, but I don't recall a brick wall.

Annnnnd there's the little fact that my arms are yanked behind my back, plastic zip ties biting into my wrists, and my butt is aching from a cold, hard concrete floor.

Oh. Right. I got *kidnapped*.

There's a groan next to me. Then a muttered, "Fucking *hell*."

Mads.

I exhale sharply, my own breath hot under the fabric covering my face. We've been hooded. Fucking fantastic. That's a *great* sign.

"Mads? You alive?"

"Unfortunately." A beat of silence. Then, "Moira. You absolute *disaster* of a human being. This is one hundred percent your fault."

I bark out a laugh. "Oh, *my* fault? *You* were the one dragging me down the street like we were late for the fucking Oscars!"

"Yeah, because I was trying to *save your life!*" she hisses. "Jesus Christ, I tell you to break up with your priest, and instead of listening like a reasonable person, you drop that little bombshell—*Oh, by the way, we got married*—and the next second, we're getting thrown into a goddamn van!"

I roll my shoulders, testing the zip ties. No give.

"That had nothing to do with this! Nobody even knows about that. He made sure the marriage certificate was confidential so it's not a matter of public record."

Not that I understood why at the time, but now I'm starting to get it. "Nobody would have even known I was with him. This is about that stupid paparazzi picture because you had to go smoke a stupid fucking cigarette when you knew there were fucking photographers around!"

Mads lets out a strangled noise. "Oh, *fuck you*, Moira. Fuck. You. I should've *left you* there. I should've just walked away and let you handle your own goddamn mess."

I snort. "Uh-huh. Because *you* were the one who got dragged into *my* bullshit, not the other way around?"

"Oh my God, I *hate* you." She shifts against the floor. "Where even *are* we?"

I tilt my head, listening. No city sounds. No people. Just the faint hum of industrial lighting and the drip-drip-drip of something that *better* be water. "Warehouse, maybe? Basement? Definitely somewhere creepy and murder-y."

Mads sighs. "Fabulous. Just how I wanted to spend my night. Tied up next to *you* in a discount horror movie set."

"Would you rather they knocked you out again? Because I could start screaming and see if they come back."

"Don't you fucking dare."

"Then shut up and let me think."

"Oh, great, Moira's gonna *think*. This is already going *so well*," Mads mutters.

I shake my head. "Why didn't you go running to your billionaire fiancé? Domhnall could have an entire army of mercs to protect him and you."

Silence. A tense, angry silence.

Then I get it. "Oh shit, this is too big for even Domhnall to fix, isn't it? But at least he could've *tried*."

"And ended up with us all dead if any little thing got fucked up? No! I won't risk him." Then she growls, "You're the idiot who fucked the son of the richest man in the world. So fuck you."

"Took the words right out of my mouth."

She groans. "Okay, well, whatever your *big plan* is, I assume it involves some level of stupidity."

I inhale deeply. "Oh, absolutely."

"Of course it does," she mutters. "This is really working out great for both of us. Just stellar planning all around. I love being tied up in a murder basement. Best day ever."

I don't answer. Instead, I take another deep breath. "Okay. This is gonna suck."

"What?" Mads asks, immediately suspicious.

"I'm dislocating my thumb."

"The fuck you are!"

"Too late!" I grit my teeth, inhale, and *yank* my wrist at just the right angle. A sharp, hot bolt of pain shoots up my arm as my thumb pops out of its socket. I swallow the scream trying to claw its way out of my throat. "Oh, *motherfucker*—"

"Oh my God, I think I'm gonna puke," Mads gags next to me. "What the *fuck*, Moira?!"

"Oh, I'm sorry. Did you have a better idea?" I hiss, blinking away tears. "Or do you just wanna keep lying here like a useless sack of shit?"

"You're insane."

"That's rich coming from you, Splitzy. And look, I'm the only one *escaping*." I flex my now-looser hand, grit my teeth, and *work* my fingers, slipping them through the zip tie one by one. It's slow. Agonizing. But then—

Snap.

I'm free.

I rip the hood off my head, blinking at the dim, flickering light overhead. It's a concrete room with a metal door and no windows. Definitely a warehouse or a back alley butcher shop. Either way, not ideal.

Mads is still gagging. "I hate you. I hate everything about you. I hope you get *tetanus* from this floor."

"Noted." I rub my raw wrists, then reach for her zip ties.

"No," she says sharply. "Moira, *no*. You can't free me. If I go with you, they'll think I helped you escape. I'm fucked if that happens. You can still stop all this. You need to run to that priest, break it off, and then disappear. If I stay, I can make sure Domhnall stays safe. I won't do *anything* that puts him in danger."

My stomach twists. "Mads—"

"No." Her voice is iron. "I mean it. You know me. You know I'm not bluffing. Domhnall's everything to me, and I'll play their game if it keeps him alive. But you have to go. Just break up with the priest, for fuck's sake! It's the only way any of us makes it out of this alive."

I hesitate, my heart hammering. "This is *stupid*."

"Oh yeah? Well, *so is love*, but here we fucking are. Now get the hell out of here before they catch you, or I swear I'll start screaming."

Footsteps echo in the hallway.

Fuck.

"You better not die," I hiss at her. "Because Domhnall will so fucking kill me if you die."

"I've got more lives than a cat," she whispers, "Now get the fuck out of here!"

I hesitate. Just for a second.

Then I run.

The hallway is dim, smelling like damp concrete and impending doom. My heartbeat pounds in my ears, and I don't have time to think about anything except *run, Moira, run.*

But of course, because the universe hates me, a door at the end of the hall swings open, and out steps a *brick shithouse* of a man. Bald, beefy, wearing a scowl like he was born with it. And he's got a gun in one hand.

"Well, well," he drawls, cracking his knuckles like some dime-store henchman. "Looks like the little rabbit got out of her hole."

Oh, he's one of *those* guys. Big. Dumb. Likes to intimidate. Probably has a really complicated relationship with his mother.

I plant my feet and tilt my head. "Oh, wow. A scary man with a gun. I'm *so* frightened." I clutch my chest like some old-timey fainting maiden. "Please, sir, don't hurt me!"

His eyes narrow. "You think this is funny?"

This is the problem with feeling ambivalent about death. It really makes you lose a proper scope of situations. I realize, somewhere in the back of my brain, I ought to be shitting my drawers right now.

But all I register is being pissed the fuck off.

"Oh, no. I *know* it's funny." And then I *charge*.

Look, I don't do things by halves. I go *all in*. So I sprint at him like an *actual lunatic*, shrieking at the top of my lungs, flailing my arms like a windmill in a tornado.

It works.

The guy's brain short-circuits, his gun goes up, and that's all I need.

I *launch* myself at him, clawing at his face like a feral raccoon that's just been evicted from a dumpster. I get a handful of his ear, yank, and he *howls*. The gun wobbles in his grip, and I slam my knee right between his legs.

"Oh—FUCK—!" he grunts, doubling over, and I use the opportunity to rip the gun from his hand.

I take two steps back, leveling the barrel at his forehead while he groans and tries to collect himself.

"Damn," I say, catching my breath. "You are terrible at this. Didn't they teach you anything in goon school?"

He blinks, then scowls. "Where's Veronica?"

I freeze.

Veronica?

Who the fuck is Veronica?

For a split second, my brain does the math—and then it clicks. Oh. *Mads*. He doesn't know her real name.

Right. Time to improvise.

I let out a bitter little laugh, rolling my eyes. "That *bitch*? She's the reason I'm in this mess. She set me up! And has been bamboozling my brother. Soon as I got loose, I bolted. Fuck her."

He studies me like he's deciding whether to believe me. So I do what any good liar does: I double down.

"You think I'd waste my time saving someone who *betrayed* me and my family? Please. You're stupider than you look. And listen here. I'm not an idiot. My brother and I are *out*. I'm breaking it off with Blackwolf Jr, got it? I don't need this shit."

His lip curls, and for a second, I think he's gonna say something. Maybe call me a liar. Maybe take his chances.

Too bad for him, I don't give him the opportunity.

I swing the gun, cracking him right in the temple with the handle. His eyes roll back, and he drops like a sack of potatoes.

I step over him, adjusting my grip on the gun. "Nighty night, asshole."

It's only right as I'm about to leave him in the dust and get the hell out of there that it clicks.

Mads suggested this was blackmail or a rival for my spot who wanted me to break up with Bane.

But why wouldn't they have tried offering me money first instead of this elaborate plot?

And then my stomach drops.

Because there's only one person who has both the power and the spite to go this far just to rip Bane and me apart. Somebody who *did* try offering money first.

Fuck.

What if it's his *father*?

But I don't have time to dwell on it. Not now. Not when I still have to get out of here alive.

I lean down and riffle through the thug's pockets. Nothing but a couple extra ammo cartridges.

I shove the extra ammo in my pocket, grip the gun tight, and *run*.

FORTY-SIX

BANE

MOIRA IS GONE.

It's the first thing I know when I wake up, and it's the only thing that matters.

I sit up in bed, my hand shooting out to the cold space on the mattress beside me where she's supposed to be curled up like a little snoring kitten.

I can't believe I let those fuckers last night convince me she'd left me. I came back home and fell into bed with a whisky bottle, full of despair.

I drag a hand down my face.

What the fuck was I thinking?

Even if she ran, so the fuck what?

She thinks she can disappear on me?

She fucking can't.

She's my *wife*.

I stare at the empty sheets for a long time, forcing my breathing to stay measured. The possessive rage that coils inside me—dark, lethal, waiting—wants to tear through the walls and rip apart everything standing between me and her.

The Moira I know wouldn't just run. No note. No message.

I know I was her first... everything. Relationship. Attempt at commitment. And she can get freaked out. She can get manic, her decision-making becoming erratic.

That's just all the more reason to find her and remind her of all that's so good between us.

But I don't move. Not yet. Not until I have a plan.

Five minutes later, I finally swing my legs over the side of the bed, planting my feet firmly against the floor.

My phone is in my hand a second later, my fingers already dialing Domhnall's number. It barely rings before he picks up.

"What?" His voice is sharp, groggy. I don't care if I woke him.

"Where is she?"

There's a pause. "Bane—"

"Don't lie to me."

A slow inhale, like he's bracing himself. "I don't know."

"Find out. You run a super security business, right? Well, let's see you put it in gear. Help me find your sister."

"I don't—"

"I wasn't asking."

Silence. Then, a muttered curse. "Fuck. You think I'd let my own sister disappear?"

I breathe through my nose, forcing the fury into something sharper, something useful. "I'd fucking hope not, but I don't know what kind of man you are, do I? Help me find my fucking wife."

Another pause. Then, begrudgingly, "After you came to the club last night, I tracked her credit card."

That gets my attention. My grip tightens on the phone. "And?"

"Last charge was at a bar yesterday afternoon. She went there after lunch with Kira, and it looks like she ordered a shitload of drinks all at once at two in the afternoon. I'm sorry, man. I told you, she just went on a bender."

"What bar?"

He exhales sharply, then gives me the name. A place on the west side of the city.

I'm pulling the phone away from my face to hang up when I hear his voice again, "And Bane—"

I put it back to my ear.

"What?"

"Check back and let me know what you find. I still think she's just fucked off, probably with some bloke she met at that bar. But I do care about my sister. If she's in trouble, I wanna know."

"Could've fooled me." I hang up, furious at him for not giving a shit sooner.

I don't have any more time to waste. I'm moving with a singular purpose, jumping in my car and putting in the bar's address, then stomping on the gas.

THE BAR SMELLS like stale beer and regret. It's dimly lit, the kind of place where the floor is perpetually sticky, and the patrons have long since stopped caring about anything but their next drink. The bartender eyes me warily as I approach, polishing a glass with a dirty rag. "What can I get you?"

"Information." I slide a bill across the bar. "Moira. Auburn curly hair. She was here yesterday afternoon around two o'clock."

The bartender looks at the money, then at me. His fingers hesitate before he takes it. "Yeah, I remember her. She was with another girl. They looked close."

Another girl? Kira said she got a text from someone. Everyone at the club last night just assumed it was a man. But it was a woman?

"Can you tell me any more about the woman?"

The bartender shrugs. "Good tits."

I roll my eyes.

"You said they looked close?"

"Maybe. They were having a good time. Until they weren't."

My fingers flex against the bar. "What do you mean?"

"They left in a hurry. Looked spooked." He shrugs.

Spooked?

"What else?" I demand. "Did you overhear where they said they were going next? Anything?"

But he just shrugs again. "That's all I know. The other one was dragging your girl out and then they was gone. But your girl had a shit-ton of tequila in her. Kept ordering shots."

What the fuck has Moira gotten herself into? Why didn't she come to me? Who was the woman?

"Can I see your security footage?" I demand of the man, already pulling out my wallet. I know enough from my former life that money is the oil that smooths the hinges of the world. And there's a giant camera hung over the bar pointed straight at the register.

But the bartender just shrugs again and chuckles, silver crowns on his front teeth gleaming as he leans in like he's telling a secret. "Man, that thing's just there for show." His sour breath rolls over me, and I pull back, disgusted.

I storm out of the bar and look in both directions, wondering which way Moira and the mysterious woman went. Then my eyes go up.

The bar's cameras might be fake, but other places around here give an actual shit about security.

Like the jewelry store halfway down the block. If they went that way, maybe I can catch a glimpse. I'm heading in that direction when my phone buzzes in my pocket.

I yank it out and quickly check the text.

> Domhnall: Moira's at my door. She looks fine.

Relief floods me.

> Bane: What's your address?

I'm already halfway to my car by the time he responds.

FORTY-SEVEN

MOIRA

I RING DOMHNALL'S DOORBELL, foot tapping like I'm drumming out a rock solo on the porch.

The bad guys didn't exactly leave me with my phone when they kidnapped me and Mads, so getting here took some good old-fashioned Moira-style improvisation.

Step one: Escape the hellhole. They'd stashed us in some abandoned warehouse by the river, and let me tell you, nothing screams "high-quality hostage experience" like peeling paint, rusty chains, and the lingering scent of dead rats. But I got out. Had to jog for what felt like miles before I found a street that didn't double as a tetanus breeding ground.

Step two: Pop my thumb back into the socket. My hand was starting to go really numb. And yes, it hurts like just as much of a bitch going back *in* as it does popping it *out*.

Step three: Hustle up a ride. No phone, no cash, just my wits and a face that people tend to be generous to when I play my cards right. So I worked my magic, batting my lashes at any guy who looked both kind and gullible. Told a heart-wrenching sob story about getting robbed and needing to get back to my dear, worried brother. It took a few tries—people are skeptical these days—but eventually, some saint of a man bought it and called me an Uber. Bless his easily manipulated soul. Though, in this case, the grift was pretty damn close to the truth.

Now, here I am, standing on Domhnall's doorstep, looking like I lost a fight with a few alley cats, waiting for my so-called loving brother to open the damn door.

Finally, the door swings open. But instead of the warm welcome I deserve, Domhn plants his arm against the frame, blocking the way like he's a bouncer at a club. And, of course, he's glaring. That's his default setting when it comes to me lately.

"Where's Mads?" he demands in a voice sharp enough to cut glass.

Not "Are you okay, Moira?" Not "Holy shit, you're alive!" Nope. Straight to business.

I roll my eyes. "Lost your fiancée?"

His jaw twitches. "Mads sent me a message yesterday

saying she had to go out of town for a few days. Then you go missing. Do you know where she is or not?"

"Yes. That's why I'm here." I shove against his arm and muscle my way inside. Screw waiting for an invitation. I've been kidnapped, hustled, and half-starved for the past however many hours. I am not in the mood for his attitude. Because all that isn't even to mention what I still have to do. I've only been functioning by blocking that part out.

Domhnall barely moves, but he lets me pass, shutting the door with a heavy sigh. "Jesus, Moira."

I flop onto his couch, stretching out like I own the place. "Nice to see you too, big brother. Got anything to eat? Because I'm starving. And also, maybe, just maybe, you could show a little concern for your only sister who just escaped a goddamn hostage situation?"

His glare softens—just a fraction. But I'll take it.

"Start talking," he says, heading for the kitchen. "And don't leave anything out."

Finally. Some hospitality. "Napkins, too!"

Domhnall drops a plate of leftover lasagna in front of me with all the gentleness of a prison guard serving slop, along with a couple paper towels. "Talk."

I take a big, dramatic bite just to piss him off. The man has even less patience than me. "You sure you don't want to ask me how I am first? Maybe offer me a hug, a 'glad you're alive, sis?' No? Cool, cool."

His glare sharpens. "Moira."

I sigh, dragging my fork through the sauce. "Fine. Short version? Mads and I got snatched off the sidewalk, stashed in some abandoned warehouse by the river, and left to marinate in our own panic."

His chair scrapes against the floor as he shoots up, fists slamming on the table. "WHERE IS SHE?"

I sigh *again*. "Someone with serious connections is pulling strings, and Mads thinks it's too big for you to take on."

His voice is a growl, veins popping at his temple. "You got out. Why the fuck didn't you get Mads out with you?"

I grip my fork tighter, swallowing down the flash of guilt. "Because she wouldn't let me, Domhnall. It wasn't an option. If I'd tried, neither of us would've made it." My eyes flash up at him. "And she thought they'd come and kill you. She wasn't willing to risk it. The guys who had us were people she said she knew from—" I gesture with my fork, *"Before."*

His hands ball into fists. "That's even *more* reason to get her the hell out of there! You should've—"

"What? Magically turned into a Navy SEAL and busted her out between kidnappers with guns?" I snap. "I did what I had to do. The only way to fix this is by playing their game."

His nostrils flare, his whole body coiled like he's ready to punch a hole through the wall. "What game?"

I take a deep breath. "They want something from me. Something I have to give them. And when I do, they'll let Mads go."

He shakes his head, eyes burning. "That's not a fucking plan."

"It's survival," I say, voice flat. "And if I do it right, everyone—including Mads and *you*—comes out of this alive."

His eyes narrow. "What do they want?"

I hesitate, my throat tightening. "I have to break up with Bane."

Domhnall blinks, caught off guard for half a second before rage slams back into place. "This is about Bane? They're threatening my fiancée because of your goddamn *husband*? Who the fuck cares that much about a fucking priest? Is he in witness protection?"

I exhale, slow and controlled, like I can keep my hands from shaking if I just regulate my breathing. Like I can keep my voice steady and my head cool and my shit together. Spoiler alert: I can't.

"His father is Brad Blackwolf. That's why Mads got scared for you. I think he hired the guy who still has Mads."

I swallow hard and drop the fork onto the plate with a clatter. I shift back in my chair, needing space, needing air. "He's not exactly thrilled about me as a partner for his son. He tried to pay me off to leave Bane a little while ago, but I didn't take it. And now, if I don't walk away from Bane, bodies are gonna start dropping."

Domhnall stares at me, breathing heavily, obviously still furious. His mind's working, and I can see the exact moment the pieces click together behind those dark eyes.

"Shit," he mutters. "Mads didn't tell you to come here, did she? She didn't want you to tell me at all."

I shake my head, a sharp, jerky motion. "No. She thinks we should handle it ourselves. She thinks getting you involved will make things worse."

"Well, she can fucking forget it. Because I'm fucking getting involved." His growl is low and lethal, his entire body coiled tight like he's about to launch himself into battle. "And if you think I'm sitting back while you try to handle this alone—"

"You have to." I cut him off before he can go full raging bull. "Because if this goes wrong, you're the only one who'll know what happened. You have to find Mads and tell Bane it's his father if my leaving doesn't call off the attack dogs. Do something to fix this clusterfuck. But let me try to fix it first. Please."

"Why don't *you* just tell Bane?"

I swallow hard again, looking down. Then I grab the paper towel to scrub at my face. I feel dirty after spending the night in that place, even if I was unconscious for most of it. "Bane left that world behind for a reason. His father's obviously a monster. And I—" I blink hard to keep back stupid tears. "This is for the best, anyway. We both know I wouldn't be any good for him in the long run."

I drop the towel and reach out, daring to rest my fingers on his knee, a soft plea against all his hard edges.

"Please, Domhn," I whisper. "I know I fucked up last

year. I know I've disappointed you in every way a sister can. I brought the vilest piece of shit back into your and Mads's lives, and even before that, I was too much—all the time—when all you deserved was a normal sister—"

"Stop it, Moira." He snaps the words like a whip. "I never needed normal. You're my *sister*. I always knew you were capable of standing on your own two feet. I just needed you to see it, too."

I blink at him, stunned silent. He's always acted like I was a hurricane he just had to endure. To hear him say he actually believed in me? It steals the breath from my lungs.

"I'm going to fix this." My voice is steadier this time. More sure.

"Well, you should have a chance to any second because I told Bane you were here when I saw you step out of the Uber."

"What?!" I lurch to my feet so fast the chair legs screech against the floor. "Why didn't you tell me that when I got here?!"

"I didn't know what you'd have to say for yourself," he says, completely unbothered by the fact that my entire plan is unraveling before my eyes. "And he's been off his rocker since you left. If you were running from him for a good reason, I figured it was best for me to be here when you reunited."

I drag a hand down my face. "If I'm going to break up with him, I can't do it *here*. I need it to be somewhere they'll see. They've probably got us under surveillance back at the church house. I've got to do it there. Let me borrow a car and some money."

He rises to his full height, all bristling big-brother energy. "Only if you tell me where Mads is."

"Fine," I huff. "But they've probably moved her since I escaped."

"Don't care. Tell me."

"Keys first."

His eyes narrow. "They're in the garage."

"Fine, then money now, keys later." I rub my thumb and forefingers together in the universal sign for "pay up." He rolls his eyes but pulls out his wallet. Instead of handing me cash, he slaps a credit card into my palm. Even better. I shove it in my pocket.

"Give me your phone."

"Tell me where she is, for shite's sake!"

"Phone!"

He curses but hands it over, dragging a hand through his hair like he's regretting all his life choices that led to keeping me in his life as a sister. See? No matter his sweet words, it's better for everyone when I'm not around. I'll break up with Bane and cut town. Everyone will get a break from the chaos-bringer that is me.

First, I text Bane, telling him that Moira's left and she's going home. Then I text Isaak an SOS, telling him I need him and whatever security goons he's got to meet Domhn at the following cross streets in the warehouse district ASAP.

Only then do I hand the phone back to Domhn and tell him where Mads is.

We both take off for his extensive garage, feet pounding the floor in a synchronized rhythm of urgency and barely restrained panic.

"Even if they've moved Mads," I say as we run, "there could still be bad guys there. I texted Isaak for backup."

He grunts, then says, "Buy a burner as soon as you're done breaking the priest's heart. Keep me up to date."

As soon as we hit the garage, he points to a box on the left wall. "Keys." He's already got the garage door opening and is peeling out in one of his sports cars before I've even reached the box.

I look at the three cars left. My hand hesitates for all of two seconds before reaching for the keys to the shiniest, fastest-looking one.

Naturally, it is the sexy red one.

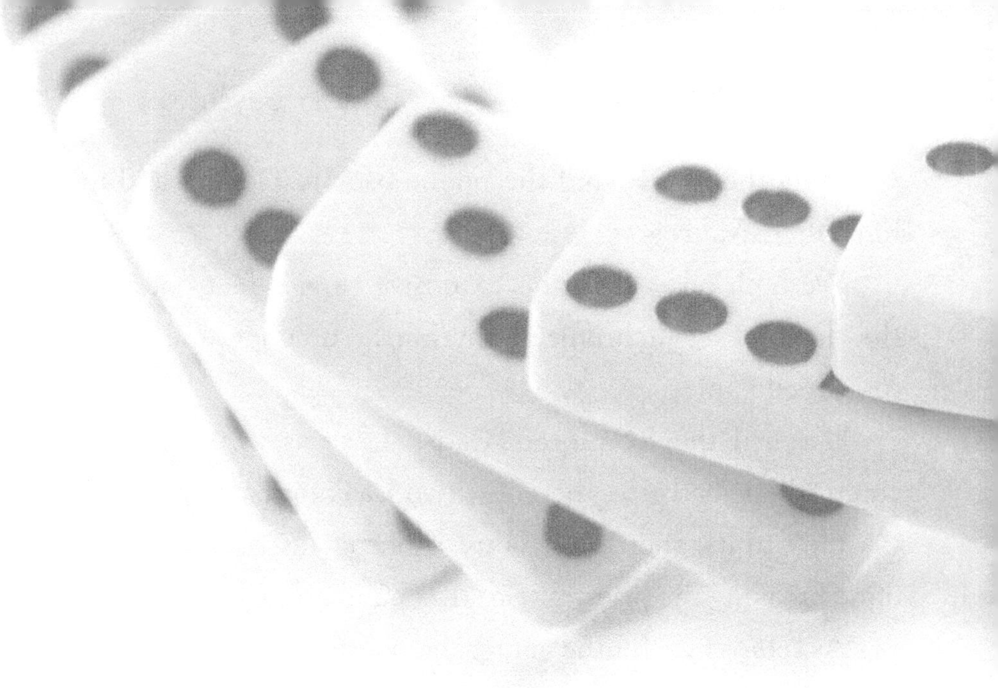

FORTY-EIGHT

BANE

I get the sporadic text from Domhn when I'm halfway to his house—Moira's left and is heading home.

Home.

I text back immediately.

> Bane: Our home or her apartment?

No response.

My jaw tightens. Is this another game? Another way to keep me chasing her, always a step behind? I don't fucking like being a step behind. I don't like being out of control.

And Moira knows it.

A roar rips out of me, raw and animalistic, as I slam my foot down on the gas. I fucking hate this. Hate not knowing where she is, what the fuck she's thinking, and what she's running from.

I am never out of control.

And right now, I don't even know what the fuck is happening, much less how to be in control of it. I should have her at my side already, not running around like she's a ghost slipping through my fingers.

When I get home, the house is empty. Silent. My body is too tight and my head too full of all the ways this could go sideways.

I pace the living room, rolling my shoulders and cracking my neck. My pulse pounds, my body primed for battle.

My phone rings. "Moira?" I bark into the receiver.

There's a pause, then a confused voice. It's a parishioner. Just the phone tree, asking me to arrange a hospital visit later this week.

I clench my teeth so hard my jaw aches. It takes everything in me to shove Father Blackwood into place, forcing my voice into something smooth and reassuring as I make pastoral assurances that yes, I will visit, yes, I'll be there, yes, my prayers are with them.

I nearly drop the phone when a sleek, overpriced red car glides into the lot outside.

Moira.

I cut off the parishioner with a quick, "My apologies, I have another incoming call," and hang up before they can respond.

She's here.

I move to the window, standing just behind the curtain, watching her step out like she hasn't shattered every piece of my sanity these last couple of days.

Whose fucking car is that?

Not hers.

A man's? A rich man's?

The idea slams into my gut like a fist. I shake it off because I know Moira. She's not like that. But then, what *is* she like anymore? Because she sure as hell isn't the woman who whispered confessions into my skin and heard mine in return.

She opens the door and steps inside, her eyes locking onto mine like she expected me to be waiting.

She exhales long and slow, raking her gaze over me, and I do the same. Her hair's twisted into some messy attempt at a bun, but strands have fallen loose. Her dress is wrinkled, her makeup smeared. She looks... tired.

And fucking gorgeous.

My hands twitch. I want to grab her, pin her, hold her still, and make her *explain* what the fuck is going on in that head of hers.

"Are you all right?" The words come out rough, edged in something lethal. I step closer.

She lifts a hand, stopping me. "I'm fine."

Liar.

"I've been calling—"

She shrugs. "I lost my phone out clubbing last night."

"Clubbing?"

Her leg bounces, fingers flipping the key fob like it's a toy instead of a weapon that's gutting me.

But she doesn't look manic, necessarily. Or drunk, or high, or anything else that could easily explain her erratic behavior.

"I was gonna just ghost you," she says, casual as anything, "but I'm trying to be better now. Figured you deserved more than that, so—"

She inhales, meets my eyes, then drops the fucking hammer.

"Bye, Bane. Thanks for all the tumbles."

I go still.

She wrestles the ring off her finger, presses it into my palm, and turns like she's already gone.

I stare at the ring. The same cheap silver ring she giggled about when I slid it onto her finger in Vegas. The same ring she's refused to take off since we got back.

The same ring she's trying to pretend meant nothing.

The door's still open.

This is what she had planned.

To walk in, break my fucking heart, and leave. Just like that.

Not happening.

I reach the door before she can step through it, grab her

wrist, and spin her back into my chest. She gasps, glaring up at me, but I don't let go.

"What the hell do you mean?" My voice is low and dangerous. "You're my wife."

She flinches, then tries to steel herself, lifting her chin. "We both know that was just make-believe for your job. So you wouldn't get fired. It wasn't real."

I exhale through my nose, slow and controlled, but inside, a storm is building.

"Not real?" I press her back into the doorframe, my body caging hers. "It felt pretty fucking real when you tied me to the bed after we got married, and we spilled our every secret to each other. It felt real when I had my cock so deep in you I was tickling your cervix, and you massaged my prostate until I came so fucking hard I almost blacked out. It felt real when I ate you out so completely you wept and called me your god."

She swallows, throat bobbing, and I see it. The flicker of doubt. The crack in the armor she's trying so damn hard to keep in place.

She's running. And I need to know why.

"You think you can just walk away?" My voice is softer now, but it's no less lethal. "After everything?"

Her lips part, but she says nothing.

I lean in, my breath a whisper against her skin. "You belong to me, Moira."

Her breath shudders, but she still doesn't move. Doesn't push me away.

Because she *knows* it's true. Still, she's threatening to go. But I don't fucking let go of what's mine.

I yank her all the way inside the house, slamming the door shut so hard the hinges rattle. The house trembles with the force of it, but she's trembling harder, breathless, chest rising and falling like she already knows what's coming.

Good. She should.

I pin her against the door, my body caging hers in, letting her feel exactly how hard I am, how fucking ready I am to remind her who she belongs to.

She gasps, eyes widening, but there's no fear in them—only raw, desperate hunger. Lust so thick it's choking the air between us.

"I don't give a damn where you've been," I growl, voice dark with possession. "And I sure as hell don't give a fuck who you've been with."

I can't even tell if it's a lie or not.

All I know is that I drop to my knees, rip her skirt up, and yank her panties down in one rough move that has her stumbling against the door. I grip her thighs, spreading them wide, fingers gripping her ass as I bury my face between her legs.

I am not a jealous man. I've shared her at the club and let others touch what's mine—under my rules, my control.

But this? Coming home in another man's car, acting like she can walk away from me?

No.

I inhale her, deep and furious, my tongue swiping

through her slick heat, searching—demanding proof she's still mine.

And all I find is Moira. *My Moira.*

Her scent. Her taste. Her perfect, untouched musk.

It sets something off inside me.

I devour her.

I don't tease or ease her in like I have before. I eat her like a starved man, tongue thrusting, lips sucking, my grip on her thighs bruising as I drag her against my mouth, forcing her to take everything I give.

She keens, thighs quivering, hands yanking at my hair. One leg hooks over my shoulder, grinding against my face like she doesn't know if she wants to escape or pull me in deeper.

"This doesn't mean anything," she gasps, voice shaking, body writhing. "I'm still leaving."

Wrong.

I growl against her clit, the vibration sending her up on her toes, and then I drive a finger into her, curling back against the spot that makes her come undone.

She screams, convulsing against me, juices flooding my tongue as I pin her there, my mouth locked around her as she shatters. Her hips jerk, slamming the door against its rusty hinges. Her moans bounce off the walls.

But I'm not finished.

Not by a long shot.

I stand, pressing her soft, spent body against the door. Her lips are parted, her breath coming in ragged gasps, her pupils blown wide with pleasure.

"Do I need to tie you to the bed again?" I murmur.

Her brow furrows, something unreadable flickering through her eyes before she shakes her head. "I'll safeword," she rasps. "I should have already." Her hand fumbles for the doorknob. "I have to go. I can't be here anymore."

"Why?" My voice is a growl. "*Tell me.*"

She shoves at my chest, but I don't move.

"That's right, dove," I taunt, voice smooth as sin. "Fight me. Get good and mad at me."

Her lips part, and for a moment, she looks like she might break—like she might confess everything.

But then her eyes harden, fury following pleasure.

"You don't always get what you want!" Her voice cracks. "This isn't how I wanted it to end, but I have to go."

She reaches for the door again, and again, I block her.

She slaps me.

Her palm leaves a sting that only makes my cock throb harder.

She knows exactly what she's doing.

Then she groans, fists my shirt, and yanks me down, her teeth sinking into my bottom lip before she breathes against my mouth, "Just one last time."

That's all the permission I need.

She leaps, wrapping her legs around me, and I catch her effortlessly, slamming her back against the door. One hand grips her ass while the other rips at my belt, my pants, freeing my cock just enough to thrust inside her in one brutal stroke.

She cries out, nails digging into my back, and I swear, Heaven and Hell collide inside me. She's so tight, so wet, squeezing me like she never wants to let me go.

She moves to take control, but I growl, slamming her harder against the wood, gripping her hips tight. Making her take every inch just the way I want her to.

She gasps, shudders, and then—

She slaps me again.

Something snaps inside me. I lose every ounce of restraint.

I tear her dress open, baring her breasts, and take one in my mouth, biting the hard tip of her nipple just enough to make her jolt.

She clenches around me, her orgasm ripping through her as she wails my name, her juices drenching my cock, my balls, the scent of her pleasure thick and intoxicating.

That's *two*.

And I'm still not done.

I lift her off the door and carry her to the kitchen, setting her on the counter. I need to see her. I need her to look me in the eyes when I ruin her again.

I slow my thrusts, grinding deep, rolling against her clit, never looking away.

"You're my wife," I whisper, my voice gravel and devotion.

She flinches, shaking her head.

"I want to worship you like this every night," I murmur, dragging my lips up her throat, sucking a bruise into her skin. "Every day."

She squeezes her eyes shut. "This was a mistake."

I cup her jaw, forcing her to face me, to meet my eyes. "No, it wasn't."

She swallows hard, and for a moment, I see it—the part of her that still belongs to me. That always will.

She just hasn't accepted it yet.

But she will.

Because Moira is *mine*.

She tries to wiggle off my cock, but I just start thrusting deeper, hitting that spot I know she can't resist.

Her head falls back, ecstasy contorting her features. I swear she mouths, *not fair*.

Then her hips lift, responding without thought, eyes locking onto mine, full of conflict. Full of what I'm terrified of is a goodbye.

I grab her hips and kiss her furiously, wanting to trap her, to keep her locked away where only I can have her.

But she pulls back, sinking her teeth into my shoulder, ever the wild thing.

I can't hold back anymore.

I wrap my arms around her, and I come.

One heartbeat. Another spasm.

Two heartbeats.

Three.

Two bodies, together as one.

Man and wife.

And then she squirms away, and I refuse to let go.

Until she whispers her safeword in my ear.

"Domino."

FORTY-NINE

MOIRA

HE LETS ME GO, but it doesn't mean he's done arguing with me.

Not that he cares that he's ripping my heart out with every word. Or that I was just devastated by making love one last time with my husband.

Just one last fuck, I thought. I'll still do the right thing and leave. Just one last fuck that will ruin me forever.

Pretend, pretend, let's play pretend.

Moira's just a wind-up toy with no heart. She feels nothing.

I'm just feet walking back to the front door with the bag I

threw some of my shit in. So what if I can still feel him dripping down my inner thigh?

It doesn't mean anything.

Nothing means anything.

Fucking him was definitely *not* in the plans, but then he was eating me out and we were up against the door, and before I knew it, his cock was inside me, and I was riding him to kingdom come.

"Tell me *why*," he demands, on my heels.

"Because I don't do monogamy."

I yank open the front door. I can tell he wants to slam it shut again, but the safeword was effective. He stayed hands-off the entire time I was throwing whatever I could grab into my bag.

"I told you, I don't care about that!"

Good. Let him yell. The louder and more public for whoever may be watching, the better.

"Too bad. I do. And I just can't stay here like this with you anymore!" I start down the stairs of the front steps. My heart's beating too loud in my ears.

"No!" he shouts. "No. I don't accept it. I'll find you and make you change your mind."

My mouth drops open as I spin back to look at him. "You can't say no. And that's called *stalking*!"

"So what? I've stalked you before. I'll do it again." He sprints down the steps until he's right in my face. "Especially since I don't believe a word out of your mouth."

My breath immediately gets short, chest heaving. Damn him. Why is he making this so hard? Just let me break up with you already!

"You want me," he demands, eyes dark as they search mine. He jams a pointer finger back toward the house. "You just proved in there how much you still want me."

"That doesn't mean anything!" I toss my hands up. "I *want* all sorts of guys."

He lets out a bitter laugh, but there's nothing amusing about it. "Bullshit. You think I don't know you by now? You think I don't see right through you?"

Oh shit. Panic floods my chest. What if he really does? Everyone's in actual *real* fucking danger. Right this second, for all I know, Domhnall could be tromping into a hornet's nest of bad guys, thinking he's invincible like he always does.

And here I've been, taking one last ride. I should never have let myself be seduced by Bane again in the first place. What if I've already fucked everything up?

Because that's what I do, isn't it?

I fuck shit up.

I ruin things.

And, given enough time, I'd ruin Bane.

This is for his good, too.

I lift my chin and force my eyes flinty. "You don't see *anything*."

His nostrils flare, and his hands curl into fists at his sides like he's holding himself back from grabbing me and shaking the truth out of me. "I see a scared woman. A woman who's running. From herself. And from me."

I force down the lump in my throat. "How poetic. And completely fucking wrong. I'm walking away because I *want* to."

"Bullshit," he snarls again, stepping closer, heat radiating off of him. "If you wanted to go, you would have left before I ever touched you again. But you didn't. You let me have you. You took everything I gave you and then some. And now you expect me to believe this is real? That you don't love me?"

I blink but try not to let him see he's just punched the air out of my lungs. *Love.* Oh god. He's told me he loves me before, but just that once. I think he's afraid he'll scare me if he says it too much. Because I haven't ever said it back.

I force myself to laugh caustically. "Love?" Meanwhile, I'm dying inside. "Whoever said anything about *love*? I thought we both knew what this was. We were both just using each other."

His face darkens, and his voice drops dangerously low. "You're a coward."

I inhale sharply, then point in his face. "You knew exactly who I was since the moment you met me. It's not my fault you made up some fairytale about a pretty, helpless maiden who needed saving. Because that was never me."

"I don't know what the fuck's going on, but you're in trouble, aren't you? Who was that woman with you in the bar?"

His voice softens just slightly, rough with desperation. "Let me help, Moira. Let me in."

I shake my head wildly, stepping back. "I don't need help."

"The hell you don't." His eyes flick over my face, searching, pleading. "You love me, Moira. Say it. Because I love *you*. See? I'm not afraid."

I steel myself against the panic that's like a thousand bats screeching and flapping in my ribcage.

Then I raise my chin.

For once in your goddamn life, Moira, don't fuck this up.

He always did love it when I hurt him.

So I devastate him.

I lean in. "I don't *want* you, Bane. You're nothing to me."

Bane flinches like I just carved the words into his flesh.

His grip on my wrist goes slack, and I take the opening, pulling free. The moment I step back, his whole body changes; his face goes blank, his posture is locked in rigid control, and the Bane that loves me disappears behind a mask of cold, impenetrable steel.

It's working. Now, I need to make sure it sticks.

"I used you," I continue, voice sharp as a blade. "You were a fun distraction. But I'm done now. I don't want you anymore."

He doesn't speak. He doesn't move.

I push harder. "You're too intense. Too *much*. And frankly, it got boring."

A muscle ticks in his jaw. But still, he says nothing.

Good.

"Go back to your perfect little church house," I snap, turning my back on him. "Find some sweet, devout thing who'll let you own her like you want. Because it's not me."

Silence.

Then, softly, so quietly I barely hear it—

"You're a liar."

I walk away.

I force one foot in front of the other, my vision blurring, my chest a gaping, open wound. He doesn't chase me anymore. He doesn't call my name.

I break him and leave him standing there.

It's for the best.

But then why does it feel like I just killed the only thing that ever made me feel alive?

FIFTY

BANE

WHAT DO you do after the love of your life stomps on your heart and leaves you broken on the floor?

I begged her to stay. I put everything on the line. I fought for her. Told her I *loved* her. Looked her in the eye and would have sworn I saw it in her eyes, too.

But was she right?

Was she just a story I made up in my head?

Was the real Moira just a body inhabited by my dream woman for half a year before she stepped back out of the Pygmalion version of her I'd shaped in my mind? Far too real to ever be caged by my foolish imagination?

Far too wild.

Far too magnificent to ever truly *want* me.

She volunteers at the women's shelter because she loves people. Because she sparkles from the inside out. Whereas *I* volunteer at the prison to purge my soul. Because it was where I should've ended up if my father hadn't stepped in. Because I am and always will be a privileged little prick. My path always smoothed before me.

No one ever says no to me.

Until her.

And here I am again.

The entitled little shit. Sad boy. All alone.

Like my father, who could buy the whole world, but there's still not an actual soul in that world that genuinely loves him. Like father, like son.

At the end of things, I'm back at the beginning.

So I do the only thing I can think of because drowning myself in a bottle of whisky is so fucking cliché I can't even bear to crack open the bottle.

I don't want to feel numb.

I want to *hurt*.

I go to the club. And I stomp in with a purpose.

The club is alive.

Not in the way a church is alive—breathing with whispered prayers, the rustle of hymnals, and the gentle clinking of a chalice.

This place pulses. It throbs. It beats like a second heart,

its rhythm discordant with the one already hammering in my chest.

The bass rattles the walls.

Bodies move in the dark.

Writhing. Submitting. Taking. Giving.

The scent of it, the *weight* of it, presses against me like an invitation, and I breathe it in.

I don't belong here.

Not tonight. Not in this headspace.

But I came anyway. And without my mask. I'm done pretending I'm two people. Consequences be damned.

I scan the room, my pulse a steady, punishing thrum beneath my skin. I know who I'm looking for. A particular person clad head to toe in latex, booted heels tipped in a wicked spike.

Quinn.

She's easy to spot. In all black, confidence rolls off her as she sits on a throne-like chair with a man kneeling at her feet, his head bowed, his body slack in surrender. She runs a hand through his hair absentmindedly as if he's a pet. The room seems to orbit around her without her even trying.

I cross the floor in measured steps.

When I reach her, I don't hesitate. "Mistress Quinn. I'd like to engage your services for the night."

"Father Blackwood," she purrs, dismissing the man at her feet with a flick of her wrist. He whines but crawls away.

She looks up at me and takes her time raking her gaze over my frame. *Reading me.*

"You look like hell, Father."

I roll my shoulders, feeling the tension coil tighter. "I need your services."

Quinn leans back in her chair, crossing her legs, the movement lazy. Unbothered. "Oh?"

"I need you to hurt me."

She stills. Not a dramatic pause, not a tease—just pure, assessing silence. Then, slowly, she exhales, setting her drink down on the table beside her.

"You're not my usual clientele."

"I don't care." My voice is raw, scraping against something inside me that feels close to breaking. "Just do it."

She studies me, taking her time, eyes slicing through my composure like a scalpel. She sees too much. She always has.

"This about *her*?"

My teeth clench, and my pulse roars.

"Questions aren't part of the bargain." My voice is low with warning.

Quinn smirks, tilting her head like she's debating. "Oh, I think they are." She stands, stepping closer, the scent of expensive perfume curling around me. "Because you, *Father*, are not a man who gives up control easily. And yet, here you are."

I don't flinch. "Are you going to help me or not?"

She lifts a hand, trailing one perfect, red-tipped nail down my chest. Slow, deliberate.

"I could break you," she murmurs, a whisper of a promise.

I meet her gaze, unflinching. "That's the point."

She lets that hang between us. The music pounds, distant, like it belongs to another world—one where I haven't lost everything. One where Moira still calls me hers.

Then Quinn laughs. A quiet, knowing sound. She steps back, shaking her head.

"No."

The word slams into me harder than any whip ever could. It lodges deep, where the wounds are still open and bleeding. My body locks up.

"You're refusing?" My voice is even, but barely. "Why?"

She shrugs. "I don't play with men looking to run from their pain."

I exhale through my nose. "That's not what this is. I *want* the pain."

She tilts her head, amusement flickering in her eyes. "Oh, really? So tell me, *Father*. Are you here because you *like* submission?"

I stay silent.

"Are you here because you want to *serve*?"

My jaw tightens.

"Or are you here because you think if I beat the hell out of you, it'll erase what's already been done?"

Something in my chest twists violently. "Don't act like you know me."

"Oh, but I do." She steps closer again, pressing a single, manicured finger to my sternum. "I know *exactly* what you are. A man who takes. Who dominates. Who breaks others, piece by piece, until they're nothing but offerings at his altar."

My teeth clench. I don't respond.

She leans in, lips just brushing my ear.

"And now? You want someone to *break you?*"

The breath I take is sharp, burning its way down.

"I need to feel something else," I grind out. "I need to be punished for my sins."

She pulls back, meeting my gaze again, something knowing in her expression. "No, you want to feel *her*. You want to replace the pain of losing her with another kind, but you're not built for that, Father. You don't bend."

I clench my fists, every muscle in my body screaming for violence, for anything that isn't this truth she's carving into me. "If you won't do it, I'll find someone who will."

Quinn sighs, stepping back. "You could. Plenty of people here would love the chance to put their hands on you."

She sits again, taking her time crossing her legs and picking up her drink.

"But that's the thing, isn't it?" she murmurs. "You don't want *them*. You want someone who can *actually hurt you*." She takes a slow sip, eyes glinting.

Then, with the smallest tilt of her head, she gives the order.

"Kneel."

It's not a request. Not an invitation.

It's a command.

My body locks up. A muscle in my jaw ticks. I've only kneeled before one person in my entire life.

But Quinn just waits, patient, her lips curling slightly. Daring me.

This is what I'm here for, isn't it?

So I do it. Even though it feels like a betrayal. *Because* it feels like a betrayal. Slowly. Deliberately. I kneel.

The floor is cold beneath my knees. I feel the weight of the moment pressing on my spine. My hands settle on my thighs, fists clenched, every muscle in my body going tight as steel cables.

Quinn circles me, the click of her heels barely audible over the thrum of bass.

"Look at you," she muses, her voice smooth as silk and twice as sharp. "So eager to run from your pain, you'd rather crawl to me than face it."

I grit my teeth. "I don't run."

She laughs. It's not kind. Not cruel. Just knowing.

"Then say it." She stops in front of me, tilting her head. "Say why you're really here."

I exhale, slow and measured. "I told you—"

A sharp snap of her fingers cuts through the noise. "No. The truth, Bane."

My chest rises and falls. The music presses against me, a suffocating rhythm. "I need—"

Another snap. "Not good enough."

My throat tightens. I *won't* give her what she wants. I *won't* say it.

But Quinn? She's a professional. And she's ruthless.

She crouches down, leveling her gaze with mine, amusement curling at the edges of her lips. "You're pathetic like this," she muses, her nails dragging down the side of my face, slow and deliberate. "Look at you, kneeling like a good little submissive, thinking I'll give you what you want."

I breathe through my nose, refusing to react.

"Your wife left you."

Her words are a wrecking ball to my ribs.

I don't move.

She hums, tapping a manicured nail against my jaw. "Say it."

I swallow, pulse in my throat. "No."

Her smirk deepens. "You think pain will fix it? That if I mark you up, break your skin, make you bleed, it'll drown out the ache in your chest?"

Silence.

She drags that single finger down the center of my chest again, slow, like she's peeling me open. "You don't want pain, Bane," she whispers, eyes locked on mine. "You want absolution. You want someone to tell you this isn't your fault. That she was always going to leave, no matter what you did."

I force my breath to stay steady.

"But you don't get that," Quinn continues, her voice almost gentle now, almost kind. "No one's coming to save you from this." She leans in close, lips brushing my ear. "And you *know it*."

My hands tremble. I curl my fingers tighter, nails biting into my palms.

"Say it."

I shake my head.

She sighs, almost pitying. "What are you afraid of? That saying it out loud will make it real?"

I don't answer.

She crouches again, so close I can feel the heat of her body, the sharp scent of her perfume. "It's already real. She's gone. She left you. She walked away, and you let her."

Something inside me snaps. My hands slam down on my thighs, my breath rushing out like I've been punched in the gut.

Quinn smiles, slow, triumphant. "That's it, isn't it?"

My pulse roars in my ears.

"You don't need my hand on you," she continues, her voice softer now. Deadlier. "You need to sit in this pain. You need to feel it. Acknowledge it. Stop trying to outrun it."

She paces around me, taking her time, savoring it. "That's why she left, isn't it? You tried to make her something she wasn't. And when she finally had enough, when she walked, you came here—hoping I'd erase her from your skin."

I squeeze my eyes shut.

"But she's still there, isn't she?" Quinn crouches down in front of me again, lifting my chin with two fingers. "Every inch of you is still hers."

I grind my teeth. "You're enjoying this."

"Immensely," she purrs. "Because I see you, Bane. And I know this won't be the last time."

I rip my face away from her grip, my entire body tight with restraint.

She leans in, almost gently. "You will sit with this pain. You will feel every second of it. The weight of her absence. The finality of it." She smiles like she's handing me my death sentence. "And when you've had enough of pretending, when you're ready to actually *face* it, maybe then—*maybe*—you'll finally understand why she left."

I breathe hard through my nose, my body shaking with something violent and raw.

"Until then?" Quinn rises to her full height, looking down at me like I'm already broken.

"You'll be back," she says simply. "Again and again. Because you don't want release. You want punishment." She leans in one last time just to whisper, "But your true punishment is facing the pain inside you."

Then she turns and walks away, leaving me on my knees, drowning in everything I refuse to say.

FIFTY-ONE

MOIRA

THE SPEEDOMETER NEEDLE quivers just under a hundred.

The engine roars beneath me, the whole car vibrating as if even the machine itself is terrified of the way I'm treating it. But the road stretches long and busy ahead of me. Red taillights flicker in the distance. Brake lights flare as I weave between cars.

But I don't slow down. I don't lift my foot off the gas. I don't even blink.

I can't. Because if I blink, if I stop, if I even let myself breathe too deeply, I'll feel it.

The gaping, sucking chest wound where my heart used to be.

I did the right thing.

Right? Right. Of course, I did. I saved Domhnall. I gave Bane back his life. I did what I had to do.

And all it cost me was everything.

"FUUUUCK!" I scream into the night, slamming both palms against the steering wheel so hard the whole car shudders. The headlights ahead of me wobble with the impact, but I don't care. Cars whip past on either side, a blur of silver and black, some honking as I cut too close, but I don't give a shit. It's just me, the moon, and my absolute, unrelenting regret.

I yank my phone out of the cupholder and jab at the screen. Domhnall's name. Again. Ringing. Ringing. Straight to voicemail.

I throw the phone onto the passenger seat. "Pick up, you useless bastard!"

I need to know. I need to hear him say it. That it worked. That everyone's safe. That I didn't just burn my whole world to the ground for absolutely fucking nothing.

But the silence stretches, and my fingers twitch against the wheel. The itch starts low, right in my bones, crawling up my arms and wrapping around my throat.

I'm burning. I need—

To scream? To smash something? To fuck? To crash this fucking car into the nearest concrete median just to feel something else?

The highway curves, and I take it too fast, tires screeching. There's a thrilling, terrifying tilt of gravity before the car corrects itself. A truck blares its horn behind me, its lights flashing as I cut in front of it.

Adrenaline spikes through my veins, but it's not enough. I press harder on the gas because fuck it, why not? Let the whole world try to stop me. Let the cops come. Let someone do *something* because I sure as hell don't know how to stop myself.

"God, you're such a fucking idiot, Moira," I snarl to myself. "You had it. You had *him*. And you just—what? Threw it away? Maybe for fucking nothing!"

You loved him, didn't you? whispers a quiet, traitorous voice in the back of my mind.

"Shut up," I snap back out loud as if I can banish my own thoughts through sheer force of will. "Love isn't fucking real. Love is a goddamn bear trap hiding under the grass just waiting to snap shut around your fucking ankle the second you get comfortable."

The tears come hot and fast, blurring the road ahead. I blink hard, shaking my head like a dog.

I did the right thing.

But what if I didn't?

What if I just threw away the only real, good thing I ever had in my entire life?

"NOPE. No, we're not doing that." I sniff hard, knuckling my eyes before gripping the wheel again. "We are not having a mental breakdown on the road, we are not careening off into a ditch, we are absolutely, positively not going to cry over a man. Nope. No, sir. Not today, Satan."

I nod firmly to myself and then slam my palm against the horn for no other reason than the fact that it feels good to make noise. The driver in front of me flips me off in the rearview mirror. I grin wildly, teeth bared, and floor the gas to pass them.

The itch gets worse. My body vibrates with it. I press down on the gas again, foot shaking. One hundred. One-ten. One-fifteen. The world outside is a blur, just streaks of light and shadow, and inside my head, it's even worse. I'm spinning out. I'm spiraling. I need to do something—

My phone buzzes.

I lunge for it, barely glancing at the screen before swiping to answer. "Domhnall?!"

"Moira, what the fuck—"

A car flashes toward me in the opposite lane, horn blaring, headlights glaring like judgment. I yank the wheel hard to the right, tires screeching as I barely correct in time, my stomach slamming into my spine from the sheer force of it. The car beside me swerves, its horn blaring in a long, angry note.

"Jesus fecking Christ," Domhnall's voice barks in my ear. "Where the fuck are you?"

I pant, white-knuckling the wheel, chest heaving. "Driving."

"Driving?! Driving where? Are you drunk?"

I laugh, high-pitched and unhinged. "Oh, I wish. That'd be way more fun than this."

"Moira."

His voice changes. No more bluster, no more exasperation.

I swallow hard. "Just tell me. Did it work?"

A long pause. "Yeah," he says finally. "Mads called and said she's all right. We're all safe. Whatever you did, it worked."

I squeeze my eyes shut for a brief second. Relief crashes through me so hard I nearly choke on it.

"Okay," I whisper. "Okay. Good."

Domhnall exhales on the other end. "Where are you?"

I glance up just in time to see the giant green highway sign flash overhead.

Austin.

"I—uh. Apparently, I'm about to be in Austin."

Domhnall mutters a long stream of Gaelic curses under his breath. "Jesus, Moira. You need to—"

But I don't hear the rest because suddenly, the itch is worse than ever. My hands shake as I hang up on Domhn. My whole body thrums with electricity. I don't know what I need. To fight? To break something? To break myself?

All I know is that I can't stop. I can't slow down.

Everyone's safe, but it doesn't change anything. I can't go back to Bane or it just starts all over again.

I yank the wheel to take the 6th Street exit.

Losing myself in the famous Austin bar scene sounds perfect just about now.

FIFTY-TWO

BANE

I SIT at the club's bar, my fingers wrapped around a glass of whisky I'm not drinking. The ice has melted, diluting the amber liquid into something weaker.

Quinn told me to feel my fucking feelings. To sit in them. To let them do their worst.

I have a better idea.

I could drink myself into oblivion. Numb it all out. Let the alcohol cauterize the gaping wound Moira left in me. It would be so easy to slide back into old habits. To drown in the dark instead of facing it.

But what's the point?

Tomorrow, the pain will still be there. The hole inside me will still be a bottomless, black fucking void that not even the best whisky can fill.

So I sit. I breathe. I let it settle in my chest like a second heartbeat—pounding, pulsing, demanding my attention.

Punishment.

This is what I deserve. To be left. To be hollowed out and wrecked.

Quinn's whip could tear the flesh from my back, and it still wouldn't compare to this. This pain is deeper, a sickness in my soul I can't sweat out or bleed away. This is the kind of agony I've spent my whole life outrunning.

And now, I have to sit in it.

Like a good little boy taking his medicine.

I stare down into the glass. My reflection stares back. A stranger. A man who let the only good thing he ever had slip through his fingers.

Moira.

No, that's not true. She wasn't the *only* good thing I've had and lost.

A face flickers behind my eyes. Another loss. Another woman I failed.

My mother.

I inhale sharply, forcing my fingers to unclench from around the glass before it shatters.

I spent years resenting her. Hating her. Believing she

abandoned me. That she left me behind without a second thought.

She hadn't.

She loved me. And I was too much of a selfish, angry little bastard to see it.

I close my eyes, swallowing against the tightness in my throat. She was good. Too good for the life she was handed. Too good for the son she had.

I never let myself grieve her. Not properly.

Grieving felt like a privilege I hadn't earned.

I was a shit son. I didn't fight for her. Didn't tell her what she meant to me when she was alive. And by the time I was ready to stop being a fucking coward, it was too late.

Am I making the same mistake with Moira?

Did I not see her?

The thought grips me like a vice, squeezing so tight I can barely breathe.

I should've seen it. Should've fucking felt it in my bones. She wasn't right today. Her eyes were wild, her body vibrating with an energy that wasn't hers. I was so obsessed with keeping her and holding her down and making her stay that I didn't stop to ask the one question that mattered.

What did she *need*?

Not me. That's for fucking sure.

She ran from me like the devil was at her heels. Like I was the devil.

I drag a hand down my face. It's not the first time I've been someone's worst nightmare. But this—this is different.

Because she wanted to stay. I know she did. I felt it in every desperate kiss, every shuddering breath, every broken gasp of my name.

But she still left.

I frown, the pieces shifting, rearranging. Something doesn't fit. Something is wrong.

The excuses she threw at me weren't real. They crumbled the second they left her lips. A woman like Moira doesn't run from what she wants. She grabs onto it with both hands and holds the fuck on.

So why did she let go?

Something else *was* going on.

I grit my teeth. The answer is there, just out of reach. Taunting me.

I slam the whisky back in one burning gulp and set the glass down with a sharp crack.

But I don't move.

My instincts scream at me to act. To track her down. To hunt, to chase, to take what's *mine*. That's what Dad always said to do, right? You want something, you take it. It's what I've always done. It's what I know.

But what if that's not what she *needs*?

The thought sits in my stomach like a stone, heavy and unwelcome.

I don't know the answer.

And it fucking kills me.

For the first time in my life, I have to stop. To think and try to understand instead of react.

I fucking hate it.

I feel Caleb's eyes on me from behind the bar before he even says a word. I'm aware of everything tonight—the weight of my own body in this chair, the burn of whisky down my throat, the fucking hollowness stretching wide inside me. So when he finally speaks, it doesn't startle me.

"Hey, man," he says.

I lift my head. My body is slow and heavy, like it resents being pulled back to reality. I meet his gaze, and he immediately hesitates, stepping back a little like he just realized he approached a caged animal.

"Uh, sorry," he mutters, glass in hand, rubbing at it with a clean white towel. "Didn't mean to disturb you."

"No, it's fine." My voice is rough, and I sigh out a breath, running a hand down my face. "Just noodling on a puzzle I'm not sure I can solve tonight. What's up?"

Caleb keeps rubbing at the glass, even though it's already bone dry. "Well, the other day, Moira mentioned you do some volunteer work at the prisons? I was wondering if you ever go down to the state prison near Waco."

My mind sharpens, the mental haze clearing just enough to latch onto something that isn't Moira. A problem that isn't my own.

"Is that where your father's at?" I ask.

He nods but doesn't look at me. Just keeps polishing. "Yeah."

I watch him for a long beat, noting the tension in his jaw and the way his fingers tighten around the glass like it's the only thing holding him together.

"Have you changed your mind about visiting him?" I ask.

He shrugs. Stares down. The silence stretches long enough that I could leave it there and let it drop. But I've been a pastor long enough to recognize shame when I see it. I know that look. I see it in the mirror every goddamn day.

"It's my fault he's there," Caleb says in a rush. "And I— I just don't know how to face him."

I don't press. I've heard it before—people thinking if they'd just done something, just reached out, they could have stopped a desperate family member before it was too late. As if they had some kind of divine foresight, like they were supposed to know what was coming.

"That's okay," I say. "You know that, don't you? I know everyone was pressuring you the other night. But it's fine if you don't know how to feel right now."

Caleb exhales, the sound short and sharp, like a laugh that got choked on the way out. His Adam's apple bobs as he swallows hard, eyes darting to the left. I catch the sheen in them before he looks away, the flicker of tears he's trying his damnedest to fight.

Fuck.

The way his pain sits right there, just under the surface, makes something claw up my throat. Seeing his pain so close to the surface drags up mine. The grief I've been pretending I'm dealing with when all I've really done is shove it further down.

Quinn was right.

I am a fucking coward.

The man standing in front of me is doing a better job confronting his demons than I am.

"I guess that's what you're doing right now, huh?" I say, clearing my throat. "Talking to someone."

Caleb lets out a short, wet laugh and swipes his forearm across his eyes. The universal fucking sign of men everywhere trying to pretend they're fine.

"I could take a trip down to Waco and check in on him," I offer.

The words are out before I fully think them through, but I don't regret them. Not when the alternative is sitting in my own misery, waiting for answers that won't come. At least this is something tangible. Something I can fucking *do*.

"Yeah?" Caleb looks at me, eyes wide—the first time he's looked me in the eye this entire conversation. "Oh my god, man, you'd save my fuckin' life. That would be amazing. I just want to know he's okay and—" He swallows again, looking away. "And for him to know that I love him. That I'm pulling for him. And that I'm so fucking sorry."

I nod, feeling the weight of his words, of his guilt, of his pain. They settle into the air between us, heavy and unspoken.

They're his words, but they might as well be mine.

Wherever you are, Moira, I love you. I'm pulling for you. And I'm so fucking sorry.

FIFTY-THREE

MOIRA

BAR-CRAWLING on 6th Street on a Friday night is practically a fucking tradition in Austin. They close the whole street to traffic, turning it into a river of sweaty bodies and pulsing music spilling from bar to club to rooftop to gutter.

When I used to regularly come down to 6th Street for a good time, I'd just turned eighteen and had no patience to wait three more years for access to all the fun. Thank god my fake ID guy was still in business since bad guys took my wallet yesterday. Fuck, was that yesterday? The day before?

I shake my head.

It's officially time to get fucked up and let all this shit go.

The hours pass, the drinks flow, and I give into the electricity of the city on a Friday night. I finally find the perfect club—electric with bodies that move like a single, chaotic organism. It's not just alive; I can feel it breathing. It pulses through me like a second heartbeat.

The mayhem is me, and I am the mayhem.

The fabulous insanity only escalates as the night deepens. The music thumps louder. Drinks get sloppier. Bodies press closer.

By last call, the whole street will be a writhing mess of drunk, horny, half-dressed heathens stumbling toward whatever bad choices will carry them into the morning.

I throw my arms up and spin.

Someone hands me a shot, and I toss it back, laughing. Liquid fire coats my throat, and heat spreads through my limbs. I move back into the center of the full, writhing dance floor. The crowd roars. A great undulating beast—pressing, pulling, moving as one.

I am everything and nothing, just sensation and sound and motion.

The bass from the club shakes the floor beneath my feet, vibrating up through my spine. *Toxic Love* comes on, SZA's voice dripping like honey, Kendrick's words slicing through me like a whip. The DJ mixes it with a dark, thrumming techno beat that turns my veins electric.

The pain in the lyrics doesn't just seep into my skin—it fucking burns.

It's in the way I move, in the roll of my hips, in the arch of my spine. My fingers dig into the air like I can pull something from it. Like I can rip myself open and let the music swallow me whole.

I feel Bane's fingerprints ghosting over me. The bruises he left on my hips, my waist, my thighs. I hear the heat in his voice as his voice breaks, demanding the truth from me.

Say it. Tell me you love me.

My body remembers. The way he pinned me against the door. Then the countertop. Oh god, the way he filled me. He held me together even as I shattered in his hands.

And I remember the way his eyes burned when I lied to him and broke us apart with my own two hands.

Tears stream down my cheeks as I fling my arms up to the music, to the ceiling, to whatever god wants to take me.

I am a dark, broken angel, cracked down the center, wings outstretched as I plummet.

Fly, fly away, dark angel.

The lights strobe too fast. The floor tilts under my feet.

I blink, and the neon signs smear across the walls like wet paint. The air is crackling and alive, making my skin prickle.

I press my hands to my temples. Oh shit. I know this feeling. I'm not right in the head. This happens sometimes. When I get pushed too far. Too far. Too far. Too far. I don't tell anyone. *Shhh. Don't tell don't tell.* They already think I'm crazy.

The crowd moves around me, liquid and distorted,

shifting in ways that don't make sense. A man brushes my arm, but when I turn to look, his face isn't right. His eyes are too dark, his mouth stretched wide in a grin that doesn't end.

The music warps and deepens, twisting into something hungry.

A woman in a red dress is dancing near the bar, except her feet aren't touching the ground. She's hovering. Her feet dangle inches off the floor, her arms limp at her sides. Her hair floats around her like she's underwater. Her head tilts too far, and her black, endless eyes find mine.

My breath stutters.

Her lips part, and even though the club is still pulsing with music, I hear her whisper like she's inside my head.

You can't run forever, Moira.

A maniacal giggle sounds right in my ear. *Inside* my ear. Inside my *head*.

The walls stretch. Breathing in. Breathing out.

Hands snag at my dress, fingers tangle in my hair. The air is heavy, pressing down, pushing me into the floor. The bass is inside me, rattling my ribs like they're going to crack apart.

I can't breathe.

I need out.

I push my way through the bodies, gasping, shoving, tripping over feet and knocking into strangers. I burst through the exit into the cool Texas night, hands on my knees, sucking in air like I just crawled out of a grave.

The city is still wild—still alive, still burning. But I am not.

I am unraveling. I am breaking.

I press my palms to my face, to my temples, squeezing.

BREATHE.

But the music is still inside me.

Bane is still inside me.

And I don't know how to get him out.

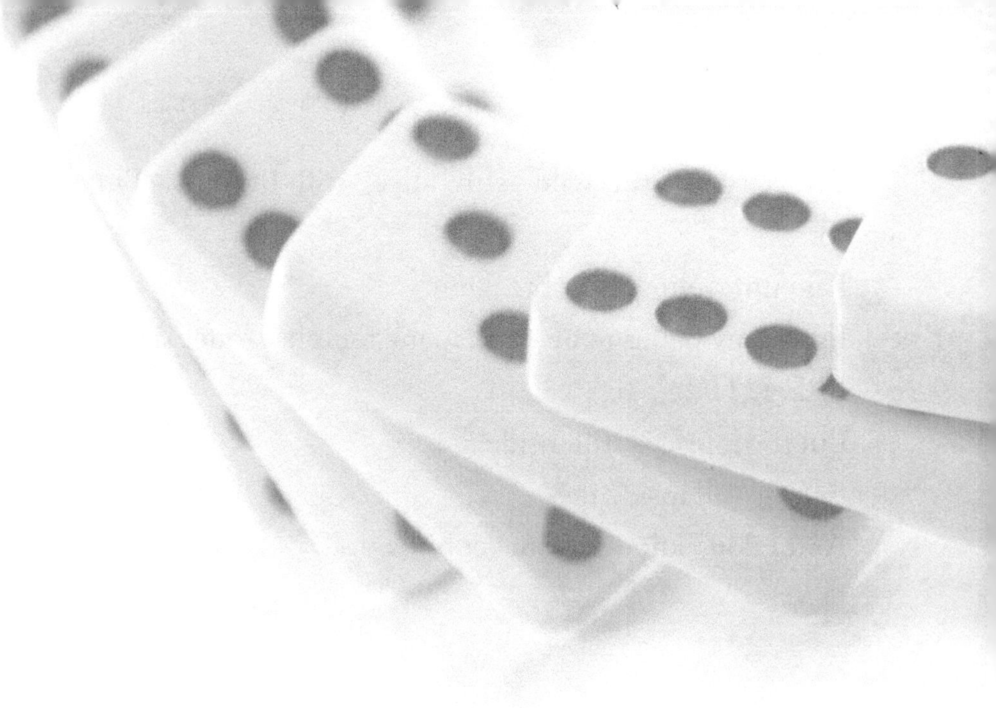

FIFTY-FOUR

BANE

I SPENT all night with my phone in hand, staring at it and waiting for Moira to text. I typed out a hundred messages to her.

Where are you?
Are you okay?
Just let me know where you are and that you're all right.
Moira, damn it, let me know you're okay.

But I deleted each one, letter by letter, hands dragging through my hair as the clock ticked onward—two a.m., three a.m., four.

I lie in bed, but I don't sleep. I can't imagine that sleep is something that's going to happen anymore. Not without her beside me. Not with this clawing, empty ache sitting inside my chest like something gaping and bottomless.

The sheets are ice-cold. My body is stiff, restless, clenched with the need to do something, *anything*, to chase away the ghost of her warmth. My stomach twists with hunger, but I don't eat. My throat is dry, but I don't drink. My body demands, but I refuse it. What's the point of anything if she's not here?

I haven't shared a bed with a woman for twenty-seven years, and suddenly, I can't imagine sleeping alone for the rest of my life. No one will ever replace Moira. No one ever could. She's a gemstone with a million unique facets, brilliant and dazzling and completely irreplaceable. The hole of her absence in my life is a wound that will never heal.

So I do what Quinn said.

I let myself feel it.

I let the grief swallow me whole. I wallow in it like a pig in mud.

Because at least in the pain that stretches my chest like a doctor's chest spreader, I can feel her presence.

She's there in the ache, in the absence, in the all-consuming devastation of losing her. She is the pain, and that's the only satisfaction I will get tonight.

But the salt on the open wound is the fucking *wondering*. The not knowing. She exists somewhere in the world, but God only knows where.

Is she sleeping peacefully right now? Is she missing me?

Or is she tucked up in some warm bed without me—in some other man's bed?

The thought sears through me like acid, burning a hole straight through my gut.

Or is she just back at her apartment, our time together meaning as little to her as all the men who came before me? Was I just another flavor to taste?

Or maybe—maybe she just needed time away from me.

You fucking egotistical, self-involved bastard.

I turn over in bed and punch the mattress, then do it again. Harder. Again. Until my knuckles sting and the ache in my hands is something solid. Something real. Something to ground me in this stupid goddamned night that won't ever fucking end.

I squeeze my eyes shut and try to sleep again. I try to block out the images of her in my mind. But she's everywhere—in every inch of this bed and every shift in the sheets. She is everywhere, but she's gone.

Oh fuck, she's fucking *gone*.

I shove my face into the mattress and howl in fury and rage and grief.

When the sky begins to lighten, I give up.

The night is done with me. Sleep never came.

I move to the shower, stripping off my clothes and stepping under the hot spray. The water scalds, but it doesn't cleanse. It doesn't burn away the phantom weight of her body against mine.

I scrub harder. Hard enough that my skin turns red. Hard enough that my muscles strain with the force of it. Hard enough that if I just keep going, maybe I can scrub the ache from my bones.

She's not here. I have to face it. And I can't show up to the prison today looking like a whiskey-soaked wreck.

I promised Caleb.

Wallowing isn't getting me anywhere. I don't think I even know how to sit in my pain right. I think Quinn intended some sort of meditation, some sort of quiet reckoning.

But I am not a man who sits still. I am not a man who finds peace in stillness.

Fuck sitting still. Fuck meditation.

Movement is the plan of the day.

Soon enough, I'm on the road to Waco, two hours away.

The drive should be a distraction. It should be something that pulls me out of my own head. Instead, it's just another reminder. I have to slap myself awake several times when my eyelids grow heavier and heavier as exhaustion sets in. Each slap is a punishment, a reminder—Moira should be here. She should be in the passenger seat, chattering away and filling the car with her endless energy.

I never thought I'd miss her chatter.

But my life is so fucking quiet without her.

Finally, I arrive at the prison.

It sits atop a hill, cold and imposing. I know the routine. I know what to expect. The sign-in process is smooth. It always is. I've done this for years.

Prison ministry is an ostentatious title for what I do. I don't lead Bible studies. I just offer volunteer chaplain services. I talk to guys one-on-one who want to talk. I just listen. Offer counsel if it's asked for.

These men are different from my usual congregation. They don't have the luxury of pretense. They don't get to hide behind status and wealth and reputations.

As much as I like to pretend I have any sort of control, I know it's all a lie. There's no rhyme or reason to the hand we're dealt in life. Some are born into privilege. Some are born into suffering. Some fight their way out. Some never get the chance.

It makes me furious. Furious at the structures and systems that push some down and elevate others. Furious at the world, furious at my father, furious at myself.

But anger is useless unless it transforms into action. So I do what little I can. I show up. I sit down. I shut up and listen.

"I'd like to talk to a particular inmate, Silas Graham, if he's up for a visit. Tell him that his son, Caleb, sent me."

I sit in the waiting room for a while, staring at the walls and letting the sterile quiet fill the hollow spaces in my chest.

Finally, they call my name and nod me through the system of locked doors and hallways.

I take my seat across from the thick glass, waiting.

A man appears on the other side. Grizzled, salt and pepper at his temples, dark eyes that are weary but sharp.

He picks up the phone.

So do I.

"Caleb sent you?" Silas asks, voice gravelly.

I nod. "Yes. He's been worried about you."

Silas snorts, shifting in his chair. "Well, then he could drag his ass down here and check in on me face to face, couldn't he?"

I tilt my head, meeting his steely gray eyes. "He feels guilty, and he's young."

Silas exhales heavily, running a hand through his thick, graying hair. "Yeah, I know. He's just a kid, still."

"I don't know. Twenty-six is hardly a kid," I say wryly, considering I'm only a year older.

Silas lets out a rough laugh. "The way that kid was raised... it was chaos. He didn't have a father until his mom and I hooked up."

I nod. "It's difficult growing up without a parent you need." I swallow down my own shit and try to focus on the man in front of me. "How are *you*?"

His mouth presses into a hard line. "Been doing hard time, going on a dime—ten years. That's a long time to be on the inside."

"That means you went through COVID in here."

He shakes his head, eyes darkening. "That was a shit-show. Place is understaffed as it is. Everyone all but went feral. Never seen so much death, and I was with the fucking Kings for a few years back in the day."

Shit. If he's talking about the Lone Star Kings, they're a legendary ruthless MC—mostly underground these days. When you hang out in prisons, you learn the local landscape. La Eme, Bandidos, not to mention the warring cartels active in Texas.

I do a pretty good poker face even though I now realize that Caleb's father is a man seriously not to be fucked with. "How have you handled things? Do they have a counselor in there for anyone to talk to?"

He barks out a laugh. "Mental health? What's that?"

I nod, understanding. "I know short-staffed is an understatement for most prisons." Seventy-five percent staffed is a good day for most facilities in Texas. Some are as bad as fifty-five percent.

Silas straightens, muscles stretching the fabric of his faded orange jumpsuit. The man is built like a fucking tank. "I keep things in line on my block."

I bet he does.

"Is there a message you wanted me to pass along to Caleb?" I ask.

"I told him not to visit when I first went away, and," he sighs, dragging a hand through his thick hair, "that's still probably for the fuckin' best. But at my last parole hearing, there was some talk about letting me out early." His eyes snap to mine. "But don't tell Caleb that."

I raise a brow. "But that's good news. How soon—?"

He shifts, his gaze sliding away, like even saying it out loud might jinx it. "Six months."

"Six months? That's great."

He shrugs. "Won't believe it's real 'til I'm walking out those doors. Sunshine on my face."

I nod. Understandable for a man who's been on the inside so long. "Is there anything I can get you? Anything you need?"

He shakes his head. "Caleb supplies me with a good stipend each month so I can get the things I need... and the things I need to trade."

I get it. Prisons have their own internal economy, and Silas has no doubt learned it well after so many years inside.

"That all?" he asks roughly.

I relay Caleb's message—his love and support. "Do you have any messages you want me to give Caleb? Or anyone else?"

"Don't tell him about the possible parole," he reminds me again. It sounds like a warning.

I hold up my hands. "My lips are sealed. I'm a priest, after all. If you can't trust me, who the hell can you trust?"

He nods. "All right, priest. Yeah, there is someone I'd like you to reach out to for me. She changed her number, and I haven't been able to get ahold of her."

"A sweetheart?"

His eyes narrow. "No. My daughter."

His daughter?

Caleb never mentioned a sister. Or stepsister, I suppose, if she's Silas's natural-born daughter.

"She kept in contact for a few years, but... then we had a falling out, you could say."

"You want to talk about it?" I offer.

"No." His eyes are like flint.

The entire man is hardened—cut muscle and sharp edges. A survivor.

"But now that I'm about to get out... potentially," he adds quickly, "it might be time to try to reconnect."

He gives me her name, and I take it down on my phone.

"Where did she live when you were last in contact?"

"Austin. But she was talking about moving out west." His eyes go distant. "California. She always said she wanted to see a real ocean. One that was blue instead of brown like the Gulf. So maybe she made it out there, finally."

His voice gets gruff again when he says, "Don't mention this to Caleb, either. They used to be close, but... I don't know now."

He looks away again, settling back in his chair with his arms crossed over his chest. His muscles bulge, making clear again that he's one intimidating motherfucker. And that the subject is done.

"I'll see what I can do about contacting her," I say.

He nods, then studies me long and hard. "If I do get out of here..." He hesitates, uncomfortable. "They have halfway houses for fuckers like me, but it's better if family gives you a place to land. The parole officers prefer that kind of shit."

I nod. "From everything I've seen of Caleb, I think he'd be more than happy to accommodate."

"Well, since I still own the club, I'd fuckin' think so."

I blink. "Wait—you own the club?"

He nods. "Half, anyway. Caleb inherited the other half when his mama passed. Whole thing was a clusterfuck."

Considering he's in prison orange, across an impenetrable barrier of glass, I'd say whatever happened back then was.

The guard calls his name, and he stands.

But I say quickly into the receiver, "Silas."

He pulls the phone back to his ear.

"I'll do my best to find your daughter. And you're going to get out of here." I meet his gaze. "I'll come back and visit you."

He nods, but he doesn't let any emotion show before he hangs up the phone.

FIFTY-FIVE

MOIRA

THE PHONE RINGS on the other end as I hold the old-school handle of the receiver up to my ear. Like they have in movies. A strange, almost haunting sound echoes in my ear. I never call people. I text. But here I am, swallowing around the desert-dry ache in my throat, listening to that dull, repetitive tone.

Waiting.

The Travis County Jail is too bright. Fluorescent lights buzz above me, flickering faintly, casting the gray walls in a sickly, bluish hue. The linoleum floor beneath my pinched toes is sticky despite the overpowering scent of industrial cleaner that clings to every inch of this place. A bulletin board to my left is crammed with outdated flyers—bail bond advertisements, victim advocacy pamphlets, something about "finding Jesus."

The acrid scent of stale sweat and regret lingers in the air, thick as the exhaustion that presses into my bones.

I'm just about to give up when the line clicks.

"Hello?" Kira's voice on the other end is groggy. Confused.

I blink, my brain lagging behind my body like it's buffering.

"Moira," I croak, then clear my throat. Try again. "It's Moira."

Silence. Then—

"Jesus. Moira? Bane was looking for you at the club a couple nights ago. Are you okay?"

My stomach clenches, and I squeeze my eyes shut, pressing my forehead into the cool metal receiver. *Bane*. He was looking for me.

But now—

I swallow the ache clawing its way up my throat and try to ignore the glaring officer looming over me, arms crossed over his Kevlar vest. His badge catches the light, and he taps his watch impatiently, spinning his finger like I need to wrap this up.

"Not so much," I say, my voice hoarse. "I had a bad night. Can you come pick me up?"

A pause. Then, softer, "Where are you?"

I close my eyes, pressing my fingertips to my temples. My head pounds.

"They impounded my car," I admit. "Well, Dohmn's car."

"Moira." Her voice sharpens. "Where *are* you?"

I exhale through my nose. "Austin. Travis County Jail, to be exact."

A beat of silence. Then—

"Oh my god, Moira. What the hell happened?"

A muscle in my jaw twitches. I glance up at the officer, who's now all but tapping his foot.

"Nothing exciting," I mutter. "Just... I might have mistaken a mounted cop's horse for a unicorn. And then, uh, tried to ride her off into the sunset."

My eyes flick to the dull gray walls and the rows of empty plastic chairs in the waiting area beyond the payphone. A vending machine hums in the corner, blinking a red 'OUT OF ORDER' sign.

I hate gray.

I stare down at my scuffed Mary Janes. "Turns out she wasn't a unicorn. And I wasn't exactly sober."

I don't mention the part where I'm pretty sure someone dosed my drink with Special K at some point in the night.

Like, yeah, things can get shimmery when I get that bouncy manic shine, and sometimes I think I'm a re-incarnated oracle from an ancient, alien civilization, seeing everything at once but forgetting it at the same time in some terrible form of karmic punishment.

But last night went *extra dextra*, and it's just a whole disjointed mess of colors and laughter and then—cold, gray walls.

Did I mention I hate gray? There are just *so* many other colors to choose from.

"Moira," she sighs. "I'll be there soon. Give me a few hours, okay?"

"Yeah." I drop my head back. "Thanks, Kira."

I hang up before my throat can close up again.

Officer McGrouchy-Pants jerks his chin, ushering me back to the cell where my new, temporary family is waiting.

I smile and wave at Big Mama, the plus-size sex worker who cradled me in her lap last night like a drunk little baby bird. She blows me a kiss as she's led out for her own phone call, and I mime catching it. Damn, she's a good cuddler.

Making friends wherever I go is one of my few talents.

If only I could keep them.

I sink down onto the cold bench, pressing the heels of my hands into my burning eyes. My head is still foggy, but fragments of last night flicker through the haze. The unicorn. The way the world glowed—the streetlights haloed, the laughter like wind chimes. The officer's stunned face as I vaulted onto his horse—

Backward.

Her tail was so pretty, though.

I huff out a soundless laugh, but it fades fast. Because when I woke up this morning—

No unicorn. No magic.

No Bane.

Just cement walls, iron bars, and the yawning, endless ache where he used to be.

I slump against the wall, exhaustion sinking into my bones. Man, I'd give my left arm for a Barcalounger. Hell, even one of those crusty office chairs with lumbar support.

I must doze off at some point because the next thing I know—

CLANG.

A flashlight slams against the bars.

"Moira Callaghan," a female officer calls.

I jerk upright, my stomach pitching. My head is still a fucking mess, and my shoes—god, why was I wearing these tight-ass pinchy Mary Janes when those fucking assholes decided to kidnap me?

Pushing to my feet, I swallow against the nausea. Then I clench my fists, nails digging into my palms as I follow the officer out.

A grim-faced worker hands me my belongings in a sad little plastic bag.

Domhnall's credit card.

My key fob—to a car I currently don't have.

A half-empty pack of cinnamon gum.

A ponytail holder.

Don't remember where I acquired those last two from but

shrug and pop a piece of gum in my mouth. Cinnamon. My favorite.

Then, with all the grace and dignity of someone definitely *not* arrested for public intoxication and unauthorized unicorn theft—

I skip out of the jail.

It's tradition.

For luck.

What can I say? I've had a few drunk and disorderlies in my day. A handful of indecent exposures.

But FOMO?

Yeah. That's never been my problem.

Kira is waiting when I get outside, leaning against her car like some kind of sleek, put-together goddess of competence and emotional stability. Unlike Dom, she's not here to give me the world's most disappointing TED Talk about my life choices. She just smiles and pulls me into a hug so big and warm that I half expect her to absorb me like an amoeba of goodwill and expensive perfume.

"I'm so glad to see you're okay."

Tentatively, I smile back. "Thanks," I say, voice quiet, but my body already betrays me by sinking into her hold like an exhausted cat.

She gestures toward the car, but before she can get inside, I remember Domhnall's car and launch into an explanation about how we have to go break it out of car jail. Kira just waves me off.

"Isaak can send one of his guys to do it later in the week. Domhnall's got, like, five cars, right? He's not going to miss it."

I stare at her. Then, before she can dodge, I give her another hug, squeezing the stuffing out of her.

"You beautiful, competent, problem-solving genius!" I announce, squeezing tighter. "If you were a cake, I'd stuff my face with you."

She laughs, but it's the indulgent kind like she's used to dealing with me at full volume.

She lets me hold on for far longer than socially acceptable, her arms tightening around me at just the right moment before finally pulling back.

"I'm so sorry you had a bad night, Moira."

I swallow hard. My throat's gone tight, and I hate it. I hate how easily she gets past my defenses. How she doesn't even have to try.

When we let go, she holds onto my forearms, pinning me down with one of those therapist looks I can already tell are her secret weapon.

"You know, over the phone, you asked me for help. I'm happy for that help to extend as far as this car ride, but I can also connect you with people who could do more than that. We could get you *actual* help."

Every muscle in my body goes rigid. "I'm not going back to one of those fucking… uh, places."

"No, no," she says quickly, shaking her head. "Nothing

like that. Just a therapist. Everybody does therapy these days. It doesn't have to mean anything."

I squint at her, suspicious. "Everybody? Even serial killers? Even billionaires? Even... Batman?"

"Probably Batman needs it the most."

I consider this, then squeeze her forearms back. "I'll do it if the therapist is *you*. You just started your practice, right?"

She blinks, clearly caught off guard. "Well... there are some ethical considerations. I can't take on close friends as clients."

"Perfect. We're not close friends yet. I just met you."

"Thanks. Love your bluntness."

Her eyes flick up and to the left, obviously thinking. I hold my breath without meaning to, already bracing for rejection, for the gentle letdown—

"I can't be your therapist, per se," she says, finally, "but there is some wiggle room if we consider me a life coach."

I exhale. "Fucking perfect. I like the sound of that way better, anyway. Life coach me, babe."

"I'm happy to help you get on the right track."

Then her expression softens, turning serious. "But part of that track might be..." She hesitates again. "As your friend, I can't ethically diagnose you, but have you noticed certain... um... ups and downs in your moods?"

The Texas heat beats down on us, but her words make my skin go cold. A bead of sweat slides down my spine. Fuck.

"You noticed." I swallow hard.

I try so hard for no one to ever notice.

"Well, *yeah*," she says with maximum side-eye energy.

My mouth drops open.

"Fuck, does everyone know?"

"I mean, I think most people have noticed something. Did you think it was a secret?"

I scrub my hands down my face, groaning. "Well, that's just fucking fantastic. Might as well put it on a billboard. 'Welcome to Dallas, home of the Cowboys, the best barbecue, and Moira's Fucking Unstable Brain Chemistry.'"

"Moira..."

"No, no, it's fine. I love being predictable. It's my favorite."

Kira sighs. "You want to get in the car and talk about it on the way home?"

"Maybe," I whine.

She grins. "You can do this, Moira. You're the strongest person I know."

The only other person to ever tell me that was—*Bane*. I swallow hard against the grief that makes me want to crumple to the ground at even thinking his name, then blink at her. "Yeah?"

"Yeah," she says. Then she tips her head slightly back and forth. "Well, it's a toss-up between you and MadAnna." She holds her hands up. "She told me to call her that."

I give the window of her car a couple of raps before heading to the passenger seat.

"Fair," I call back as I point over the car at her. "Very fair."

FIFTY-SIX

Two Weeks Later

BANE

THE PHONE RINGS again and again. I ignore it.

It's only Rotterdam, my father's lawyer. I've been ignoring his calls and texts all week, just like I've been ignoring the letter that landed in my mailbox last week from my father. He's the last fucking person I want to deal with right now. The man doesn't understand the concept of going no contact.

So I continue to stonewall him. If you give an inch, he'll

take a mile. He'll take a hundred miles. And try to drag me back into his orbit, where love is a transaction. No, thank you.

I block Rotterdam's number. He keeps calling from different ones within the firm, and I keep blocking them as soon as they come in.

I'm trying to focus on this week's sermon, and the constant interruptions are a fucking annoyance. My modus operandi for the past two weeks has been to bury myself in work. I've spent more days doing prison visits and checked back with Silas. Took communion to parish members who were too elderly and ill to make it into service and let them chat my ear off all afternoon.

Anything to fill the time so the clawing chasm of grief at her absence is numbed. Besides my self-destructive vices, that is. Which I've avoided every day except last Sunday after service when I gave in and drank an entire bottle of Glenlivet Twenty-five and spent the night violently vomiting and regretting my entire life.

Since then, it's been strictly a course of filling my time with work and avoiding being alone. Except for the endless nights that I can't escape. When I'm lucky, I manage a few hours of restless sleep, tossing and turning as my subconscious tortures me with memories of her in my arms—her happy laughter, her kinky quirks, her fingers in my hair, nails digging into my scalp—

I slam my pen down on the desk, about to go for a punishing jog, the other activity I've taken up to fill any hours not consumed by work. But my phone buzzes again—another text from an unknown number. I pick it up, ready to stab the block button.

My eyes dance across the quick four-word message.

> Unknown: Your father is dying.

That stops me in my tracks and has me sitting back down heavily in my chair.

Dying? Mad Blackwood?

A strange sensation bites at my ribs, something tangled and messy I can't name. The old man was always larger than life, a force of nature in a bespoke suit. He can't just die. He wouldn't.

I glare down at the phone. Is this just a ploy? I wouldn't put it past my father to demand my attention with a lie.

After a sharp exhale, I punch my finger against the number to call it.

Rotterdam immediately picks up.

"Bane! Thank God you finally picked up."

"Is it true?" I bark. "Is the old bastard actually dying?"

"Yes," comes the immediate response. "That's why we've been trying to reach you. He wants to see you. He doesn't have much time left." He's speaking rapidly as if to get the main points across quickly in case I hang up on him.

I'm still trying to process the concept of my father, a bull of a man his entire life, being *sick*, much less dying.

"What the fuck happened? He's only sixty-three, and

God knows he can afford the best doctors money can provide."

"It's a hell of a thing," Rotterdam sighs, sounding exhausted. Considering how much my father leans on him, I can only imagine. My father is notoriously cruel to anyone he considers an underling, but Rotterdam has stayed longer than any of the others. I know it's only for the money, not out of any love for my father.

He gives me the name of the disease, and I only register that it's something other than cancer. I scribble it down haphazardly. "The doctor only gave him a few months to live."

My hand clenches on the phone. A few *months*?

I swallow hard, my jaw tightening. I hate the man, but hating him has given me structure and defined a large portion of my life. And now he's just going to die? Just slip away, without giving me a proper target to throw my rage at?

My breathing gets shorter.

"Where is he? What hospital?"

I open my laptop and start pulling up airlines to get a ticket back to London.

"He's there. In America."

I pause, frozen. "Here?"

"They were trying some experimental treatments. He participated in a clinical trial at a research hospital in London, and now he's in San Francisco. But between you and me, he's desperate, and nothing is working to stop or slow the progression of the disease."

I pause. "Is it hereditary?"

"No. Their best guess is that he got it either from something he ate or from a contaminated implement during one of the experimental cosmetic surgeries he's gotten during one of his trips abroad during the last six months."

I shake my head. The old man was always so goddamn vain.

Fuck. This is so much information all at once.

"I'll get on a plane to San Francisco."

Rotterdam sighs in relief. "That would be great. The disease affects his cognitive function. You're all he can talk about. But he's starting to lose it."

I swallow hard and nod—not that Rotterdam can see it.

"Got it."

I get the rest of the details and hang up. Then sit there long after the phone call, even though I know I need to be making arrangements. At least I've been practicing grief lately, though I don't know if grief is exactly what I'll be feeling after my father passes.

Maybe it will feel more like relief.

Maybe I'll feel sad.

Maybe I'll feel nothing at all.

I can't name the emotions I'm feeling right now. There's just a lead weight in my chest and a clench in my belly, wishing Moira was here, wishing I could hold her and bury my head against her stomach—her fingers in my hair, her whisper in my ear, telling me that everything was going to be okay.

By nightfall, I'm landing in SFO and catching an Uber to the hospital. I'm exhausted after two weeks of barely getting any sleep. My body is running on fumes. This feels like a dream. Or a nightmare.

I'm still not sure this isn't all just a hoax—another manipulation to get me where he wants me.

He's done worse. Far worse. To his employees. To his wives. To his children. I've seen firsthand the wreckage he leaves behind. He grinds people to dust beneath his polished shoes. If it were any other situation than him dying, I'd be far more wary. His gaze has landed on me once more, and when Mad Blackwood sets his sights on someone, it never ends well.

It's chillier than I expected. A damp, coastal cold that seeps through my clothes and my skin and settles in my bones. I shove my hands into the pockets of my jacket as I walk through the endless, gleaming-white hallways of the premier hospital wing where my father, no doubt, spared no expense to be housed.

Money can buy a lot of things. But it can't buy time.

Or redemption.

"Bane!" Rotterdam sits in a chair outside the room, his laptop perched precariously on his knees. He looks up at my approach, and a wave of relief washes over his exhausted face.

He slaps the laptop closed and tucks it under his arm as he stands to shake my hand.

"You don't know how glad I am to see you."

I eye him warily, giving only a grunt. "Is he awake?" I look toward the door.

Because of the time difference between Texas and California, it's only seven at night, but I have no idea what I'm about to walk into.

Rotterdam nods. "He told me to send you in as soon as you got here. When I checked on him a half hour ago, he was *very* eager to see you."

I nod. No point in avoiding the inevitable.

I knock on the door once and then push inside.

I freeze.

Holy shit.

Rotterdam wasn't lying.

My father looks... already half-dead. His skin is parchment-thin, stretched too tight over sharp bones, veins dark and bulging beneath the surface like cracks in marble. His once-imposing frame has collapsed in on itself, his body devoured by this disease until all that remains is a ghost of the man who once ruled with an iron fist.

I've seen death before. Up close. I've prayed over men whose bodies were already cooling and given last rites to people who had nothing left but regret and time slipping through their fingers.

But nothing prepared me for this.

Nothing prepared me for seeing the monster diminished.

"Well? What are you doing just standing out there glaring at me from the doorway?" he barks, his voice low and rough, but the weakness is there. The frayed edges of it. The decay.

I realize I'm being rude, gaping at him like this. I force myself to step across the room, closer to his bed.

I'm supposed to be playing the role of dutiful son. But it's a role I've never played before.

A good son—someone who has taken an oath to serve others—should bow their head and offer grace, even to a vile man in his last hours.

I've spoken to criminals with life sentences, offering them counsel and a listening ear.

But my father?

Why, God?

Why one test after another of my faith?

First, you took Moira. And now you ask me to forgive this man?

My fists clench at my sides. I swallow hard, still unable to look him in the eyes, my gaze landing somewhere in the landscape of his sunken chest.

He's dying.

The words echo in my head, but they don't feel real.

This is Mad Blackwood. The man who made himself king. The man who controlled every room he walked into and every person in his orbit. A man who bent the world to his will because he could.

And now he is frail. Mortal. *Small*.

For years, he was the shadow looming over me, and now...

Now he's just another dying man.

I tell myself I should feel relief. I tell myself that this is justice.

But I don't know what I feel.

I don't know what I'm *supposed* to feel.

His tired eyes finally look my way again, the only acknowledgment that I've entered the room.

"Your mother was the only one of all those bitches who wasn't grubbing after my money," he says, voice rasping like dry leaves against the pavement. "That's why I married her. That makes you the only one of my children who's not a bastard. Which means"—he hacks out a rough cough—"you're my only true heir."

I close my eyes.

Of course.

Of course, even now, he can't stop playing God.

"If this fucking thing gets me," his fists clench weakly, and he slams them against the mattress in an exhausted fury, "it'll be up to *you* to take on the mantle—to marry and produce sons who will continue the name. I've had Rotterdam compile a list of women from acceptable families who'll produce good stock to continue our legacy."

My stomach turns.

He didn't want to see me for some last-gasp father-son reconciliation.

Of course not.

Even now, it's about power.

Even now, it's about control.

Even now, I am not his son. I'm an asset. A pawn. Just a thing to be wielded as an extension of himself, even after death.

The realization settles in me like lead.

I should have known better.

But somewhere, buried deep beneath all the fury, all the scars, all the years of distance—I wanted to believe.

Just for a moment, I wanted to believe.

And that's the worst part of all.

"Would you like to pray, Father?" I ask, voice hollow.

He sneers, his lips twisting. "Did you listen to a thing I just said? I'm giving you instructions, boy. Listen!"

I nod once. "I heard you. But you're also in this bed, and it might be one of the last times you and I ever speak."

His glazed gaze sharpens for just a moment. "I'll see you married and bedded to one of the women I've chosen for you before I leave this damned earth."

I shake my head slowly, exhaling. "You? How are you going to manage that from this bed?"

He tries to lift himself onto his elbows but falls back from weakness. Still, his eyes are ice cold.

"I have my means. I'm not dead yet. I'm the most powerful man in the world."

I let out a slow breath, forcing down the rage crawling up my throat. He's always been like this. Clutching at control like it's the only thing keeping him alive. Maybe it is.

"You'll have to get an annulment from that little slut you ran to Vegas with, of course," he sneers. "But that's mostly taken care of. I'm the most powerful man in the world," he repeats, full of impotent rage. "Don't you know who I am?"

My breath stills in my chest. Because my attention is still frozen on the first part of his maniacal little rant.

"What do you know about Moira?"

I stand, towering over the deranged old man with his lingering delusions of power.

And then I remember the fear and confusion in Moira's eyes as she left me that day. The way her hands trembled when she packed her bags. The way she wouldn't—couldn't—look me in the eye. And the fact that this fucker already tried to pay her off once to leave me.

Realization crashes into me, painful as needles spiking into my skin all over my body. Why haven't I kept my eyes on him? I should have known he wouldn't stop. I just saw no reason for him to press the issue. I didn't realize that suddenly there was a deadline.

It's all so clear now.

She didn't want to leave me.

She *had* to.

Because of him.

Something inside me breaks. A tether snapping loose, untamed rage surging up like a tidal wave. My hands are on him before I can stop myself, shaking his frail body like I can rattle the truth out of him.

"What the fuck did you do?"

His eyes shift slightly sideways, unfocused. And then he starts moaning.

"Sarah... Sarah, I didn't mean it... You were my best bitch. Sarah, come back... Don't leave me alone... You're the only one who ever loved me... Sarah, listen..."

His arm reaches out to the side, grasping at nothing. At the phantom of my mother. As if she'd waste her afterlife haunting him.

My stomach twists. He isn't here anymore. Not really. He's back in whatever hell he crawled out of. But he can relive his past sins and cling to the ghosts of the women he broke another time.

"Hey!" I cry, shaking him again. "Don't fade on me now, you fucker. What did you do to Moira?"

He finally looks back at me, his eyes widening in confusion.

"Who are you?" he asks.

Something dark and rotten unfurls inside me.

This is the first time in my entire life my father has ever looked at me and not seen a piece of himself. His possession. His legacy. His puppet. He sees nothing. And somehow, it's so satisfying even as it cuts deeper than anything he's ever done.

He starts flailing, reaching for the call button.

"Help! I'm being attacked! Who let this man in here? I should have the best security! Do you know who I am? I'm the richest man in the world! I'll get all of you fired!"

I step back, staring at the crumbling ruin of the man who spent his entire life trying to play God.

Frightened. Frail.

I did some research on the disease on my way here. Cognitive decline—rapid, unforgiving—often happens when the disease is acquired externally, the way my father did.

But the bastard stayed lucid just long enough to destroy the only thing that ever mattered to me. Just long enough to make sure I'd suffer.

I step forward again, leaning down until I can whisper right in his ear.

"I hope you die a slow, painful death. Terrified and alone, like the little boy you made me my entire life, you sick fuck."

His breath hitches.

His lips tremble.

And then I turn my back on him while he continues to shout pathetically, his voice already cracking apart under the weight of his own decay.

FIFTY-SEVEN

March, Six Weeks Later

MOIRA

FUCKING DRUGS, man. And not the fun kind, either. I've been taking the kind a doctor prescribes for the last two months, and they're total ass. This is what I get for letting Kira talk me into seeing her psychiatrist friend. I mean, at least they had something more novel to call me than sex addict.

Bipolar is my new shiny diagnosis, and the head doctor was sure he could get me all sparkly and new by swallowing these pills more and more every two weeks until I was at optimal dosage. Well, I finally reached the magical dose last week.

I thud my forehead against Kira and Isaak's kitchen window in a slow, repetitive motion until Kira comes back in and catches me doing it.

"Moira! What are you doing?"

"Nothing." I let the side of my face smoosh into the cool glass of the window. "All I ever do is nothing." Then I roll my eyes. "And no, before you ask, I don't feel like harming myself or others today."

That's everybody's favorite question.

She puts her hands on her hips, which is especially effective because of her cute, round belly bump.

"I see you didn't quite make it up from the breakfast table, but look, you ate!"

I slither like a slug from the glass onto the table, my body completely flat.

This is all I can seem to manage to do lately—slug from one place to another.

I don't think it's the meds, necessarily. Just... the sad face part of sad face me.

"Mama, help me to the couch," I whine, wiggling my hands at Kira.

She sighs. "Well, at least I'm getting some training for when I have a baby around."

I cry dramatically, but she stays where she's standing, arms on her hips.

"What if I told you Bane was asking around about you again at the club last night?"

I pull my arms in and bury my head in them.

"Doesn't matter," I grumble into my sleeves, face still hidden.

"Oh yeah?" she challenges. "Even if he told Isaak to give you a message?"

I shake my head, mumbling into my arms again. "I don't want to hear it."

It's too painful.

My chest squeezes in on itself because what I just said is a lie. Of course, I want to hear it.

The fact that he's still thinking about me—even after all this time, even after I broke his heart—makes my stomach twist.

But then I think, *You didn't break his heart, you ninny. Yeah, he married you, but that was just because he had to. That's probably what his message is—just letting you know he found some way to let you off the hook or got the marriage annulled.*

"He said to tell you that his father is dead."

I spring fully upright in my chair for the first time in weeks, blinking up at her.

"Mad Blackwolf is dead?"

Kira's mouth drops open. "Bane's father is Mad Blackwolf?" Her eyes go round. "Wow. I had heard that he passed."

"What did he die of?" is my immediate follow-up question.

She waves a hand. "It was all hush-hush with the media at first, but apparently, he picked up some wasting disease from his travels. It took him out in just a few months. There was nothing they could do."

"And... he just died?" I ask again, still unable to fully wrap my head around it. "Where's my phone?"

Kira glances down at me, eyebrows raising. "Are you going to call Bane?"

"I need to call Domhn."

Kira suddenly bites her fingernail.

"What?" I ask suspiciously.

"Nothing."

She jerks her hand down, but I catch the hesitation.

"It's just... we've all been worried about you. You've been in kind of a fragile state."

"What the fuck does that mean?" I snap. "I'm fine."

I stand up.

Oily curls fall into my face, reminding me that I haven't exactly been the best at showering lately. I push them back and tie them at the base of my neck with the ponytail holder that's always around my wrist.

"Why? What's up? What's going on?"

"Well..." Kira hesitates. "You know how MadAnna wasn't at my baby shower? Oh, wait—neither were you. Anyway. Apparently, she's taking another "leave of absence" for her mental health," Kira continues. "That's what Domhn's been calling it, anyway."

"What?!" I shriek. "And you're only just telling me this now? Where's my phone?!"

"I think you left it by the couch."

I scurry over, my limbs feeling only slightly less heavy at the unusually quick movement. Depression is a bitch when she gets her claws into you.

Immediately, I dial my brother's number.

"Moira?" Domhn answers, surprised. "Hey."

His voice gets all gentle and weird—which is never a good sign.

"How's everything going?"

"Where's MadAnna?" I cut to the chase.

He sighs, and I can just imagine him dragging his hand down his face.

"Uh... she said she had to go take care of some things."

"When?!" I all but shout into the phone. "How long ago?"

He sighs heavily, and that tells me I'm not going to like what he says next.

"Ever since she and you..." He doesn't finish the statement.

"But she came back, right? After we got kidnapped, she came back home. We've had a few video calls..."

And then it lands.

Oh, shit.

"Domhn, is she on the run because of what I did?"

"You didn't do anything, Moira," he says firmly. "You fell in love with a good guy who just happened to have a psychotic father. It's nothing you or anyone else could have controlled."

"But—"

"She says there are some things she needs to clear up from her past before she can come home and we can get our happily ever after."

"Fuck, Domhn!" I cry. "Oh my God, I fucked everything up again!"

"No, you didn't," his voice is stern. "I know you love to take the whole world on your shoulders, sis, but this one has nothing to do with you. She's running from people she pissed off in a former life. She doesn't feel like she can ever be safe until she deals with them."

"Then we have to help her," I say immediately.

He chuckles low.

"Don't you think it's killing me that she won't let me?"

Right. Of course, it is.

If there's one thing my big brother lives for, it's to be the big, burly savior.

No wonder she never went home. He would've locked her up in a golden cage—probably in whatever new dungeon he installed in their new place.

It only hits me now that he's actually talking to me—really *talking*. Like we used to. Like he doesn't hate me anymore. Do I really have my big brother back?

"She knows what she's doing," I whisper, trying to believe it—as much for my sake as for his. I want to be here for him in the way I know I wasn't before. I'm not going to be the little sister who takes him for granted anymore.

"Yes, she does," he says thickly. "But I barely survived her being gone last time when she was safe and under my security."

"Oh, Domhn... Is there anything I can do?"

"It's been hell being out of contact with both of you," he admits. "Kira said you needed some quiet while you got better."

"I'm better," I say, sitting up straighter. "Bitch finally got me on meds. Can you believe that? So I'm all good now. Swearsies."

Kira eyes me from the other side of the room, lips pursed, face telling me I'm full of shit. Yeah, yeah, I know it can take like months and months for shit to regulate and start to actually feel... right.

"Has he heard about Bane's father?" she calls, reminding me why I reached out in the first place.

"Oh, yeah," I say distractedly. "Kira says Bane's dad is dead. Is it true?"

Domhn sighs. "I've been working on confirming it all morning. Just got intel from inside the hospital—it's true. He died three weeks ago. Asphyxiated in his own fluids."

Holy shit.

"So does that mean..." I hesitate, my heart plummeting through the soles of my feet.

"Yes," he answers for me. "Barring any end-of-life retribution, which I'll make sure is seen to... nothing is standing between you and Bane anymore."

"I—I—" I stammer. "Domhn, it's really so good to talk to you again. And I wanna talk all morning, really, but I—"

"You've got somebody else to call," Domhn interrupts. Then softer, "And, sis?"

"Yeah?"

"Maybe drop by sometime."

My whole chest fills with happiness at the request. "Absolutely."

As soon as we hang up, I immediately dial Bane's number—which I deleted from my phone after memorizing it—but then I freeze, thumb hovering over the green call button.

What the hell am I going to say?

Hey, saw your dad's dead. Will you take me back now after I crushed your heart and stomped it to pieces? So sorry about that. Plus, I'm all whacked out on meds now, I know, what a prize!

I slump in my chair and delete each number, digit by digit, staring listlessly out the window.

Later, when Kira and Isaak are back in the baby's bedroom attempting to put the kid's baby furniture together, the doorbell rings, and my stomach doesn't drop or twist or clench or do any of the dramatic bullshit it used to.

Well, yeah, 'cause I'm expecting it. I ordered a pizza. But I also like to think it means that as much as the meds suck, maybe they're starting to work. I have to admit; I have been feeling a touch less wanna-crawl-out-of-my-own-skin lately.

I stretch, yawn, and shake out my hands as I push off the couch. My tea sits cold and forgotten on the coffee table, a half-hearted attempt at self-care that never quite sticks.

Whatever. Pizza is better.

The bell rings again, sharp and insistent. Jesus, impatient much? I'm already halfway to the door, tugging my hoodie straight and reaching for my wallet.

I yank it open with a breezy, "Yeah, yeah, keep your pants on—"

And then I freeze.

Because it's not a delivery guy standing on Kira's porch.

It's Bane Blackwolf.

My ruin. My obsession.

My *husband*.

My stomach does *drop* then, so fast I feel like I'm plummeting off a cliff, wind rushing past my ears, heart slamming against my ribs.

He's so goddamn gorgeous in a black suit, hands in his pockets, looking so sharp he could slice right through me. Like he's been waiting for this moment. Like he *planned* this moment.

The world tilts, and I grip the doorframe.

I wasn't ready.

I *thought* I was. I thought the pills and the therapy and the trying would make me immune to this.

But no. No, because my body is already betraying me—heart racing, breath catching, fingers twitching with the memory of what it feels like to touch him.

"Moira."

His voice is a slow drag of gravel and heat, and it wrecks me.

I wet my lips and force a smile that doesn't fit. "Bane."

His eyes darken. He expected something else. Sharp words. A flirty jab. The old Moira, crackling and unhinged. But she's gone. Or caged. Or sleeping.

Or maybe she's still here, pressing up against the bars, waiting for him to get close enough to sink her teeth into.

"What the fuck are you doing here?" My voice is hoarse.

His lips press together, a flicker of something unreadable crossing his face. Then he exhales, slow and steady, and says, "You're coming with me."

I laugh. Short, brittle. "Yeah? And why's that?"

"You're tangled up in my inheritance." His gaze never wavers. "As my wife, you have to come to England."

There's a sharp crack inside my skull. Like something snapping back into place.

As my wife. As if it's something real and not just a thing I dreamed up that one time.

As if it's binding.

My pulse skitters. I scrape a hand through my hair, fingers catching in the knotted curls. "You're shitting me."

"No."

"Christ." I squeeze my eyes shut and press the heels of my palms against my temples. "Did you *make* this happen?"

Silence.

He's just *watching* me, that quiet, steady, terrifying way he does.

Oh my god, that was just a shot in the dark, but he *did*, didn't he?

"You fucker." It comes out on a breath, a laugh, a goddamn whimper.

He steps closer. Just a fraction. Just enough to make the space between us feel like a living thing, thick and hungry. "Pack a bag."

My stomach clenches. "And if I say no?"

A ghost of a smirk flickers across his lips. *There* he is. The man who owns me. The man who *knows* me. "You won't."

I let out a sharp, shaky breath. Because he's right. Because I never say no to him. Because I don't *know* how to.

But I don't want to.

"Fine. But if you think for one second I'm just gonna fall in line—"

"I would never." His voice is too smooth. Too certain. "I *know* you're going to fight me the whole way."

His lips twitch. Like he's *looking forward to it*.

And God help me, I think I might be, too.

FIFTY-EIGHT

BANE

SHE'S QUIET. Too quiet.

I expected claws. Teeth. That vicious mouth lashing me open the second we sat down. I expected either a fight or to find her on her knees weeping in apology and begging for me back now that my father's dead.

But instead, Moira is calm. Moira is distant

And I fucking hate it.

The jet hums around us, a soft undercurrent to the silence between us. It's not just any jet—it's a Blackwolf jet. A thing of obscene wealth, all buttery leather seats and polished mahogany paneling, with gold accents that catch the dim cabin lighting. It smells of expensive whiskey and money.

Money I never wanted, money that came with a legacy I've spent years trying to run from.

But now? Now I've got a kingdom built from my father's sins waiting for me in England, and I made sure to drag Moira with me.

She's curled up in the window seat, her knees pulled up, bare feet tucked beneath her. She should look out of place here. This jet was built for politicians and billionaires, not for the girl who used to drink three dollar wine with me in parking lots at three a.m., her bare feet on the dashboard, laughing like the night belonged to us and no one else.

But she doesn't. She looks like she belongs everywhere and nowhere and like she's made peace with being untethered.

She doesn't so much as blink when I unbuckle myself from my original seat across the aisle and slide in beside her. If she notices the way my thigh presses against hers in the too-close space, she doesn't react. She doesn't roll her eyes when the flight attendant asks if we want anything, and I order whiskey, neat. Or even flinch when I say, "And whatever she wants."

And then—

Instead of talking to me or even looking my way, she pulls out a notebook.

A fucking notebook. It's very *Moira*, the cover a chaotic mix of dark pink and black splashes. And it's clearly well-used.

I watch, rigid, as she flips it open to the middle and starts writing.

"What's that?" I ask, my voice low and rough.

"My journal." She doesn't look up; she just keeps moving the pen across the page.

"Since when do you journal?"

"Since I started tracking my moods."

Her voice is clinical. Distant. Like she's talking about the goddamn weather.

I don't like it. I don't like the way she sits there, perfectly composed, writing her thoughts like they aren't meant to be torn out of her, spat at me, and fought over until we're both raw.

She used to be all jagged edges, sharp and wild and impossible to hold without getting cut. Now, she's smoothing herself down. Filing away the parts of her I used to clutch like a lifeline.

I lean in, close enough that my breath ghosts over the shell of her ear. "You don't have to pretend with me," I murmur, dark and quiet, the way she used to love. "I know exactly who you are."

She pauses. Just for a second. Just long enough for me to think I've cracked through. Then she exhales. Slow. Even. Like she's past it. Like she doesn't crave me anymore.

And that's when I feel it—

Real fear.

Not for her. For *me*.

What if this isn't just about her getting better? What if she's outgrowing me?

I sit back, jaw tight, and watch her hand move across the page, logging things I don't understand. Moira never used to write things down. She used to scream them out into the world.

I don't know this version of her.

And I don't know if she still wants me.

Hours pass in silence, and at some point, she dozes off against the window. I study her, trying to make sense of the sight. Moira asleep. Moira still. Not tossing and turning, not mumbling half-crazed thoughts in her sleep. Just… peaceful.

It unsettles me more than anything else.

I reach out before I can stop myself. A curl has slipped over her cheek, and I want—need—to tuck it behind her ear. To touch her. To make sure she's real. But my hand stops inches from her skin. I let it hover there, suspended, before curling my fingers into a fist and pulling back.

Then, an alarm goes off.

Moira stirs and blinks, then reaches into her bag. She pulls out a bottle, dry swallows a pill, and tucks it away like it's nothing.

I watch. I wait. I feel the words scrape up my throat before I can stop them.

"What was that?"

She arches a brow, the ghost of her old smirk dancing on her lips. "My meds."

Silence.

"What kind of meds?"

"The kind that makes me less fun."

I hate the way she says it. Like she's taunting me, daring me to react. Daring me to admit I *do* miss the fun. The fire. The chaos.

I don't answer. Because I don't fucking know the answer.

She watches me, something sharp in her gaze, and then, finally, she says it:

"You don't like me like this, do you?"

I freeze.

She exhales and shakes her head, then looks away. "Not that it matters if you like me anymore, I guess. I'm just here for paperwork."

And that? That's what makes me snap.

I grip the armrest between us and lean in, my voice low and razor-sharp. "You think I'm dragging you across the fucking ocean for *paperwork*?"

She doesn't answer. Doesn't blink. She just holds my gaze, so fucking steady and unshaken.

Then she shifts, stretching her legs out and rolling her neck like she's settling into a throne instead of a seat. She lets her gaze wander the cabin—across the sleek walnut bar, the plush recliners, the gleaming brass light fixtures—and then, without looking at me, she says, "You must like having nice things now that you're rich again."

I don't take the bait. Because the truth is, I don't give a

fuck about the money, the jet, the legacy. None of it means anything.

She's the only thing I ever wanted.

And for the first time since I met Moira Blackwood, *I* am the one unraveling.

I stare at the woman in front of me and wonder if I ever really knew her at all.

FIFTY-NINE

MOIRA

Dear Journal,

I'm on the fanciest fucking plane I've ever ridden, and Bane just slipped into the seat beside me.

What do I feel???

Not gray. That's for damn sure. All I've felt for weeks since I started those dumb meds is gray-fucking gray. I hate fucking gray. At least I did.

But now Bane's back. A burst of red.

I see it in his eyes. He wants something from me.

But I'm afraid.

Fear feels like blue—the blue-black of a bruise.

I'm not an idiot. I see the lust. The want.

But what if he wants something I can't give him anymore?

Everybody loves the bouncy, shiny girl.

The shadowed, sad girl—I've always tried to tuck her away.

Hide in the cabinet. Cower down. Mam's fucking again. Hide in the cabinet. Put your sad thoughts away there, too. Just a crack of light in the cabinet-dark.

Men wanted Mam for an hour or two at a time.

Domhn had friends at school—or at least people who respected him and wanted to be like him.

No one wants you.

Bruise blue girl.

Petals plucked, one by one.

Who's going to want you now?

HOLY FUCK, Bane is *rich*.

I mean, I *knew* it. I knew it in the way you know the ocean is deep or that the sun is hot. But there's a difference between *knowing* and *standing in the middle of a goddamn castle* while some starched-up butler with an accent straight out of a period drama asks if I'd like my tea with honey or lemon.

Castle. *Castle.* With turrets. With a hedge maze. With an *actual suit of armor* in the hallway that I swear shifts slightly every time I walk past it. The whole place smells like old books, old money, and the kind of secrets that don't stay buried, no matter how many silk curtains and imported Persian rugs you drape over them.

And somehow, in the midst of all this gothic nonsense, I'm supposed to be here to "figure things out" with Bane's father's estate. Which—newsflash—I *shouldn't even be part of.* I did my research. We don't live in California. And Texas doesn't do that whole 'Congrats, you married a man and now you own half his empire!' bullshit.

So when I bring this up at dinner, where I sit across from Bane at that absurdly long table like we're starring in a high-budget enemies-to-lovers adaptation, he just *smiles.*

That slow, deliberate, *I already know how this ends* kind of smile.

Then he says something about our joint bank account.

And I frown. "You mean the joint account we made so we could, like, split the cost of ramen and toilet paper?"

He nods. Casually. *Too* casually. Like he isn't about to say the most batshit thing I've ever heard in my life.

"Why would you put anything in there?" I ask because someone needs to inject some logic into the conversation.

He just gives me *that look*. The kind of look that makes my goddamn bones itch with need, along with every sinew and nerve ending, too. I didn't know I could still feel *that* itch through the medical gray.

"Because we're man and wife," he says, voice smooth as sin. "And what's mine is yours."

I choke on the amazing soup—the first of several courses, by the way, all prepared by the Michelin-star chef who apparently lives here.

Bane doesn't even blink. Just waves a dismissive hand. "I'll see that you get a fair settlement."

A fair—

I swear to God, my brain is short-circuiting. My hands tremble with the effort it takes to not launch my soup spoon at his stupid, smug, *infuriatingly perfect* face.

"I told you from the beginning I don't want your money," I snap.

And he—

He chuckles.

This man—this infuriating, impossible bastard—just chuckles to himself like I'm a child and just said something *adorable*. Then he scrolls through his phone, completely unbothered, while I'm seconds away from flipping the entire table over.

"Tomorrow, Rotterdam and the rest of the family will show up," he continues, voice cool. Commanding. "You should try to sleep off the jet lag tonight."

Oh. Oh, should I? Should I just *sleep*? Like I'm not trapped in a stone mansion that probably has secret passageways? Like I'm not currently lying in a bed that could fit four of me, staring up at a chandelier worth more than my entire life, while somewhere down the hall, he's probably sleeping like a king who just conquered the last piece of land he had left to claim?

So no. No, I can't sleep.

Instead, I'm here, scribbling in this stupid journal, trying to make sense of any of this, trying to wrap my head around how I went from splitting bills with Bane in his tiny little parish house to being an actual pawn in some old money inheritance nonsense.

And the worst part? The absolute worst part?

I felt something when he said it. When he smiled like that. When he mentioned a settlement like I was already his to take care of.

So no, I can't sleep.

Kira says I'm supposed to write down my big feelings when I have them, but I don't know what the fuck I'm *feeling* right now. I need a canvas the size of Dallas and even then I don't think I could *paint* out what I'm feeling. Especially when Bane comes around and scrambles up everything just when I thought I was settling into a nice numb gray I was starting to embrace.

She says if I need help, I should look up the *Feelings Wheel*.

Feelings are stupid.

The *Feelings Wheel* is stupid.

I don't know what I fucking feel.

Nothing.

I'm about to slam the journal shut. Or better yet, throw it across the room until its spine cracks against the brick wall.

But I don't.

I sigh, then take a forced breath.

Inhale for three. Exhale for six.

I pull open that goddamned color wheel on my phone and try to find a word for whatever the fuck this emotion is.

Inadequate. Alienated. Empty. Apathetic.

I try each one out. But no, none of the outside wheel words are quite right. So I head inward to the more basic emotions.

Sad.

Afraid.

Angry.

Oooh, angry, my old favorite.

But now that Bane's not here, I can't even work up a tenth of the buzzing, bright fury I used to be able to call on at the twitch of my fingers.

I feel like a witch whose magic was stolen.

But I do think about unaliving myself a lot less often lately.

So, you know.

There's that.

Dear Journal,

I don't know how to want things without wanting to swallow the entire world whole.

I don't know how to want things like a person on a canoe with strokes so even.

I don't know how to want things like a sane girl.

I miss the chaos.

The kaleidoscope of such pretty, wild colors ever-shifting.

Today, I'm still just black and blue.

Today, I meet the rest of Bane's family.

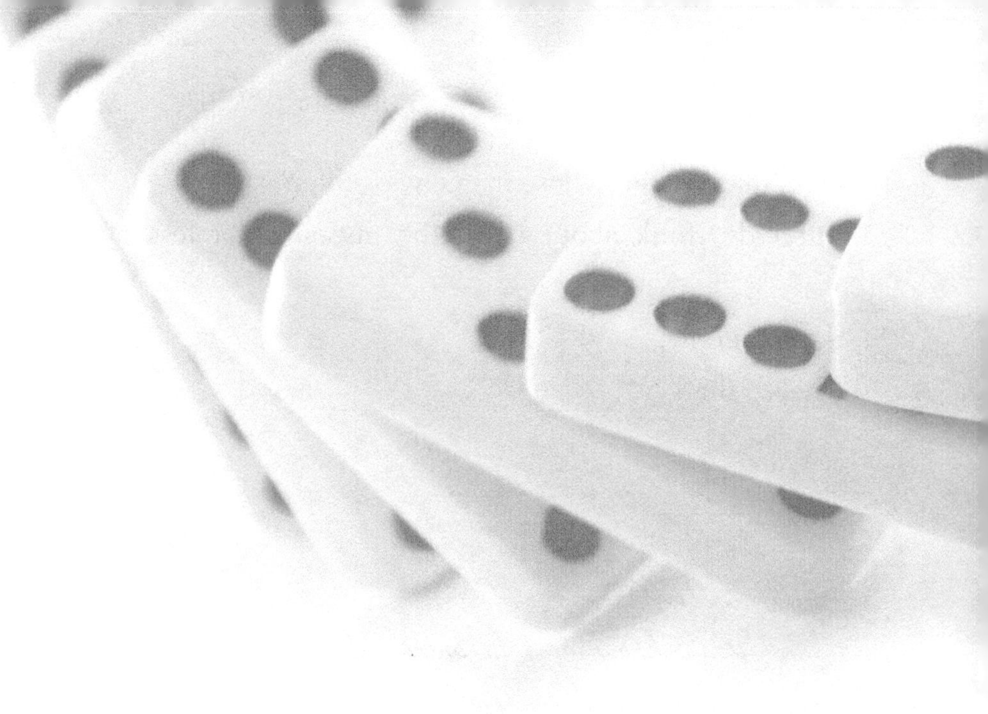

SIXTY

BANE

I KNOCK ONCE.

Moira opens the door before I can knock again, her expression sharp, unimpressed—until her gaze drops to the ring in my hand. Then, just for a second, something flickers in her eyes. Something she smothers fast, locking it down behind that wicked mouth and defiant chin.

I haven't been able to read her face since I got her to agree to come here with me, and we haven't spoken a single word about what happened. I haven't told her I know why she left. She hasn't offered any information about her swift departure or anything else. She's barely spoken two words to me.

At least on the plane, I had ten straight hours of being

near her. Of watching her every twitch and squirm. The way her hand so gracefully held her pen as she scribbled furiously in that bright fuchsia notebook of hers with black paint splatters on the cover.

Yet whatever's changed between us, my obsession with her remains as deep as ever.

"They're here," I say simply.

She crosses her arms, leaning against the doorframe. Deliberately casual. "Who's 'they?'"

I let the corner of my mouth lift, slow and deliberate. "A den of Blackwolfs."

She scoffs, but I catch the way her throat moves when she swallows. I don't miss a single thing. She's hidden in her extensive suite in the castle since we got here yesterday, and I'm hungry to drink in the way her fingers twitch where they're tucked under her arms.

I lift the ring, this one heavier than the last, something meant to be *seen* and send a message. The sconce light catches on the deep-cut facets, the gold of the band gleaming. I clock the way her breathing subtly changes, just enough for me to notice. Just enough for me to *feel* it.

"You'll need your armor."

Her expression doesn't crack, but her pulse jumps at her throat, a betraying little flutter just under her skin.

She takes her time answering, gaze locked on the ring like it's a loaded gun. Then a wry eyebrow pops. "You're upgrading me?"

I tilt my head, drinking her in. *Savoring* her. "Let's see how it fits."

She doesn't move. Doesn't reach for it.

But she doesn't pull away when I take her hand, either. The immediate electric sizzle is still there the second we touch.

I have to force myself not to hold my breath as I press the ring onto her fourth finger. Slow. Deliberate. Watching the way her breath hitches. Watching the way her lips part just slightly before she seals them shut again, locking up whatever reaction she refuses to give me.

But I *feel* it.

She can pretend all she wants. Pretend she's indifferent, that this means nothing. But her body betrays her in the quietest ways. The tension in her fingers, the way she lets me slide the ring all the way to the base of her finger without a single protest.

Satisfaction roars in my chest.

Her armor may be up, but she still lets *me* in.

It's still there between us. That living flame that bursts to life whenever we're near each other. If she's getting help for her mental health, I want to celebrate and support her.

But I won't let her deny the inferno that is *us*.

"Ready?" I ask, voice low, dark, meant only for her.

She exhales through her nose, then makes a show of examining the ring like it's just another accessory. "Let's get this over with."

But when I offer my arm, she takes it.

We descend the grand staircase together, the murmur of conversation below growing louder with each step. The dining hall stretches before us, dripping in excess. Dark wood gleams beneath the glow of chandeliers. A fire roars in the massive stone hearth, casting flickering shadows across the long dining table that's ostensibly set for dinner but that's really set for war.

The air is *thick*. Every eye in the room is on us as we approach. A meal fit for kings stretches across the table, untouched apart from the wine glasses. Everyone here's ravenous, but not for food.

They're waiting. Watching. Calculating.

I lean down, my lips close enough to brush Moira's ear if I let myself. I exert maximum self-control, though, and stay a millimeter away from her precious skin as I whisper, "Rotterdam's at the head of the table. He's my father's lawyer and a professional vulture. He'll smile, but only because he enjoys picking people apart at the bones."

Moira's lips press together, her spine straighter now. Good girl.

"To his right—my eldest brother, Charles. He's got my father's ambition but none of his charm. Next to him is Gabriella. Sharp and vicious, and she'll smile while she's shoving an icepick in your ribs. She's one to watch."

Moira's fingers tighten slightly where they rest against my arm.

"The blond, three seats down? That's Simon. He's had everything handed to him, so he compensates by making everyone else miserable. Don't engage."

She exhales, muttering under her breath, "I wouldn't dream of it."

"And the woman at the end, swirling her wine like she'd rather shatter the glass than drink from it? That's Miriam. One of my father's many discarded lovers and Simon's mother. She'll call you *dear* while digging the knife in."

Moira lifts her chin, eyes bright with something reckless. "So many pointy objects."

I glance down at her, noting the fire in her eyes. My blood heats.

Conversation around the table slows as we reach the last steps. Every head turns. Every gaze sharpens. They're ready to carve Moira up and see what she's made of.

I slide my hand over hers, fingers settling firmly over her knuckles. When she squeezes back, my entire chest expands.

Let them look. Let them wonder. Let them think what they want.

She's *mine*.

And I'm about to show them exactly what that means.

The moment we sit, as expected, the knives come out.

Moira sits beside me, her spine straight, her chin tipped up in the way she does when she's already prepared for a fight. She thinks she's ready. She doesn't understand yet—this isn't a fight. It's a slow, deliberate unraveling. And they'll enjoy every second of watching her come apart.

I immediately want to protect her, but I can see by the way she shoots a quick glare my way she won't welcome it. I need to let her find her footing on her own first. It won't do her any favors with the wolves if I don't let her parry some first strikes and show them what she's made of, either.

So grudgingly, I just nudge my chair closer and stare down my family.

Simon is the first to punch, his voice dripping with lazy cruelty. "Well, well. The stray he picked up finally made it to the big kid's table."

Moira doesn't flinch, but I see it—the way her breath catches, the fraction of a second where she has to decide whether to ignore him or slit him open with her words.

She picks the latter. "I'd say it's nice to meet you," her brow scrunches adorably, "but I was raised not to lie."

Gabriella lets out a sharp little laugh into her wine glass. Charles merely raises an eyebrow. Simon's smirk widens, but there's something mean curling at the edges now. He leans back, stretching out like he owns the room. "Feisty. Shame that won't help you here."

Moira's fingers tighten around her fork. She's still trying to play it cool, but I know her. I know how hard it is for her to sit still when she's under attack. She'd rather throw the first punch and draw first blood. Fuck, I love her. Even as I know she's in *my* world now, and here, we don't waste effort when words can kill just as easily.

Still, it's nice to see some fire back in her eyes, even if I instantly feel protective of her in this room of vipers.

Miriam, ever the elegant executioner, tilts her head, smiling with a mouth full of hidden razors. "I must admit, darling, I was expecting... well, someone *else*. Bane's tastes have always run a bit more... polished."

Moira turns to her, eyes sharp, but before she can fire back, Miriam keeps going, voice smooth. "But I suppose every man has his rebellions. And who could blame him? You're such a *delightful little scandal.*"

The way she says it—delightful like an insult, scandal like a disease.

Moira's eyes narrow. "And you're his father's *what*, exactly? Beloved companion? Kept woman? Longest-running mistake?"

A hush falls over the table. Gabriella's lips twitch. Simon grins outright. Even Rotterdam, ever the composed observer, flicks his gaze toward Miriam to see how she'll react.

Miriam only smiles wider, but there's something venomous underneath. "Oh, darling," she murmurs, her fingers gliding over the rim of her wine glass. "If you have to ask, then you really *don't* belong here."

Moira's fingers twitch toward her knife.

I know the moment she's about to snap—the tension in

her shoulders, the tight breath, the way her eyes flash like she's on the edge of lunging across the table and cutting this woman open with something sharper than silver.

I could stop this. Step in. Shut it down with a word.

But I don't.

Not yet.

I let it simmer. Let her feel the weight of them pressing in. Let her make the choice—does she lash out? Does she rise above it? Does she play the game or let them tear her apart before the first course is even served?

And then Charles, ever the patient predator, finally speaks. "This is all very entertaining," he says, voice as smooth as the whiskey in his glass. "But I think we're all still wondering the same thing." He turns his gaze on me, but his words are meant for her. "Why is *she* here?"

Rotterdam doesn't react, but I know he's listening closely now. He flips open his leather folder, ready to lay out the details of the inheritance. But Charles doesn't care about legalities. He cares about power. About hierarchy. About reminding everyone at this table where they fall in the Blackwolf pecking order.

Moira squares her shoulders, her lips parting to answer, but before she can, Simon scoffs. "She shouldn't even be here."

That's when I move.

Not loud. Not aggressive. Just a slow, deliberate reach for

my whiskey. I swirl the glass, the scent of oak and fire curling under my nose.

"Neither should most of you," I murmur, my voice lazy and edged with amusement. I lift the glass to my lips. "But here we are. Brothers and sister. *Ladies*," I give a sardonic raise of an eyebrow Miriam's way so she feels my sarcasm like a whip, "and gentlemen, may I introduce my wife, Moira Blackwolf."

Moira exhales sharply beside me, irritation rolling off her in waves.

She doesn't *need* me to fight for her.

But she's realizing something now, something that's been creeping up on her since the moment we walked into this room.

It doesn't matter how sharp her tongue is or how fast she can strike—

Because in this world, power isn't about speaking the loudest. It's about making everyone else fall silent. I decide when the knife twists and when the room bends to *me*.

And right now, they're learning what Moira already knows—this was never a fight. It was always a foregone conclusion.

I'm just making damn sure they know it.

Silence never lasts long in a room full of predators.

I let them have their fun. Let them snap their teeth at Moira, let them think they could toy with her, let them believe—for one last, fleeting moment—that they still hold power here.

But the game is over.

I set my whiskey glass down with a deliberate *clink* against the polished wood, the sound slicing through the low hum of conversation like a blade. "Rotterdam."

The lawyer looks up, unfazed but already moving. He knows. Of course, he knows.

"It's time."

Moira stiffens beside me. Her fingers are curled tight against the edge of the table, white-knuckled like she's bracing for impact. She should be. They all should be.

Rotterdam clears his throat, unfastens the leather clasp on his folder, and pulls out a thick sheaf of documents. He adjusts his glasses, scanning the first page. "As per the last will and testament of the late Bradford Blackwolf—"

The name alone sends a ripple through the table. A sharp inhale from Miriam, Charles's jaw locks tight, and Gabriella's fingers tighten around the stem of her wine glass. My father's ghost is still in the room, his phantom hand still wrapped around their throats.

Rotterdam continues, his voice cool and measured. "All assets, including Blackwood Hall, all financial holdings, and controlling interest in Blackwood Enterprises are hereby transferred in full to Bane Blackwood."

For a second, there's nothing. Just the weight of those

words settling like lead into the marrow of every person sitting at this cursed table.

Then, the explosion.

Miriam is the first to react, shoving back from the table so hard her wine glass tips, red spilling across the pristine linen. "That's impossible."

"Surely, there's a mistake." Charles's voice is tight, but there's an edge of desperation beneath it. "My father wouldn't—"

"He did." Rotterdam flips a page, adjusting his glasses. "The will was amended six months before his death. The paperwork is in order."

Gabriella exhales a sharp laugh, dark and bitter. "So that's it? We get *nothing*?"

"Correct."

Simon is less elegant about it. "That *fucking bastard!*" He slams his fist onto the table, silverware rattling. "He left us scraps? What about the company? What about—"

"All holdings." Rotterdam doesn't even look up. "Including the company."

"You expect us to believe that?" Charles snaps, voice finally cracking. "You expect us to just accept that Bane gets *everything*?"

I take my time swirling the whiskey in my glass, watching the amber liquid catch the firelight. Then I meet his gaze, slow and deliberate. "Yes."

Chaos erupts.

Miriam hisses something under her breath, venom dripping from every syllable. Gabriella is laughing again, wild and mean. Simon is half out of his chair, face red, furious, looking like he's ready to launch himself across the table. Charles is already plotting, I can *see* it—the calculations running behind his eyes, searching for any loophole, any way to claw back what was never his to begin with.

Moira hasn't moved.

She's watching them, expression unreadable, but I can feel the tension in her body. It's different now. Before, they were attacking *her*. Now, they're devouring each other.

And me?

I sit back, relaxed, and let them.

Simon finally rounds on me, voice furious. "What the fuck did you *do*?"

I blink at him. "Inherited."

Charles rakes a hand through his hair, exhaling sharply through his nose. "This doesn't make sense. Father wouldn't just leave everything to you."

"Wouldn't he?" I arch a brow. "I was the only one who never needed a leash."

That lands. A direct hit. Charles's fingers twitch like he wants to throw his glass at my head. Instead, he turns to Rotterdam. "There has to be a way to contest this."

Rotterdam is unbothered as he slides the papers forward. "You're welcome to try. But I assure you, there is no avenue to contest."

Gabriella scoffs. "Oh, come now. The old man was losing his mind at the end. He probably didn't even know what he was signing."

Rotterdam lifts a brow, turning a page with infuriating calm. "The will was amended before he contracted Creutzfeldt-Jakob disease. His mental faculties were intact. The paperwork is sound."

"So you're saying Bane *didn't* blackmail him into changing it?" Simon sneers, crossing his arms. "Because that seems more likely."

Rotterdam doesn't even glance up. "I'm not exactly sure what you imagine a man on a lowly priest's salary could do to influence a man like your father, but I assure you, there was no coercion, no undue influence. Your father made his wishes explicitly clear. And as your father so often loved to remind anyone in his vicinity, as the richest man in the world, he could afford the *best*."

He continues shuffling papers. "And I *am* the best. The will is iron-clad against contestation, lawsuit, or any other infringement the lot of you might think up."

Miriam lets out a cold laugh, eyes glittering with something sharp. "Of course it is. Even if it wasn't blackmail, I still suppose we're meant to believe Bane had *nothing* to do with it? That he didn't whisper in his father's ear and poison his mind against the rest of us?"

"Believe what you like," I say, tipping my glass toward her. "It won't change the outcome."

Silence again, but this time, it's different. This time, it's heavier. More dangerous.

I exhale slowly, stretching out my fingers against the table. "Are we done?"

Miriam scoffs, shaking her head, her nails digging into her palm. "You don't even *want* it, do you?"

I tilt my head, smiling slightly. "Want has nothing to do with it."

The fire crackles. The wine knocked over earlier still bleeds across the tablecloth. The wolves are restless, snapping their teeth, realizing too late that the hunt is already over.

I have everything.

And they have *nothing*.

I let them stew in it. Let the weight of their loss settle and their desperation sink into their bones.

Then I break the silence.

I push back from the table, slow and deliberate, and glance at Rotterdam. "You know," I say, amused, "you're right that Father only ever hired the *best*."

Rotterdam, professional to his core, does not react, but I see the flicker of dry amusement in his eyes.

I swirl my whiskey, watching it catch the firelight. "And as luck would have it, he was *right* about that. Which is why, as of today, Rotterdam is no longer *our* father's lawyer." I lean forward, placing my glass down with a measured *clink*. "He's *mine*."

The eruption is immediate. Reactions explode around the

table again. Only Miriam just studies me quietly, her eyes narrowing like she's recalibrating everything she thought she knew.

Moira shifts beside me. I don't look at her. Not yet.

Instead, I nod to Rotterdam. "Read it."

Rotterdam clears his throat, straightens his cuffs, and flips to a fresh set of documents. "As the sole heir of Bradley Blackwolf's estate, Bane Blackwolf has allocated the following financial distribution."

The room quiets immediately and holds its breath.

Rotterdam continues, voice unshaken. "Each legally recognized child of Bradley Blackwolf is to receive a payout of one billion dollars."

Charles stills, Simon's mouth parts slightly, and Gabriella, for the first time all evening, looks *genuinely* surprised.

Rotterdam barely pauses before continuing. "Each partner who maintained a domestic relationship with Bradley Blackwolf for six years or more is to receive a payment of fifty million dollars."

Miriam's grip tightens on her wine glass. She lived with my father for eight. I don't miss the way her lips part slightly or the way she catches herself before reacting.

"I, Bane Blackwolf, will retain one billion dollars for myself." Rotterdam turns the page. "The remainder of the estate and holdings will be transferred to an investment portfolio to be donated to charitable organizations both of my choosing and by a board I will personally appoint to determine further allocations."

Rotterdam folds his hands neatly over the documents. "This offer expires in one hour."

A breath of silence.

Then, the room *erupts*.

"You're out of your *mind*." Simon's voice is incredulous, but beneath it, greed hums like a second heartbeat. He *wants* the deal. They *all* do.

"Only a *billion* dollars." Charles's voice is furious. "You'd really cheat me out of—"

"Yes." My tone is final. "Take it. Don't take it. It makes no difference to me." I lean back in my chair, tapping my fingers idly against the glass. "But let me be very clear: once the hour is up, the offer is gone." I let the words settle before delivering the final blow. "And you go back to getting *nothing*. Feel free to ask questions."

Miriam exhales slowly, setting her wine glass down. Her nails click against the crystal. "You're enjoying this."

I tilt my head, considering her. "That," I murmur, "is not a question."

A muscle in her jaw flexes.

Gabriella laughs, the sound rich with something *almost* admiring. "Well," she says, lifting her glass. "I'll drink to that."

But Charles—Charles is calculating. Simon is vibrating with barely contained fury. And Moira, beside me, is watching *everything*.

Tick, tick, tick.

The clock is running down.

And the wolves are *cornered*.

Beneath the table, Moira squeezes my hand. It sends a wave of electricity that tangles with the adrenaline of the moment and at finally facing off with my toxic family.

SIXTY-ONE

MOIRA

THE MOMENT BANE takes my hand to take me upstairs, my heart cracks wide open.

Not from fear. Not from panic.

From *him*.

From the sheer overwhelming weight of what just happened downstairs. The absolute *power* he wielded in that room—like a king granting mercy to his enemies, deciding whether to devour or dismiss.

And I watched it all.

Watched him shut them down with a single look and make them break with nothing but his silence. I watched him let them destroy themselves while he sat back, untouchable, unbothered, and completely in control.

God, that was sexy.

And now the warmth of his fingers curls around mine, so steady and grounding, the total opposite of the chaos inside my head.

Upstairs, the halls stretch long and dim, shadows spilling from sconces mounted on the walls. The air smells like old books, stale air, but also *him*—whiskey and heat and danger. He makes colors start to seep back into the edges of my world, and I'm afraid, but not in a sad blue kind of way.

I'm afraid with excitement. With orange and yellows, fire flickering at the edge of my vision again. Which makes me even more afraid.

I should let go. I should say something sharp to break the spell and remind both of us that I don't *need* him to take my hand.

But I can't. I just... *can't*.

Because this is it. This is the moment. I *feel* it.

My chest aches with the force of what I want to say. It presses against my ribs.

I stop walking.

Bane does, too, turning to face me in the luminous glow of the sconces.

His gaze rakes over me, dark and unreadable, but there's something different in his expression now. Something softer. Something *devastating*.

Something like *realization*.

"I know my father did something to make you leave."

The words slam into me. I jerk back slightly, my pulse roaring in my ears. "You... you do?"

He nods, gripping both of my hands now, his voice low and certain. "I always knew it wasn't you."

My throat closes. I can't breathe.

I've spent weeks believing he hated me. That he thought I *chose* to leave him. That he looked at me and saw a woman who walked away without looking back.

My fingers tremble as they tighten against his. "I—I wanted to tell you. But he—he threatened my brother, Bane. He *kidnapped* me and Mads."

Bane lets go of my hands and steps back, dragging his fingers through his hair. I just keep spewing excuses. "He said if I didn't disappear, if I ever came near you again—"

"Fuck. Now I wish I had murdered him. Just to see the light go out of that motherfucker's eyes."

"So you didn't? It wasn't you?" I ask because I can't deny the thought had crossed my mind.

"No." He shakes his head. "He really did have a disease. They said it was just a matter of months, but I guess it progressed even more quickly than any of us thought."

Then he shakes himself and rushes back toward me, wrapping his arms around me. "Oh my god. You were kidnapped. I'm so fucking glad you're okay." His arms squeeze tighter. "Holy shit, that's why you couldn't pick up the phone that day."

I bury my face in his chest, letting myself melt into his warmth for just a moment. Just one moment of weakness where I can pretend I'm still the old Moira—the one who would've launched herself at him, clawed her way up his body, and demanded he take her right here against the wall.

But I'm not her anymore. I don't know if I can ever be her again.

"They drugged me," I whisper, the words spilling out now that I've started. "I woke up in some warehouse by the river. Mads—she told me to run and leave her behind. She said they'd kill both of us and Domhn if I didn't break it off with you."

I pull back, meeting his eyes, needing him to understand. "I didn't want to hurt you. But I had to make you believe it. I had to make it real. And I am so sorry. It felt like I was choosing my brother's life over you."

His jaw tightens. "You did the right thing. I know my father was ruthless enough to do it." His hands come up to frame my face, thumbs brushing over my cheekbones with such tender reverence that my knees nearly buckle.

"And I knew it," he says again, voice rough. "I fucking *knew* it. I could feel it in my bones that you were lying that day. Your eyes..." His thumb slides across my bottom lip. "You've never been able to lie to me without your eyes giving you away."

I exhale sharply, my heart rabbiting against my ribs. "But you let me go."

"I didn't have a choice. You used the safe word. I had to respect that."

My throat tightens. He's right. I'd weaponized our trust against him. The one thing that had been sacred between us.

"I'm sorry," I whisper. "I'm so fucking sorry."

"No." His fingers tighten, tilting my face up. "Don't you dare apologize. Not for protecting the people you love. Not for sacrificing yourself. The dominos were always going to fall. But I'll be damned if I don't set them back up again. I love you, Moira."

His words pierce through me.

"I missed you," I confess, the admission torn from somewhere deep. "I missed you so much it nearly killed me."

His expression breaks, something raw and vulnerable crossing his face before he pulls me tightly against him again. I feel the shudder that runs through him and how his heart hammers against mine.

"Moira." My name feels like a prayer on his lips. "I thought I'd lost you."

My arms slide around his waist, holding on like he's the only solid thing in a world that's been spinning out of control for too long. The meds made everything gray, but somehow, in his arms, color seeps back into the edges. Dangerous, beautiful color.

"I'm not..." I swallow hard, forcing myself to be honest. "I'm not the same."

His hands stroke up my back, one tangling in my hair. "Neither am I."

I lean back just enough to look into his eyes, searching for any sign that he's lying—any sign that he's disappointed in what I've become. But all I see is that same intensity, that same desperate hunger that's always been there when he looks at me.

"I'm on meds now," I say, the confession hard to push out. "They help. Sometimes. But they make everything... duller. Quieter." I bite my lip. "I don't know if I can be what you need anymore."

His eyes darken, and for a moment, I think I've ruined it. I've shown him too much of the broken parts of me. But then he cups my face between his hands again, his gaze burning into mine.

"I don't need you to be anything but *mine*." His voice is a growl that sends shivers racing down my spine. "Just like I'm yours. We'll figure out the rest."

"I love you," he says, the words simple and devastating. "I've always loved you. I will always love you."

"I don't know how to be steady," I whisper, my voice cracking. "I don't know who I am without the highs and lows."

His thumbs brush over my cheekbones, catching my tears. "Then I'll love you through all of it."

I shake my head, squeezing my eyes shut. "What if I'm not the same?"

Bane's lips hover over mine, his breath mingling with mine, his fingers strong, *sure*. "Listen to me. Your brain makes you who you are. Who I *love*. You are Moira fucking Callaghan, the most unique, fascinating, infuriating woman I've ever known. And I will want you, need you, and *worship* you, no matter what. Medicated or not. High or low. In sickness and in health. That's what those vows meant to me."

Her eyes fill with tears. "You're sure?"

"I've never been more sure of anything in my life." I brush away a tear with my thumb."

Something in me *collapses*. "I love you too. I always have, and I always will."

And then, finally—

He *kisses* me.

Not a slow, careful thing. Not something delicate.

My hands fist in his shirt, pulling him closer, closer, until there's no space left between us.

It's *brutal*.

It's *wreckage*.

A hunger, a devastation, a reclaiming.

And I let myself be *taken*.

SIXTY-TWO

BANE

I SLAM the door to my father's study—my study now—and lock it behind us. The sound echoes through the room like a gunshot, ricocheting off leather-bound books and mahogany panels.

It's a declaration. A line drawn.

The world outside this door doesn't exist anymore. Not the inheritance. Not my venomous family downstairs. Not the years I spent hating my father while he plotted to tear apart the only good thing I've ever had.

There's only Moira.

Moira, who didn't leave me. Moira, who was fucking

kidnapped. Moira, who sacrificed herself to protect the people she loves.

I want to hunt down every person who touched her. I want to make them bleed. I want to set this whole fucking estate on fire and dance in the ashes of my father's legacy.

But Moira is watching me with those eyes that see everything—that always have—and I force myself to breathe.

"Take off your clothes," I say, my voice barely controlled. "All of them."

Her breath catches, and her eyes widen just slightly before narrowing again, that familiar spark of defiance igniting. "Why?"

"Because I need to see every inch of you." I step closer, close enough to feel the heat of her but not touching. Not yet. "I need to make sure they didn't leave a single mark on you."

"I'm fine. I swear."

"I'll believe it when I see it," I promise, voice dark with certainty. "And kiss every perfect part of you."

She shivers. I watch it travel down her spine, watch the way her pupils dilate and her lips part on a shaky exhale.

"But this isn't a command, Moira." I keep my voice even now despite the maelstrom inside me. "I don't want you naked because you think you owe me. Or because you feel like you have to prove something."

Her chin lifts. "What if I want to?"

I step closer, letting her feel just how much *I* want it. "Then take off your clothes."

She doesn't move right away. She's still measuring me and trying to decide if this is the right choice. A kiss is one thing, but is she ready to give herself completely to me again?

The old Moira would have already been naked and halfway across the desk. This new Moira thinks before she leaps.

I love the measured calculation just as much as the wildfire.

Because when she finally moves, it's deliberate. She kicks off her shoes. Unzips her dress. Slides it down her body until it pools at her feet. Finally, she stands before me in nothing but black lace underwear, vulnerable and exquisite.

"All of it," I remind her, my voice rougher now.

Her fingers tremble slightly as she unhooks her bra, letting it fall away. She hooks her thumbs in her panties and slides them down, never breaking eye contact.

I can't hide how she makes me breathless.

And then she's bare before me. Completely exposed.

Mine.

God, she's beautiful. Still Moira.

I let my gaze travel over every inch of her. Her skin is unblemished except for the scars I already know, the ones I've traced with my tongue in the dark hours of the night.

"Turn around," I command softly but firmly.

She does, slowly, arms wrapped loosely around her middle. The pale curve of her spine, the little dimples at the base, the birthmark on her right hip—it's all exactly as I remember. I let out a breath I didn't realize I was holding.

"They didn't hurt you."

It's half question, half statement.

"No." She turns back to face me. "Not physically."

The implication hangs between us. The mental damage. The trauma. The way she's had to rebuild herself in my absence.

I close the distance between us in two strides, pulling her against me, one hand tangling in her wild curls, the other pressing into the small of her back. I want to devour her. I want to wrap her in my arms and never let her go.

"I shouldn't have let you out of my sight," I growl, my mouth at her ear. "I should have known he'd try something."

"You couldn't have." Her hands slide up my chest, over my shoulders.

I pull back just enough to catch her gaze. "No more secrets between us. Not ever again. Promise me."

Something shifts in her eyes—a flicker of uncertainty. "I don't want to make promises I'm not sure I can keep."

She's being honest. The old Moira would have promised me anything just to feel my body against hers again. This new Moira understands her limitations. Respects them.

I brush my thumb across her lower lip. "I've never expected perfection from either of us. Just promise that you'll try, and I'll do the same."

She nods, solemn. "I promise."

Fuck, I love her honesty.

I kiss her then, finally, desperately.

My hands roam her bare skin, relearning every curve, every dip, every place that makes her gasp against my mouth. She clings to me, her body arching into mine like she can't bear any space to exist between us.

When our lips break apart, both of us panting, I press my forehead to hers.

"I've missed you," I repeat. I know I already told her, but the words feel pathetically small against the enormity of what I've felt these past weeks.

"I missed you too." Her voice breaks on the words. "Every fucking day."

I should go slow. I should be gentle. She's been through hell. She's been fucking medicated. I should treat her like glass.

But then her hands are at my belt, her eyes wild with need, and I know—

She needs this as much as I do.

Still, I capture her wrists, pinning them behind her back with one hand. With the other, I tilt her chin, forcing her to look at me.

"Not like this," I say, voice rough with restraint. "Not quick and desperate."

She trembles in my grip. "Bane, please—"

"No." I tighten my hold just slightly. "I've spent weeks thinking I'd lost you forever. I've grieved you. I've fucking *raged* over you. And now I have you back." I lower my mouth to her ear, letting my breath warm her skin. "I'm going to take my time with you. I'm going to worship every inch of you until you're begging. Until you're screaming my name. Until you remember exactly who you belong to."

Her pupils dilate so wide her eyes look nearly black. "I never forgot." The words are barely audible.

And then she sinks down, graceful and fluid, her knees hitting the thick carpet. Her gaze never leaves mine, and I have to fight for control. I was the one who said I didn't want this quick and desperate, but—

My Moira. On her knees. For me.

The sight nearly undoes me.

I slide my fingers into her hair, cradling her head in my palm. "You have no idea how often I've dreamed of this." My voice is hoarse with want. "How many nights I woke up reaching for you."

She leans into my touch like a cat, eyes closing briefly. "I used to pretend you were still there, too," she whispers. "On the bad days. I'd wrap myself in that hoodie you left at my place and pretend you were holding me."

Something in my chest cracks open. "You're never going to need to pretend again," I promise, fierce and certain. "I'm not letting you go. Not ever."

Her hands move to my belt again, and this time, she undoes it slowly, deliberately, never rushing despite the need I can feel thrumming through her body.

When she frees me, her breath catches, and the sound goes straight to my cock.

"I've thought about this so many times," she whispers, her hands sliding up my thighs as my pants sink to the floor. "About you. About us."

I brush a curl from her face, gentler than I thought myself capable of being in this moment. "Tell me what you need, dove."

Her eyes flick up to mine, and there's a vulnerability there I've never seen before. "I need to know it's real. That you still want me. Even like this."

Even medicated. Even different. Even with the highs and lows smoothed out into something less chaotic.

I cradle her face in my hands. "I told you, I just want *you*, Moira. Not just the parts that are easy or fun or wild. *All* of you."

Something shifts in her expression—relief, maybe, or resolution. And then she takes my cock in her mouth, and all coherent thought dissolves.

Oh fuck. The wet heat of her mouth. The barest scrape of her teeth. The flutter of her throat as she takes me deeper and hums.

I groan, my head falling back, my hand moving to tighten in her hair. She moves with purpose, with devotion, her nails digging into my thighs.

When I feel myself getting too close, I pull her back. "No. Not yet."

I help her to her feet, relishing the flush on her cheeks, the swell of her lips. "Not until I've tasted you, too."

I lift her onto the massive oak desk, shoving aside papers and pens without a care. Let them fall. Let the whole fucking world burn. Nothing matters but the woman in front of me.

I drop to my knees between her legs, pushing her thighs apart, exposing her pink, perfect cunt to my gaze. She's already wet.

Mine.

I dive in without preamble or gentleness. I devour her like a starving man, my tongue flat against her clit, my hands gripping her thighs to keep them spread wide. She cries out, back arching, fingers tangling in my hair.

"Bane—fuck—"

I growl against her, the vibration making her gasp. I suck her clit between my lips, flicking my tongue against it as I slide two fingers inside her, curling them to find that spot that makes her—

"Oh my god—"

There.

She comes apart on my tongue, her thighs trembling and her cries echoing off the walls. I don't stop. I keep going, relentless, dragging her through one orgasm straight into another. She writhes above me, her hands alternating between pushing me away and pulling me closer.

"Too much," she gasps, voice broken. "Bane, I can't—"

I pull back just enough to meet her gaze, my lips slick with her arousal.

"You can." My voice is dark, commanding. "And you will. Because I say so."

Her pupils dilate even further. She swallows hard, then nods, surrendering.

I dive back in, adding a third finger, stretching her, preparing her. By the time I rise to my feet, she's a trembling, incoherent mess. Her skin flushed. Her eyes glazed with lust.

Perfect.

I shed the rest of my clothes, never taking my eyes off her. When I'm naked, I step between her legs again, sliding my cock through her wetness, teasing just the head of my cock at her entrance.

"Tell me you're mine," I demand, voice rough.

Her gaze locks with mine, clear and certain despite the haze of pleasure. "I'm yours." She wraps her legs around my waist, drawing me closer. "I've always been yours."

I thrust into her in one swift, deep stroke, burying myself to the hilt. We both groan at the sensation. She's tight, so fucking tight. Like her body has forgotten the shape of me.

I'll remind it.

I set a brutal pace, fucking her hard and deep. The desk creaks beneath us. She clings to me, nails now digging into my shoulders, leaving marks I'll wear proudly. I want to be marked by her. I want everyone to know I belong to this woman just as much as she belongs to me.

"I love you," I growl into her neck. "I fucking love you, Moira."

She gasps, clenching around me. "I love you too. God, Bane, I love you."

The words send me over the edge. I come with a shout, emptying myself inside her, marking her in the most primal way possible. She follows a heartbeat later, her body arching against mine, her cunt milking every last drop from me.

We collapse together, sweat-slick and panting. I cradle her against my chest, her head tucked under my chin.

Her breath is warm against my skin and for the first time in weeks, I feel whole.

I carry her to the leather sofa in the corner, settling her in my lap. She curls against me, boneless and sated, her fingers tracing idle patterns on my chest.

"I thought I'd never have this again," she murmurs. "You. Us."

I press a kiss to the top of her head. "There will always be us."

She shifts, looking up at me with those eyes that have haunted my dreams. "Even with everything changing? You inheriting all this?" She gestures vaguely at the opulent room. "Me being... different now?"

I brush my thumb across her cheekbone. "The money doesn't change anything. We'll use it to do good. To build something better than my father ever could. And as for you being different..." I tilt her chin up, making sure she's looking me in the eyes when I say this. "You're still Moira. Still the woman who challenges me, who drives me fucking crazy, who makes me feel more alive than I've ever felt. The core of who you are hasn't changed."

She bites her lip. "But what if... what if the meds dull everything too much? What if I'm never as fun or exciting as I was before?"

The vulnerability in her voice breaks my heart. I pull her closer, cradling her face in my hands.

"You're it for me, Moira. The beginning and the end. My fucking salvation."

She laughs softly, the sound warming me from the inside out. "That's blasphemous, Father."

I grin, my hand sliding up her thigh. "Wait until you hear what else I plan to do to you tonight."

She shivers, her body already responding to my touch. "Tell me."

I lean in close, my lips brushing the shell of her ear. "I'm going to take you to the bedroom—our bedroom—now."

Her breath catches. "But what about... everyone downstairs?"

"I'll tell them to text me their answer. I've got more important things to attend to."

"Like what?" She arches an eyebrow sexily at me.

I tug her closer. "Like laying you out on that massive four-poster bed and fucking you in every way I've been dreaming about for the past six weeks."

"That sounds... thorough."

"Oh, it will be." I nip at her earlobe, relishing her gasp. "By morning, there won't be a single doubt in your mind about who you belong to."

She tilts her head, giving me better access to her neck. "And who's that?"

I growl against her skin. "Say it."

Her fingers tangle in my hair, pulling just hard enough to send a spark of pleasure-pain down my spine. "You," she breathes. "I belong to you, Bane."

Satisfaction rumbles in my chest. I stand, lifting her effortlessly in my arms. She curls into me, trusting, yielding in a way the old Moira rarely did.

But as we reach the door, she suddenly stiffens, pulling back to meet my gaze.

"Just so we're clear," she says, eyes glinting with that familiar spark of defiance, "you also belong to me. And I plan to stake my claim just as thoroughly."

I laugh, deep and genuine, feeling something tight in my chest finally release.

There she is. My Moira. Still wild. Still fierce. Still perfectly, gloriously *mine*.

I carry her through the door, toward our future, leaving the ghosts of the past behind us.

EPILOGUE

December, 9 Months Later

MOIRA

DOMHNALL'S new house is fucking ridiculous.

I mean, I'm not one to talk anymore. I'm literally staying in a castle right now. An honest-to-God British castle with towers and turrets and creepy suits of armor that I still swear move when I'm not looking.

But Domhn's place is ridiculous in a different way—all sleek lines and sharp angles and more security than the Pentagon. It's a fortress disguised as a modern architectural wet dream. He moved again after everything went down. I know he keeps hoping that if MadAnna comes back—no, *when* she comes back—he doesn't want her to worry about being in danger ever again.

"Stop bouncing your leg," Bane murmurs, his hand settling on my knee like a warm anchor.

I hadn't even realized I was doing it. I glance down at his fingers splayed across my skin, and something inside me settles. Just a little. Just enough.

"Sorry," I whisper back, but there's no real apology in it, and we both know it.

Bane's lips twitch. "No, you're not."

"Nope." I pop the 'P' because I know it amuses him.

Across the room, Domhn is pacing. Again. He hasn't stopped since we arrived twenty minutes ago. Back and forth, like a caged tiger. Is this just what he does all the time now?

Isaak watches him with the patience of, well, Isaak, while bouncing his and Kira's four-month-old daughter on his knee.

Baby Lily is a squishy, perfect little thing with Kira's eyes and Isaak's perpetual look of mild concern. She's got a jumble of dark curls and the kind of cheeks you just want to *nom nom nom* on.

"Would you sit the fuck down?" I call to my brother. "You're making me dizzy."

Domhn glares at me. "I'll sit down when I feel like sitting down."

Bane's fingers squeeze my knee in warning. I ignore him.

"So... never, then? You gonna just wear a trench in your fancy floor by the time MadAnna gets back?"

"Moira," Kira interjects, her voice that perfect blend of gentle and firm that only seems to work when she uses it. "Let's give him some space."

I flop back against the couch with a huff. "Fine."

It's hard to believe it's been three months since Bane and I reunited. Three months of figuring out this new us. Three months of learning how to be together again, but differently.

I fidget with the gold band on my finger—the proper one Bane got me after we returned from England and sorted out all the legal bullshit with his father's estate. He officially said goodbye to his congregation, though he remains ordained. All his time is spent heading his new charity board as we work to give away the *billions* left in the trust after the inheritance was distributed. It's still weird being married to a billionaire.

No, scratch that. It's weird being married, period.

Me. Moira fucking Callaghan. Settled.

Well, as settled as I get these days.

"She'll come back," I say suddenly, because I can't help myself. Someone's gotta say something. The silence is unbearable. "MadAnna. She always does."

Domhn stops pacing just long enough to skewer me with a look. "It's been nine months, Moira."

"And? She disappeared for what—a whole year last time? And still came back."

"That was different." He speaks through his teeth, neck veins strained.

"Was it, though?"

Bane's hand slides subtly up my thigh. A squeeze. A warning. *Don't push too hard.*

But pushing is what I do. It's what I've always done. Being medicated doesn't change that; it just... smooths out the edges. Makes the pushing less erratic, maybe.

That's the thing nobody tells you about meds. They don't fix you. They don't even change you, not really. They just make you more... manageable. Less likely to fly off the handle or buy a one-way ticket to Bali on a Tuesday at three a.m.

Sometimes, I miss that wild, careening freedom. The way the world used to feel so sharp and bright it cut my retinas.

But then I look at Bane, and I remember the way his eyes went dark with terror that day I told him I was leaving. The way his hands trembled when he found me again. And I think maybe... maybe this middle ground isn't so bad.

"Do you want some wine?" Kira asks, already heading for the kitchen. She's gotten so good at defusing tension. I wonder if that's a side effect of living with Isaak, the human equivalent of a controlled explosion.

"God, yes," I reply, ignoring the way Bane's eyebrows lift slightly.

What? I'm allowed. The meds don't play nice with too much alcohol, but one glass won't kill me.

Probably.

Domhn finally stops pacing and drops into a chair, his head falling into his hands. I've never seen my brother like this. So utterly demolished. It's fucking unsettling. Domhn has always been the solid one. The mountain. The absolute immovable object to my unstoppable force.

"She's coming back," I say again, softer this time. "She loves you."

He looks up, eyes red-rimmed. "You don't know that."

"I do, actually." I mean it. I might be chaotic, but I know love when I see it. And whatever MadAnna is—assassin, enigma, avenging angel—she loves my brother with a ferocity that rivals my feelings for Bane.

Speaking of.

Bane shifts beside me, his arm sliding around my shoulders, drawing me against his side like he can't bear to have me too far away. Even now, after everything, he still touches me like I might dissolve into smoke at any moment.

To be fair, I did kind of pull a Houdini on him once. Can't really blame the man for his attachment issues.

Kira returns with wine for me and Domhn, water for herself and Bane. Isaak is still occupied with Lily, who's attempting to grab his nose with sticky fingers.

"She's got your smile," I tell Kira, gesturing at the baby with my wine glass.

Kira beams. "You think so?"

"Definitely. Look at those dimples."

Shit, I sound like a normal human having a normal conversation. Progress!

Baby Lily chooses that moment to let out a gurgling laugh that does weird, squeezy things to my insides. Like my organs are being hugged.

"Do you want to hold her?" Isaak asks, and my stomach drops through the floor.

"Oh, uh—"

"She won't break," he adds with a rare smile. "Trust me, we've tested it."

Kira slaps his arm. "Isaak!"

"What? She rolls off things all the time. She's resilient."

I glance at Bane, panicking. He just smiles, that knowing, infuriating smile that says *I see you, I know you, and I love you anyway*.

"I don't think—"

But Isaak is already moving, and suddenly, there's an eleven-month-old being deposited in my lap like a warm, squirmy loaf of bread.

Holy shit.

Lily stares up at me with huge, curious eyes. I stare back, frozen.

"Support her head," Bane murmurs, his hand sliding beneath mine to show me.

His fingers are warm and steady against my own. I follow

his lead, cradling the tiny human in a way that apparently won't result in permanent damage.

Lily reaches up to grab a fistful of my hair, yanking with surprising strength.

"Ow, fuck—I mean—shoot!" I wince, trying to untangle her grip without hurting her.

Bane chuckles, the sound rumbling through his chest and into my side. "I think she likes you."

"Yeah, she's expressing it through violence. Takes after her dad."

Isaak actually laughs at that, which makes me unreasonably proud. Getting the stoic giant to crack is my personal Olympic sport.

Domhn watches us from his chair, something unreadable on his face. For a moment, I wonder if seeing me—wild, unstable Moira—holding a baby is just too bizarre for his brain to process.

But then his expression shifts, softening. "You're not awful at that," he says, which might be the closest thing to a compliment he's given me in years.

"High praise," I retort, but my voice lacks bite.

The truth is, holding this tiny human is terrifying. And kind of amazing. And has my brain spiraling in about sixteen different directions.

Could I do this? Could I be responsible for a little life?

A month ago, Bane found me curled up in the bathtub at

four a.m., weeping because I couldn't remember if I'd taken my meds. I was convinced I'd taken too many, or none at all, and that I was about to either die or lose my mind completely.

He sat on the bathroom floor for an hour, just holding me, breathing with me, until the panic subsided enough for him to show me the pill organizer. Monday's compartment was empty. I'd taken exactly what I was supposed to.

And then there was the day I ran out of the house in nothing but his shirt and my underwear because I'd seen a fox in the garden and was suddenly, irrationally convinced it was my spirit guide trying to tell me something.

Bane found me twenty minutes later, halfway down the lane, still trying to chase down and talk to the bewildered animal.

So, yeah. Probably not Mother of the Year material.

"What are you thinking so hard about?" Bane murmurs, his lips brushing my temple.

I look down at Lily, who's now attempting to eat my necklace. "Nothing."

"Liar."

I sigh. "Just... life stuff."

His eyes soften, seeing right through me as always. "We have time," he says quietly. "For all of it."

He means kids. We've danced around the topic, never quite addressing it head-on. His gentle "we have time" is both permission to wait and the promise that he's not going anywhere while I figure my shit out.

Sometimes I wonder if I'll ever feel stable enough, sane enough, to be a mother. If the meds will ever balance out just right, if therapy will finally click and make me whole. If the fear of passing on whatever genetic time bomb sits in my DNA will ever fade.

Other days, I think maybe I'm overthinking it. My own mother was a complete disaster, and I turned out... well, I turned out.

Lily suddenly decides my lap is no longer the place to be and makes a grabby-hands motion toward Kira, who swoops in to reclaim her offspring.

"She's probably getting hungry," Kira says apologetically.

I hand over the baby, ignoring the strange emptiness I feel once my arms are free again. "She's amazing," I say, and mean it.

Kira's smile is pure sunshine. "She is, isn't she?"

Bane's hand reaches out, fingers threading through mine. A silent *I'm here*. A wordless *whenever you're ready*.

The thing about Bane is, he never pushes. Not about the important stuff. He might dominate me in a thousand delicious ways in the bedroom, but out here? He waits. He watches. He offers his steady strength without forcing it on me.

It shouldn't work, this thing between us. The wild girl and the controlled priest. The chaos and the order. But somehow, it does.

We've spent the last months building something new

from the ashes of what we had before. Something stronger and more honest.

There are days when I miss the mania—that electric euphoria, the feeling that I could conquer worlds. Days when the meds make everything feel flat and gray and I wonder if Bane secretly longs for the untamed girl he fell for.

But then he'll look at me like he is now, like I'm the most fascinating creature he's ever encountered, and I remember—he never loved me for the chaos. He loved me despite it. Because of it. Through it.

"We should probably head out soon," Bane says, checking his watch. "We've got an early flight tomorrow."

Right. Back to England for another round of meetings about the foundation. Bane's determined to put his father's blood money to good use, funding mental health research, prison relief programs, and supporting programs for at-risk youth. It turns out my formerly penniless priest has quite the head for business when he wants to.

I've been tagging along, finding my own place in this new world we're building. Turns out, my unique perspective on mental health systems is actually valuable. Who knew?

"Stay for dinner," Domhn says abruptly. It's not quite a request, but it's softer than his usual commands.

I glance at Bane, who nods slightly. "Okay," I agree. "But I'm not eating any of that keto shit you're always pushing."

Domhn almost smiles. Almost. "We'll order in."

"Pizza," I demand.

"Fine."

Kira and Isaak exchange a look that I can't quite decipher, but it's something like surprise mixed with relief. Maybe they've been worried about Domhn, too. Maybe they've been trying to pull him out of this funk for months without success.

Bane's thumb traces circles on the inside of my wrist, right over my pulse. It's a habit he's developed. Like he's checking that I'm here, that I'm real, and that my heart is still beating.

"Lily needs a change," Kira says, grabbing up her packed baby bag.

Isaak immediately jumps to his feet to help, but Kira waves him away. "I got it." She hefts her infant in her arms and sweeps out to another room.

For a moment, no one speaks.

Then Domhn sighs heavily. "You look... good, Moira."

I blink, surprised. "Uh, thanks?"

"I mean it. You seem..." He struggles to find the right word. "Steadier."

I don't know whether to be flattered or offended. "Meds will do that to a girl," I say, trying for lightness but hearing the edge in my voice.

Bane's hand tightens around mine.

Domhn's gaze shifts to Bane, something like grudging respect in his eyes. "You're good for her."

Okay, now this is fucking weird. My brother, admitting

that Bane is good for me? Next thing you know, pigs will fly and hell will freeze over.

"She's good for me too." Bane's voice is quiet but firm.

The two men look at each other for a long moment, some unspoken masculine understanding passing between them. I roll my eyes.

"Jesus Christ, just hug it out already so we can order pizza."

Domhn snorts, but the tension breaks. He gets up to grab his phone, presumably to call in our order, when the doorbell rings.

We all freeze.

No one rings Domhn's doorbell. Ever. He has more security than Fort Knox, and visitors don't just *drop by*.

"Expecting someone?" Bane asks, already shifting slightly in front of me. The protective gesture would be annoying if it wasn't so goddamn endearing.

Domhn frowns. "No."

He moves to a panel on the wall, checking the security feed. His entire body goes rigid.

"Domhn?" I push to my feet, suddenly on high alert. "What is it?"

"Stay back. My security feed's glitching." He strides to the door with purpose, his shoulders set in a hard line.

Isaak immediately jumps to alert, hurrying behind Domhn, hand hovering at the gun on his belt—a new addition since he's gotten all his licenses in.

Bane and I exchange a look, then follow, too. Whatever—whoever—is on the other side of that door, we're facing it together.

Domhn yanks the door open, and for a moment, there's only silence.

I peek around him, trying to see what's got him frozen like a statue.

At first, I don't understand what I'm looking at. There's no one there. Just a wicker basket sitting on the doorstep, covered with a soft blue blanket.

And then the blanket *moves*.

Oh.

Oh *shit*.

Domhn drops to his knees like his legs have given out. With trembling hands, he pulls back the blanket to reveal a tiny, perfect face. A baby—no more than a few weeks old—with a shock of black hair and eyes the exact same shade as my brother's.

There's a note pinned to the blanket. Domhn unfolds it with shaking fingers, reads it silently, and then reads it again as if he can't believe what he's seeing.

"What does it say?" I whisper, unable to tear my eyes away from the infant, who's now making adorable gurgling sounds.

Domhn looks up, and I'm stunned to see tears in his eyes. Real, actual tears. From my stoic, unshakable brother.

"It's from Mads," he says, his voice rough with emotion.

"She says... she says this is our son. That she'll be home soon. That she loves me." His voice breaks on the last word.

The baby—my nephew, holy shit—lets out a tiny, indignant cry, and Domhn gathers the baby into his arms with the kind of reverence usually reserved for religious artifacts.

Bane's arm slides around my waist, pulling me against him. I lean into his warmth, my heart so full it feels like it might crack my ribs.

"What's his name?" I ask, peering into the tiny, scrunched-up face that somehow manages to look exactly like Domhn already.

My brother blinks clumsily and cups the back of his baby's head in astonishment, glancing down at the note again, a smile—a real, genuine smile—breaking across his face like a sunrise.

"Connor," he says softly. "His name is Connor."

As if recognizing his name, the baby's eyes blink open, staring up at the giant man holding him with a kind of solemn curiosity that's almost comical on such a tiny face.

Bane's lips press against my temple. "You okay?" he murmurs.

I nod, leaning into him, letting his strength support me while I process the hurricane of emotions swirling through me. Joy. Wonder. A strange, fierce protectiveness. And deep, deep relief that MadAnna is alive. That she's coming back. That she hasn't abandoned my brother after all.

"Family just got more complicated," I whisper back.

He chuckles softly. "Family always is."

I watch as my brother—my fierce, terrifying, overprotective brother—cradles his son against his chest for the first time. His face is transformed by a love so raw and immediate it takes my breath away.

And suddenly, I get it. Why people do this. Why they take the risk.

Love is worth it. Love is always worth it.

I turn in Bane's arms, looking up at the man who has seen me at my absolute worst and still looks at me like I'm his miracle.

"I love you," I tell him, because it's true and because life is short and unpredictable and magical.

His eyes crinkle at the corners. "I love you too, little heathen."

Maybe someday we'll be ready for this—for tiny humans with Bane's gray eyes and my wild curls. Maybe we won't. Either way, we'll figure it out together.

For now, I have this: my husband's arms around me, my brother finding his way back to hope, and a brand-new little person who's about to discover that being part of this family means being loved fiercely, protected ruthlessly, and accepted completely—just as you are.

Imperfect. Complicated. But never, ever alone.

. . .

DON'T MISS A THING: to read the beginning to Domhnall and MadAnna's tumultuous love story, **one-click 7 DAYS.** Seven days to make her remember. Seven nights to make her beg.

ISAAK AND KIRA'S love story releases May 1, 2025, preorder RUINED VOWS. See how the silent, brooding bodyguard and the prim young professor fall in love in *Ruined Vows*.

ALSO BY STASIA BLACK

CARNAL GAMES

7 Days

Unholy Obsession

Ruined Vows

TABOO SERIES

Daddy's Sweet Girl

Hurt So Good

Taboo: a Boxset Collection (Boxset)

BREAKING BELLES SERIES

Elegant Sins

Beautiful Lies

Opulent Obsession

Inherited Malice

Delicate Revenge

Lavish Corruption

MONSTER'S CONSORTS SERIES

Monster's Bride

Thing

Between Brothers

Hunger

MAVROS BROTHERS SAGA

Who's Your Daddy

Who's Your Baby Daddy

Who's Your Alpha Daddy

Mavros Brothers Saga Boxset

MARRIAGE RAFFLE SERIES

Theirs To Protect

Theirs To Pleasure

Theirs To Wed

Theirs To Defy

Theirs To Ransom

DARK MAFIA SERIES

Innocence

Awakening

Queen of the Underworld

Cruel Obsession (Boxset)

BEAUTY AND THE ROSE SERIES

Beauty's Beast

Beauty and the Thorns

Beauty and the Rose

Billionaire's Captive (Boxset)

Love So Dark Duology

Cut So Deep

Break So Soft

Love So Dark (Boxset)

Stud Ranch Series

The Virgin and the Beast

Hunter

The Virgin Next Door

Reece

Jeremiah

Freebie

Indecent: A Taboo Proposal

Draci Alien Series

My Alien's Obsession

My Alien's Baby

My Alien's Beast

Alpha Alien Beasts (Boxset)

ABOUT STASIA BLACK

STASIA BLACK grew up in Texas, recently spent a freezing five-year stint in Minnesota, and now is happily planted in sunny California, which she will never, ever leave. She recently got married, is wildly in love, and has the cutest cat on this side of the Mississippi.

Stasia's drawn to romantic stories that don't take the easy way out. She wants to see beneath people's veneer and poke into their dark places to find their twisted motives and deepest desires.

Want to read or listen to an EXCLUSIVE, FREE book/audiobook? Indecent: a Taboo Proposal, that is available ONLY to my newsletter subscribers, along with news about upcoming releases, sales, exclusive giveaways, and more?

Get **Indecent: a Taboo Proposal** at www.stasiablack.com

When Mia's boyfriend takes her out to her favorite restaurant on their six-year anniversary, she's expecting one kind of proposal. What she didn't expect was her boyfriend's longtime rival, Vaughn McBride, to show up and make a completely different sort of offer: all her boyfriend's debts will be wiped clear. The price?

One night with her.

Get it at stasiablack.com

Website: www.stasiablack.com
Tiktok: @stasiablackauthor
Instagram: @stasiablackauthor
Facebook: facebook.com/StasiaBlackAuthor
Goodreads: goodreads.com/stasiablack
BookBub: bookbub.com/authors/stasia-black